Her Missing Pieces

Her Missing Pieces

A Moonshine Romance

Susan Sands

TULE
PUBLISHING

Prologue

I SMELLED SWEAT *and the putrid odor of alcohol on his breath. The look in his eyes terrified me—like he was possessed. He was going to kill me this time.*

He drove his fist into my right shoulder blade. It would have been my face if I hadn't slithered out of his grip and turned at the last second. I didn't scream, even though the pain nearly split me in two. Tears streamed down my face, along with mud from the dirt floor of the barn. His body odor and the home-brew moonshine he'd swilled just before he'd gone on this current rampage gagged me. I fought to catch my breath.

"I'm gonna kill you, you little bitch, and cut out those devil eyes. Gonna cut 'em out." He came at me with a screwdriver. Usually, it was only his fists. The screwdriver told me he meant business. I rolled aside, just as he plunged it in the ground right next to my head. That was too close.

Chapter One

MY BEST FRIEND Jenny arrived just as the paramedics were rolling my precious mom, or Thelma, as I called her, out in a body bag on a gurney. Its wheels squeaked repetitively as it trundled by, headed out the door. I couldn't look. My horror over finding her like that this morning would never cease—I was sure of it.

I was currently sitting on the floor of the living room of our home, where Thelma and I had watched TV for the final time together last night. I held the remote in my hand. Early this morning, my beagle mix, Daisy Mae, had alerted me that something was wrong. I shivered. I still couldn't believe this was happening.

Now, only a few hours later, there were strangers in our house—our sanctuary. Completing paperwork, making calls, and taking photos. We didn't *do* strangers, but here they were, invading our precious privacy. It was only me now. I was thankful for Jenny or I would be completely alone in this.

"Oh my God, Randi. I'm so sorry." Jenny nearly sprinted to cover the space between us. She wrapped me in a tight hug. Her embrace was welcome but didn't change anything.

"She's gone, Jenny," I whispered, sounding as broken as I felt.

"I can't believe it." Jenny was obviously trying not to cry as she sniffled and dashed tears from her eyes. "And I'm sorry you had to find her like that." Jenny pulled a tissue from the box beside the sofa. Jenny had known Thelma since we had attended the local college together. Jenny was like family to both of us.

"Thanks for being here."

"Excuse me, ma'am." One of the paramedics handed me a paper to sign to release the body. Thelma was a body now. I cycled from crying to being numb and back to crying. This overwhelming flood of emotion surprised me. I wasn't an overly emotional person—or hadn't been that I could remember, but that was the thing: I didn't remember anything from before my sixteenth birthday. Retrograde amnesia. Dissociative amnesia. Those were the terms that doctors had used to describe my very strange condition. I didn't even remember why I called my mother by her given name. Or why, until now, that I hadn't tapped into my emotions like a normal person. I didn't cry or even laugh out loud, despite the fact that I found things sad and amusing.

"Of course." Jenny happened to be a clinical therapist. Ours wasn't a doctor-patient relationship, but she still gave great advice and had seen firsthand what I'd gone through, not knowing anything from my childhood. "I'm so glad you called."

I burst into sobs, my shoulders racking as I wept. "Jenny, what will I do?" I meant now. And forever. But mostly right now. I had no idea how to live a day without my Thelma in my life.

"You'll breathe. And I'll help you get through this."

An hour later, they were all gone except Jenny. I'd closed

Thelma's bedroom door, leaving everything as it was. Always neat and tidy, but I couldn't find the courage or strength to even glance inside today. My head ached and nausea sat in the pit of my stomach.

My disbelief warred with the sobbing realization of today's dreadful nightmare. *How could this be happening?*

"Do you want me to spend the night?" Jenny asked, clearly worried about me.

I shook my head. "I know you have to work tomorrow. I-I'll be okay. Daisy Mae is here with me." I didn't want to burden Jenny. I honestly didn't know if I would ever be okay.

Jenny frowned. "I'm not convinced but call me anytime during the night if you need me. I'll come."

"Thanks for everything, Jenny. I don't understand any of this. Mom was so healthy and fit, especially for her age. How does somebody like that die without any warning?"

Jenny shook her head, her eyes sad. "Sometimes people do."

Once I shut the door, I remembered Daisy Mae in the backyard. When I let her in, her tail wagged and she seemed just as happy to see me as always, like every other time I'd opened the door to let her in. But she'd found Mom just hours ago and had alerted me. Dogs were so simple but complex at the same time.

Daisy Mae set to sniffing around the house, smelling the scents of everyone who'd been in and out in the past couple of hours. Then, she searched the entire place, every room. For Mom, I was sure. Which set forth a new torrent of tears and sobs. "She's gone, girl."

Chapter Two

IT HAD BEEN just over a week now since I'd discovered my mom, Thelma, deceased in her bed. She'd simply stopped breathing at some point during the night. I'd never lost anyone, and I wasn't handling it well. I shook my head at the memory of how Thelma had looked when I'd found her. She'd been so cold. I didn't think I would ever get that day out of my head.

I missed Thelma sitting beside me eating popcorn while we watched our shows and laughing at the funny parts, which made me cry again. *How did people do this?* This heavy emotion? It was exhausting. Now, the thought of watching any of our favorite streaming shows filled me with sadness.

Mom and Daisy Mae had taken up my whole heart, and now half of it was gone. There was an empty space where Thelma used to be. All I had left were the past thirteen years filled with memories. Not a lifetime together, though. Since the car accident as a teen where I'd suffered a severe head injury. The only lasting effect was that I couldn't remember my childhood—that, and my flat affect. I wondered what I'd been like before the accident.

Thelma was always super-weird about protecting me and I'd been living here with her still, at the age of twenty-nine.

Jenny, Thelma, and Daisy Mae made up my circle. I had a few casual acquaintances, but I'd lived a sheltered life with Thelma.

Jenny and I were going to spread Thelma's ashes in her garden today. I'd been dreading this all week so I didn't want to delay it any longer.

I'd called the attorney's office number on the card under the magnet from the refrigerator the night after Thelma had passed. A few days before, she'd mentioned the card and said, "The attorney's card is on the refrigerator, darlin'. If anything were to happen to me, he's the one you should call immediately." She'd said this out of the clear blue as we sat together in the garden, sharing a glass of iced tea, and enjoying the nice weather. I'd blown it off as one does when one thinks nothing bad would ever happen. When I'd called him, the attorney was equally stunned at learning of Thelma's passing.

Arnold P Whitaker, Esq. had kindly provided me with details to have Thelma cremated per her wishes and send the bill to his office. I'd had no idea she'd already planned for her untimely death.

Mr. Whitaker insisted we meet as soon as I'd spread the ashes in the garden out back. He'd been helpful and expressed his condolences. I wondered when he'd met and done business with Thelma. She hadn't gotten out much besides going to the bank, the garden center, and the grocery as far as I knew. Maybe when I'd been working on a design project? Somehow she'd set up her estate and final wishes without my knowing anything about it.

Jenny touched my shoulder and nodded toward the urn.

"Are you ready? Do you want to say anything?"

Should I say something? I shook my head. My mother knew how much I loved her. I hadn't even thought to bring in a minister. Thelma hadn't been a churchgoer, though she kept a Holy Bible beside her bed and a rosary hanging on her bedpost. She'd never taken me to church, and I wondered if she'd attended Catholic mass when she was younger—before I lost my memory. Something else I'd never asked her about when she was alive.

"Do *you* want to say something?" I asked Jenny. I didn't want to prevent her from expressing any sentiments if she felt the need.

Jenny seemed to think about it for a minute. "No. There's no need to be formal. I can't imagine her wanting formality."

Thelma had surely been the most unpretentious, plain-spoken woman on earth. I meant that in a good way. She wasn't coarse, but direct. She said what she'd intended and didn't waste words or stand on ceremony. As I spread the ashes in her beloved garden, I couldn't help but think that my canine might roll in them the first chance she got. Considering the love between the two of them, I guess that wouldn't be the worst thing, although the idea of bathing human bits off the dog made this whole experience even more dreadful than it had been thus far.

"Are you all right, Randi?" I figured Jenny knew I wasn't, but it was sweet of her to ask.

"Just trying to get the rest of this out." I tilted the container and shook it a little, careful not to inhale. Fortunately, there wasn't a strong breeze today. Ashes didn't spread nearly as well in real life as they did in the movies.

"Here, let me help." Jenny tilted the heavy container more and shook it a little, causing several clumps to tumble out onto my open-toed shoe. I made a face and shook my foot.

"Sorry." I noticed Jenny suppress a small grin.

It was a weird and morbid situation. Thelma would have appreciated the strange humor here. I replaced the lid once the container was empty and set it on the edge of the porch. "There. It's done. So glad it's done."

It had taken this whole week to get the ashes back from the crematorium. I'd been living in limbo waiting for them. The entire time, I'd moped, cried, and revisited the night before Thelma had passed, trying to figure out if she'd shown any signs of illness or changes in behavior.

I hadn't gone for a run once this past week as I'd done most days of my adult life. I knew I would likely feel better, at least physically, if I did. Maybe later.

Tomorrow, finally, would be my appointment with my mother's lawyer.

"The garden is gorgeous." Jenny pulled me out of my thoughts, causing me to look around the yard.

The grass was nearly green now that the springtime weather had finally arrived, and there were daffodils and tulips pushing their way in the raised beds all around. I nodded at Jenny's comment. Thelma had known the name of every plant and shrub she'd ever encountered. We'd ordered seeds online and patronized garden centers and nurseries outside of town. Thelma had dedicated years to curating our outdoor space into this amazing showplace.

Sadly, no one ever saw it. It was our private wonderland.

I would never see a plant, tree, or flower again without reliving our many memories together, side by side, planting and digging. That made me sniffle—again.

Jenny hovered, likely uncertain whether to mother me or let me be. I was a little funny about physical contact. "When will I stop crying?" I asked, hoping for a good, solid answer.

Jenny sighed. She was trying to *therapy* me because she knew I'd not had any experience with death. "Things are super raw right now. You'll work into managing the strong reactions as they hit you."

"I'm going to take your word for that." I was sure she might be right eventually. But not yet. It was taking a new form of self-control that I hadn't yet developed to keep it all in check right now.

We sat on the porch together in the Adirondack chairs Thelma and I had refinished last year, the same ones where Thelma and I had sat almost every non-rainy evening since then. I remembered her teasing me that I should stick to art rather than refinishing furniture. That gave me another hard punch in the gut.

"Do you want me to go with you to the appointment with the lawyer? I can make it work."

I dreaded the meeting. I had a strange feeling that after it, my life would never be so simple as it had living here with Thelma, and as much as I hated to inconvenience Jenny, I conceded it would probably be a tough day. "I would appreciate it, Jenny."

"Sure thing. I'll pick you up at nine thirty."

I inhaled deeply, almost breathing my mother in the air.

Her presence here was strong. There were so many questions left unanswered between us.

"Do you think I'll find out anything new tomorrow?" I stared at the beauty around me and wondered how things might change.

Jenny knew about me and what I knew of my history, so I didn't need to explain what I meant by that. "It's about time to learn something new, don't you think?"

Chapter Three

As Jenny drove me to the attorney's office, I allowed myself to consider new possibilities. Maybe I'd not been as curious about my past before because I preferred the status quo. It was comfortable and safe to live in the bubble of Thelma's making. But something now ate at me.

I was beginning to question who I was—*before* my memory had been snatched away in a way I'd never done before. Like an itch I needed to scratch badly, whereas previously it didn't seem to matter as the years rolled by pretty uneventfully. Maybe I'd been the same, only younger. But something told me the before was different. That there were memories I was missing that mattered. Being head-injured and having experienced complete amnesia made me question what else about myself had been different.

I knew Thelma worried about me, which was normal for moms, I guess. She'd mentioned her concern that I might be out one day and remember something traumatic about my accident. Nothing scary like that had ever happened before, so I wasn't exactly afraid, just curious over the possibility of finding out something unusual.

I didn't know much about my early childhood, besides the facts that Thelma had supplied. We'd lived in Georgia at some point and moved when my dad died, shortly before the accident. Because I didn't remember, I didn't have a connection to it. Thelma hadn't pushed me to remember my past, taking her cue from doctors and therapists I'd seen initially after the accident.

Jenny spoke then, pulling me out of my head. "I don't think I've ever been to this area." We were a few miles out of town. "It says we've arrived."

The small red-brick building was nearly hidden behind the thick canopy of heavy juniper bushes that had been allowed to grow beyond the neatly trimmed boundaries normally found around the in-town office parks. This wasn't an office park though, more like a house converted to an office.

"I wonder how she found this place." I said it out loud but didn't really expect an answer.

There were four parking spaces, and one other small dark car was parked in the tiny lot besides ours. Aside from the overgrown greenery, the place appeared well-kept, with freshly painted white shutters and doors. There were two bright red doors: one was marked *private* and the other bore the gold lettering of Arnold P Whitaker, esquire, LLC.

A bell jingled as we entered. The place was more like the living room of someone's granny rather than a professional office, with an afghan across the back of the sofa and with numerous crocheted doilies on the coffee table, under the lamps, and on the arms of the overstuffed chairs. Someone here had a hobby.

"Come in, come in. Mr. Whitaker is expecting you. I'm Mrs. Whitaker." The woman's voice matched exactly my idea of someone who was an expert with the crochet needle.

"Thank you. I'm Randi Collins."

"Of course you are, dear. My deepest condolences on losing your mother. Mr. Whitaker knows you're coming. He's finishing up with his nine o'clock call, so you have a seat. Can I offer you some hot tea or coffee?" The tiny woman sat low in her office chair behind the partition window. She had a tight gray ballerina bun and wore the expected shawl. And yes, it was crocheted.

"No thank you. We're fine," I answered for both of us.

I dared not make eye contact with Jenny for fear of snickering. Partly because of the massive displays of yarns, and because I was nervous enough to giggle. I didn't usually giggle, but since Thelma's passing, my emotions were causing me odd responses to things.

"Mr. Whitaker will see you now." The tiny woman was even more petite now that she stood before us. And round as a peach.

Jenny and I followed her into the office of what could only be Arnold P Whitaker, esquire. A shock of pure white hair framed his bespectacled bright blue eyes.

"Randi. It's so lovely to finally meet you in person. Thelma—your mother—has told me so much about you in recent months."

I shook his warm, firm hand, comforted immediately, as if I knew I could count on this man. I guess Thelma had, and she had trusted no one.

"Y-yes. Thank you. I'm surprised she never mentioned you other than pointing out your card on our refrigerator just before—"

He grinned knowingly, his deep dimple on the right making him reminiscent of Santa Claus. "Thelma was a true woman of mystery, wasn't she?"

Was she? I pressed my lips together to try and prevent tears.

"I'm thrilled you brought your friend with you. Jenny, right?" he asked, but clearly already knew the answer.

Jenny's eyebrows shot up. "Yes. How did you know?"

"Thelma described your friendship, and hoped that if there was ever a need, Randi would turn to you for comfort and consult. Of course, none of us knew the *time* would be so soon upon us."

"Was she sick and didn't tell me?" I was suddenly dying to know the answer.

"Not as far as I knew, so she didn't keep you in the dark there." He smiled that lovely, calming smile again. "I think she simply wanted to prepare for the improbable."

"But she *did* keep something from me?" I pushed a little because I could tell he had far more to say.

"Please understand that what we will discuss today wasn't meant for you to discover in this way, or at this time. There was a plan, but since Thelma has left us so unexpectedly, I must share information that will surely change your perspective and cause you to question…things."

I stared at the lovely man, my eyes wide. His words set off my radar. "Question what?"

He sighed as if he were speaking with a small child. "This is going to be a trying day for you, and I'm afraid there's no way to prevent it. Thelma's passing without warning took away her opportunity to transition your finding out the way she'd hoped."

My stomach lurched. "Finding out what?"

"Your memory loss kept her from telling you something very important. She continued to wait for the right time. She'd been planning a trip for the two of you as a way to reintroduce you to your childhood and maybe jar your memory."

"What in the world do you mean? We never went any-where." This wasn't getting any better. It was as if everything became still. I held my breath. This was it.

"My dear, Thelma wasn't your mother." He said this as if it was some huge bombshell.

I nodded. "I realize she wasn't my birth mother. I was adopted as an infant."

He shook his head, a sympathetic expression on his kind face. "Thelma only came to know you after you lost your memory at age sixteen." His gaze held mine.

Bombshell.

He could have said anything else. But he didn't. He'd just told me that my mother wasn't my mother. "Sixteen? That's not possible. No. Th-there was a c-car crash." My teeth began to chatter. "She a-adopted me when I was an infant."

"I know what a shock this is. Your finding out this way is the last thing Thelma wanted."

"Oh, Randi." Jenny grabbed my hand and passed me a tissue from the corner of the desk.

Mr. Whitaker continued. "The real truth is that she *rescued* you from a bus station. She found you wandering and injured. From what she's shared, she had very good reason *not* to bring you to the authorities."

Jenny moved closer. "I don't understand, Mr. Whitaker. Are you saying Thelma found and *kept* Randi? Without letting anyone know?"

A realization hit then. I'd been sixteen. *She'd kidnapped me?* I thought the words but dared not say them aloud.

He cleared his throat and didn't quite look either of us in the eye. "Thelma was my client, and all she would tell me about that night is that she refused to return you to someone who might hurt you again. She hoped you would regain your memory but couldn't take the chance with your safety. So, she planned to keep you safe until you remembered. But you never did."

"She *kidnapped* me?" I choked out finally, repeating my thoughts. "But she was my mother. She loved me."

But she wasn't my mother. Or even my adopted mother.

He nodded. "Yes, she came to love you dearly. She believed you to be in grave danger the night she found you."

The years of Thelma urging me to keep my head down and not make eye contact with strangers saturated my brain then. It hadn't ever made sense until that moment. Our move to Hickman from the South. Maybe the part about the South was all a lie too. Had I had an accent? I didn't now.

There was a low-level buzzing in my brain. Like it was about to shut down. My heart was on fire. Thelma was the only mother I'd known, certainly that I remembered, and I loved her with all my heart. And I'd cried and cried at losing her.

But she wasn't even my adoptive mother. Well, she had been for thirteen years into my adulthood, but it had all been total BS. I wanted to slide into a puddle on the floor.

"Randi, are you okay?" Jenny asked. "Of course you're not but tell me what you're thinking."

"I don't know *anything*. I don't remember *anything*. Everything I thought I knew...is wrong." My chest threatened to cave in on itself.

Mr. Whitaker cleared his throat. "Wait, hold up now. Thelma adored you. Can you honestly say you doubt that? Think about your years together. How she loved you wasn't a lie; I know this much. The actual mother-daughter relationship didn't start out the way she told you, but you needed her, and she was a mother to you, though I can't say I agree with her methods in keeping you in the dark all these years."

"How could you know her well enough to judge our relationship?" I nearly spat the words at the messenger.

Mr. Whitaker held his hands up as if to ward off my anger. "I know this is hitting hard, Randi. But Thelma and I spoke at length about her concerns should she pass unexpectedly, and what that would mean for you if it happened before she had the opportunity to carry out her plans. The odds of this happening were very low, but I've lived long enough to recognize authentic love and emotion, and that woman loved you to her core."

I took a shuddering breath. "How could she not tell me the truth? And why?" I whispered the last word as my voice failed.

He smiled gently. "Thelma shared that she didn't want to hurt or confuse you. She told you the kindest things initially when you were so fragile, with the belief that eventually you would remember on your own. There was something you'd locked up that your brain and body were protecting you from. Thelma feared what might happen should she one day break the news that everything you knew to be true was based on a false background."

"What on earth will I do now?" Because that was what this became. A sudden stop to my life. The life I thought I had that had changed so drastically in an instant and now showed me no path ahead.

⚬❦

MRS. WHITAKER BROUGHT in a tray with hot tea and coffee. I wasn't usually a drinker of either, but the tea seemed like a soothing idea right now. Sugar, honey, and lemon were all things that made people feel better, right?

This was all so complicated. I muddled and tripped toward the magnitude of what this really meant, trying to digest the information. "So, if I wasn't ever her daughter, who am I?" I asked quietly. "And how could I have gone by the name Collins all these years? Did she change my name from whatever it was before legally, and how could she even do that?"

Mr. Whitaker frowned. "This is all a bit tricky, you see. As Thelma's attorney, I strongly advised her to keep the information confidential of how she aided you in coming by your identity. It would have proved legally compromising to her. Protecting you was her number-one priority, and she couldn't do that if she was in legal trouble."

Tricky? *Um, yes.* "I don't understand." Because he still

hadn't told me anything. "So, you're saying I'm *not* Randi Collins?"

He furrowed his brow and shifted in his chair. Signs of his discomfort. "You have a *borrowed* identity. From a deceased person. It's never been an issue because a death certificate was never applied for in this case."

I stared at the man. "I'm pretending to be a dead person? As in, I took over somebody's identity?"

"Technically, yes. Though you were a minor and unaware of the situation, so you can't be held accountable. I mean, you couldn't then. This was part of Thelma's way of protecting you from legal difficulty. You were an unwitting participant in the situation, and now that she's deceased, well, *she* can't be held responsible. But if it came to light that you were aware of the deceit, then you would need to take steps to clear this up."

He continued, "Apparently, she maintained all the birth records, social security documents, et cetera to pass you off as her own child, which allowed you to move to a new place and finish high school and enter college. And to live as Randi Collins," Mr. Whitaker addressed me.

Jenny cleared her throat. "Randi, I'm concerned that this is too much information for one day."

She turned to Mr. Whitaker. "Can we come back in a day or two once she's had a chance to digest all this?"

Jenny looked at me. "Are you okay with us taking a break and coming back?"

I nodded. I didn't have a clue how I felt about much right now. Empty. Too full. Who knew?

"I have one more item I believe will begin to help Randi

see this from Thelma's point of view. I have a letter, Randi. I'm hoping it will show some idea of Thelma's heart."

He handed a sheet of paper over, written in Thelma's own scrawl. I would have recognized it anywhere. I took the paper, my hand shaking.

Ma Chère Randi,

If you are reading this, it means I've died before completing my work for you. I wanted so much to help you find your way home and your path to the future. I've treasured you greatly, and hope you've felt safe with me as your mama during our years together.

I hope you will understand and forgive me for protecting you so tightly. Please, darling, return home and regain your former self. I had hoped we could go on this journey together. For as much as I've protected you, I've kept you away from those you love and those who love you. I'm sorry for that. Tell them of my apology, and that it wasn't your fault. Your loss of memory was a blessing and a curse. Without it, I couldn't send you back. But the time has come, and you must find your family.

You became my Randi after Randi died. You saved my life and my sanity. We saved each other. Be safe and well, my heart.

Trust Mr. Whitaker. He is a good man and holds the information you will need on your journey home. Be patient. Someday, you will understand...

Thelma

Jenny handed me the box of Kleenex. I was trying to get

my breathing under control as another huge sob racked my frame. "H-how can she be g-gone?"

Jenny held my hand. I handed her the letter to read.

"Holy moly," Jenny said when she finished reading the letter.

Another family? There were a lot of things in that letter I tried to digest. "How could she not have told me she was pretending I was her child? Or even that she'd lost a daughter?" These things were all so surreal I couldn't wrap my mind around them. Terrible and surreal.

Jenny asked, "Wouldn't Thelma have needed a death certificate to bury her daughter, or cremate her?" Jenny, at least, was thinking with her brain and not her emotions, and I was grateful to have her there.

Mr. Whitaker shook his head a little. "She didn't share this information with me. I helped her only with the very specific items she requested. When I asked questions she didn't wish to answer, she simply didn't answer."

That sounded like Thelma.

WE LEFT MR. Whitaker's office at Jenny's insistence. She'd been right—there was too much to take in.

Once I'd arrived home, I stared at the place. It was like viewing every room, every item with new eyes. Even our beautiful garden held secrets. Hearing what I had, I couldn't ever go back to the blessed ignorance from before. Before, when I'd believed every word Thelma told me and trusted that all was well. That life was simple and pleasant.

But so many things made sense now and so much more didn't. Things I simply hadn't bothered to address in all these years. Having no memory meant complete trust in the one who holds your truths. I could never be blissfully ignorant again, though I still knew very little.

As upset and angry as I wanted to be with Thelma, Jenny reminded me that just before she died, she'd been working hard toward helping me find my past and get to the truth. So, surely this shroud of lies had all been to protect me. I couldn't condone it, but at least I had proof from her letter that I was meant to discover what I'd forgotten. Knowing all of this didn't go far to change the knot in my stomach or the constant drumming in my head.

It hurt. It hurt knowing Thelma wasn't my mother, adopted or not. It horrified me to uncover the fact that she'd kept me away from a family who might believe me dead. I couldn't even think about that right now. It was overwhelming.

I sighed. The emptiness I carried in my heart was only second to the anxiety of what was to happen next—the great unknown. The future.

I spent two days thinking, and crying more, and wanting to be angry for all the lies I'd been told, yet my anger felt counterintuitive next to what I believed Thelma wanted for me—what she'd shown me. Love and protection. Words weren't as strong as actions. I wanted answers but was afraid of what might come of them. The world had suddenly become huge. I sifted through memories of our time together, but I couldn't bring myself to actually go through Thelma's physical things yet.

Chapter Four

WE HEADED BACK to Mr. Whitaker's office two days later.

"First of all, you are the sole benefactor in Thelma Collins LaFleur's will." He handed me a packet of papers. "But we have a few other things to discuss first."

"Wait, LaFleur?" I asked. "But her driver's license says Collins."

Mr. Whitaker peered at me over the top of his glasses. "I couldn't say. I prepared the will based on legal documents. Most of her papers referred to Thelma without LaFleur, so perhaps it only shows up on her social security information."

I was living someone else's life when I had a life out there someplace I'd been taken from. "How do I get back to where I came from?" I asked, though I wasn't at all sure that was something I wanted to do.

"Thelma said she'd mapped out the journey to Moonshine, Georgia, with stops along the way, the last time we spoke. But so far, I don't have that information. Maybe she has it on her desk at home?" Mr. Whitaker asked.

"Moonshine, Georgia? Where is that?" Another secret. Would they ever stop coming?

"It's your origin story, Randi. It's where Thelma planned

to take you. My suggestion to you as her attorney is to get hold of the itinerary she'd planned for the two of you."

"I'm not sure it's a good idea." Now that my curiosity had kicked up, so had my fear of finding out the unknown. "Do people there think I'm dead?"

"I assume so, Randi. And as for the trip, it was what Thelma wished for you. With or without her," Mr. Whitaker said gently.

"Do you have any information about my family, or if I even still have one?" I asked, barely able to wrap my lips around the word. Thelma was the only family I remembered. I'd dared not dwell on the possibility of the things I couldn't recall. "How do I show up someplace and say, 'Hey, I'm back!'"

"I have the name of a contact in Moonshine that Thelma left in the packet," Mr. Whitaker shared. "Understand, I was directed to open this specific information about your past only if Thelma passed away unexpectedly. She'd shared the conundrum of your identity switch, and I added your prior name into the will not long ago, but I didn't have specifics about your full background."

"So, who am I?" I asked, not at all sure I was ready to know the answer.

Mr. Whitaker cleared his throat as if he was about to make a large pronouncement. He opened the other envelope and pulled out more papers, having a look first. "You, my dear, are Sadie Brubaker, missing, presumed, and now declared dead from Moonshine, Georgia. A true milk carton kid. Fascinating." He slid a photocopied newspaper article across the table.

It was grainy, but there was a picture of a young girl—me. The headline read, "*Moonshine Teen Vanishes. Leads Grow Cold.*" A chill ran through my body. "How could she—I—have disappeared with no clues?" The story suggested that Sadie Brubaker had simply vanished in the night. Her mother had raised a ruckus the next morning when she'd discovered her missing. *My* mother.

I blinked. Missing and presumed dead. Now declared dead, apparently, according to a later article with the same photo. "How horrible."

Jenny scooted closer to me on the sofa. "How could Thelma let the family believe such a thing?" she asked Mr. Whitaker.

"She believed Randi—uh—Sadie was in grave danger from someone all these years." But he sounded uncomfortable with his answer. "She didn't confide in me in this regard."

"But to never give them closure? It's hard to accept." Jenny appeared horrified.

I had to agree it was awful. And the idea that the woman who'd been my mother had actually picked me up randomly at a bus stop and kept me without finding out where I came from—it was too much. Or maybe when she had, she'd decided not to send me back.

But I *knew* Thelma. She'd raised me to adulthood, fed me, made sure I'd been educated, and put me on the path to success. She'd taught me how to garden and build things. She'd *loved* me. That, I conceded. "Whatever else she did, she took care of me and protected me. I can't ignore that."

Jenny nodded. "The woman I've known all these years

would have broken the law to put *your* best interests first." When Jenny had gone through a divorce five or six years ago after her brief marriage, she'd spent a lot of time at our house. Thelma seemed to consider her an extension of our tiny family. I could see where Jenny would defend Thelma almost as fiercely as I wanted to.

But *did* I want to defend her? Depended on the moment.

"I tend to agree with you both, but the authorities wouldn't have seen it that way, unfortunately. I don't know all the details, but there will be two sides to this story. And the other one isn't going to like Thelma's version," Mr. Whitaker warned.

"What's your first memory, Randi? I mean the very first thing you remember after the accident?" Jenny hit me with the question.

I squinted my eyes. She and I had discussed this in the past, but I hadn't given it much thought in a long time. "I vaguely remember lying in a hospital bed, but I'm not sure how long. I had headaches for what seemed like forever. Thelma sat in a chair beside my bed saying her rosary. I hadn't known who she was, but everyone said that was okay because it would all come back in time. She referred to me as her daughter and nobody questioned it."

We'd left the hospital and driven for days, it had seemed. To Hickman. "Since I didn't remember anything before Hickman, I didn't question it. She fed me a story about my father dying when I was little."

"I can't imagine how this all transpired. What a baffling web," Jenny said.

"Thelma hoped you'd find your way home quickly in the

event of her death. She didn't specify her motives, but it was clear she wanted things to be made as easy for you as possible. She asked me to expedite the release of funds and get your inheritance to you so that you could leave as soon as possible and not have to worry."

"I make a good living from my online design firm," I reminded the attorney. "I don't need her money to take a trip." I'm not sure that mattered to him, but I felt the need to say it out loud.

"I'm sure she didn't want to cut into your finances," he replied.

"But what about the house? I can't just close it up and leave it indefinitely." I thought immediately about Thelma's beautiful garden. I couldn't let it fall to ruin, no matter how upset I was at the moment.

"We're to handle all details regarding mail forwarding once you arrive in Georgia, as well as house and garden maintenance, and such while you're away. We will be in contact should there be anything that requires your attention. Shall we read the will now?" he asked.

"I...guess so," I answered and opened the tri-folded sheets that were my copy.

Mr. Whitaker began: "*To Whom It May Concern: I leave all my worldly possessions to my daughter, Randi Collins, aka Sadie Brubaker. This includes the house at 212 Jacoby Lane, Hickman, Nebraska, and its contents...*"

There was a cash sum in the amount of two hundred and fifty thousand dollars. There was life insurance I hadn't known about. Property was mentioned in Louisiana in Lafourche Parish in a place called Galliano. That came as a complete surprise as well. I never knew the source of Thelma's income, but there had always been enough money for the things we'd needed.

The will made the lies official, almost clinical, though less personal than the letter from Thelma. At least the location had been real in Louisiana, though I'd never heard of it.

"I don't know how to even begin this trip. How can I leave and head someplace where I don't remember anything or anyone? What if they would rather I stayed dead?"

"There's no one in the world who wouldn't love a second chance with someone they've loved and lost, Randi," Jenny said.

I thought about that for a second. I guessed it might be true.

Mr. Whitaker read from a sheet of paper. "Looks like you'll have a contact there once you arrive. He is the sheriff of the town and knew you when you were a girl. Thelma hadn't yet informed him that you're alive, but she'd worked all this out. She did her research in recent days. This Chase Blackburn would know everyone in town, and he worked the case when you disappeared. He'll likely be very happy to know you're safe and sound."

"Why wouldn't she have already contacted him? Or my family for that matter?"

Mr. Whitaker shook his head. "I guess she couldn't take the chance of anyone finding out. Remember, news of your reappearance will cause quite a stir in Moonshine. At the time, this homecoming was in the planning stages. No timetable had been established. There were too many legal issues for this to get out prematurely. For Thelma, especially. Not so much now that she's gone. But still there are legal concerns until your identity is settled."

I let that sink in. I was breaking the law by just being me. Until I settled my true identity, I couldn't go back to the way things were.

"Sadie. Sounds like a country bumpkin." I wrinkled my nose at the thought.

"I don't think they'll call you Randi in Moonshine, Georgia, since they all knew you as Sadie." Jenny reminded me this was all too real. She was practical. And that made sense, as much as I hated it.

"I haven't said yet whether I'm going." My name was Sadie Brubaker. I was from some Podunk town in Nowhere, Georgia, apparently. That wasn't *me*. No. My name was Randi Collins from Hickman, Nebraska, where I didn't make eye contact with anyone, and they probably thought I was pretty strange. Where I was invisible.

My pronouncement created silence in the room. Jenny's expression showed compassion. Mr. Whitaker appeared confused.

"We'll take care of everything here, Randi." Mr. Whitaker said it in a way that made clear what was expected of me, no matter my feelings on the matter.

"Is my name Randi, or is it Sadie?" I asked. "Legally?"

"It was never legal for you to be Randi, but I'm not sure how you can un-Randi yourself until Sadie is declared alive again by the Social Security Administration. And that is a whole ball of bureaucracy we'll need to carefully navigate. And it will take time. I'll look into the process, but until you get back to Moonshine, we'll not start any legal action. Otherwise, you won't have an authentic and legal identity."

"This is complicated. I'm Randi and I'm Sadie. But I'm neither."

"Sounds like fodder for a Lifetime movie," Jenny said.

"Yeah. A weird one," I agreed.

"Continue with Randi until we work out the transition. You'll need to access bank accounts and such. And don't tell anyone who you are yet, at least until you get to Georgia. They'll recognize you there or find out soon enough."

This must have been the change I felt was coming eventually. I'd lived in this no-memory limbo for almost half of my life. Thelma would have gotten me there sooner rather than later if all had gone as she'd intended. I'd pushed against it, maybe because I sensed impending doom?

"Randi, I believe you should go on this journey. Thelma wouldn't have planned it so carefully unless she believed it was the right thing for you to do." I could see the worry in Jenny's expression.

"You're talking about the woman who didn't return me to my family and kept me a thousand miles from home, and then lied about being my mother for thirteen years." Even as I muttered the words, I rejected them. But I continued the thought because the facts didn't lie. "And then she died before she could explain. You'll forgive me if I'm not completely sold on this idea of trusting her plan." I'd been going back and forth, almost hourly. Angry and sad. Disbelieving.

But I *was* going to do this, and we all knew it.

"You've a right to feel that way." Jenny gave me permission to express myself like a good therapist. Her skills had come in quite handy since this storm of confusion had struck my world.

"You could come with me." I tossed this out to Jenny like a ridiculous idea, but part of me hoped she would drop everything and agree to come with me and Daisy Mae.

Jenny gave me a small smile. "I would if I could. But I've got patients to see. You're more stable than many of them, but I promise we'll FaceTime every day. If you get cell service there."

I didn't know what a place without cell service might be like. What kind of people lived in that sort of place? My people?

I guess the decision was made. Thelma had already prearranged this journey before she died. It was a final labor of what? Love? It seemed ungrateful to turn my back on her efforts. Because then, where would I be? Still living alone in her home, running my business, still with no memory and no friends besides Jenny. Sounded tempting.

Chapter Five

I LOADED UP the last of my necessities for the trip to Georgia. Only two days had passed since I'd learned of my real identity, and my stomach fluttered with nerves. I could have researched more about Sadie Brubaker and her family. Maybe I should have. The internet was a powerful tool, and I was certain much could be learned from utilizing it in my case. But I had a fear of finding out too much before I left and not being able to unsee it. And it might leave me more confused than ever if I started remembering.

I'd found the courage to go back to the place I was born with no memory of it or anyone, or would by the time I arrived, hopefully. I assumed I had a family there, since Thelma alluded to it in her letter. I didn't want to know the bad things that caused me to leave—at least not yet. I didn't want to lose my nerve and my momentum. Maybe the sheriff could supply information once I arrived. Thelma would have checked him out thoroughly if she trusted he would be a good contact.

I had just under a thousand miles to travel between here and Moonshine, according to the file I found in Thelma's top drawer of her desk. Hopefully, the nerves would calm down by then, or maybe I'd get used to the name Sadie, and prepare myself for anything.

I was terrified. And still so sad and missing Thelma. And even with Jenny's help and support, and the constant companionship of my Daisy Mae, I was more alone than I'd ever remembered being in my life. Lonely.

"Do you have enough water? A bowl for Daisy Mae?" Jenny asked. At least my dog's name would fit right in at my destination. Maybe somehow I'd known deep down when I named her where I'd come from.

I nodded. "I've got a cooler on the floor up front with a gallon of water to pour into my bottle, and several gallon jugs in the back. Daisy Mae's dish is right over there." I pointed to a space by the cooler. Half the items in the Jeep belonged to my buddy. I wanted her to feel as comfortable as possible along the way and in strange places. So, I had all her favorite toys, bed, and various other things she required.

I'm sure I was projecting. My worry about the immediate future could be controlled through Daisy Mae's comfort and security. I couldn't control anything about what was coming for me.

"Well, I guess this is goodbye for now," Jenny said.

"I don't think I'm ready yet." Leaving everything and my only friend was like untethering myself in space and heading out into a vast unknown with no control.

"I'm not sure how you could be, honestly. I wish we'd had time to do some more hypnosis and work on getting your memory back."

"Um, we tried that, remember?" Yeah, we'd tried that early on. And then again a few years back with no luck. I was blocked. My memory was locked up tight. Whatever it was my mind wanted to forget was a doozie, I guessed.

"I know. I wish I'd had time to give it another shot before you headed to the place where whatever caused you to lose your memory in the first place happened. Remember, you're not sixteen anymore. Anything from then isn't a threat now." Jenny sighed. "I don't know if you'll ever be satisfied until you get your missing pieces back. Scents from the past, familiar sights, or even voices can trigger memories out of the clear blue. Since you've been here, you've not been exposed to anyone from your past. Anything's possible."

Without a thought, I moved forward and hugged Jenny tight, which got me a startled gasp from Jenny. The old Randi wouldn't have shown such spontaneous affection.

"I feel like my firstborn is leaving the nest." Jenny was a little teary-eyed. "I'm going to miss you, my friend."

I sniffed. "I'll miss you too. Thank you for putting up with me."

"Honey, you'd better blow up my phone every chance you get."

"It's not like I have anybody else to call." It was a sad truth.

"You've got the sheriff's number, right? Chase Blackburn? When are you going to contact him?"

"In about a thousand miles, maybe. Whenever I get the nerve." I laughed a little nervous giggle. The idea of calling a complete stranger and announcing my impending arrival intimidated me. As it was, I'd avoided strangers intentionally, so it went against the grain.

"Okay, off with you. Call me every two hundred miles, or whenever you feel like it. If I can't answer, leave a message. No texting and driving."

I gave her the thumbs-up. "Got it."

She watched me as if waiting for me to make the next move.

"First steps, right?" I climbed into the Jeep, quite literally taking the first step.

"I'm going to watch you drive away so you can't chicken out. Remember, we've got everything covered here. The house is secure. The garden will be watered and cared for. Think of this as a vacation. I'll be here when you get back."

Between Mr. Whitaker, his lovely bride, and Jenny, it seemed they did have things covered. So, I tried not to worry about the house, the bills, or the garden. Of course, no one could care for Thelma's garden the way she would have, not even me.

Tears were threatening in a big way now. I nodded and waved through my open driver's side window, not trusting myself to say anything else.

I took a mental snapshot of our house—my house—as I put the Jeep in reverse. When would I return? How different would I be when I did? I'd walked every corner, inside and out. I'd touched things, absorbing any leftover memories, hoping to take them with me. My heart was full, more so now that I could gain access to the places in it I'd wished for before Thelma died. But the lies hung over everything. The secrets.

I backed out of the driveway slowly, wanting to savor this moment and remember every detail of the house. Thelma *had* been a mother to me for the past thirteen years, whether or not she should have. And I tried to trust that she'd made that decision in my best interest. That was my gut instinct. But there was so much more to consider now. And soon I would learn things I'd never imagined.

Jenny and I waved until I was out of sight. My cranky navigation lady stated the obvious while I drove the familiar roads toward the unknown. Daisy Mae settled into her new throne bed/seat-belt contraption meant for pups whose owners cared deeply about their safety while riding shotgun in automobiles. And she promptly fell asleep.

Leaving the safe haven of Hickman *with* Thelma's blessing seemed surreal. For so many years, she'd worried and fretted that I might expose my identity, or some long-ago danger might find me. Maybe her fear had become a habit, or maybe she'd been afraid that if I'd gone on my quest sooner, she might have lost me to another life, which now totally made sense, given what I knew.

I was scared to death. Was there still danger? Did I have a family left in the area after so many years? Questions and worries were imbedded in my mind. Maybe I should have done a little digging online to prepare for my destination.

The old newspaper clipping I had tucked away in my bag that Mr. Whitaker had given me was from right after I'd apparently disappeared from my home at sixteen. There had been speculation about a stranger in town around that time, but no evidence had supported the theory of kidnapping. Or there hadn't been proof of any. The reporter mentioned my mother, Mary Frances, and my stepfather, Hank Brubaker. I wondered about my real father as I drove. Was he still alive? I had been referred to as Brubaker, so I suppose I'd been adopted by Hank Brubaker.

Clearly this kind of disappearance had never happened in the town of Moonshine, Georgia, as they'd touted it as a safe, God-fearing community. I wondered at the wording, and how a God-fearing place might be to live in. Hickman certainly didn't have that vibe—at least what I'd known of it. Up in Nebraska, people didn't say things like that.

I wasn't sure I wanted to walk around fearing anyone, let alone God. Hopefully it was just an expression. I knew from watching that small-town Southern show, *Sweet Magnolias* on TV, if the show was to be believed, that life would be far different than what I was accustomed to. Even though I hadn't wholeheartedly participated in society these past years, I liked to think I had a decent handle on what went on around me. I'd observed, after all, even if I didn't get involved.

As I drove, I listened to the playlist I'd taken some time to assemble. I loved music of every genre and I'd carefully chosen popular country music songs both past and current because I assumed the Moonshine, Georgia, population might generally be familiar with the genre. I didn't want to assume too much about the town or its people, but the stereotype was strong in my mind after so much television over the years.

My mind wandered to Thelma then and to how trying the years with me must have been with my handicap. I wondered what her life might have been like if she'd not found me and had my oddities to maneuver. Not that she ever complained, because she seemed to take it as her life's mission to make certain I had everything I needed, and even wanted.

I guess I had some guilt hanging around for possibly keeping *her* from something else—whatever she might have done all those years had she not finished raising me. I simply couldn't find a sinister motive for her to keep a brain-injured teen loosely captive as her own daughter.

But I didn't have a clue how I'd changed her life's course, because she'd revealed very little about her past, besides allowing me to know we'd come to Hickman, Nebraska, from Georgia. She'd certainly cooked Cajun and Southern food like a native, and spoke with her soft, odd lilt, throwing in the occasional French word, here and there. And her skin had been the color of coffee with a splash of cream. I guess I should have asked more questions.

Why would a woman of color save a white teen wandering around? Not that it should matter, but I still found it an odd detail to add to the curiosity of my tragic and confusing story. And she'd left me property in Louisiana, so there was another mystery. The one of her past as well as my own.

A whisper passed through me. *Because she loved you.*

Chapter Six

THE BELL JINGLED on the front door signaling the arrival of a visitor. Before he could even look up, the unmistakable cloud of Vanilla Fields perfume smacked him like the nineties in the face. Chase Blackburn winced at the *tap, tap, tap,* of Cindy Hayes's heels approaching on the linoleum floor. He looked up from his newspaper toward the woman who now stood in front of his desk.

"Hey there, Sheriff. You got a minute?"

The voice grated, like somebody ripping Velcro apart—really slowly. He hated that sound. "Yep. I've got a minute." It was a courtesy because his elected position called for courtesy.

"Well, good. Because I need to know what you plan to do about that pothole in the middle of Main Street? It rattles my teeth every time I drive through town, and it's gotten so big, there's no way around with oncoming traffic."

He folded his copy of *The Moonshine Herald* and slowly placed it on his desk before addressing a tired subject with the woman. "Potholes are part of city maintenance, Cindy. I would go and fill it with my bare hands if I could, but it's already been reported, requisitioned, and put on the work schedule, according to Josie at the front desk. You'll have to contact the folks at city hall if you want to give them a nudge." As she well knew. They'd already had this conversation, or a similar rendition of it a week or so ago.

"I believe in hitting problems from all sides. If I bug you about it, then you'll light a fire under somebody who can make it happen—hopefully sooner than later. Ya know what I'm saying?"

Cindy needed to be heard; he got it. But her kind of prodding on the issues in town wasn't as productive as she might believe. He meant what he'd said about filling the damn hole himself to reduce this kind of harassment. But Cindy was a specifically strong irritant. He would need to air the place out from her perfume when she left. He'd been hungry before, but lunch no longer held the same promise.

"I'll pass along your displeasure should I run into anyone who has any real influence in the matter." Hopefully that would be the end of it.

"You would think with all the tourists about to come through here they would want to get this place ready." Cindy pursed her lips. She wasn't finished.

"I believe that's what the new plantings around the fountain and fresh paint is in anticipation of around downtown." The tourist season was revving up, and this year promised to be more active than last if the local hotel and bed-and-breakfast reservations were any indication.

The whole town and lake area were booked up solid for the summer season, and it was barely mid-April. Here in the North Georgia mountain region, spring and summer were second only to the fall festivals and Christmas season. The glorious changing of the leaves began in early November, but the town and outlying areas booked up starting in mid-October through the Thanksgiving and Christmas holidays.

"I guess." Her doubtful tone and hand-on-hip posture communicated that she wasn't convinced. They'd gone to school together. Cindy was single now since her husband discovered his recent love of Moonshine's former Baptist preacher's twenty-year-old son. The two men had moved away together, and no one spoke out loud of it out of respect for Cindy. Well, not quite out loud.

"Anything else I can help you with?" he asked, hoping she would move on and find someone else to take out her general unhappiness on.

"The Brubakers." Two words with lots of meaning behind them.

He sighed. "What about them?"

"What are you going to *do* about them?" she asked, narrowing her eyes.

Chase had enough then. She'd moved from potholes to pure malice. "Cindy, unless you've come to help solve a problem, or report a crime, I suggest you move on."

"I'm just sayin'—"

Chase admitted a sensitivity to the topic of the Brubaker family. "Not liking the way someone lives or behaves doesn't mean you can have them removed from town, and that goes for your social circle as well. So, leave it alone." He stood and stretched his six-foot-four frame to full height to show their conversation was over.

"But—"

Chase made his way around the desk and grabbed his jacket from the hook on the wall. "I've got an appointment in a few minutes, so if you'll excuse me, I need to lock up." That was a lie, but he'd do almost anything to get rid of the woman at this point.

He didn't want to hear another word about the Brubakers, especially from a gossip like Cindy Hayes. And he certainly didn't want to add any fuel to her fire when it came to spreading hateful information.

"If you don't do something about them, someone else just might." There was a threat there, he was sure of it. And he didn't take threats lightly.

He quirked a brow in question. "Please explain that."

"*I* wouldn't ever do anything un-Christian-like, but there are others who've gotten fed up with *those people*."

"*Those people* are citizens here and are not to be bothered or harassed in any way, do you understand? And spread the word to any others who might have other ideas."

"Well, fine. But you might want to go out there and see what's what. That's all I'm saying." She sniffed in obvious disdain.

"I'll check it out."

A victory smile spread across her face. She'd won by managing to get her digs in and bring the Brubakers front and center once again.

Once he'd made certain Cindy was well on her way, Chase took a step back and shut the door. He paced a bit and then stared out the front plate-glass window through the canopy of oak leaves from the old tree that sat tight just behind the office and provided shade on the hottest days. The town of Moonshine sat on the edge of a large valley, the mountains surrounding. Fannin County bordered Tennessee at the northernmost part of the state, not far from Chattanooga. It was beautiful and breathtaking. But it was small, and everybody knew everything and everyone.

Chase sighed as he considered the Brubaker family, something he tried to avoid doing, as it was complicated and the memories were difficult. Back when the oldest daughter, Sadie, had disappeared, they were all the talk. The name Sadie Brubaker was still legend to some of the long-time residents around here. Sadie had been several years younger than him in school. A knife twisted in his gut—like it always did when he remembered.

The Brubakers were poor and often teased for wearing ragged clothes. Their farmhouse was old and in need of repairs, though the land itself was a nice backdrop, framed as it was by hardwoods out back. It was a crying shame the condition it had fallen into. Some folks prayed for them, and some whispered behind their hands about the family. None of it was good.

And it was now on this community, on him, to make certain Mrs. Brubaker lived as well as she could, considering she still had to deal with Hank. He wasn't able to work now, and hopefully wasn't strong enough to harm her or anyone else anymore.

He should have already followed up with the Brubakers. Two weeks ago, Hank Brubaker had a stroke, and Mary Frances found him unresponsive near his tractor. Hank had been so drunk, he'd passed out, and it was unclear whether his brain bleed was caused by the fall or the years of heavy drinking and poor nutrition. It was likely a combination. The poor woman had been a miserable mess when they'd gotten them both to the hospital. The emergency staff insisted she be admitted too. They'd checked her out and done a few simple blood tests. The results found her to be severely dehydrated and malnourished. They were both on Medicaid, but the wheels moved slowly for the poor, and the woman likely had already given up based on what he'd seen.

He doubted she'd followed up regarding treatment for Hank's recent stroke. Mostly because she wasn't in great shape either. The hospital here in town was small but drew from a good-sized, though sparsely populated region to serve the needs of the rural population in and around Moonshine. Considering how hard it would be for the Brubakers to travel the two hours to Atlanta for the most up-to-date treatment in Georgia, Chase figured that any care Hank might need would be local. Chattanooga was only an hour and a half from Moonshine, but it was in Tennessee, so health insurance across state lines was an issue. Access would always be a problem for a town like Moonshine because of its location and topography. At least they weren't stuck with dial-up internet anymore, as was the case for far longer than most of the country.

This was a small town, but they took care of their own. Both Hank and Mary Frances were released and sent home the next day. The church women were called in to help provide meals and compassionate charitable services until Mary Frances got back on her feet. The very capable, but not-so-compassionate Cindy Hayes unfortunately was the head of the women's auxiliary.

He understood that the Brubakers weren't the most inviting souls to deal with, but they were humans, and after all, weren't they the ones who church people were supposed to minister to? Yes, Chase had been remiss in his duties concerning the Brubakers and he was feeling pretty guilty about it. He mostly hated that Cindy was the one to point it out.

Chase sighed. His was a charming and scenic town, but it certainly wasn't without its challenges. At least the crime rate was low, though they'd not escaped some of the opioid issues that led to meth addictions in the area. Somehow the dealers had made their way here with enough of a supply to wreak havoc among a small percentage of their population.

The phone on his desk rang then, startling him out of his ruminations. "Hello?"

"Hey there, son."

"Hi, Mom." His mother's voice was like a drink of water on a hot day compared to Cindy Hayes's grating presence. Somehow Mom knew most everything happening around here. "I've gotten word through the sewers that Cindy Priss Pot has taken to whining about poor Mary Frances Brubaker and that louse, Hank, using up too much of their Christian time and resources."

"Yeah, she left here a few minutes ago. She started in on me, but I showed her the door."

"Hey, why don't you head over here for lunch and we can talk about what to do for them. I made meat loaf."

"Thanks, Momma. I'll be there soon."

His mother was the most capable woman on this planet, Chase was certain. She took no guff from anybody, him included. If anybody could get poor Mrs. Brubaker moving in the right direction, it was Becky Blackburn.

Chase locked up the office on his way out. His office assistant, Hannah, was still on maternity leave for another week. Hannah had given birth just over a month ago to the most adorable baby girl. Chase would be lucky if she came back to work at all. Hannah was efficient, and even better, could handle people in crisis. Drunk, angry, scared; you name it and Hannah had them cooing like her newborn before they realized it. Most folks didn't sashay into the sheriff's office for a chat. They stormed in. He was missing Hannah right now.

Chase couldn't complain too much. His was a satisfying job in a great town. Moonshine was laid out like so many other small towns in America. The town square, complete with a tree-lined park with benches and a central fountain that ran year-round, unless it froze solid in winter, was the heart of Moonshine. The area was rich in its history for gold mines and moonshine stills during prohibition. The people who lived here were hard workers; they gardened, hunted, and prepped for winter months. Sure, there were a couple small local grocery stores, but the closest big city was Chattanooga about an hour and a half away, so local economics and good sense often prevailed.

So many of the young people in town consistently headed off for higher education and greener pastures near and far, but this place would endure so long as the people had jobs and their quality of life didn't decline. Coal mining had played a part here years ago, but they'd diversified by bringing in the rubber plant and the cotton yarn-spinning factory. Both those industries had meant long-term security for residents in Moonshine.

The thriving arts community and tourism were the underlying engines that drove the local economy here over the past ten years. Visual artists and musicians visited for inspiration and now made their home. Galleries and gift shops sold artwork, pottery, and hand-tooled jewelry. There were outdoor venues for live music and an extensive concert schedule line-up throughout the season.

And there was moonshine, quite literally. The comeback of the high-alcohol-content liquor with new regulations and savvy minds pulled hundreds, if not thousands of visitors to their tiny town these days.

Blue Ridge Lake was a hub of activity and required boat police a full seven days a week from April until October. Chase had his hands full and was on the hunt for another deputy in addition to the two already on the payroll.

Chapter Seven

SHOWING UP FROM the dead was likely best done in person. I was considered a true "milk carton kid," according to the old news reports I'd read regarding my disappearance from Moonshine, Georgia, at age sixteen. Missing and declared dead, apparently.

I'd been on the road to get here from Hickman, Nebraska, for two days. I'd stayed at an adorable B&B just outside of St. Louis that was listed in Thelma's notes. She'd planned the entire trip down to our stops. So strange that she'd been planning all of this without my having a clue.

As I crossed the border into Georgia, the drive became excessively hilly, winding, and thick with green vegetation and trees. I spent every moment focused on the road in front of me, maneuvering the next sharp curve through the mountains.

This was considered the North Georgia Mountain region, according to the map online. Every now and then I caught sight of a waterfall between the trees beyond the guardrail. I concentrated on not plunging to my death as the road disappeared beyond my eyesight.

I gripped the steering wheel and wondered how I'd ever escaped as a sixteen-year-old from a place so treacherous to navigate. Had I gotten a ride with someone? Stolen a car? For someone without a memory before the age of sixteen, the questions were endless.

The GPS in my Jeep had gone quiet. No service up here in the middle of nowhere.

Then, I noticed a small green road sign up ahead that read: *Moonshine 10*. Ten miles to go. Ten miles until I reached the destination I'd been kept from for the past thirteen years. *What had happened to me there? What* would *happen to me when I arrived?*

The Jeep veered near the edge of the guardrail, causing me to snap out of it. I pulled the wheel sharply to get us back between the lines. Going over a cliff ten miles from the answers would be incredibly counterproductive. I spared a quick glance at my sleeping travel companion and whispered, "Sorry, girl."

The rain began pelting my windshield as I hit the outskirts of Moonshine, Georgia. I slowed as the speed limit became thirty-five. Moonshine was situated in a valley surrounded by mountains. And it was breathtaking. At first, the homes were sparse and plain by Hickman standards. But as I drove farther, the population thickened toward the center of town. The fronts of the small shops appeared freshly painted in pastel colors and adorned with window-box planters overflowing with color. Hand-lettered signs hung from above announced the names of businesses. It was all very neat and clean. Picturesque.

The tree-lined town square was complete with a large fountain in the center. Miss Fannie's Bed-and-Breakfast was around here someplace. I was registered as Randi Collins, so no one would be the wiser. My childhood name, Sadie Brubaker, might've raised questions, since this was a small town. Fannie told me I was lucky there'd been a cancellation just that morning on the day I'd called, as they'd booked up already for the season. I wondered at such an out-of-the-way location having such a robust tourist business, especially since it was still spring.

I found the bed-and-breakfast at the corner of the square overlooking the middle of town. I was charmed despite my butterflies at what might come next. Next, as in meeting with the sheriff of Moonshine, Chase Blackburn, if I could catch him in his office. I hadn't called ahead, though I'd meant to every day leading up to this journey. Truth was, I was terrified and overwhelmed by all of the sudden changes in my life.

The rain was steady now and my check-in time wasn't until three o'clock. I didn't need to look far to find the sheriff's department, as it was only a block down and across the street from Fannie's B&B. I parallel-parked a couple of spaces from the sheriff's office, which meant there wasn't far to go in the rain. I had an umbrella, but no idea where it was packed beneath all my things in the back of the Jeep.

Should I leave Daisy Mae here in the Jeep or bring her with me? I'd let her out to relieve herself about twenty miles back, so she should be okay. Plus, it was cool enough.

She stared at me with such soulful, pleading eyes that I snapped on her harness, convincing myself it wasn't because I needed the backup of the one who loved me most. We climbed out, and I was thankful for the covered awnings of the shops that prevented us from being soaked beyond the distance we'd already run from the car.

Daisy Mae shook off the water—on me. "Thanks, girl."

As I approached the sheriff's office, my feet became lead. It was a similar sensation to the morning I'd found Thelma deceased. I still shuddered at the shocking memory.

I suddenly had a strong urge to take my dog and run back to the Jeep, to safety and ignorance from the moment I stepped onto the street in Moonshine. There were secrets here. I hesitated for a few seconds, frozen with a sudden sense of dread. I took a couple of deep breaths and made eye contact with Daisy Mae. Her kind brown eyes encouraged me.

We slowly made our way along the sidewalk as I gathered my courage. I saw the star on the front door and took a deep breath. But before I reached for it the door swung open.

I retreated a step as bells jingled. A man wearing a gold badge stepped out and our eyes connected. For an infinitesimal second, I swore I'd known this man at some point in my life.

As Chase stepped outside and was about to lock up and head to his mom's house for lunch, he turned to his right and noticed a woman outside. She was slim with striking blue eyes and dark hair. As their gazes connected and held, Chase experienced a jolt of recognition. Yet, he didn't immediately identify her.

They both stood for a moment until a dog yipped and broke the strange connection. "Hi. Can I help you?"

Her strangely blue eyes widened. "Y-yes. Are you Chase Blackburn?"

He nodded. "I am. Do you want to step inside?"

"Can I bring Daisy Mae?" She motioned to her dog.

"Fine with me as long as she minds her manners." He stepped back holding the door for them to enter ahead of him.

"She'll be fine." Her voice was soft, but without the local accent. She wasn't from around here; that was for sure.

Once they were inside, he offered her a seat across his desk, while he took a seat in his chair. Having the desk between them felt official. And someplace deep inside he knew this was necessary.

The woman cleared her throat, in a nervous way. "I have a feeling what I'm going to tell you is going to be somewhat unbelievable."

"I've heard my share. Give it your best shot." But even as he said the words, something was working on his brain as recognition of those blue, blue eyes and black hair creeped inside his soul. *No. Freaking. Way.*

"I'm Randi Collins, but you might've known me as Sadie Brubaker." She said it as if it was no big deal. As if sashaying into this town over a decade since she'd disappeared hadn't mattered.

"H-how? How are you here now?" His hands were actually shaking.

"I came here first. I was told you could help me." She showed no recognition other than that odd moment their eyes met on the sidewalk.

"I know this is a shock, and I realize that's likely an understatement—"

He stood abruptly as it began to sink in. Then he rushed over to lock the door. "I can't have anyone come in here and see you."

"I don't want to upset anyone but I also didn't come here to be locked inside." Her tone sounded calm, but Chase could tell she was struggling as she tapped her foot on the floor and took deep breaths.

"Listen, I know this seems extreme, but give me a minute to let this sink in." He worked to calm his heartbeat and breathing. "People in town are going to be shocked to see you again. I have so many questions and so will they."

"Are you okay?" she asked, frowning slightly, seeming somewhat confused by his over-the-top reaction.

He breathed deeply and asked, "How are you here? Where have you been?" he demanded. "I'm sorry. It's just— Sadie Brubaker, as I live and breathe."

"Hickman, Nebraska," she said, as if that explained it. "I've been driving for two days."

"No. *Where* did you come from? All these years? Were you kidnapped? Did you run away? We've been killing ourselves trying to figure it out. How are you here now? You realize everyone believes you're dead, right? You've been officially *declared* dead." Chase realized he must sound like a crazed person instead of a professional who protected citizens in this county.

She put her hands up at his verbal onslaught. "Please. Let me try to explain. I can't imagine how this must be for you. How it's going to seem for some people here who knew me…before."

Chase nearly bit his tongue not to shout at her, so he merely motioned with his hand for her to continue speaking.

"I need you to understand that I've had no memory since the day I went missing. None. I don't know how or why I left, or what happened to cause my disappearance. I only know I was found wandering at a bus station outside Oklahoma City by my mom, Thelma, who picked me up and took care of me."

Chase stared at her, his mouth hanging open. "Your mom's not Thelma. Who's Thelma? How can that even be true? Any of it?"

"I thought Thelma was my mom—my adoptive mom. Now, I don't know who she was really. I understand this is hard to believe and I expected to be doubted." But she appeared confused by his reaction. "I have a letter from her from before she died." She reached into her purse. "Here." She slid a letter across the desk.

Chase tried not to snatch it away and rip into it. He managed to pick it up and open it without obvious urgency.

Ma Chère Randi,

If you are reading this, it means I've died before completing my work for you. I wanted so much to help you find your way home and your path to the future. I've treasured you greatly, and hope you've felt safe with me as your mama during our years together.

I hope you will understand and forgive me for protecting you so tightly. Please, darling, return home and regain your former self. I had hoped we could go on this journey together. For as much as I've protected you, I've kept you away from those you love and those who love you. I'm sorry for that. Tell them of my apology, and that it wasn't your fault. Your loss of memory was a blessing and a curse. Without it, I couldn't send you back. But the time has come, and you must find your family.

You became Randi after my Randi died. You saved my life and my sanity. We saved each other. Be safe and well, my heart.

Trust Mr. Whitaker. He is a good man and holds the information you will need on your journey home. Be patient. Someday, you will understand...

Thelma

Sadie waited patiently until Chase finished reading and looked up. "I still don't quite understand. Not yet. Mr. Whitaker was Thelma's attorney who I'd not even known about until she died. Learning that she wasn't my mother was shocking—but learning that my entire life as I'd known it since age sixteen was a lie... Well, you can't imagine."

Chase read the letter a second time. "You can't fathom the years we spent—the manpower—trying to locate you." He could hear the frustration in his voice. But the way she stared at him, her large blue eyes like deer in headlights, made Chase realize he hadn't done enough to temper his response, and Daisy Mae's low, protective growl confirmed this. "I'm sorry. This—this is so unbelievable. I've imagined this scenario—your coming back one day. I can't believe it." He shook his head.

She seemed a little less nervous then.

"I'm sorry for your loss—I think. Did *Thelma* tell you

anything about your history here? Did she kidnap you?"

"No. She rescued me. I was hurt when she found me, but I don't remember what happened to me—before that."

"Well, we don't know anything about the night you disappeared, or where you went."

"I wish I could answer your questions." She shrugged.

But Chase still couldn't wrap his mind around the fact that Sadie Brubaker was sitting at his desk. "I can't believe you're here, Sadie."

"Randi."

"Pardon?"

"My name's been Randi Collins for the last thirteen years. There are legal things going on behind the scenes while the attorney works to figure out how to declare me *undead* now that we know who I am. I just found out my real name a couple of weeks ago when Thelma passed away. It's all very confusing."

Mary Frances's face swam into his mind. "Your mother—" He dragged a hand through his hair. "You don't remember her?"

Sadie paled, real emotion showing now. "I've been told my mother lives here, but I don't know anything else."

"Yes. But Sadie—Randi, things haven't gone well, generally, since you've been away. Not that they were great when you were a kid—"

"I don't know anything—or anyone, Sheriff. That's why coming to you first was so important. I was told I could trust you, and I need someone to help me navigate all of this if my memory doesn't return."

He stared at her and worked to put himself in her shoes

if she was to be believed. She didn't even remember her own mother or her sister, Julie? Or Hank Brubaker?

What a mess. This was going to be confusing and possibly unbelievable for many of the folks in town. When she'd disappeared, it had gone national very quickly. All the major newspapers and television networks had shown up to interview the locals. Back then, a missing child was a big fat hairy deal. It still was, but now it was a more commonplace occurrence and less of a national story.

He took a deep breath then. *Sadie Brubaker is back. Now, isn't that something?* It was finally sinking in.

"Sheriff, why are you smiling at me like that?" she asked.

"Sorry, Sadie. I spent over a decade trying to figure out what happened to you. And here you are. You'll have to forgive me for appreciating the moment."

"Oh. Thanks?" She gave a nervous laugh. Maybe like he was a little crazy.

He managed to gather his wits and get down to business then. "What *do* you know about your past?" he asked.

She pressed her lips together and shook her head. "Not much. Like I said, it's only been a couple of weeks. I was afraid to do too much research ahead. I've been a little...scared...of what I might find out. I-I've lived a pretty sheltered life." She dropped her gaze.

Sounded pretty messed up, but one thing at a time. "Right now, we've got to figure out how to handle this situation. Where are you staying?"

She pointed out the window. "At the bed-and-breakfast a couple of doors down."

"Fannie's place? That's good. She's trustworthy. I assume

you registered under Randi Collins?"

She nodded.

"Okay. First things first. Are you hungry? I was just on my way out to get some lunch."

"Starving. Is Daisy Mae going to be an issue?" She indicated the animal by patting her on the head.

"Nah." He stood and strode over to the coatrack, grabbing a cap. He handed it to her. "You might want to wear this to be safe."

"Safe?"

"Bad word choice. Wear it so nobody will recognize you. Believe it or not, you still look very much the same. Once a whisper starts that you've come back from the dead, things might get complicated around here. I mean, obviously, the town has moved on, but your story was a big deal around here for a long time."

She nodded. "Makes sense."

He was sure she would have remembered him. It stung just a little that there wasn't even a glimmer of recognition in her eyes, well, maybe a glimmer when their eyes met outside. He was four or five years older than she was, but he'd liked to think he'd been a protector of sorts toward her when she was young.

She still bore an innocence that made her appear vulnerable. Vulnerable and naïve as a newborn babe. She didn't have a clue what sort of havoc she'd left in her wake.

"Whatever happens, keep your head down and don't make eye contact."

She burst out laughing, startling Chase. Her teeth were white and even, and her blue eyes sparkled.

"Was it something I said?"

"You've repeated something I've been told every day for years by Thelma," she said. "I've had plenty of practice keeping my head down."

Chase was glad to see a bit of spunk from her but it also made him sad for her, being held under somebody's thumb. The Sadie he remembered wouldn't have put up with it. But he was trying to be careful how he approached what came next. "Not for much longer. We need to get you over to your momma's house before anybody else recognizes you. She deserves to be the first one to know you're back—besides my momma, who's got lunch waiting. We shouldn't do this on an empty stomach." And he wasn't up for explaining to all those folks how Sadie Brubaker came to be his dining companion.

Sadie's belly growled at that moment, loud enough for them both to hear. She placed a hand over it. "Um, agreed." She pulled on the cap and adjusted the size then pulled it low.

He nodded as he ushered her and Daisy Mae into the passenger's side of his large SUV, marked with Moonshine's logo. Daisy Mae hopped in back without being prompted.

Chapter Eight

I'D WORKED TO keep my emotions in check the entire time in Chase Blackburn's office. And I'd done a fine job until he'd quoted Thelma almost verbatim, when I'd burst out laughing like a loon.

Maybe I'd fall apart later, but right now my stomach was eating a hole in itself. The anxiety and anticipation of meeting my mother had to stay put until the time came.

I'd had a tiny spark of recognition when my gaze connected with the sheriff's. But nothing real specific. I got the sense he was a kind man, and not someone I should fear. "Are you sure your mother won't mind you bringing a guest to lunch?" It seemed rude to me that he wouldn't call ahead and make sure.

It was his turn to laugh. "Are you kidding? She's gonna be so tickled to see you. She and your mother are friends of sorts, and nothing goes on around here without Becky Blackburn knowing about it. She'll feed us and head over to the Brubaker farm with us."

"I lived on a farm?" I hadn't thought about where I'd actually lived. My home.

"In a farmhouse. It wasn't ever a real working farm beside a few chickens and goats. There was a nice garden out back when you were a kid. Not so much anymore."

I wasn't sure what he meant by that, but it didn't sound comforting. "Is my mom sick?" I was getting antsy now. His concern for my reaction worried me.

"She isn't well. But I don't know how much of that is from living with your stepdad—Hank."

"What's wrong with him?" But I knew then that he was the yelling man. The one who'd so viciously attacked me. I'd had one single memory and that was it.

His mouth compressed into a straight, tight line. "It's probably good that you don't remember. He's been abusive to her and anyone else who's gotten within his bad graces for the last twenty-five years. Before that, I wouldn't know. The bastard's sick and dying."

Something about how he said that jolted me. I gripped the armrest and heat rushed to my face. A man's face flashed in my mind. Bloodshot eyes. Bloated, ruddy cheeks. Hate. Glaring at me.

"Are you okay?"

"I-I think so." I took deep breaths.

We pulled into a gravel driveway of an old, but freshly painted white farmhouse with a bright blue door.

"Are you sure you're okay?"

I nodded, but anger had filled every part of me in the instant I remembered his face, and this time I was having a hard time putting it away. "I'm pretty sure I remember Hank."

He cut the engine and sighed audibly. "If anyone could bring back a memory in the worst possible way, I imagine it would be Hank—especially for you, Sadie. And I'm sorry.

He's a real shithead. Pardon my language."

"Randi." My identity was my life preserver while it seemed I was circling a huge drain.

"Okay, Randi. But around here it's going to be hard to convince anyone to call you anything other than Sadie. They're going to call you by your given name."

He opened the door and climbed down. Before I had a chance to do the same, he was beside me offering a hand of assistance. I'm sure I stared at him like he'd lost his mind. Then it dawned on me. *Manners.* I'd not been very familiar with those kindnesses. Thelma treated me very well, but besides her and my friend Jenny, I hadn't had a lot of experience with good manners—or men.

Shaking off the flash of memory and its surge of bubbling rage, I pushed the intrusive emotions into the compartment where they belonged until I was ready to pull them out and examine them later. I'd had to do a lot of that these past weeks.

Daisy Mae and I followed him up the porch steps toward the bright blue front door with the large floral wreath. I silently wondered if my family home was similar to this one. Somehow I doubted I would've run away from a place this nice and tidy. Bad things couldn't happen here, could they?

Chase knocked a couple quick times, then shoved the heavy door open. "Momma?"

"Oh, hey there, honey. You're right on time. The meat loaf just came out of the oven—oh, my." She dropped the potholder she been holding and her face paled.

The woman stared at me wide-eyed, still with my cap on. But she *knew.*

"It's—she's—" Then she stared at Chase as if for an explanation.

"Momma, it's Sadie Brubaker." He bent down and retrieved the potholder from the polished wood floor.

"Hi, Mrs. Blackburn. It's nice to meet you—or, to see you again?" So awkward.

"Let's go into the kitchen and have a look at that meat loaf, okay?" Chase suggested, as Mrs. Blackburn continued to stare at me—as if I'd come back from the dead. It gave me an idea of what might happen over and over now that I was back in Moonshine.

We moved into the kitchen, which was just as lovely as the foyer and living space, I noticed. Everything was updated, but still held the vintage farmhouse feel. It was homey and cozy. I felt secure in a way I hadn't since leaving my home in Hickman. I'd watched enough HGTV to appreciate how well loved this home was.

"Have a seat, Mom. Sadie—Randi."

"What on earth is going on here, son?" Mrs. Blackburn demanded now that she'd come out of the trance my appearance had put her in.

"Well, obviously, Sadie isn't dead like we all thought. She's been living in Hickman, Nebraska, all this time with a woman named Thelma."

"But—" she began.

Chase put a hand up. "Let me explain. Then you can ask her any questions you want, or as many as she's willing to answer."

Mrs. Blackburn nodded. "Okay."

Chase filled his mother in on my whereabouts for the

past thirteen years from what I'd told him.

Mrs. Blackburn appeared to let the information sink in a minute. She was an attractive woman, dark hair, with a few gray threads. She looked to be in her early sixties, fit, in her slim jeans and button-down top. No-nonsense in her dress and hairstyle. A little makeup.

A huge grin spread across her face, and she was transformed. "Welcome home, Sadie." She pulled me into an unexpected warm embrace. I really wished people would give me a heads-up before they did that. I'd watched how friendly people were in the South on television.

"Call me Becky. I'm sorry for your loss."

"Thank you, Becky."

"Your momma's gonna be over the moon to see you."

Then, she noticed Daisy Mae. "Hi there, girl. Would you like some water?"

Becky patted her and led her to a bowl on the floor in the kitchen. Daisy Mae wagged and whined in happiness at being welcomed.

"Hey, Momma, could we get something to eat before we head over there? We're both starved."

Becky frowned at her son. "Of course, son. You're always starved, but everything's better on a full belly, for sure."

She served us heaping plates of meat loaf, mashed potatoes and gravy, and corn bread. And some kind of unfamiliar green vegetable cut in small rounds that appeared to be dipped into a batter and fried. It wasn't something Thelma had ever cooked. "Thanks. This looks delicious."

"I have so many questions for you, honey. We've wondered about you for so long. People around here aren't gonna know what to do with themselves."

"Yeah. We've got to figure out how to get accurate information out before everyone sees her passing by and the rumors get started." Chase frowned.

"Why such a mess once they understand I can't remember?" I asked.

"Let's just say, folks here have made up their own truths over the years about what might have happened to you. Your coming back with no memory safe and sound is rather—anticlimactic."

My ending up living quietly in Hickman was far less dramatic than being murdered, kidnapped into a cult or sex trafficking ring, or held against my will in a cage for the last thirteen years. "I see your point." I'd watched a lot of crime drama with Thelma over the years. I suppose it was strange now how I could make jokes about captivity and murder. I was odd that way, I guess.

My past away from Moonshine had been mostly calm and completely unthreatening, and my early therapist said that I had a *low affect due to trauma*. Thelma always seemed so supportive despite the fact that she encouraged me to keep my head down. But she'd also taken me from a bus stop at age sixteen and not contacted the police. I didn't have those answers yet—maybe I never would.

"We'll have to put it out in *The Moonshine Herald* tonight if we can get the mayor to agree," Becky Blackburn said.

That caught my attention. "The mayor? Why does he have to agree? And why put my return in the newspaper?" I truly didn't understand these people and their thought processes. Maybe I was missing something. No, I was *definitely* missing something.

"The mayor and Chase aren't the best of friends. They've been rivals since they were kids, but mostly because Jason Weston is married to Chase's ex-wife, Annie. Oh, and Jason owns the local paper."

"And *everyone* in Moonshine reads the newspaper. We even have it online now. But mostly it's delivered twice a week early in the morning for folks to read with their coffee before they start the day."

"It must be filled with exciting information," I said, remembering how Thelma got the local paper and read it with her coffee. But when I tried to read it, all I noticed were a few headlines about protests, new stores opening nearby, some national stories, and tons of ads. Certainly nothing that would make it a priority before starting my day. My online graphic design business was much more exciting and satisfying.

They both snickered a little at that. "Mostly who got speeding tickets or drunk and disorderly, who killed what wild game with a picture of the animal laid over the hood, and whatever local businesses are running specials for the week trying to outdo the next," Becky said.

"Then there's the gossip along with some community information and concert and art festival schedules thrown in. It's like people checking social media everywhere else in the world. They do that here too," Chase added.

"Oh. I see." I didn't have a personal social media page, but I had one for my business and though I didn't use my name, only my business logo, I understood online sites and what they meant to people. In my internet work life, my clients talked about it. But online communication and conversation meant rarely ever having to see another person's face, so I'm sure I seemed pretty normal in that realm.

"We'll need to give them just enough of the truth to keep the tongue-wagging to a minimum," Becky said.

"I'll answer any questions I can. But I guess we should go to my mom's house first?" I asked. I didn't want to appear too impatient, but I was getting antsy.

"Yes, so sorry. Of course you want to see your mom." She turned to her son. "But Chase, what about Hank? Do you think we can keep him in another room or something?"

"His recent stroke has him in bed most of the time so keeping him out of the way might not be an issue."

There was definitely a theme here. Hank was a terrible human being. I felt it. They said it. But I needed to know more.

"What exactly did Hank do?"

His answer hit me like a punch to the stomach. "He's a violent alcoholic, Sadie. He has been known to send your mother to the emergency room, but she won't ever press charges. And he's someone who's tangled with a good number of locals as well—though they don't take him seriously anymore."

The acidic taste of bile rose in my throat. I swallowed several times to get rid of it. I had a sudden flash of Hank coming at me with murder in his eyes. A memory. "He nearly killed me," I said matter-of-factly. I couldn't call up the exact recollection, but it wasn't far away. "I'm starting to have some small flashes of memory here and there. The night

I ran away—he and I fought. He nearly killed me. I don't know about anything before that."

Chase and Becky stared at me.

"You remember about that night? You ran away? We knew Hank hit your mother regularly, but we weren't sure that he'd ever hit you," Chase said.

I didn't know what to say to that. "I-I guess we should go," I suggested, because tears threatened out of nowhere.

Becky took my hand. "Please know that we wanted to help your mom. Chase was young at the time. He even took on Hank once, before he became a deputy. Landed Chase in the hospital, and Hank in jail."

Then I did understand a little better. Hank had been strong then, and Chase not yet quite a man. "Thank you."

Daisy Mae had been a lovely lady and sat at my feet the entire time. She and I now climbed into the back seat of the SUV while Becky and Chase took the front.

"How far is my mom's house?" I asked.

"About two miles," Becky answered. "And since you don't remember, I want to warn you that it's not in good repair. It's gotten worse over the years as Hank's drinking's increased. He's been on disability for about ten years, so there's not a lot of money coming in."

Nothing about my family sounded good. "What about my mom? Does she work?"

"She tries to as much as she can. Mary Frances is a clerk at the dollar store. They've been pretty good about giving her time off to take care of Hank lately from what I hear."

I wondered how she knew details about my family. About my mother's work schedule and her employer.

"Sounds like she ought to let him die," I murmured. The man who'd shown the females in his life the business end of his balled-up fist didn't get much compassion from me.

"You wouldn't be the only one in town of that mind," Chase said. "Just be aware that things are in a sad state. But your coming home now will be good for your mom."

But will it be good for me?

What kind of mother didn't report the abuse of her child?

They pulled off the paved road down one that was a mixture of dirt and gravel. It was bumpy, and I pictured how muddy it got when it rained. I'm not sure why that was the first thing that occurred to me. Memory? Maybe, but there wasn't any emotion tied to it, just the knowledge of mud, and maybe walking down this road in it.

The road, or driveway might be a better term, ended after about a half mile. I stared ahead, wanting a first glance of what had been my home. The term *farmhouse* had been used to kindly identify this property. Ramshackle was more accurate.

"I'm sorry, Sadie," Becky said when our eyes met.

"Randi," I corrected her.

"Pardon?"

"I've been Randi Collins for the past thirteen years. I have no real memory of being Sadie."

Becky nodded, her eyes filled with sadness for me. "Life has done a number on you, hasn't it, baby girl?"

I had two lives. I was a split person. I was Randi, but here, Sadie. I had the feeling I wasn't going to change their minds.

This was it. I stared at the old farmhouse from the back seat. It was a stark contrast to Becky's well-kept home. Thelma, with her DIY skills and can-do attitude would've see this as a fixer-upper.

I was about to meet my mother. The woman who'd given birth to me and who'd believed me dead for over a decade. My hands shook, and I fought tears—again.

Chapter Nine

A S WE CLIMBED out of Chase's vehicle, Daisy Mae ran over to the porch and sniffed at something underneath. Then, she relieved herself in the grass.

"Are you ready?" Chase asked me.

I took a deep breath and thought of Thelma's wisdom and calm in most situations. It steadied me. "I'm ready."

"Might be best to give Mary Frances a heads-up. We'll go on inside and make sure Hank's off in another room before you come in." Chase got out and headed up the steps of the slightly sagging porch.

I nodded and tried to smile, to show them I had faith in their plan.

Becky touched my shoulder. "Coming back from the dead is a good thing."

I wasn't so sure right now, so I stayed back around the side of the car. I was terrified that this was a step I couldn't take back. I heard Chase knock on the door and a woman's voice greeting them. I wanted to look but didn't dare yet. So far, I had no memories of this place besides the dirt road when it rained.

I heard her cry out then. It was terrible and sad, more animal than human.

"Mary Frances—wait—" Becky called.

I moved from behind the car and saw her. My mother. "Momma?" Flashes of childhood ran through my rusty brain like a video montage. Momma sewing my dress, cleaning my skinned knee, kissing us good night. Sunday dinner passing potatoes, and Hank's yelling.

She looked the same, but different. My heart bled inside my chest. I tried to inhale, but the pressure was a lead weight.

She threw herself on me and dragged me to the ground. "S-Sadie. God brought you back to me. I prayed—I prayed every day—"

"Momma?" I breathed then. "It's really you." I pulled back from her shaking embrace. I touched her hands. The ones from my childhood with Julie. *Julie!* Where was Julie? But my mind couldn't understand what my eyes saw. My stomach ached, or was it my stomach? I wanted to throw up the huge meal I'd just eaten.

"M-my baby girl." Tears streamed down her cheeks. She touched my hair, my face. "He didn't kill you after all. You managed to get away. How—where did you go for all these years while I've been missing you?"

My tears matched hers. It was raw and it all hurt. "Momma—" I sobbed until there weren't any more tears in my body. We both did. Momma's cornflower-blue eyes were tired and sad, but she wasn't broken all the way. He hadn't killed her either.

"My sweet, strong girl. How I've missed you." Momma's voice was familiar and filled a little of the void where so much nothing had been before.

"What the fuck is going on out here? Get the hell outta my way before I kick your ass, Sheriff." That hateful voice threw me to another place and time.

I smelled the tears, the sweat, the putrid smell of alcohol on Hank's breath.

"I'm gonna kill you this time, you little bitch, you, and those devil eyes. Gonna cut 'em out." He came at me with a screwdriver. Usually, it was only his fists. The screwdriver told me he meant business. I rolled aside, just as he plunged it in the ground right next to my head. That was too close.

I felt Daisy Mae lick my hand then, pulling me out of the horrible memory.

"Sadie. Can you hear me? It's Momma." I felt the rush of relief flow over me. I'd found my momma again.

"Sadie. He can't hurt you." I heard Chase Blackburn's voice.

I was sitting on the ground, my mother and Becky on each side of me. Chase stood about fifteen feet away and held a frail, bony old man, his arms behind his back. *Hank.* He looked nothing the same—besides the eyes. The hate behind them was exactly the same. *He'd* been the danger Thelma had kept me from? But before, he *had* been a danger. A big, strong angry danger who'd been intent on hurting—even killing me—that particular night.

"Goddamn my soul. Where—*how* did you get back here? You're supposed to be dead where you belong." He slurred and I noticed that the left side of his face drooped. His right arm was pulled up and curled at the wrist.

Daisy Mae growled then, low and deep.

I stared at him, the evil from my childhood. The reason

for the way my life had gone up until now—my memory loss. "You tried to kill me," I said quietly.

His face lost what color it had. "You can't prove anything. Nobody's gonna believe anything you say." His words were somewhat garbled, but I understood them.

Because I didn't have a full memory of the event yet, I let it go. He appeared weak and old, and a tiny part of me felt sad about that.

Momma's hand shook on my arm. Her fear of him was real, as sick and frail as he was. Even though he could barely stand on his own.

In that moment, I understood the threat he'd been to me—to us all.

Then, I saw Julie again in a flash of memory. In my mind she was blonde and petite. Thirteen years old or so. I asked, "Momma, where's Julie? Where's my sister?"

Momma hung her head, and the tears began anew. "They took her, baby. When you disappeared, the state came in and claimed us unfit—well, they said as long as there was any suspicion, Julie couldn't live here. And Hank—he wouldn't leave." She glared at her husband for a moment, but he didn't seem to be paying attention. In fact, he was now staring blankly.

"Suspicion?" I asked, still uncertain of what had happened beyond the memory I'd just experienced.

"The police thought Hank might have something to do with your disappearance but didn't have any proof. They were investigating."

"It was my fucking house," he snarled then. Clearly, he remembered some of it.

Momma stiffened. "It's not your house. It's my house."

I took a deep breath and wondered how this came to be my reality. This is where I came from. Then I asked Momma, "They took her, and you don't know where she is? Like you never saw or heard from her again?" I pictured my sweet little sister being ripped from our home by strangers. I imagined how scared she must have been.

And it was my fault because I left. "I'm so sorry, Momma. If I hadn't left—"

Momma's gaze was steady when she looked into my eyes. "If you hadn't left, *he* would've killed you." She pointed a finger at Hank, who'd taken a seat on the front porch. "I still pray every day that my Julie went to a nice, clean home with people who loved her and took good care of her and where she didn't have to be afraid or ashamed of being our daughter in this town."

But Hank hadn't ever laid a hand on Julie that I could remember. Of course, I still didn't remember much. I tried to process her words.

Hank was breathing hard and sweating. His skin had a yellowish tinge to it, as did the whites of his eyes. It was clear he was very sick.

This man had hurt me—tried to kill me even—and he'd hurt my family. I believed he was pure evil, if such a thing existed. But now, he was pathetic. I would never forgive him for hurting us. Was forgiveness for such a thing even possible?

Chase, who seemed to understand exactly what Hank was made of, did his civic duty despite that, and led the dying man inside, even allowing Hank to lean on him for support. I experienced a pang of emotion at his kindness. I was...touched by it. Not on Hank's behalf though. Chase was a good person, and I'd not been around enough people for any length of time in recent memory to process my response to his kindness right now.

"Sadie, I'm so sorry we lost Julie—that she's gone. I would do anything to bring her back to us," Momma said. Her eyes were downcast.

I didn't understand how I could've come from such a violent household after my years living with love and support from Thelma. How could Momma not have turned over every rock to find us both? I didn't say any of that though. I was still trying to catch up to all the memories. Taking a deep breath, I pulled my mother's hand into mine. It was dry and aged, though she couldn't be that old. Thelma had been in her early seventies. I had the feeling Momma had been young when I was born, which would make her still in her, what? Late forties or early fifties?

Hank was older, by ten years maybe? The drinking had aged him well beyond the calendar gap. When I left town, he was still quite capable of violence and murder. I was absorbing these things, these memories. There were things I just knew now, coming back here. And these things horrified me. Especially, that Momma was still with Hank after everything he'd done to her—to us—during my childhood.

"Momma, we'll find her, okay? There's got to be a way." My heart was filled to bursting with emotion, but I was equally confused. I remembered Momma's love—feeling it, knowing it. Leaving her and Julie had been the only way for me to stay alive, I was certain. The memories were foggy and jumbled, but that night was inching its way back in my mind one bad memory at a time.

I wasn't quite ready though. How much more was there that I couldn't remember? How much worse could it be?

Momma put her arms around me. "It's all gonna be all right now. You're back, thank the Lord. My heart knew you were out there someplace, but my mind kept telling me Hank had killed you and buried you somewhere."

I stared at her. *And you didn't kill him yourself?* Were they only talking about that night? How many other times had he hurt me? Beaten me?

"He swore it was all his blood on the floor and that you'd run off after the two of you had fought in the barn."

I stared at her, not knowing how to respond. I got that she was scared, even deathly afraid, but to not come out with a shotgun and blow him to hell if she had any inkling what might be happening to me was beyond my understanding of what mothers should do to protect their children. Though I had no children, I knew what Thelma would've done to save me, without a single doubt. She'd changed her whole life for me—that I knew.

Momma bowed her head and continued. "I never knew if he was telling the truth. He told me I wouldn't ever see you again, and I didn't know what he meant and was so afraid he would kill me and Julie too. I wasn't scared of dying, mind you, but I needed to be here for the two of you. Not that I was any help—"

I didn't have any real ideas on how to comfort her at the moment, not sure I even wanted to, but I could be honest. "My memories are all jumbled right now, but I feel it coming back. He did try to kill me that night, but I ran. I got away." I remembered riding a bicycle on an old dirt road in the pitch-dark for what seemed like miles. It was the first time I'd had a glimpse of memory of leaving my home.

Chase stepped down from the porch and approached. "He's back in bed. I gave him a pain pill. He's likely out for the night, so you'll have some peace, Mary Frances."

"God bless you, Chase," Momma said. "He's gotten so weak, but he still has such an angry mouth on him."

"Are all the guns out of the house, or at least locked up where he can't get hold of them?" Chase asked.

Momma nodded. "I did that last week. I got rid of the knives and the fire poker too. He's too weak to hurt me with his fists, so I'm not as worried about him hitting me any- more."

I felt her words strike me like blows. "I can't believe you've lived with him like this all these years."

Momma shrugged. "I couldn't let him take my house. He told me if I left, he'd find me and kill me. And that he'd hunt Julie down. I don't know if he would've done that, but I know he wouldn't have let me live a day in peace. Not that he ever has."

Now that my memories of Hank were returning, the sense of hopelessness and being trapped seeped back into my being. Momma must have believed she had no choices, no options. I found my way out when I ran. But it hadn't been without consequences for Momma and Julie. This was all so confusing.

But I kept quiet. Hank's abuse was soaking back into my soul, and I wasn't ready to share that with anyone yet. I felt shame. A secret, even now, like back then. *Sadie, don't tell anyone about Hank's bad temper. They'll take you and Julie away. Hank will get fired and we'll lose the house.*

I thought suddenly about Thelma's picking me up at the bus stop and taking me away. Of course, she didn't have any way of knowing what had happened with Hank, but *had* it been the best thing for me at the time? If I'd been returned home by police with no memory, would Hank have gotten rid of me, especially if he worried about my randomly remembering what he'd done? No one would have been the wiser.

Becky stepped up and offered, "Mary Frances, would you like to come and stay at my house tonight? I've got a meat loaf from lunchtime and a clean bed for you."

Momma shook her head. "If I leave and don't come home all night, he won't let me back in the house. It's *my* house. No matter what he says. My first husband—Sadie's daddy—bought us that house."

I didn't remember anything about my father, so that raised even more questions. I wanted to scream at her but also comfort her. "I'm staying at the bed-and-breakfast in town, so I'll come back tomorrow if you think that'll be okay." I wasn't sure how this all should go. Maybe I would bring a baseball bat *and* my dog with me when I came back, just in case. I knew Daisy Mae wouldn't let Hank lay a hand on me. Plus, I'd knock his old, sick ass out if he tried.

Now, where had that come from? That urge to fight? To defend? That was new to me. It wasn't me. I'd never really had those urges. Were they part of the me I left behind? Were they the sixteen-year-old Sadie who'd fought off grown men wielding screwdrivers?

That wasn't Randi; that was Sadie. I remembered her for a moment. How it had *been* to be her. Me. The old me. Spunky, feisty, and filled with rage and the need to keep my momma safe from Hank.

Randi was calm and rational. Kind and smart. But what if there was more to me than I knew?

Part of me wanted to stay here in my childhood home and sleep at my momma's side to protect her from Hank. The other part wanted to drag Hank outside and make him sleep in the dirt. It's like there were two of me. I guess if I thought about it, there were: Randi and Sadie.

I was exhausted. My days of driving, sleeping in a different location each night, and the adjustment of meeting so many new people had already worn me down. Add that to the surge of memories and emotions I'd been overwhelmed with this afternoon and it all threatened to shut me down right here.

"Let's get you back into town, Sadie. You look like you're about to fall over." Becky pulled at my arm gently.

Chase nodded. "You do seem a little pale." His eyes met mine then, and he seemed to stare at me for a moment, which made my skin suddenly sensitive and tingly. What an odd sensation.

Their concern reminded me of Thelma's years of care and mothering, which made my eyes tear. And I looked over at Momma, which made me want to bawl, because I didn't know how to feel.

Daisy Mae moved over next to Chase, almost as if the drama here was too much. He obliged her by crouching beside her and laying a hand on her back to soothe her.

Momma put her arms around me then, like she used to when I was a little girl. "Sadie, you listen to me. We're together now. I don't know what happened to you or where you've been all this time, but you're home. I didn't do a good job protecting you from Hank, but I loved you girls, and I love you now. You're my girl, and I'm still your momma. We'll take it from here, okay?"

I melted against her then despite my conflicting emotions. "Okay. I'll see you tomorrow."

"And you bring your sweet puppy back too. I can tell she's your best friend."

I smiled and glanced over to where Daisy Mae had ditched me for Chase. "She's my saving grace."

Leaving Momma there with Hank was terrible. But she'd been with him every day for all these many years. It was her normal. She hated him, but I guessed she loved him too. Maybe that's how they defined co-dependent. Unbearable to stay and impossible to leave. Maybe like a captor with a rope tied around his victim crossing a rickety bridge with sharks in the water below—or some such tragic horror show. Somehow, she'd borne it, though I would never understand.

"You okay back there, Randi?" Becky asked once we were back in the SUV.

I nodded. I didn't dare speak right now. My brain was too full and messy. I hated messy. Daisy Mae sat up on the seat tightly against my side.

Maybe Hank will die in his sleep.

That was definitely a Sadie thought. But even as Randi, I swear I wouldn't waste my newly found tears on him should that be the case.

It was evening now, and I wondered if Miss Fannie thought I was a no-show since I hadn't yet checked in to the B&B. As we pulled up in front of the sheriff's office, it occurred to me that Chase had yet to take Becky home.

"I'm sorry to keep you out all day, Becky," I said from the back seat.

She turned. "Nonsense. I thought I would help you get settled and whisper into Fannie's ear while you unpack. We need all the allies we can get. And then there's the call to the newspaper. We've got to get ahead of this homecoming before people start to recognize you and fire up the phone tree."

"Sounds like something from an old Andy Griffith rerun Thelma and I used to watch together."

Becky snorted a little laugh. "You have no idea. This town's come a long way in recent years, but the mindset of many is still small and terribly set on spreading gossip. And I wouldn't call your coming home gossip even. This is going to be the biggest news since—well, since ever. If it goes badly from the start, it's going to be hard to reel back in."

I nodded. I was beginning to get some idea how impactful my unexpected return might be to some members of the community. After all, they'd believed a terrible crime had happened the night I'd disappeared. I was guessing that nobody felt safe for a while since they had no idea what had happened to me. Maybe some of them believed a stranger carried me off. That would've been unsettling for sure.

"No time like the present," Chase announced as he climbed out then opened my door. "Might want to pull your hat down a touch. Shield those blue eyes."

I tugged my cap down and moved from the vehicle as incognito as possible toward the entrance of the bed-and-breakfast. I clipped on Daisy Mae's leash, and she walked beside me like a perfect lady.

"Hand me your car keys and I'll grab as much of your stuff as I can on the first trip."

"Oh, thanks." I wasn't used to anyone carrying my things for me.

"Let's get you inside." Becky put a hand on my back and hustled me forward.

They were serious about getting me off the street. I assumed there was the normal number of people around, both residents, and likely several tourists. Several nodded or spoke greetings to Becky and Chase. I tried to keep my head down and not make eye contact with anyone. But I noticed a few curious stares. No one said anything to me directly, thankfully.

We slipped inside Fannie's establishment with a loud jingle of the door's bells. What was with the bells around here?

"Well, howdy, ladies. Lord Jesus, Becky, it's been a coon's age." A tiny, skeletal woman with purplish-gray hair in a yellow muumuu cackled. I recognized her voice from our phone call confirming my reservation. She appeared far older in person.

"Oh, nonsense, Fannie. You saw me last week at the market."

"Oh, yeah. You were stocking up on booze. Now I remember." The woman cackled again. "Who you got here?"

Fannie moved quite close into my space and stared at me with cataract-afflicted eyes.

"This is your new guest. Her reservation is under the name Randi Collins."

"Randi! I thought maybe you'd gotten lost or fallen off the side of the road on one of our dead man's curves. So glad to see you made it here." Fannie grinned and stuck out her hand in greeting.

I shook it. "Me too. And yes, those curves were pretty sharp."

"I'd like to say it keeps the drunks off the road, but it doesn't."

Her words brought Hank to mind, and Momma. A tiny spout of joy followed by a punch in the gut, or vice versa hit me. I'm not sure which order it happened, because thinking of them caused both. Having what little bit of memory that had returned still freaked me out a little. The blank part of my brain felt like it was working in overdrive to fill itself in.

"This must be Daisy Mae. She's well behaved, I see."

Daisy Mae was sitting beside me waiting her turn. "Yes. She's probably ready for her dinner and a nap."

"Well, let's get y'all settled in."

The bells jingled and Chase entered laden with what appeared to be everything from inside my Jeep. "Good Lord, son, you could have made more than one trip." Becky rushed over to take some things off his load.

I watched how his arms strained under the weight of it all and didn't move for a moment. "He's a real looker, don't you think?" Fannie not-so-quietly whispered into my ear. Her eyes were obviously good enough to see me staring at

Chase's muscles.

Horrified at the new sensations that caused in my body, I frowned. "Uh, no. I'm amazed he could carry all of it in, is all."

Fannie grinned. "Right. Say what you want, but if I was sixty years younger, I'd be all over that. He's single, you know?"

I didn't know that. Becky had mentioned he had an ex-wife, but it wasn't of any interest or consequence to me. I was so weird and broken, the idea of a normal relationship with a man was ridiculous.

"You'll be in room 6B at the end of the hall on the first floor. It's a corner suite. Best room I've got. The cancellation was a honeymooning couple, so lucky you."

I handed her my debit card. I thought about my name then. And how I now knew it wasn't real. It reminded me to call the attorney back in Hickman to check the legal status of my situation next week.

"All righty then. You're all set."

Becky approached then. "Chase can follow you up to your room."

Then, she turned her attention to Fannie. "Can you and I have a word in private?"

"Sounds serious. I'll put the 'out to lunch' sign up and we can talk in my office." Fannie sat the sign right next to the *Please ring bell for service* one.

Chapter Ten

AS I DRAGGED my feet and my dog toward 6B with Chase on my heels, my thoughts suddenly registered, *I'm home.* What an odd thing.

After today's events, part of me wanted to climb right back in my Jeep and return to Hickman and the house I'd shared with Thelma. I wasn't certain moving forward with all this mess was in anyone's best interest.

I unlocked the door with a real key to the room, which was more like a suite, complete with a sitting area and kitchenette. I stood back as Chase hefted my bags and such inside. I'd packed for the unknown. Having the things I needed calmed me. There was very little within my control. I could control how I dressed and how I cared for Daisy Mae.

"Are you going to be okay here by yourself?" he asked. There was an odd expression on his face. I wasn't great at reading such things, but it seemed as if maybe he was a little worried about me.

"I'll be better after I sleep for about twenty hours. I've been driving for several days now, and I think it's caught up with me."

"Remembering your mom is kinda huge, huh? And Hank, and what happened. Before, you said you didn't remember anything."

Oh. Yeah. I had told him all of that. I pulled off the cap he'd loaned me and dragged the elastic from my ponytail, allowing my hair to drop to my shoulders. It was giving me such a headache.

"Things are running together. I've spent years with no memory, and now I have a momma. I don't remember everything: some really bad smells, yelling, and Hank attacking me and threatening to kill me. We fought with a screwdriver, and I was able to get it from him and stab him, uh, in his private area. He bled—a lot. I thought I'd killed him. I remember riding my bicycle for what seemed like miles on a dirt road in the dark."

Chase's expression changed as I described the events. His eyes became dark and angry. "I didn't know Hank hurt you, Sadie. Was it the first time the night you left? Or had it been going on throughout your childhood?"

"I know it wasn't nearly the first time. It was a culmination of past abuse, because I remember believing *this* was the time he would finally follow through and end my life."

"How did we miss the signs?" Chase asked, his gaze tortured. "I was young, but I saw what he was doing to your momma. That wasn't a secret."

I didn't have a clear picture yet of how often or how severe the abuse had been at Hank's hands, but the memory of the night I left was crystal clear, and it was intense and violent. "I honestly don't know how the situation presented itself to others, but it felt like it was our dark secret to protect the family."

He shook his head as if trying to clear it. "I've seen it too many times. I'm so sorry we failed you."

"I'm sorry my momma didn't make it stop. How could she allow it?" I asked him, though I knew there wasn't an answer.

"I wish I could explain it. She lived in terror. Scared of losing everything in an instant. Then, she did one day."

I nodded. "Yeah, I guess she did."

"I hope you can get some rest tonight. It's been a big day."

"I'm exhausted, so I think I should be able to sleep it off until tomorrow. I guess I'll have to *come out* tomorrow, huh?"

He gave a little laugh. "Another huge hurdle to face in a day. It's a lot. I wish I could prepare you."

"I hadn't thought much beyond just getting here, so I'll plan to deal with things as they come, I guess." What else could I say? That I was already completely overwhelmed at remembering and seeing my mom and Hank after all this time? That the uncorking of my firmly locked past was beginning to seep out in spurts that confused and terrified me? No sense dumping all my drama on him. Not that I hadn't already. He didn't ask for any of this.

"No way this is going to stay quiet. You were national news in a big way for a long time. So, as much of your story as you can piece together that can be proven or backed up with evidence, the better. There will be some doubters."

"Oh, you mean about who I am?" I hadn't thought about someone not believing me.

He nodded. "I recognized you immediately, but it's been a number of years since you lived here."

"I guess I'll have to prove my identity eventually to be declared *undead*. Maybe that will be enough."

"Should be."

"I guess Becky is going to speak with the newspaper owner?"

"They'll print something tonight for the morning edition if she has to go to the newspaper office, write the article, and supervise the printing herself. It's amazing what can happen overnight when the right pressure is applied."

"I'm glad you were the one I was directed to on my arrival. Sounds like you and Becky know how to get things done." Mr. Whitaker had given me Chase's contact information. I'm not sure how he knew that Chase was the best person to intercept me as soon as I got to town. I'm assuming Thelma knew something about my past and the people here in Moonshine.

"It sounds like Thelma did her research about our town. As a lawman, I have so many questions about what happened to you. I know you've still got lots of blanks to fill in. Let me know if I can help in any way. And I'd like to know more about this Thelma and why she didn't bring you to law enforcement immediately. You should prepare for the circus once word gets out that you are among the living."

I shrugged, trying not to reveal my angst at the mention of Thelma's choices. I was split in two when it came to that topic and wasn't ready to take a side. "I'm still unclear about a lot of things, and one of them is why Thelma handled things the way she did. I don't doubt her affection for me, and I believe she wanted to keep me safe."

"It's an important question, along with piecing this all

together."

I nodded. "I'll let you know as I remember anything new."

"Anyway, if the right information, or just enough gets into the paper, you'll be able to move freely around town without being bothered so much. Don't get me wrong. Folks aren't likely to keep their distance or respect your privacy, so decide what you want to tell them and stick to it. You're in charge of what they know at this point, so if you change your story or give more information to one person than the other, you'll find trouble."

"Thanks for the advice."

I felt my eyelids drooping, and Chase must have noticed because he said, "I'll let you get some rest. Here's my card with my cell number. Text or call in the morning once you're up and around. I feel kind of responsible for you since Thelma sent you to me, no matter her role in keeping you away from us all these years."

I smiled. "Thanks for all your help today. I couldn't have managed this without you."

He nodded. "Sure thing. Sleep well."

As I closed the door behind him, the phone in my room rang, nearly shooting me through the roof. "Hello?"

"Hello, Sadie! It's Fannie downstairs. Welcome home, honey. Becky told me who you are. I won't tell a soul. I'm so happy to hear that you're alive and kicking, dear."

"Um, thanks." This was so strange.

"Breakfast is from seven until nine in the morning. If you want to sleep in, I'll leave you a little something on a plate in the fridge down here. There is a gallon jug of filtered water in your mini fridge and glasses next to the coffee cups and coffee maker in your room. I put some fresh fruit and cheese in the fridge in case you're hungry tonight. Sleep well, dear. This is so exciting!" The line went dead.

I pulled out Daisy Mae's food and water dishes and she ate while I unpacked and settled in as much as possible for now. I nibbled on the food Fannie had left for me, God bless the woman. The meat loaf at lunch had been hours ago.

By the time I'd turned down my bed, it was dark outside, so I took Daisy Mae for a quick walk before bedtime. The air outside was warm and humid, and fragrant in a totally different way than the Midwest. It was sweet-smelling instead of pine-scented, though I'd noticed there were different varieties of pine trees here.

It occurred to me that after so many years away, this environment should seem foreign, but it surrounded me like one of Thelma's old handmade quilts. A peace and calm enveloped me unexpectedly. And relief that I was finally going to learn about my past.

I should call Jenny, but I wasn't quite ready to share today's events yet. Instead, I texted her a quick: *Arrived at the bed-and-breakfast in North Georgia safely. Met the sheriff. Exhausted. Will call first thing tomorrow morning. Love you.*

The little dots flickered and jumped for a few seconds, then Jenny answered: *I'm dying to hear all about it! Call me as soon as you wake up. So glad you made it!*

I had no idea what tomorrow would bring, but right now I was too tired to think beyond my drooping eyelids. Daisy Mae was one step ahead of me, if her snoring was any indication.

The bed was comfortable, thankfully, because I'd slept

on a few in the last couple of days that hadn't been. I pictured Thelma's face briefly as I closed my eyes, feeling her with me.

NEITHER CHASE NOR his mother spoke for a few minutes as they left Fannie's place. "I don't know how to make this go easy for her." There was worry in his mother's tone.

Chase had been thinking along the same lines. "What did they say at the paper?"

"I spoke with Nancy, the editor. Once I got her jaw off the floor and managed to stop her babbling reporter questions and make her listen, I think she got the facts straight. I hope. I encouraged her to get it done before she called Jason. I told her I would take the heat if he gave her a hard time. Told her you would find her a job if he fired her."

He stared at his mother. "You what?"

"Just in case. He can't fire the editor who's got the byline on the story."

"I'm surprised I haven't heard from Jason yet." And Chase was—surprised. Of course, getting first scoop in Jason's paper that Sadie Brubaker was still alive and back in Moonshine might keep him from being a jackass simply because Chase was involved.

Sadie's immediate future depended on this article informing the citizens of her whereabouts and a basic explanation of what had happened the night she'd disappeared. The details could be filled in later.

"I didn't tell Nancy where Sadie was staying, though she

did ask. Couldn't risk Jason barging in and demanding more details than she was ready to give."

"Do you think Fannie will keep a lid on it?" he asked.

"Yes. I might have threatened her a little. No violence, but maybe a tiny bit of embarrassment." Judging by her expression, his mom was only a little ashamed.

"I'm not going to ask if this blackmail was illegal or immoral because the thought of arresting my own mother right now doesn't sit well. Sadie is going to need you to help run interference in the coming days. I have a feeling Mary Frances won't be in a position to help much."

She shook her head. "That poor woman has enough on her plate dealing with a dead daughter coming back to life and a husband everybody wishes was dead."

"Won't be long now if he's as bad off as he looks." Chase didn't believe in ushering folks to their graves, but if anybody deserved an early sendoff, it was Hank Brubaker.

After all the hell on earth he'd served up to those weaker than him, a small part of Chase hoped the asshole lived long enough for his sins to catch up with him before he shed his mortal coil. The entire town would enjoy watching him get what he deserved. Over the decades, Hank had insulted, offended, or spat on anybody who'd pissed him off. Pretty much everybody had pissed him off.

"I hope Sadie has her chance to finally stand up to him after everything he did to her momma," Mom said. "And especially now that we know he hurt Sadie, though I'd not heard that before."

His mother was fierce when it came to protecting those she loved, him especially.

"Sadie's got a lot to work through, I guess, since she's just starting to remember who she is, or was. Can you imagine forgetting your entire life before age sixteen?" Chase shook his head.

"That poor girl's got a good deal more than her memory to worry about."

Chase agreed. So much more.

"We'll stay close for a little while. How about I meet you at Fannie's for coffee at seven. That way, we'll be there when she comes down."

He nodded as he pulled up beside her front porch. "Thanks for your help today. I'm not sure I could've handled this one without you."

"Nonsense. But I was glad to help. And I'm tickled pink Sadie Brubaker is still among the living. It is very exciting—certainly doesn't happen every day."

"No, it doesn't. Night, Mom."

She blew him a kiss as she got out of the car.

As Chase drove toward his house, his cell phone rang. The caller ID showed Jason Weston's name.

He took a deep breath, then answered. "Weston. I guess you heard the good news."

"Who the hell do y'all think you are?"

"Excuse me?"

"How dare you feed a story like this to my editor without running it by me first? This is too important to take the word of a woman who's been missing and declared legally dead—it's a risk for my paper," he huffed over the phone.

Chase could understand his irritation but couldn't help feeling it was partly because the story had come from Chase's direction. "Sadie Brubaker's not dead. I just left her an hour ago very much alive."

"How can you be sure it's her? She disappeared when she was sixteen. This could be an imposter." Leave it to Jason to cause a ruckus and not trust Chase.

"It was her. Her own mother recognized her. I recognized her. Don't you remember her blue eyes?"

Silence.

"You'd better not be wrong about this."

"Listen, we're trying to get ahead of the gossip by letting folks know she's back." Chase gave few details but explained about her lost memory. "You have nothing to gain by refusing to help, and your newspaper gets the scoop."

"My editor took Becky at her word and pushed forward with the story, so I can't stop it from coming out since it's already on the presses to print and on servers for the online edition. Most people fire employees for stunts like that."

"Don't be a dick, Jason. Sadie Brubaker's coming home will be a shock to everyone, but it's not a bad thing. The newspaper's story will announce her return to the community in a way that can give a basic explanation and cut down on rumors."

"You're taking this woman's word for everything. That's dangerous reporting for a newspaper." Jason's tone was terse and lecturing, as if he were speaking to a complete idiot.

"I can verify her identity, being the sheriff, and having recognized her as who she says she is. And you can call it her personal account. *She's* the only one who can verify what happened to her. You can run a follow-up with more details as we get them *if* Sadie agrees to share. She may decide to let someone else have the scoop."

"You'd better be right about this, or I can guarantee you won't be re-elected next term." That was always Jason's threat, as if he could change the vote of every citizen in the county.

"I'll take full responsibility," Chase said. And then he couldn't resist slinging, "Tell Annie I said hi."

Jason's family was old money, and Jason had been born with a silver spoon so far up his ass that Chase and everyone else mostly tried to ignore his pompous attitude and automatic assumptions that he could, would do, and get anything he pleased. He did rash things and didn't worry about consequences.

Chase's parents had frequently cautioned him about the possible risk when he attended anything hosted by Jason in high school. Chase had seen enough questionable behavior that he rarely participated when Jason was involved, especially his behavior toward girls. He'd been a player and had dated half the town at one time or another. Luckily, Chase had started dating Annie his junior year of high school, and she'd been his one and only girlfriend, so he and Jason hadn't fought over girls.

Both Jason and Chase had played football and baseball, and were strong academically, but Jason went Ivy League and Chase dropped out of the University of Georgia his junior year to help his mother take care of his dad.

The same year Chase joined the Moonshine Sheriff's Department, Sadie Brubaker disappeared. Annie, who'd always seemed so unaffected by Jason, continued at UGA and graduated with a degree in social work while Chase slowly watched his dad succumb to dementia. He and Annie got married right after she'd graduated.

Annie was his greatest regret. Allowing his marriage to decline along with his dad's health said very little for Chase as a man. Considering the deep depression he'd slid into after the funeral, he didn't blame his young wife for finally giving up on him. She'd now been married to Jason Weston for just over a year.

They were still cordial with one another, but Chase could see a sadness in her gaze whenever they made eye contact on the occasions they ran into one another in town. The very idea that she actually saw anything good or redeeming in Jason was the cruelest part of it. Of anyone she could have ended up with, Jason was the *worst*.

Chapter Eleven

"TELL ME *EVERYTHING*!" Jenny was evidently on her second cup of coffee based on her level of enthusiasm and alertness. She'd waited for me to rest and recover from my trip to fill her in, so I could understand her demands for information. I silently applauded her patience.

"Okay, so as soon as I got into town I met with Chase Blackburn, the sheriff. He's a very nice person and he—remembered me."

"That's so exciting. Did you remember him?" she asked. I could almost feel her anticipation through the phone. Jenny was my friend, but she was also a clinical family therapist. She rarely "therapied me" but I could imagine how much she'd wanted to over the years after learning of my odd condition.

"Maybe. I had a familiar feeling for a moment, but nothing specific. He brought me to meet his mother, who also remembered me. They're worried about the reaction, or maybe the overreaction of some of the people in town about my coming back, I think."

"Hmm. Small towns have long memories. They likely know a lot more about your life there at this point than you do, I guess. It might be good to find out as much personal history as you can quickly."

"Oh, and I met my mother—and I *remembered* her."

Silence. "Wait—you met your mom, and you didn't lead with that? Holy shit, Randi, are you all right?" Jenny's voice held threads of barely controlled worry and excitement.

"I'm okay. I'm confused. I'm filled with all sorts of feelings and emotions I can't put into words. I feel split in two. I've had the brief sensation of what it was to be Sadie for a few minutes at a time. But then I revert back to myself completely."

"This is what I was most worried about. The confusion. How's your mother? Is she well? How did she react to your coming back?"

"She was emotional, loving, relieved. Part of her wondered if my stepdad, Hank, had killed me, and the other part believed, or hoped maybe, deep down that I'd escaped."

"What about the stepdad, Hank? Is he there?" Jenny asked.

I paused, gathering my thoughts regarding Hank. "He's here. He's very ill and dying, I think. I remember him too, and his violence. He tried to kill me the night I left. I've had a few flashbacks."

Jenny was quiet for a moment. "I'm sorry, Randi. This is so much for you to deal with at once. You were abused. How are you handling that?"

I had to think for a second. "My mother kept the abuse as our family secret. I'm struggling with that. Her not protecting us. But I'm actually doing pretty well considering everything that's happened since yesterday."

"Secret abuse is common but maddening and so wrong.

Your mind has been searching for the truth all these years, and you've known it but couldn't access it. Promise me you'll continue talking to me about all this and how it's affecting you as things unfold. Please." Her therapist self was kicking in hard.

"I promise. I know this is only the beginning. There's so much more to learn and fill in. I hope this foggy confusion lifts."

"I can't imagine what that feels like," Jenny said.

"At least I finally slept off my trip in a comfortable bed. I feel alert this morning and ready to see what happens next." I tried to keep it upbeat with Jenny because I didn't want her to worry.

"Good for you. It's still early here but I'm determined to get a workout in before I begin my day. And I recommend that you keep up with your running to burn off steam too."

I completely agreed. "I need to map out a running route here for Daisy Mae and me once I get a handle on things."

"What does it look like—I mean the area? Is it safe for you to run alone? I've never been down South."

I thought about it for a second. "It's not that it looks so different, but it *feels* different. It's very green and hilly—lusher. The air is humid, but a different kind of humid than there. It's heavy and warm, and fragrant with a hundred flowers and pine trees. The air is sweet, for lack of a better word."

"Sounds interesting. Good or bad?"

"I'm comfortable here. I don't feel out of place in this climate. I have yet to interact with people in town besides Chase and Becky, and my mom and Hank, and the bed-and-breakfast owner, but I guess it remains to be seen how that will go."

"Have a good day, Randi, and take this one memory at a time. It won't be all bad."

"Thanks—you have a good day too, Jenny. We'll talk later."

I checked the time. Eight o'clock. Daisy Mae stretched and yawned. I should be able to grab a quick breakfast downstairs before Fannie stopped serving.

"C'mon, girl. Time to go outside and potty." She didn't appear convinced, but slowly stood, stretching each leg for a moment as she moved toward me and her leash.

I was dressed in running clothes, as was my habit first thing in the morning, hopeful I might get a run in before I faced the uncertain day ahead.

I'd already made the bed and replaced the mountain of pillows on top of the white matelassé coverlet.

As we made our way down the narrow staircase of the old building, I heard voices below. I was mildly surprised to find Chase and Becky sitting companionably on the comfortable furniture in the lobby area sipping coffee.

"Good morning, you two," Becky said to Daisy Mae and me as we walked up. Daisy Mae's tail wagged, and she moved to greet them both.

Then I heard the voices. I looked up and saw people lined up against the front window of the bed-and-breakfast. They were staring through the glass at me. Some had their hands cupped and eyes against them straining to get a better look.

"I was about to warn you," Chase said. "Pay them no

mind for now."

"What's going on?" I asked. But I didn't think I wanted to know the answer.

"You've been discovered. Someone told someone you were here. And of course, they got up early and read the morning edition of *The Moonshine Herald*."

I suddenly felt like a zoo attraction through the glass. "Daisy Mae has to go outside to the bathroom. She hasn't been out since last night," I said, almost as an afterthought.

"I'll take her." Chase stood and gently slid the leash from my fingers. His touch made my skin tingle. There was that odd feeling again. "Have some breakfast in the dining room. They can't see you in there. Fannie has the doors locked. They aren't animals. They won't break them down."

"It's like I'm some sort of freak show."

Chase nodded. "To them you are, I'm sorry to say. They had to come over here and see it for themselves."

"Should I wave or something?" I asked.

"Ignore them for now. Pretend they're not here. What they're doing is rude. I'm going to go have a talk with them and hopefully get them to simmer down."

"Come on, dear, let's go into the dining room." Becky took my arm gently. "Chase will take good care of Daisy Mae."

❧

CHASE LED THE dog out the front door on purpose. There was a back exit, but it was time to face his constituents head-on. When the door jingled, all eyes were on him. "Sheriff, are you sure that's truly her?" And then: "When's she coming out? I want to say hello. We went to school together."

He put a hand up to try and get their attention. "Folks, I'm assuming most of you read this morning's paper, so you know Sadie Brubaker is back home in Moonshine. I can confirm that it's the same young woman we all knew thirteen years ago. As you might've read, she lost her memory that night and hasn't yet regained it. Hopefully, being back here will help with that. At least that's what she's hoping. So, let's all be patient and kind, as I know you all will."

"We'd like to say hello and welcome her back," someone called out.

"And I know she will appreciate that. I'm asking that you give her some space and go easy, okay?" Chase looked around, making eye contact with the fifteen or twenty people who'd gathered, waiting for their response.

Most nodded, or mumbled assent. "Okay, Sheriff. We can do that," Merilee Bell agreed out loud.

"Merilee, you better be glad she doesn't remember you." There was a snicker.

Merilee frowned, clearly bothered by the comment from someone in the crowd. "People change, Buddy Jackson. You ought to know." There were a few more comments.

"Listen up, everyone. Spread the word that Sadie is back but likely won't remember anyone. Welcoming her home is fine, but don't press her too hard to recall the past. Let's be supportive as a community. It's not every day somebody comes back from the dead." More murmurs and nods of agreement.

Daisy whined a little. "That her dog?"

Chase nodded, realizing his reason for coming out here. He walked over to the grassy area at the end of the block to give the poor animal a bit of privacy. "Here's a baggy in case she goes number two."

Chase heard the hard Southern twang that wasn't quite the same as the locals here in Moonshine. He looked up and noticed the big-haired blonde and her giant purse with a tiny animal's head sticking out. "Thanks, Bree. I didn't think about it when I brought her out here. Hi there, Tiny." Tiny yapped, distracting Daisy Mae, who came over and sniffed at Bree's purse.

"Let her go potty, Tiny," Bree addressed her purse.

Chase led the bigger dog a little farther down the sidewalk.

"Sounds like y'all've got a big mystery on your hands around here. Poor gal. I can't imagine what she must be going through."

"It's a mess to say the least."

"You haven't given the emotional impact of her coming home much thought, have you? Not to say you're not a good guy, but you're thinking like a sheriff is all." Bree was smart and she was waiting for an answer.

He shrugged. He had given Randi's emotional well-being quite a bit of thought, actually, but he didn't want to get into that conversation here on the street with Bree. There were so many things Bree didn't know about all this yet. But maybe speaking to another woman, who was a professional, might help Randi as she was learning about her life as Sadie.

"You mean a *man*?" he asked, laughing a bit. Bree didn't hurt his feelings. They were friends. She was a Southern transplant, but from a different part of the South. Alabama, he remembered. She'd recently hung her shingle as the town therapist. Different, he was informed, than a counselor. She'd worked in a hospital setting, but he wasn't sure what exactly she'd done. He did know she worked with addicted patients, which Moonshine had plenty of, whether in or out of the closet of public knowledge.

"You said it, not me," he answered. "I'll be sure to intro-duce you."

"I'd like that. I think she's finished."

"Huh?"

She pointed to the smelly pile on the grass. "Oh. Thanks."

"Sure. You have my cards at your office if Sadie needs someone to talk to."

BECKY AND I entered the dining room where Fannie was fussing over several platters of bacon, scrambled eggs, biscuits, and a large bowl of what I knew to be grits. Thelma had made grits. But she'd mostly made shrimp and grits when she'd cooked them. Grits for breakfast weren't found anywhere near Hickman.

My stomach rumbled, reminding me of my light dinner last night. I loved a big breakfast after a good run. But today it appeared I would be doing without the run. So, just breakfast this morning.

"This looks delicious, Fannie," I said.

"Eat up, Sadie. You'll need your strength to deal with

those damn vultures out there."

"T-thanks."

A twentyish man with a beard and wearing biking gear, his helmet hanging from the back of the chair, was seated at the table. His mouth was full, so he waved a hand and pointed to his mouth. I smiled slightly in greeting.

There was also an elderly couple at the table, whispering with one another and not looking toward me as I sat down with my plate. Were they avoiding eye contact?

That was okay with me as I was an old pro at it. But it made me wonder if they were locals or people worried that I might be some sort of troublemaker since they'd been locked inside their bed-and-breakfast with a mob outside staring in the windows.

Since they appeared unlikely to do me physical harm, I said, "Good morning."

They looked up in unison as if caught being naughty. The woman cleared her throat. "Oh, hello, dear."

"I'm Randi Collins." I introduced myself, refusing to give over to full-time Sadie.

"We're the Donahoos from Dahlonega," the man piped up. The way he said it told me it wasn't the first time they'd introduced themselves that way.

"I thought your name was Sadie," bicycle dude chimed in and pointed to the newspaper article I hadn't noticed lying on the table beside his plate. "This is you, right? That's why all the people in town are trying to spy you through the front window?"

I flushed. "Y-yes, that's me. Well, that was me as a child."

"Cool. Glad you're not dead," he said and gave me a two-fingered rock 'n' roll hand gesture.

"Dear, if you don't mind my saying, your story is fascinating, if it's *true*," Mrs. Donahoo from Dahlonega said.

Randi wondered for a moment if the woman doubted her story. "I haven't read the newspaper story yet, but everyone here thought I was dead until this morning's edition, so yes, it's true."

"Well, let us add that we are also glad you're blessedly alive." Mr. Donahoo tried to make a similar hand gesture as the bike dude, but it looked more like he was flipping me the bird. But hey, A for effort there.

I smiled my thanks. This was awkward, but at least we were discussing the elephant sitting on top of the breakfast table.

The bacon was amazing. Crispy, smoky, and thick, just the way Thelma always made it. It was strange. I could almost feel her here with me as my silent support. Bolstering me with bacon. It wasn't the worst way to support someone; in fact, right now, it was perfect.

I wondered what was taking Chase so long. Surely he hadn't been overcome by the mostly geriatric crowd outside. Daisy Mae was with him, and though she was a sweet soul, she was protective too. And then there was the fact that he was armed, and the sheriff of the town. If he couldn't simmer them down, his lawman days were numbered around here, I'd bet.

This town reminded me of a setting in an old Western movie that Thelma and I had watched, with Chase as the sheriff trying to keep the peace. It felt like a throwback to days of old. The accents here were similar, and I'd noticed several cowboy hats, Western shirts, and cowboy boots. These were not things one observed on the streets of Hickman unless they were shooting a movie.

As odd as they appeared, somewhere in the back of my mind, there was a familiarity to this place and the look of these people. They were right behind the dam I felt about to burst in my brain. I knew them, but I didn't—yet.

Chase came back in then. Daisy Mae's tail was wagging, and she appeared no worse for wear. Chase, however, looked a little frazzled. His thick, dark hair wasn't lying down neatly as it had been when he'd left the room twenty or so minutes before.

"How did it go?" Becky asked him. She'd been speaking quietly with Fannie in the corner of the dining room while I ate with the other guests.

"They had a few questions. The newspaper story did its job in getting the word out. I asked them to go easy on you. Mostly they want to welcome you home and give you their regards—lay eyes on you."

"That's nice of them, I guess. It seems strange that they even care after so many years. Can't they just be glad I'm not dead like they thought?" I asked.

"When you disappeared, folks created their own stories about what became of you. They even pointed fingers at your momma for not keeping you safe. Of course, nobody expected Hank to keep anybody safe," Becky said.

I nodded but dared not correct her about how things really went down. Maybe it would all get out, but I wasn't ready yet.

"It terrified folks that nobody could stop this from happening in our own community, and that if the law couldn't keep a little girl from disappearing then no one was safe from similar things happening. People began pointing fingers at neighbors. Finding you was an obsession. Getting closure was an obsession," Becky explained.

"So, all this time, it's been in the back of people's minds that there could be a killer out there, either familiar or unfamiliar," Chase added.

"So, my coming back has reopened some wounds," I said, beginning to get the gist of how the group-think went here.

They both nodded like bobbleheads in complete agreement.

"In the meantime, prepare for some odd interactions with people around town," Becky said.

"I've asked them to give you some space, but everybody has their own definition of the word," Chase said as he handed Daisy Mae's leash back to me.

His eyes held kindness and what appeared to be…pity? "I guess I can't expect them not to be curious." I hadn't noticed that kind of emotion in his eyes before. What had happened while he was walking Daisy Mae?

"Just to give you a heads-up, folks around here aren't big fans of Hank, as we discussed. He was ornery to nearly everyone he encountered for almost no apparent reason. With your coming back, it could stir up some ugliness."

"He isn't a likeable man." A deep dread crept into me. Since our reunion yesterday, I'd been having twinges of memory and feeling more angst toward my mother, Mary

Frances. Yes, I was still full of childish love for her, but my adult-self held contempt for a woman who couldn't shake loose a man who threatened her children's safety and her own. Then there was the question of my sister and where she'd ended up.

The dining room seemed to lose its oxygen.

I stood and carried my plate to the bin in the corner of the room where a couple others had been placed.

"Are you okay?" Becky asked.

I nodded because I didn't want to discuss the complex thoughts about my family. "I'm going to take Daisy Mae upstairs and get dressed. I'd like to head over to my mother's house in a little while." Daisy Mae had been a gem as usual. People didn't seem to mind her being there, thankfully.

"Okay, honey. We'll be happy to head over with you when you're ready. We want to make sure Hank isn't going to give you any trouble today."

I wasn't sure how I felt about their babysitting me, but I guess one more day of assistance with getting around in this strange land wouldn't hurt. I still had yet to actually deal with any of the residents, so I guess we would see how that went.

As I ducked out and headed toward the stairs, I noticed the crowd had dispersed somewhat, but there were still a few people milling about outside the front door. I inadvertently made eye contact with a curvy blonde woman about my age. She mouthed my name, *Sadie*, and lifted her hand in a small wave.

I was touched in a way I couldn't quite describe. I gave a slight wave and smiled but didn't trust myself to greet her.

She didn't seem familiar though. I broke eye contact and led Daisy Mae upstairs. That one small interaction, brief as if was, changed my perspective. I didn't expect to *feel* anything for these people. What would happen when I began to remember them in volume and our histories together?

How would it be to suddenly remember hundreds of individuals and my connection to them? I was thankful I'd yet to experience anything in that capacity. My brain and emotions currently seemed to be in decent working order and were accepting information as it came through. I hoped that would continue as the remembering did.

I changed out of workout clothes, sighing at the lost opportunity to get a run in this morning. My running had been hit or miss the past few days. I'd managed it several times during the trip when the situation presented itself. But today was not that day, apparently.

I slipped into a pair of comfortable faded jeans and a *namaste* T-shirt. I sometimes did yoga on my mat in front of the television back home. I'd ordered the shirt from a client after I'd designed the logo for them. The pale-yellow fabric was a cotton/bamboo blend that was soft and breathable. My running shoes would have to do today. Based on yesterday's experience with the gravel and dirt exterior at my mother's house, my ballet flats didn't seem like the best choice. I was comfortable at least.

"You ready, girl?" I asked my eager buddy as I grabbed a chew toy and secretly slid an extra rawhide bone in my backpack. Daisy Mae did best when occupied with her favorite things during stressful situations. I wish I had something to chew on that would distract me from what promised to be an unpredictable day.

Before I thought better of it, I pulled my hair out of its confinement. Why not? Everyone now knew who I was. I wasn't hiding anymore.

Chapter Twelve

A S WE DESCENDED the staircase, I experienced a small surge of purpose and renewal. Chase and Becky waited for us, which equally relieved and annoyed me. I was mostly annoyed because I needed their guidance and protection. Hopefully soon that wouldn't be the case.

"I'll drive my Jeep over to Momma's place. That way, you won't have to worry about bringing me back here," I said to them. I wasn't sure what the plan was, but I didn't want them to think I was incapable of taking care of myself.

"Sure. Sounds good," Chase said.

As we stepped out of the building, I noticed the sidewalk was clear. Well, maybe not clear, but everyone had stepped far enough away and were mostly pretending to focus on something else besides my exit. It was their right to be curious, I guess.

"Hey there, Sadie. It's nice to have you back." A large, middle-aged woman in a pair of denim overalls had approached on my blindside. There was kindness in her eyes that I appreciated. She might have been someone I knew once but I didn't recognize her now.

"Thank you," I said. I was going to have to get used to this. "I'm sorry, I don't remember much. Could you tell me your name?"

She took my hand in hers before I could snatch it back, and said kindly, "I'm Dodie Wilkes. I'm one of your momma's closest neighbors. We wanted to welcome you home. Please let me and Mr. Wilkes know if you need anything, dear."

Then I noticed a man behind her, also wearing overalls and wearing a straw cowboy hat, smiling at me with a twinkle in his eye. He appeared strong and weathered, as if he'd worked outdoors most of his life. "We've known you since you were knee-high to a grasshopper, girl. You've grown up to be a lovely young woman. So glad to have you back, Sadie," Mr. Wilkes said.

A warmth spread through me that caused my eyes to fill with tears. "Thank you both so much. I-I wish I could remember—"

"Don't you worry about a thing. We heard about your memory loss. We're so happy you're home."

I nodded and they walked away. A few more residents made their way over and welcomed me home in a similar fashion. With kindness.

"We were in school together up until—well, you know," the woman who'd introduced herself as Merilee Bell said. "Anyway, you were super smart and made good grades. Not like me. I didn't go to college, but I graduated from beauty school. I own the *Clip and Color* down the street. So, if you ever need my services, come see me. Not that you do, I mean, look at you. But you know, nails, whatever. Or, if you need a girlfriend." She was chewing gum.

One of those lightning bolt kind of memories hit me

then. Merilee Bell had chewed gum in school too. But she hadn't been nice.

"Aw, look at her, girls. I think I gave that dress to charity two years ago. Hey, Julie, if you're gonna wear somebody's hand-me-downs, you should at least wash them. Girls, do you smell something?" Merilee had pinched her nose then, like she'd caught wind of something stinky.

"I remember you now, Merilee," I said quietly. Sadie, the bullied, angry child, was still inside me. "Didn't I punch you for teasing my sister?"

Merilee's face fell and her shoulders slumped. She nodded. "Yep. Nearly broke my nose. Sadie, I was a terrible, mean girl. I cried for days after you disappeared, and I swear I never was the same again. That's why I wanted to tell you how glad I am that you came home. Because of how bad I treated you. I thought God would never forgive me because I didn't get the chance to apologize." She burst into terrible sobs. "I was a horrible person. I know we were young, but nobody should have treated you like that. You were a sweet girl, Sadie. You never hurt anybody in this town who didn't deserve it. I'm so, so sorry. Please forgive me."

Merilee's eyes were red and puffy, and people were staring. I shifted, uncomfortable. "I forgive you, Merilee. We were kids, like you said. And yes, it was hurtful. I didn't remember how much until now. But I do forgive you." It stung though, the memory of the meanness of those girls. And whether I'd really forgiven that hurt remained to be seen. I mainly wanted the confrontation to end as quickly as possible.

Merilee moved closer where no one could hear. "I hope

we can be friends, Sadie. I know it can't be easy to come back here and remember people like me." She looked so sorry.

"Thank you, Merilee." I did my best to smile at her before she walked away. Daisy Mae had moved close against my leg in her silent support.

"Had enough for now?" Becky took my arm and led me toward my Jeep, effectively keeping anyone else away for the moment.

I wiped my eyes with the back of my hand. "Yes, I think so."

"Let's get you to your momma's house," she said.

"I'm gonna head over to the office and make sure Hannah hasn't dropped off anything on my desk that can't wait a couple of hours," Chase said. "I'll meet y'all over there in a few minutes."

Something about Chase made me uncomfortable. Not in a bad way. He was obviously a good person who was trying to help me. But I experienced a restless and strange sort of sensation when he was nearby. He moved with purpose—always. And there was an intensity about him that I recognized from some of the leading male roles in movies. He was an alpha male, though so far, not a bullish one. He appeared to have a sensitive side.

I was a little relieved that he wasn't coming with us right then. I relaxed a little. Daisy Mae climbed in shotgun with a little help from me.

Becky followed in her pickup. Because around here, women drove trucks. Especially single, capable women like Becky Blackburn. I had such respect for her. She didn't seem afraid of anyone or anything. I couldn't help but compare her to my own mother, who had, from my limited perspective, lived in fear most of her life. That probably wasn't fair, but it was the contrast between the two women that crept into my thoughts as we headed toward my mother's house.

It felt good to be behind the wheel again. Maybe because it enabled me a measure of control. If I wanted to leave at any time I could. I would stay until I wanted to go.

I followed Becky but could navigate from town from memory if I needed to. It was two turns from the center of town. I dreaded and looked forward to going back today.

As I pulled onto the dirt and gravel driveway off the paved road, once again I had the sensation of rain and mud. I smelled it, and a chill caused tiny bumps to raise on my arms. It was a dark memory. Daisy Mae whined. Another snippet of past time. This one was only sensation and feeling though. Nothing had happened that led me to learn something new.

I pulled up to the house, same as it was yesterday. Old, dusty, with a few boards missing from the porch. I hadn't gone inside yesterday. Hank's anger and bad temper seemed to permeate the place. I felt it as soon as I approached the front steps. It was like a dark cloud.

Momma met me on the porch, her smile radiating joy. How could she even feel joy after the lifetime of anguish she'd lived? But her mood was infectious, because despite everything, I was equally happy to see her again. We hugged.

Becky looked around to make sure no one was about who shouldn't be. "Everything okay, Mary Frances?"

Momma nodded. "Yes, thanks for seeing her over here.

We'll be fine together for a while. I promise to give you a call if we need you."

Becky looked at me. "Sadie, you gonna be all right until Chase arrives? I'll be home and can get here in five minutes should you have a problem." Becky nodded toward the interior of the house to make her point.

"Yes, I'll be fine. Thank you, Becky," I said.

"Chase won't be long." She bent down and gave Daisy Mae a quick rub on the back and stepped off the porch.

The truck kicked up a small trail of dust as she headed down the driveway.

"Here, baby. Let's sit on the swing and visit. Hank's asleep inside. No need to disturb him. I made your favorite blackberry pie. Do you remember? You loved when I baked blackberry pie." Momma beamed.

I smelled it then. And I did remember. I don't think I'd eaten blackberry pie since then. Did we even have blackberries in Hickman? Thelma baked apple, cherry, and peach pies, and I did love pie. "I remember. It smells wonderful, Momma. Thank you."

How could I have such warm and comforting thoughts, while at the same time know what had happened to me here, in this family?

She touched my hair and then ran a hand down the length of it. "Your hair is still so beautiful and shiny. I'm glad you're wearing it down."

I remembered something else then. Something sad and terrible. I could see myself as a young girl, scraping my hair up, slicking it to my head so it would hurt less when Hank yanked it when he walked by. I was always careful about his pulling my hair. I hurt less to have a ponytail or bun pulled than a thinner, more vulnerable piece on the side or up front.

Was that why I'd always worn my hair in a ponytail since going to live with Thelma? To protect myself? A nasty urge bubbled up in my gut to go inside and drag Hank's sick, sorry butt out of bed and kick him in his rotting liver. For what he'd done to a little girl. Me. Sadie.

I quickly wiped the tear that tracked down my cheek. I cried for Sadie. "I wore my hair up because it didn't hurt as much when Hank pulled it." I wanted her to know.

Momma hung her head. "I should have killed him years ago," she said bitterly. "Nobody would have batted an eye."

I silently agreed. "I'm trying to understand. Hank beat me and I fought back. But you didn't fight back, for either of us. It was our dark secret." I'd seen documentaries about abused women. I guess we'd reacted and responded to the violence in opposite ways.

Momma's mouth was now set in a tight line. "You know people around this town have been saying the same things—but worse for all these years. Telling me I was a bad mother because my girls were gone. I've believed them. I blamed myself for all of what happened to you and to Julie because it was my fault. I'm sorry for being a scared coward. I want to make it up to you."

I wanted to forgive her on the spot as quickly as I told Merilee she was forgiven. But I'd done that so I could walk away from the situation and avoid any more awkwardness. This was different. If I said the words too quickly but hung on to the anger, I would be dismissing something too important. So, I said instead, "I left because he would have killed me. I tore our family apart that night to save my own life. So, I'm sorry you lost your protector."

"You were right to run, and I'm glad you did. You saved yourself because I couldn't do it. I wasn't strong or brave enough. I failed you."

"You were a victim. I was a victim, and so was Julie."

Momma's face was rigid then. "Hank tore our family apart long before he laid a hand on you or me, beginning in little ways. He didn't start out as a raging violent alcoholic, you know. He adopted you as a little one. Took you as his own when I married him a couple years after your daddy died."

I faced her then. "My daddy. Who was my daddy?" I asked. "Did I know him?" We swayed back and forth on the front porch swing, the intensity of our conversation belying the easy movement.

Momma relaxed as our conversation took a turn from blame to something she appeared more comfortable with. "You were two years old when he passed. He loved you more than anything in this world. You cried for him for months after he left and never came back."

"What happened?" Finally, something new I could learn about myself.

"Offshore oil rig accident. He'd just boarded the helicopter in the Gulf of Mexico to come home after his two-week shift when the rig exploded, sending the copter into the water. Never had a chance. He was a petroleum engineer."

I didn't know how to respond to that. An emptiness for someone and something I'd missed and hadn't known settled around me. "I wish I could remember him." Thelma had told me a truth. How had she even known my father was killed in an oil rig accident?

"I do too. His love for us both sustains me still sometimes. When you've had that kind of love, it lasts a lifetime and allows you to get through things you might not otherwise."

"Like a life with Hank," I said.

She nodded. "Hank was different, at first. He was so kind. Until Julie was a couple years old. Until it got hard. He lost his job and became short-tempered and started to drink. You questioned him and stood up to him, even as a little girl. He hated that. And I'm pretty sure that he secretly believed he never could live up to your father's legacy."

"Why would I do something so foolish as to challenge a grown man?" I couldn't imagine a tiny person standing up to a strong, mean adult man capable of violence.

"Sadie, you were a force of nature, not a bit afraid of anything or anyone. Hank became your enemy because you let him know his behavior wasn't to be tolerated. It was as if he saw you as his conscience. It drove him mad."

I could see it now so clearly. The constant conflict between the two of us. Hank drinking until he passed out. My figuring out ways to avoid him and protect Julie and me when he was on a rampage. But as my mind worked its way through the memories, I don't recall his hurting Julie.

"Did Hank hit Julie?" I asked Momma in case I was misremembering. I didn't trust myself to believe everything that popped into my head yet.

She shook her head. "No. He never did. He scared her

plenty though. And she hated that he was constantly after you. Julie wasn't fierce like you were, honey. She adored you and followed you wherever you went, unless it was into battle with Hank, then she stayed back in the shadows with me."

"Mary Frances, where the hell did you get off to?" Our very frank conversation was cut short by a loud thud and cursing.

"There's my call to duty," Momma said. "Most likely fell out of bed again."

"Does he do that a lot?"

"Just started. I've had a devil of a time getting him up. I hurt my back last week trying to do it. Those pain pills mess with his balance."

"I'll give you a hand."

Momma pulled back, visibly appalled that I would suggest it. "Oh, I wouldn't dream of asking you to get near him."

"I don't want you to hurt yourself again, trying to pick him up off the floor. Believe me, it's not for his sake."

"Mary Frances!" Hank bellowed again.

She hadn't rushed inside at the first sounds of his distress, which made me smirk a little. Maybe I was a little bit her daughter after all.

As we entered the house, I didn't need to ask where things were; I knew without looking. It came back as if I'd stepped through the threshold of my past. The couch still sat against the wall, facing the TV, but it was brown instead of floral. Things were cluttered and I smelled sickness emanating from Hank's room. It wasn't so different from the odor when Hank had peed himself when he was dead drunk.

Back then, Momma had worked to keep things clean, despite our poverty and Hank's lack of hygiene. Now, it appeared she'd given up the fight—almost. There were handmade quilts, so like the ones Thelma made it almost made me cry for missing her then. But stepping back inside my childhood home filled me with so many other emotions, that would have to wait.

"Okay Hank, let's get you up," I heard Momma say from down the hall. I followed her voice and saw her trying to pull Hank to standing.

He raised his eyes and glared at me.

"I'm gonna kill you this time, you little bitch, you, and those devil eyes. Gonna cut 'em out." He came at me with the screwdriver.

I didn't bother begging for mercy. He'd get a kick out of that. Sadistic asshole.

I managed to grab the sharp tool as he roughly tangled his hand in my hair. I'd been in a hurry this morning and hadn't put it up. So stupid.

I clamped my teeth together, determined not to make sound. How many times had we done this terrible dance?

"Drop it, you devil." He yanked hard on my hair, causing such blinding pain, I nearly did what he'd commanded.

He would kill me today; he'd just said so. He'd threatened to kill me so many times before, but today there was unusual determination in his eyes.

But I had the screwdriver now, and nobody was cutting out my eyes. I could live without a hunk of hair, no matter how much having it yanked out would hurt. I glared at him through the black, dirty strands, and decided that if one of us was going to die tonight it would not be me.

I smirked at Hank and pretended to relax for a second. He was stronger, but not smarter. Surely I could outwit the drunk asshole, even if he outweighed me by nearly a hundred pounds.

"I knew you'd see this my way. Nobody said you were a stupid girl. Now, hand over the screwdriver."

He still had me by the hair, but I'd already decided on my next move. I was close enough, but could I execute without hesitation?

I meekly took my time getting to my feet as he let his guard down, making him believe I'd given in for the time being. But as I stood, I gave quick thanks the screwdriver had a sharp Phillips head, because when I drove it, without any warning, into Hank Brubaker's testicles, it didn't stop until the head of the tool rested on the side of his testicular area, a good four inches shoved clean through.

I wasn't prepared for so much blood. He howled, and then fell. I had killed him for sure.

I couldn't catch my breath for a moment. I believed I'd killed Hank the night I left. I saw my next moves like a grainy old movie, but there were still gaps in time. I'd been so scared. The blood. So much of it. I'd picked up a backpack in a shed someplace, maybe? Had I put it there before? There were clothes and money inside. My bicycle was hidden, waiting too.

I remembered riding fast, my legs burning, bumping along the trail. I fell down because it was dark, and I'd cut through the woods. I hit my head on a tree root and was bleeding. Then, I remember the lights passing as I rode the bus. I must have lost time someplace between. And I remember Thelma telling me gently to get in the car.

"Seeing ghosts, girl?" Hank brought me out of my deep brain fog.

I stiffened. "It's amazing what I remember." I stared deep into his yellowing eyeballs.

"You can't prove a thing," he growled.

"I'm betting you have at least a nasty scar on your left testicle, or somewhere near there, if you even still have one." I hadn't meant to say that.

His pallor turned almost gray then. "They said you lost your memory."

I tapped my head. "It's all coming back now."

"You might want to tell them that it was *you* who tried to kill *me* that night."

I shook my head. "I was sixteen and it was self-defense. Who do you think they're going to believe? A hateful child abuser and drunk or the abused child who disappeared that night so as not to be killed by her murderous stepfather?"

"Still no proof." He sneered at me. "Don't nobody know nothing, you hear?"

Momma put her arm around me and I could feel resolve emanating from her. "I'm her proof."

He laughed an ugly laugh. "What a joke, Mary Frances. You're so afraid of your own shadow, you can't sleep at night. You've only gotten what you deserved."

I stared hard at the sick, sadistic old man in front of me. The one who'd caused so much pain and destruction for so many. When I approached him to help him up, he recoiled, fear in his eyes. "Get your hands off me, you devil." He barely managed to scramble onto the bed.

And then I walked out and shut the door.

He yelled obscenities at both of us as we left the room.

"I'm going to put him in the county nursing home," Momma's voice was low and resolute.

Those weren't the words I expected to hear. "Can you do that without his consent?"

She nodded. "I got his medical power of attorney last time he was dead drunk and crying for me to forgive him for hitting me and begging me not to press charges. I made him sign the paper in exchange for not going to the police."

I stared at her in fascinated horror. "Are you serious about this? Do you think they'll take him?"

"He's on Medicaid. They have to as long as there's a bed for him. In fact, the caseworker at the hospital suggested it when he was in the hospital last time. She said it was even time for hospice care."

"Hospice care? Is he that bad off?" I wasn't sure how I felt about Hank *actually* dying before he had what was coming to him. Maybe it was best.

"His stroke has caused some kind of dementia. He's forgetting things and getting worse every day." She paused and looked me straight in the eyes. "You coming back shows me that I have reasons to live. And I want us to find Julie to let her know you're home. She hasn't come back in all these years, so I guess it's because she hates me, but she will want to see you."

I wanted to find Julie more than anything. And I didn't blame her for not coming back here. We had no idea how her life had gone once she'd been taken away. But I didn't say that aloud. Instead, I went with: "Doesn't hospice do home care?" I didn't know much about it, but a client's mother had died of cancer in her home with hospice.

"Hospice can go to a facility," Momma said. "Plus, when I hurt my back picking him up, they said he should go to the home since he's become a falling risk."

I stared at her for a minute, uncertain of what to say. "I don't have any love for the man, but he's been with you all these years. Don't do this because of me." I was glad to hear that Momma had options in dealing with Hank's illness because she wasn't doing very well having to care for him twenty-four-seven.

She smiled at me. "I'm doing what's best for both of us—finally. I didn't put you first when I should have. Now, it's the least I can do. And I feel more peace about this decision than anything since you disappeared."

"How are you going to tell him?" I couldn't imagine that going well, no matter how the information was communicated.

"I think I'll ask Becky and Chase's advice on that. They're very smart and might be able to help me get him there without a lot of hubbub."

I considered that a moment. "We can ask his opinion when he gets here."

Momma nodded.

Chapter Thirteen

"I F I HAVE his medical power of attorney, what's the problem?" Momma sat on the front porch swing. We were gathered outside the house so Hank couldn't hear our discussion.

Chase frowned. "If he doesn't want to leave and seems to be lucid, we could run into issues."

I thought we'd solved this, but it appeared we would need to come at it from a different angle. "Should I divorce him? I own the house."

I almost laughed at the absurdity of Momma's statement—the desperation in her voice. "I don't think you'll need to go through that."

She grabbed my hand and looked at me. "What if we give him the choice between the county jail and a comfortable bed at Moonshine Manor? He knows what he did to you. If he thinks you're going to have him arrested for trying to kill you the night you left, he might just agree to go on to the nursing home with hospice. At least they'll give him some morphine and he won't have to detox."

Momma was trying to honor my wishes in being referred to as Randi, but coming from her it felt wrong. But she had a great idea. "You might be on to something," I said. "It makes sense that you wouldn't have to allow the man who tried to kill your daughter in your home while he waits for his trial."

Chase weighed in. "It might work. There's no statute of limitations on attempted murder, but we have to convince him the outcome is inevitable. The last thing you need is actually having to go through the process of filing attempted murder charges. The legal process would be a giant mess."

I considered that, and my current legal status of misrepresenting myself as a dead person still.

Becky narrowed her eyes. "He'd be well cared for, so nobody has a reason to believe Mary Frances is doing anything but the best for Hank. Plus, he's at risk of injuring himself due to falling. And she can't pick him up."

They all nodded. The arguments were solid. And Momma did have his signature on the paperwork to back it up in case Hank balked once he got there.

Chase pulled out his phone. "I'll call over to Moonshine Manor and make sure they have a bed available."

Mary Frances nodded. "Thanks, Chase. I've had all I can take. I know that sounds a little late in the day, but now that Sadie's come home, I want her to feel welcome in her own house. I need to do this for her."

I still wasn't sure how I felt about this all falling on me, but if it helped Momma rid herself of daily abuse, even if it was only verbal now, then I was willing to take the blame or credit. And she shouldn't have to deal with Hank's end-of-life care if she needed physical help.

Chase moved away from the group while he made a call.

"Are you gonna be okay moving him out, Mary

Frances?" Beck leveled Momma with a stare.

"I am, Becky. I know y'all think I'm a pathetic, wishy-washy woman, but Hank's leaving this house. I guess that's tough talk now that he's weak as a two-day-old kitten. I'm not wasting another minute of my life getting yelled at by somebody who'd as well knock me around as look at me. And he would if he could and didn't need me to feed him and wipe his butt."

"I'm proud of you for finding the courage to do this, Momma," I said and squeezed her hand. We'd moved on to the porch now and spoke softly in case Hank managed to make it out of bed.

Chase stepped up on the porch, a small smile on his lips. "Okay, there's a bed waiting for him if we can make him see his options clearly."

"I think I can convince him." As much as I loathed placing myself in a room with Hank for the length of a conversation, I believed the memories of what he'd done to me were shared, and that he must be anxious about his role as perpetrator. I intended to press that worry into fear. Fear of living out his miserable days in a hellhole, shackled, arms and legs to a metal bed in the state penitentiary with no hope of a blessed fix from a merciful soul who might take pity on him and smuggle in a small sip of whiskey or vodka, or maybe even mouthwash, should his situation become so dire.

"Do you want me to come in with you?" Chase seemed concerned.

I shook my head. "Nope. This is something I'm going to do on my own. If he doesn't believe I can make the charges stick, I may ask you to come and corroborate the legal trouble he faces."

"Okay. I can do that. Let me know if you need a good cop to your bad one."

"Do you want the baseball bat?" Momma was dead serious.

I shook my head. I almost laughed at her tone, if not at the suggestion. "Thanks for the offer."

"Good luck, honey." Becky added to the collective support.

We entered the house together. Momma went to check on Hank and make sure he was awake and able to have this conversation. I couldn't say how she prefaced my entry, but he was propped up in bed when I entered.

I sat in the chair in the corner of the room. I hesitated to close the door because the smell was hard to take. But I decided to make a point to keep our conversation overtly private to give Hank the impression of gravity.

"Why are you closing the door?" Hank eyed me suspiciously.

"Because you and I are going to have a serious discussion. And I'm giving you the choice between dying in comfort or dying handcuffed to a bed detoxing in the state prison hospital ward awaiting attempted murder charges all alone."

Hank glared hard at me. I expected him to be afraid. "What are you suggesting, girl?"

"There's a bed at Moonshine Manor nursing home. Say the word and it's yours."

"You shoulda stayed dead." He glared at me like he wished he'd finished what he started thirteen years ago.

"Have you worried about where I went? Did you think

about my coming back here and pointing a finger at you for what you tried to do?"

His torso came off the bed. "What *I* did? *You* stabbed *me*! I have the scar to prove that. What proof do you have?" He had a point, but only if one didn't look at the whole picture.

I pointed at him. "You beat me every time you got drunk and were able to catch me from the time I was *ten* years old. You threatened to kill me over and over. You left so many bruises on my tiny body that I stayed away from people and kept covered up so no one could see them."

He smirked at me then. "But nobody ever saw, did they? So, you would have a hard time getting them to believe a word you said. You, with your broken memory. I took you in and put those clothes on your back. I adopted you and gave you my name. I fed you and took care of you, you ungrateful little bitch." He sneered at me. "But *you* shamed me with those devil eyes and told me to do better. You brought it on yourself, you judgy little shit."

The urge to shove him out of the bed was strong. "That's asinine. I was a child. You should have done better by us. We shouldn't ever have been afraid of you."

"You're trying to get rid of me, a dying man." His cough was deep and phlegmy, and racked his body. I wouldn't allow myself to feel sorry for him as he was cursing me and calling me names.

"No. Momma *is* getting rid of you. Finally. But it's up to you to decide your own fate. She doesn't have to live with the attempted murderer of her own child. The terrorist who's done nothing but bully and make her miserable all these years. They'll take you into custody, if only to keep you out of her home. Plus, nobody will post your bail."

"This is blackmail. I demand to speak to Mary Frances."

"I'm giving you a compassionate option and a heads-up. I'm only suggesting you take it instead of forcing me to press charges against you. And this was Momma's idea."

He stared, his jaundiced eyes filled with hate.

He had no remorse, obviously. "Do you need some time to think it over? The sheriff is outside. He will arrest you and take you into custody, or he can take you to the comfortable Moonshine Manor. Your choice."

"I have rights."

"Not really. Momma has your medical power of attorney, signed by you. She has the recommendation from your last hospital stay to put you in the nursing home due to your failing health and inability to care for yourself. So, you see, there are a lot of factors working against you. But either way, you're getting out of Momma's house today."

He appeared ready to lunge off the bed at me, the loathing in his eyes so intense, and for a split second, I experienced the old fear. "Not today, old man. Be glad I didn't bring in the baseball bat like Momma suggested." I wrinkled my nose. "It stinks in here."

I left the room on that note.

I entered the living room and stared into three expectant faces. "He's going. I mean, I assume he's going to take the easy way. I didn't give him the choice to stay."

"How did he take it?" Momma was wringing her hands, her anxiety evident.

"As poorly as you might expect."

"I packed some of his clothes this morning." Momma wiped her hands on her dress and walked over to the hall closet. There, she pulled out an overnight bag. "Can we take him now?" It seemed she couldn't go soon enough now that the decision was made.

"Moonshine Manor's intake process for nursing care is normally twenty-four to forty-eight hours. But since Hank has had a recent terminal diagnosis and hospitalization, and he's already qualified for hospice and Medicaid, they've agreed to put him in a rehab bed overnight until the hospice nurse can get there to start the paperwork tomorrow. It's the only way to get him there today. You can do private pay for the overnight bed and nursing care and then file for reimbursement."

Thank goodness for that. Greasing the wheels with a sheriff's phone call likely didn't hurt in expediting the process.

"O-okay. As long as we can get him out of the house and somebody can take care of him," Momma said. I knew she wouldn't want him to suffer unduly even though she was ready to get him out of her house. "I'll give him his medication before he leaves until they can get that settled tomorrow."

"It's not the perfect solution, but it will help you get things handled permanently in a couple of days," Becky said.

Hank bellowed for Mary Frances then.

"Coming," she called back to him, then sighed. "I'll get him ready to go."

"How about I give you a hand?" Becky suggested, then moved forward toward the bedroom. I was beginning to realize that Becky didn't ask permission when something needed doing.

"Thanks for helping with this situation," I said to Chase once they'd left the room. Our being alone together felt a little awkward. He seemed to fill the room now that we were alone.

"Of course. It feels good to finally do something to help Mary Frances. Hank's been a black cloud in her life for such a long time."

I began to fold blankets and pick up items in the living room to busy my hands. I realized I was a little nervous around Chase. He was very good-looking, and I'd begun to notice my response more and more when he was nearby. Having so little close interaction with men my age over the years made me realize how abnormal my life with Thelma had been in many ways. Some of them important and in the most basic ways.

I could speak and interact pretty well, but I'd never had a boyfriend or even kissed anyone romantically. I was staring at Chase's lips when he cleared his throat, which made me jump. "Sorry. I was thinking."

"Sit down, Randi. We can have the house deep cleaned once Hank is gone. In fact, I know a good contractor who can come and give you an estimate on having some work done around here to get this place back in decent shape."

I wanted that for Momma. She deserved a nice, clean house to live in with a porch that didn't sag and that didn't smell of Hank's putrid breath and urine. "Thank you. I can pay for the repairs."

He nodded. "I hoped you would be able to help her. The

townsfolk would pitch in, but I don't think she would want that."

"No, she should be able to get her dignity back on her own terms. I'm her family, and I'll do everything I can to help her recover her pride." Though I thought about how hard it might be in a town this small with our history. And I felt the need to show those around us that I supported Momma, even though I had plenty of reservations of my own I'd been shoving aside. She was, and had been, rather pathetic. And the Sadie in me wanted to protect her, just as I'd done throughout my childhood. But coming to this situation as an outsider, as Randi, I was still baffled by her allowing Hank to hurt me.

Didn't most women protect their children at the expense of themselves, even to the death? I continued to compare Momma to Thelma, who was a lioness in her quest to keep me safe.

And yet, Thelma had kept me away from my family, who'd suffered the consequences of my absence. If I'd returned once I was eighteen, I could have sent Hank to prison myself. But could I without a memory? The conundrum and irony of the situation sat heavily on my souls—both as Sadie and Randi.

Chase brought me out of my musings. "Kicking Hank out will be an impressive start to help change the collective opinion. She's not the only one he's hurt."

"Who else?" I was curious as to how widespread Hank's violence was.

"Do you have all day? Hank's been an equal-opportunity asshole for many years. The list is long."

I wrinkled my nose at that answer. "I can't fix that."

"Nope. But you can stand by Mary Frances, and so can we. With your return and our support, she will be okay in time."

Warmth and appreciation flooded through me toward this kind man. I wanted to—what? Hug him? That wasn't appropriate, was it? What would it be like to put my arms around him and feel his around me? I felt heat surge in my cheeks. "I keep thanking you, but I don't think I can describe how much it means to me that you and Becky have championed us. I know it might not be a popular position to some."

His grin was wide and showed nearly all his straight, white teeth. "I'm not always on the popular side of things, and you're welcome."

Goodness. Could the man be any more good-looking?

"I think we're ready to go," Becky said, thankfully interrupting my uncomfortable moment with Chase.

"I'll pull the car around," Chase said, and stood. "Bring Hank onto the porch and I'll help get him settled."

Hank shuffled out, only allowing Momma to aid him as he glowered at us all. I didn't blame him for his rage. After all, he was being forced from his home, and for the first time ever, he didn't get the upper hand and wasn't able to bully everyone around him.

Plus, he was sweating. Detoxing, I supposed. I figured hospice would give him something to help with that. They wouldn't try to save his life, so making him comfortable would be the goal. I wanted Momma not to have to deal with the physical and emotional burden of his sickness and anger in her house any longer.

This was Momma's decision and the means to his end.

Chapter Fourteen

I'D RUN INTO the local hardware store to pick up a few items. Daisy Mae was back at Momma's house sunning herself in the dirt, so I was alone to face whatever came my way. Lately, I could pretty much handle the locals. Most were polite or kept their distance now, but I was still treated like a novelty.

"Are you Sadie Brubaker?" A short, dark-haired man appeared in front of me, sticking a microphone in front of my face.

"Excuse me?"

I then noticed another man holding a large video camera on his shoulder positioned between the racks of electrical supplies and plumbing parts.

Before I had a chance to formulate any rational response, Chase burst inside and put himself between me and the man with the mic. "Miss Collins has no comment at this time." And he ushered me toward the back of the store.

"Miss Collins? I thought her name was Sadie Brubaker." The reporter hadn't missed Chase's name change and questioned it from the other side of Chase's body, still not giving up on his exclusive.

"Betsy, can we lock the front door until Randi gets clear

of the reporters outside?"

I heard Betsy, the owner, loudly ask the men to leave her establishment, as she was closing early.

Betsy returned from locking the front door and handed me a yellow and black cap with a CAT logo on it hanging from a hook beside the counter.

"I saw the jackals headed this way from my office window. Are you ready to get out of here?" he asked.

I nodded, my hands shaking.

"Thanks for your help, Betsy," Chase said.

"Sure thing, Sheriff. I'm glad you showed up when you did."

"I-I wanted to get these things," I said, indicating my basket items. I'd grabbed a water hose, gardening gloves, and some cleaning products.

Betsy quickly rung up my purchases, including the black and yellow cap. "Got it. You can pay me next time you come in." She waved us toward the delivery entrance, which would hopefully get us out of this situation temporarily.

Chase took the bulky items from me.

"Thanks, Betsy," I said. I hadn't expected that kind of trust from someone I barely knew. I had a hazy memory of Betsy from childhood. She'd been a tomboy, I think, and I didn't get the feeling she'd been hateful like some of the others.

"Don't mention it, Sadie. I'm glad to see you getting your momma's place perked up. She deserves it." I didn't stop to question how she knew I was working on Momma's house. My heart warmed at her kindness. Being called Sadie here in Moonshine by people I grew up knowing didn't bother me anymore. Sadie and I weren't quite one and the same yet, but we had an understanding.

"My office is on the same side of the street about five or six doors down, so we could get there from here if nobody's figured out our exit strategy yet," he said.

I pulled the cap on my head and experienced déjà vu at hiding my identity once again. I looked forward to the day when I no longer had a need to hide myself from anyone.

Chase put a hand on my arm, which caused me to look up at him in question. "Randi, I'm sorry you have to do this again." It was as if he'd read my thoughts.

Heat rose to my cheeks, as it tended to do whenever I was near him. "Thank you for understanding, and for helping me yet again."

"Let's try and get to my office, then we can work on a plan. It's impossible to avoid the press forever." He pushed the exit door and peered outside.

"I know." I heard what sounded like a helicopter circling overhead.

He juggled my bag of purchases in one arm and led me down the alley behind the storefronts with his other hand. It reminded me of watching a suspense movie with Thelma, except I was on the other side of the camera. She would have been pleased to know I'd had such staunch protectors since my arrival here.

"Almost there." As we crept along, I could see the frenetic activity between the buildings, though there only a sliver of space. There was indeed a helicopter circling low, likely with an action reporter inside giving a bird's-eye account of my story.

My story. My life. So fascinating and exciting to others. But it hadn't been, not even a little. Hiding out on the outskirts of Hickman, Nebraska, with Thelma was far from it. I guess the fascination for everyone lay in imagining the lure of my unknown journey. The fictional possibilities were endless until my truth was told and confirmed. I guess I would have to let them down eventually.

We entered the back door into a small, dark storage room of the sheriff's department with Chase's key. "Hannah?" he called out in whisper.

"Sheriff? Is that you?" a woman answered, moving from her desk at the reception area of the office to where we hid, and squinting her eyes to see us.

"Lock the front door and close the blinds, please."

"O-okay." She quickly grabbed a set of keys off a ring next to her desk and clicked the lock, then set to closing all the metal blinds across the front of the plate-glass windows that gave a full view of Main Street. We came out from our dark hiding spot then.

"Hannah, this is Randi Collins, uh, Sadie Brubaker. Randi, this is my trusted assistant and my right arm, Hannah Hardy."

"Hi there, Randi. Is that what you prefer? The sheriff has told me all about you and the situation. I've known about your case for years. He speaks so highly of me because he doesn't want me to quit. Knows he'd forget his last name if I did."

Hannah had long, curly brown hair and a chin dimple. She had such a pleasant demeanor, and I could see why Chase valued her as an employee. "It's nice to meet you."

"I just gave birth, so I'm in and out of the office now, but I'm still hanging in there." She shot Chase an impish look. "For now."

"Prettiest baby girl you ever saw." Chase almost glowed when he said it.

Something tweaked inside me. A baby. Becoming a mother. It was something other people did, but the very idea of it set off all kinds of emotions and odd tingles.

"Congratulations," I said.

"Listen, Hannah, the press has descended on us. As in helicopters and news vans from Atlanta and beyond. Sadie has been discovered. We need some time to come up with a plan."

"Got it, boss man. I'll keep this place on lockdown. We'll only take emergency calls. In fact, I put the phone on service while I was getting some paperwork done and noticed it was ringing a lot. No emergencies though."

"If you check those messages, I'm sure you'll find they're from reporters asking for information. There were a few calls this morning before you arrived, but I didn't realize things were getting out of hand."

"Do they know you're here in the office? Do you want to put out a statement to the press?" Hannah asked.

"I don't think they've gotten wind that we're in here yet," Chase said. "We're going to sit down and come up with something to hopefully satisfy them for now."

I suddenly got a sick feeling. "Are they going to interview everyone in town?"

"Anyone who'll talk to them most likely," he said.

"What about Momma? And Hank?"

"That's why we need to put out a statement from you. So, they'll leave everyone else alone. You'll control the narrative that way."

"If I did that, I'm afraid of the legal implications. I haven't done what is needed to solve my identity crisis. I mean, like contacting the Social Security office and the FBI."

He ran a hand through his hair. "Didn't you say you had an attorney back in Hickman?"

The last time I'd spoken to Mr. Whitaker, he'd asked me to be patient and said that he was working on it. "Yes, but he was only checking into my situation. I'm afraid the FBI will want to interview me about Thelma and everything that happened. I wanted to come here first and try to work on my memory so I could have more information to give them. It's a very sticky situation."

"The press has now escalated this to a nasty legal situation for you. I'm afraid it might be time to hire an attorney from Atlanta. It might protect you should the feds come knocking."

Just what I didn't want to have to do. "Who should I contact?" I was completely out of my depth here. Mr. Whitaker was one thing. A stranger from Atlanta was another.

"Let me make a few phone calls. I do know some good attorneys in Atlanta. Believe it or not, our little mountain town is a vacation spot for many well-connected Atlantans since we're only eighty miles away.

"Okay. What do we do in the meantime to keep them away from Momma? And Daisy Mae's with her?"

"Call her and tell her to drive to my mom's house and

stay there until she hears from us. The press won't know to look for her there. And Becky will meet them at the front door with a shotgun if they try to mess with her."

"Okay." I had a pretty clear picture of Becky standing at her front door facing down the threat of men and women with microphones.

"I'll give Becky a call and let her know what's up," Hannah chimed in.

"Thanks. I'll get on the phone to Atlanta and get things rolling on that end." Chase was already at his desk looking up numbers in what appeared to be an old Rolodex. It made me smile—almost.

I was about to call Momma when Hannah came over and said, "Becky's on her way over to pick up your mother and Daisy Mae. She's calling her on the way."

"She said something about going over to check on Hank this afternoon while I was out getting supplies."

"Becky will catch up with her either way and make sure she has your pup. She said don't worry about it, she's got them handled."

"Thanks, Hannah." I was relieved to know Becky was on it. She was someone I knew I could trust a hundred percent with those I cared about. Then I had another thought. "I hope the reporters don't figure out where Hank is. Who knows what he might tell them?"

"I can send out Dub, our deputy out in the field and have him post up at the entrance of Moonshine Manor. They won't get past him." Hannah turned to Chase, as if to check with him, but it was evident he'd heard her.

"Good idea. Do it," Chase said from his desk and gave a

thumbs-up to Hannah, as he held the phone up against his ear. He was obviously on hold for someone.

I sat staring, in somewhat of a fog, wondering what to do next. It seemed as if my hands were tied until I secured a lawyer and got some updated and more urgent legal advice on how to handle my precarious situation with the government investigators. The last thing I wanted or needed was to be arrested for impeding justice or hampering an investigation, or whatever it was when one was supposed to be dead but really wasn't and didn't contact the authorities right away.

Mr. Whitaker initially told me he was inquiring into the smoothest way to retake my identity with the least legal consequence. I didn't know how it would all work. Did I defraud the system, whatever system that was, or had I gone along with a plan because I had no memory?

Chase spoke in low tones with someone, but I wasn't paying attention to his conversation. My mind was going in so many directions right now, my brain wiring threatened to misfire.

He appeared in front of me where I was pacing. "A top attorney from a respected firm will be here in just over an hour. I quickly told him about your situation, and he is getting briefed as he flies over on the company 'copter."

I stared at him. "Company 'copter? Who has a company 'copter?"

"The attorneys at Brindle and Brindle do, I guess. Your case is big national news, and they didn't hesitate to hop on board. No charge."

"Well, that's big of them, isn't it?" Hannah asked from

where she sat at her desk. "I guess they want in the game." Then recognition flashed in her eyes. "Brindle?"

"I told them I called *them* first, but I could have easily called their closest competitor," Chase said. "Plus, it didn't hurt that the senior partner's son got in a bit of a scrape with a local girl smoking pot on the lake last summer. It was my discretion whether the situation turned into a nasty public circus or died a quiet death with a misdemeanor arrest and disturbing the peace."

"I remember that," Hannah said. "Poor kid didn't deserve to have his name dragged through the mud because his daddy was a big deal."

"I did what I thought was right, and what I would have done in the same circumstance no matter the social standing of the parents," Chase said. "Anyway, Mr. Bristol suggested should I ever need his professional assistance, he was a mere phone call away."

"Sorry you had to use your legal favor on me," I said.

"Glad I had one." He grinned. "Anyway, he's meeting us here."

"So, we wait?" I asked.

"Yes. You can't go outside. You'll get mobbed by reporters. Word's gotten out to all the news outlets that you're here."

My phone rang then. It was Jenny. *Excuse me*, I mouthed to them. "Hi, Jenny."

"I see you've been discovered. Are you okay?" Her tone sounded worried.

"What do you mean?"

"You're breaking news! I'm watching the skeezy reporters

in Moonshine, Georgia, discuss your resurrection."

"Oh, yeah. I'm okay so far. There's a lawyer on the way from Atlanta."

"Does Mr. Whitaker know about all this?" she asked.

"I haven't had a chance to call him yet. The reporters started showing up about an hour or so ago."

"Looks like they're posted up outside the front of the sheriff's office saying you're hiding inside."

I covered the speaker and spoke to Chase and Hannah. "We're on TV." It was crazy that Jenny could see where I was from Nebraska.

Chase grabbed the remote and clicked on the television that hung at the back of the room. Sure enough, we were breaking news. "Aw, shit."

"This is crazy. It's not like I'm being held hostage," I said, looking at the screen that showed a reporter standing in front of the sheriff's office right outside, pointing to where we were holed up inside. But I guess they didn't have much to go on.

Jenny said, "The reporter is giddy. She says you have amnesia and don't remember who you are and that you found your way back to Moonshine, Georgia, after all these years."

"They only have what little information we gave the local newspaper to satisfy the town. I guess I knew this could happen, but I didn't realize it would be such a big national deal. I wanted to resolve my identity issue before the press outed me like this."

"Whether it was a good idea to put your return in a newspaper, or not, it's out there, *way* out there. Nothing you can do about it now. Once you're good and lawyered up, you'll have help in working through some of the sticky stuff."

"I'd better get off the phone so we can figure out our next move. Thanks for calling. I'll keep you posted."

After I'd hung up with Jenny, Chase said, "I should have gotten clearer information from you about how Thelma gained your identity. I wouldn't have publicized your return if I'd known she'd actually given you her daughter's legal identity."

"It's complicated, but I can't be the first person who's been declared alive after being missing for years. Because I didn't have a memory and didn't know who I was, I didn't come forward. I thought I'd have more time."

Somebody tried the front door only to find it locked up tight. We all jumped in surprise. "It's a public office. They had to try," Chase said.

"I turned the closed sign face out," Hannah said.

"Where is the lawyer landing?" I wondered how he planned to get inside.

"At the hospital's landing pad. I doubt they'll expect that. The news helicopters haven't had any luck so far in getting permission to use it."

I guess being the sheriff had its perks.

My stomach growled a little too loudly. I'd been running errands and planned to pick something up for lunch and hadn't gotten the chance. "Sorry."

"We need a couple city police officers posted so we can at least get some food delivered to the back door while we're waiting for the attorney," Chase said.

He and Hannah exchanged glances.

I was missing something. "Who's in charge of that?" I asked, glancing between the two.

"The police chief, who answers to the mayor," Hannah said.

I looked at Chase, understanding. "Oh. The same one who owns the newspaper and is married to your ex-wife." Gotcha. The small-town politics here were classic.

Chase blew out a hard breath. "I'll give him a call."

I guessed it was the last thing he wanted to do, but there were a gaggle of reporters gathering outside who would compete for the story. And they were an aggressive bunch, if watching the nightly news was to be believed. I would certainly appreciate a buffer if it came to that.

"Yeah, Weston, it's Chase. I need to get a couple officers over here right away."

Chapter Fifteen

"I'VE SPOKEN TO the Georgia Bureau of Investigation. The closest field agent is on the way. We'll make a short statement to the press ASAP and give them something to chew on for a day or two until we can get you in the clear with the authorities, or at least start dialogue from a legally neutral position," Paul Bristol said. His manner was confident and competent.

"I persuaded the chief of police to give up a couple officers to help with managing reporters and their harassment of our citizens. Their job is to make sure to keep everyone in line when someone tells them to buzz off," Chase said.

"We're pretty good at letting the reporters know the citizens' rights as well. They will want to avoid lawsuits against their networks while they are here sniffing out stories," Paul said.

"When will you have the press conference?" I asked.

"We have your information. It will take me a few minutes to prepare a statement. I suggest we do it this evening, so you won't get inundated once you leave here. If we let them know what to expect in the coming days as far as our communication with them, they won't be so overzealous."

"I'll speak as law enforcement to let everyone know they have the right to decline an interview or comment should someone approach them and to let us know if anyone hassles them," Chase said.

"Good idea. This shouldn't take more than fifteen or twenty minutes," Paul said.

Hannah had already left for the evening, as she was breastfeeding still and needed to nurse her daughter.

"I'll go out and let the press know we are going to make a statement within the half hour. Jason's staff will need to set up microphones and a podium since that's normally their kind of PR stuff." Chase stood and moved toward the front door.

I realized that Chase's interactions with Jason Weston were trying his patience, but clearly the sheriff's department had a limited team, and everyone had a role when news happened in a town or city. The mayor was the talking representative for the town and the sheriff made announcements with regards to investigations within the jurisdiction. I'd learned this from watching my share of true crime and suspense drama.

Now I was the subject of a sensational news story where a press conference was required. It wasn't nearly as exciting from this perspective. I began to realize how quiet things had been since my arrival until now.

The mayor swooshed in fifteen minutes later with his gaggle of people and equipment. The van pulled up in front of the sheriff's office, and they unloaded all the items needed for a bona fide press conference. I figured the possession of podiums and such were part of running a town. I peeked outside through the side of the blinds and watched as the reporters and camera men and women began working to get their microphones set up front and center in relation to the makeshift stage.

"Unlock the damn door," someone yelled as they banged on the glass from outside.

Chase flipped the key to let the mayor in.

"Back up. No one is getting inside this office. We'll be out in a few minutes. You'll have to wait like everyone else," Jason Weston yelled at someone who'd pushed their way forward demanding answers. There were a couple of uniformed policemen with him.

"Damned jackals," he muttered as he shut the door behind him and relocked it quickly.

I stood and stared as he brushed off his starched button-down white shirt. He had curly, thick golden hair and long, dark eyelashes framed by well-groomed brows. "Well, where is she?" he asked, his tone annoyed. So much for thinking he was an attractive man.

I stepped forward then. "I'm Randi Collins. Or, Sadie Brubaker, I guess you've heard." Then I saw him in my mind. A much younger him sitting at an outdoor table in town with his arm thrown around some girl with a group of his friends. I was sitting at a nearby table with my friend, and we'd thought he was so cute.

His obvious irritation instantly transformed to charm and schmooze. "Sadie. It's great to finally meet you. I'm Jason Weston, mayor of this fine town."

He reached out to shake my hand. "I remember you now."

"And they said your memory was unreliable."

I shook my head. "It's all coming back. Just a few gaps here and there." I'd decided it was better to keep my cards close with what I did and didn't recall.

"Is everyone ready to do this?" Paul Bristol asked, addressing the small group.

They nodded. "Okay, I'll need the mayor to welcome the press and then make introductions. You know the drill. Just like we did it last summer, guys."

I assumed he was referencing a statement regarding his own son's arrest and interest by the press and public.

"Great to see you again, Paul. How is your son?" Jason asked the attorney with a wink.

Paul's response was slightly delayed, a half a beat where everyone, except Jason, understood it was received exactly as intended. "He's well, thanks for asking. I'm keeping him away from small towns with overzealous newspaper reporting."

Jason laughed as if he'd heard the most hilarious joke. Nobody else did.

"Okay, folks, here we go," Paul said, moving on.

I stayed inside the sheriff's office as instructed and hoped Daisy Mae and Momma were well hidden from today's craziness. I understood at some point the press might find her and ask her questions. Hopefully by then she would be more prepared than we were today.

"YOU READY TO get out of here?" Chase asked once the

chaos outside ended. He'd come back inside and locked the door. The lights had stopped flashing, and it appeared the excitement was dying down.

"Yes. More than ready." I'd checked in with Momma earlier and she seemed to be doing fine. She'd gone over to the nursing home to check on Hank while I'd been at the hardware store.

"She and Becky have been playing Gin all afternoon and watching the news," I told Chase.

"Sounds like they aren't any worse for wear." He laughed. "I wasn't worried about them. How's Hank?"

"Demanding to speak to the press so he can tell them how I tried to kill him the night I left," I said. "Momma said they had to sedate him to keep him from trying to escape."

Chase shook his head. "That's all we need. A sensationalized version of the truth according to your abuser."

"He wouldn't be exactly lying, but only after he'd tried to kill me with the screwdriver first. I guess he conveniently forgot about my defending myself when I stabbed him with it to get away with my life intact."

"Don't worry about it. You have so many people here who know how he was then and now. Nobody will take his word over yours if it comes down to it. He's not exactly credible."

"It's been a long day. Let's get out of here," I said. "I'll worry about Hank and his press interviews when they happen."

"You're right. My mother texted something about fried chicken and mashed potatoes for dinner."

"Sounds heavenly. It's been hours since the diner delivered those sandwiches."

I had moved out of the bed-and-breakfast and in with Momma the day after Hank left the house. We'd managed to get the smell of urine out of most things and hauled off the things we couldn't. The place was looking and smelling so much better now.

I'd moved some money to the local bank since there wasn't a branch here of the one Thelma and I frequented in Hickman. Momma had attempted to resist my financial help, but I'd insisted on paying for the repairs on the farmhouse.

"I'll take you to your Jeep since I'm parked right out front," Chase suggested.

"Okay."

It was well after dark, nearly nine o'clock now, and the sidewalks were mostly clear of reporters. There were some tourists meandering, and a couple of local bars and restaurants were still open on the square. It was a Tuesday on a normal balmy summer evening.

We drove to where my Jeep was parked down the street. I could've walked, but I had the purchases from the hardware store to transfer from his vehicle, and I didn't want to take the chance of an unexpected rogue reporter ambushing me.

"Head over to Becky's and we'll have a bite to eat."

"Sounds good." His smile was still doing things to my insides that unnerved me. But his kindness was my undoing. I liked Chase Blackburn. I mean I was starting to *like* like him. I'd never had that giddy sensation around a man before. I looked forward to being in his company. I'd seen him less since I moved to Momma's house a couple of weeks ago.

Being with him all day today, despite the circumstances, had reminded me that I'd missed him.

As a friend, but something more too. I had no idea if he had any of the same feelings toward me. I got the impression from what I'd picked up that he still had deep stuff going on from losing his ex-wife and was totally bothered by the fact that Jason Weston was now married to her.

Who was I to even entertain ideas about getting involved with anyone? I was twenty-nine and hadn't been kissed. What a joke that would seem to anyone in the normal world. It was a secret shame of mine. It hadn't been before. Before, I hadn't worried about that kind of thing. In fact, it hadn't entered my mind that it would ever change. But now, things were different. The world was opening up to me in new ways every day. My memory was returning, as were layers of my personality. I had a real sense of humor. I wasn't such a bland nobody anymore. I *cared* about things deeply, and people.

My world had been so small with Thelma. She'd worked hard to keep it that way. No big ups or downs, so no real emotional upheaval or sadness—until she'd up and died on me. Now, I felt *everything*, which helped me understand so much more than I had about people and the world.

I wanted to live life now instead of just passively allowing it every day. I'd gotten angry, and sometimes my feelings toward people, especially people who were nasty to me in my past, were shameful. I thought unkind things and regretted my impulses, something I'd never done as Randi. Sadie was inside of me. I was her. But I was also still Randi. It continued to baffle me daily.

I went about my business in town and regularly encountered people I'd gone to school with or grown up with. Sometimes memories popped up during these encounters, or not. I worked to be gracious when someone or other apologized for treating me poorly during our childhoods. A time or two I failed and pretended not to remember, and once I called the guy a dick because the memory was particularly awful. He agreed that indeed he had been a dick and wished me well. The Sadie in me was far more outspoken and prone to calling a dick a dick. Randi had never used such language.

As I drove to Becky's house, I was aware of an emptiness still. Was it because I missed Thelma so much? I couldn't quite put my finger on it. Was I lonely for the first time? But how could that be? I had my mother, and now I'd been connecting with people who seemed to genuinely like me and want to further our friendships. I worked at night on client accounts here and there, keeping my hours at a minimum as I considered myself still in vacation mode as I worked to figure all this out.

I wanted to love Thelma like I had before, but the stark fact that she'd kept me from my home and people who cared about me kept a wedge driven between me and my old feelings for her. I knew she'd wanted to take me here before she died, but only after thirteen years. Why? Nothing about our relationship made sense still.

I pulled into the drive at Becky's house, eager to see Daisy Mae and lay eyes on Momma. I'd begun to feel somewhat like I belonged here again. Not all the time and not completely, but it hadn't taken long to get comfortable here in this small Southern town. I thought about my home in

Hickman, and Thelma's beautiful garden. What was I going to do? How could I reconcile the two places? How could home be in two parts of the country so far from each other?

A soft knock on my window made me jump in my seat. Chase offered a hand and helped me out of the Jeep. He had the nicest hands.

"Thanks." It seemed like I was constantly thanking him for something.

"It would have been rude if I'd gone inside without you, so if I'm rushing you, it's because you haven't yet tried my mother's fried chicken."

"Oh. Gotcha. Makes perfect sense. Everything else she's cooked has been award-worthy. And fried chicken is one of my favorites." Thelma hadn't made fried chicken often, but when she had, it was an event rather than a meal.

We were greeted by an enthusiastic Daisy Mae and lots of questions by the women as we entered, along with the glorious aroma that made my stomach protest the hours since I'd last eaten.

Chapter Sixteen

RUNNING IN THE summer in Moonshine was different than in Nebraska. My lungs screamed at the heat and humidity. The hills made my thighs ache, and I had to focus on where I stepped, as the surface wasn't paved, but I loved every minute. The sweat, the fresh air, and the blue skies.

There were more critters of every kind here it seemed. Birds, squirrels, and chipmunks abounded, but there were also venomous snakes, spiders, and so many mosquitos. I'd been warned to keep one eye on the ground by everyone. In Nebraska, we had critters, but they didn't seem to be part of my life. The trails were paved and the spiders were nicely behaved in Thelma's garden—or so it had seemed. Here, I was in the woods a good deal of the time sharing space with nature.

Daisy Mae had to be convinced lately to accompany me on my runs. She'd taken to country life, well, like a tick to a hound, as the expression went. Gone was my clean, sweet-smelling girl. She'd gone to digging holes in the red dirt and rolling on anything dead she could find. Mice, bugs, birds—didn't matter. Her world had expanded exponentially in all the fun, gross ways.

She and Momma had developed quite a bond. Momma

put out scraps after dinner or small food bits for Daisy Mae while she was cooking. I'd protested this practice, but neither had an interest in my opinion on the matter.

I'd come back from a run with Daisy Mae, who was breathing as hard as me when my phone vibrated. I'd somehow missed a call from a local number. And a text from an unknown number from a woman named Stacey at the bank stating to please call as soon as possible.

The hair raised on my arms. After the whole press fiasco a few days ago, I'd been looking over my shoulder at every turn. Paul, my new local attorney, and the Georgia Bureau of Investigations special agent had met to discuss my situation yesterday regarding my identity and the legal issues I faced through no fault of my own. I was supposed to hear something about a formal sit-down sometime today.

I filled a bowl of water for Daisy Mae and then wet her down with the hose to cool her. She needed a bath this afternoon due to another encounter with a no-longer-alive reptile, so she could hang out in the shade on her bed on the porch until I could give her one.

Momma met me at the door, a worried expression on her face.

"What's going on?"

"Chase called. He and your lawyer are on the way. Something about the feds and your identity."

I showered off and then made my way to my childhood bedroom thinking I should call Mr. Whitaker, my attorney from Hickman, when I heard a car door slam outside. I peeked through the curtains and saw Paul and Chase had arrived in Chase's truck.

Mr. Whitaker had suggested I keep my Randi Collins documents with me at all times as proof that Thelma had given them to me. It was how I had opened bank accounts, registered for schools, and gotten my driver's license. And now I knew it had all been illegal. But it was the only identity I had at the moment until I could clear up being dead as Sadie Brubaker.

I quickly pulled on a soft green T-shirt. It was old, but clean, and smelled way better than the one I'd run in. Admittedly, I freshened up because Chase was on his way. Otherwise, I'd have waited until after bathing Daisy Mae.

When Paul noticed my entrance, he switched whoever was on the line to speakerphone.

The male voice listed reasons why all of this was a problem. "Listen, this case gives us a black eye, and my boss wants to get it cleared up as quickly as possible. We're not looking to fight with local authorities or the FBI. We've got a long list of living people swearing they're not dead, and dead people whose identities have been stolen by people who are alive. It seems Miss Collins/Brubaker has done both."

"It's a complicated situation, and she's not to blame for either," Paul said.

"Like I said, we're not looking to make a stink, just to get this one behind us," the speaker said.

"How do I know my client is protected against prosecution if she makes a statement to you?" Paul asked.

"You don't. We need to get her information on record so we can move forward. If she's been defrauding the government intentionally, she will go through the process."

"My client won't make a statement at this time without

some kind of guarantee she won't be arrested," Paul said, and then switched the call back to his ear and walked outside.

"Could I offer some coffee?" Momma asked. She'd never acted the part of hostess much, seeing how Hank wasn't a hospitable sort.

Chase nodded. "Sure. That'd be great."

I excused myself to help Momma with the coffee. Chase followed me. "Hey, are you okay?"

"I'm okay. Just wondering who else might show up here out of the blue."

He laughed a little. "Yeah. I know what you mean. It's been an eventful couple of weeks, hasn't it? Don't worry, Paul will handle this." I tended to trust Chase and Becky but wanted to get the green light with Mr. Whitaker who'd been with me from the beginning of this ordeal. I'd spoken with him the day the press had descended on us. He'd reassured me that Paul had an excellent reputation.

Chase excused himself to the dining room then.

"Sadie, could you hand me the pie out of the fridge, please? Might as well heat it up to go with the coffee."

"Sure, Momma." I grabbed the two-thirds apple pie we'd had last night with dinner and passed it to her. Momma had finally given up calling me Randi, at my request. It wasn't fair asking her to do that when I'd been Sadie to her from the moment of my birth.

"I'll take this to the young men," she said.

I realized I was hiding out in the kitchen then, avoiding the conflict about my identity and perceived threat from the government. It's strange how I was willing to physically challenge Hank as a kid but ran like a scared rabbit at this kind of threat. This was mostly a Randi problem. I was glad to see that Momma wasn't shrinking away from people anymore. I couldn't believe the difference in her demeanor over the past couple of weeks. The change in her appearance was astonishing. It was as if twenty years had been erased from her age. She stood straighter and taller. The worry lines were less pronounced, and I heard her singing and whistling around the house.

She'd taken on shifts at the dollar store and seemed cheerful and energetic when she arrived home after work. Gone was the beaten-down woman I'd always thought of as Momma. Except when she went to the nursing home to check on Hank. It took her a little while after she got home from seeing him to shake the melancholy.

I couldn't bear to spend time wondering how much she might have been spared had I been able to return years earlier. Even with large men in her house, she managed to conduct herself without cowering and offer refreshments. I couldn't lie, I was nervous about all of this despite my very confident attorney.

Paul had taken a lengthy statement from me regarding my memories of the night I disappeared, and the events leading up to that night. He'd been especially interested in my history with Hank and how I'd managed to get away without anyone ever solving my case. I'd done my best to fill in as many details as possible, but honestly, there were gaps.

I suspect that falling and hitting my head on the tree root went pretty far to erase some of what happened before and after my grand escape. And it likely had a lot to do with my memory loss. That and the trauma. When I told Jenny about the fall from my bike and the head injury, she was almost relieved because it better explained my condition.

"Paul's giving them the business out there." Momma's return snapped me out of my musings.

"I'm lucky to have him running interference on this for me. I'm way out of my depth," I said.

"Did you manage to get that client's logo worked out?" She changed the subject and asked about something I'd mentioned last night.

I'd been working again in the evenings on smaller projects that didn't require a lot of time. Running a small business meant I couldn't afford to take too much time off. My clients expected me to respond to them should they need my services.

"Yes. They wanted to rebrand and update their look for signs, business cards, and website."

"Do you do any printing?" she asked.

I guess she didn't have a clear picture of what I did for a living, so I tried to fill her in a little. It would take all day to give a complete job description.

I nodded. "When a client wants something special. I have some pretty fancy equipment back home. But mostly I'm the one who designs the look they want. There are printing companies who handle a lot of the basics."

"I'm so proud of you, Sadie." Momma's eyes watered just a little, and she dashed the wetness away with the back of her hand.

Her words gave me a flush of pride. "Thanks, Momma."

Thelma's smile flashed in my mind. She'd been such a supporter of my education and work. Sometimes missing her was so fresh and painful still.

"You said home. Are you going back to Hickman to live?" Momma asked. I could tell she was trying to not show her worry about that.

My face likely showed my confusion. "Um… I'm not sure what my plans are. I'm kind of taking things a day at a time right now."

"You have a house there, right?"

"Yes, I have a nice house. I would love for you to come and see where I've lived," I said.

"Oh, I don't know if I could go all the way to Nebraska." She said this as though it might've been the North Pole or someplace on the other side of the world.

Paul and Chase entered the kitchen, cutting off our conversation.

"What happened?" I asked, not sure I wanted to know.

"They're going to do their due diligence to figure out what happened to the real Randi Collins. I gave them as much information as we had on her."

Momma appeared curious. "What happened to the real Randi Collins?" she asked.

"She apparently passed away sometime before Thelma met me, but that's all we know," I answered. "I didn't know anything about her until after Thelma died."

"Didn't Thelma get help for you when she found you? She must have known somebody was looking for you." Momma hadn't asked any questions like this until now. I wondered maybe if it just occurred to her to wonder about Thelma's motives.

I moved next to her at the table. "Momma, I was hurt

and confused when I met Thelma—when she found me. So, according to her letter, she wanted to wait until I'd healed up and got my memory back. But it never came back."

Momma frowned. "So, when she was still alive, did she pretend to be your momma?"

"She did. Well, she pretended to be my adopted mother. I'd assumed that meant since I was a baby. So, she lied to me all those years trying to keep me safe and happy while we waited on my memory."

"Do you think you would've come back on your own if you hadn't lost your memory? Because Julie never came back, and her memory is probably just fine."

I nodded. "I don't remember what I was thinking back then besides that I knew Hank had murder on his mind, but there's no way I wouldn't have planned to come back when I was able to help you both." I couldn't say anything on Julie's behalf.

"But you didn't know where home was for all that time." Momma covered her mouth with her hand and bowed her head. "Excuse me." She stood and moved to the sink, busying herself with the dirty dishes.

Chase and Paul had sat silently while this exchange had taken place. "If you'll excuse me, I need to contact the GBI agent and let him know about what's happened with our friends at Social Security. They will want to communicate. The hardest part will be proving the amnesia."

"I have a friend who is a clinical therapist, and she knows my entire history though she isn't my therapist."

Paul nodded. "Has she treated you at all?"

"Just some hypnotherapy years ago. I'll call her tonight."

I knew Jenny would do whatever was necessary to support me and help me shed this difficult situation.

Paul's phone rang and he stepped out of the room to take the call.

Chase spoke then. "I'm sorry about that. This will get worked out, Randi—I'm sure of it. Those guys from Social Security seemed like they want to get to the bottom of the issue, but there's so much red tape involved in government investigation."

"Mr. Whitaker warned me it would be complicated," I said.

Paul's booming voice carried from the next room. "That's bullshit! You'd better figure out a way to fix this immediately or you'll have a media shitstorm and lawsuit on your hands like you've never seen."

Then a pause.

"How long?" he demanded.

Another pause.

"Fix it, goddammit."

A few seconds later he entered the kitchen, cheeks bright red with obvious fury. "We've got a problem."

Chapter Seventeen

"THEY'VE FROZEN YOUR accounts and assets, I'm afraid," Paul said.

I blinked. "Who has?"

"The IRS, via the Social Security Administration. Apparently because you're not who your credentials say you are, it gives them the right to seize your accounts and lock up your assets until further notice. Additionally, you've taken the identity of an assumed-deceased person, which is another crime altogether. And there's no record of the death of the original Randi Collins."

An invisible claw of dread and fear closed around my throat, nearly strangling my breath.

"What about my house?" I asked, a bit breathless. I pictured Thelma's garden falling to ruin overnight at the hands of strangers and it made me nauseous. "How can they do this?"

"*They* can do whatever they please when you don't have a leg to stand on. Until you can prove what needs proving, apparently, this is their move." He blew out a breath. "I should have seen this coming, but they don't typically work this fast."

"What can I do to protect my home? Right now, someone is taking care of things. Getting the mail, watering and caring for the garden. I don't want it all to end up a mess."

"They will likely intercept your mail for a while, but if the money isn't coming directly from your personal accounts, it may not be affected," Paul said.

"I've got an attorney who is handling those things with money from Thelma's estate." Mr. Whitaker's reassuring countenance flashed in my mind, sitting at his desk surrounded by all those crocheted doilies.

"You might want to call and give him a heads-up. It's possible he can help you with whatever funds are in a trust for the estate maintenance. Find out how the trust was set up. The government can only take over bank accounts and assets it knows about."

"I'll call Mr. Whitaker now."

Chase put a hand on mine when I pulled out my cell phone. "Use mine and don't forward his contact. Write down the number in case your phone is being monitored."

That made sense, but I couldn't believe this was happening. "Okay. Thanks." I didn't have Mr. Whitaker listed as an attorney, so maybe his contact wouldn't raise red flags.

I made the call to Arnold Whitaker in Hickman. "Hi, Mr. Whitaker, this is Randi Collins."

"Hello there, Randi. I've been wondering when I would hear from you." I could picture him, with his white hair and beard, a furrow between his brows.

"Uh, yeah, that's why I'm calling." I quickly told him what was happening.

I heard him sigh loudly. "I've already made a few minor and temporary adjustments to your, uh, situation, so the house maintenance would continue uninterrupted."

I frowned, not sure what he meant. "Oh? Are you concerned someone is listening?"

"I can never be certain, but you haven't anything to worry about. You'll hear from me soon, dear. Take care."

The line went dead.

"What did he say?" Paul asked.

"He was oddly unspecific and said he would be in touch. And that I hadn't anything to worry about regarding the house."

Paul nodded. "Sounds like lawyer speak to let you know he's moved around some money as best he could. I guess he saw you on the news?"

"Yes."

"Mr. Whitaker sounds like a sharp guy. We'll hear from him," Paul said. "Do you have some cash in the meantime?" he asked.

"Enough to get by for a while. Thelma didn't trust banks and always insisted we keep emergency cash on hand for a rainy day. In fact, Mr. Whitaker had handed me an envelope full of cash before I left town and suggested I tuck it away. I'd put it in the hidden compartment of my suitcase and hadn't thought that much about it until now." I never understood why Thelma was so wary of everything and everyone, but now that I'd hit this snag, I was grateful others were a step ahead of me.

"Let me know if you get in a financial bind during this process," Paul said.

"And me," Chase said. "You've got friends here, you know." His eyes were soft and warm. And the kindness in them caused my insides to respond in the unique way I often did to him. Thus far, it hadn't happened with anyone else.

"I think now might be a good time to get some kind of corroboration from your psychologist friend if you have any proof that she's treated you professionally. The more verification we have to show that you've been blameless in this whole identity fraud from the beginning, the sooner the mess will be cleared up," Paul said.

I checked the time on my phone. "I'll give my friend Jenny a call at the end of her workday." I knew if I called, she would interrupt her schedule to pull up my records but that wasn't fair to her or her patients.

"Have you had a recent psychological evaluation by a licensed therapist to prove that you've only just begun getting some of your memories back?" Paul asked.

"No. Jenny and I don't really do that. We talk but we're best friends, so she isn't my therapist."

He shook his head. "It might be better to get someone who you don't consider your best friend to do an unbiased report, and something current."

"That means bringing someone new into this mess who doesn't know anything about me or my past," I said. And the very idea of starting from scratch with a therapist made me queasy. Baring my soul to a stranger wasn't appealing at all.

"Maybe not," Chase interjected. "We have a local therapist, Bree Hawthorne, who's recently come to us from Alabama, so she couldn't have known you from before. She is capable, and people seem to like her. She is kind and smart. I mean, she doesn't know everything about what's happened, but she's definitely heard about it."

"If she's here in town and she's got the credentials, I say let's give her a call and set something up. It would be complicated to arrange for a therapist from Atlanta," Paul said.

"Okay. I'm agreeable to meeting with Bree if she is qualified to do the kind of evaluation needed. Do you think putting her in touch with Jenny would be helpful?" I asked.

"I'm guessing Bree will need to approach this with complete impartiality, and without any backstory from your friend initially. I'm sure she will get in touch with Jenny when she's ready."

"I'll give Bree a call and ask if she can meet with you," Chase said.

We were all still sitting around Momma's dining room table. She'd long since gone into the kitchen and was banging dishes, ignoring what was happening out here. I didn't blame her; I found myself wishing for an escape too. The pleasant days of waxing her floors and making home improvements seemed as if they'd been months ago instead of last week.

Right now, I wanted to give my dog a bath and then sit on the porch swing with a glass of sweet tea and watch the sun set. How had things gotten this much more complicated in such a short time?

Chapter Eighteen

S OMEONE KNOCKED AT the front door. All I could think was, *now what?* It seemed like every time somebody came out here to the house it was bad news or more bad news. "I'll get it," I called out to Momma who was watering the two red geraniums I'd purchased on the back porch.

A woman stood outside the screen door. She was taller than me, and blonde, and shaded by the porch. I squinted to get a look at her features.

"Sadie?" the woman questioned softly, voice husky. "Is it really you?"

The voice was familiar, but I'd struggled to remember so many voices and people since I'd been home. I smiled in that blank idiotic way I did when I struggled to place someone. Until my eyes adjusted to the shade and I really *saw* her.

Then she grinned at me like she had when we were kids, and I fumbled with the latch on the door because I couldn't open it fast enough. "Julie? Oh, my God, Julie. You're here."

I'm not sure exactly what happened next except we became a hugging, crying mess. I touched her hair, lighter than I'd remembered. *"How are you here?"*

My question to Julie was an echo of Chase's to me when he saw me in his office that first day back.

"How are *you* here? I've spent my adult life believing my sister was dead—wondering every day what terrible thing happened to you that night." Tears were streaming down her cheeks along with her mascara.

"As soon as I got back and saw Momma, a picture of you flashed through my mind. They didn't know what happened to you, where you'd gone. Since I've been back, we've been searching but the records are sealed," I said. Chase had put out feelers for me through some of his contacts. "Momma—she's going to be so happy to see you—"

Julie grabbed my arm then. "No. I'm here for you, not her." But I could see the pain in her expression.

"But Julie… She's been so worried about you, and she's missed you," I said. But then I knew. I'd felt the same.

"She gave me up willingly without even saying goodbye, Sadie." Julie's voice was angry.

I took a step back. There was a lot here that I couldn't fix. "She's on the back porch—" I pointed. "Can you at least say hello?" I wasn't sure what to do. I didn't want to force Julie onto Momma if she wasn't ready.

Julie's tortured expression told me she was torn. "I have a lot of family now, no thanks to her."

The conflict still ate at me often with this whole mess. I didn't need Julie's homecoming with Momma to be perfect. How could it be after what she'd gone through? "I'm sorry. You're right. I've struggled with a lot of the memories of what went on when we were kids. It's not fair to ask you to act or feel a certain way. But I do hope you know how much she's prayed for this day—to see you again."

"You can't imagine what it was like when they took me

away, Sadie. It destroyed me." Julie obviously couldn't explain this in thirty seconds to me, so I nodded and grabbed her in a hug. "I've missed you every day and didn't even know it. Thank you for coming."

"I wasn't sure if you would even remember me. I'm so thankful you do," Julie said.

"Me too. I can't always be sure who or what I'll remember."

Julie took a step back and looked around her. Her expression became pained.

"Are you okay?" I asked.

"I-it's just. I didn't know how I would react if I came back." Tears dropped from her lashes. "The house—it's so much the same, and I've missed it since the day they took me away."

My tears mirrored hers. "I know you're hurt, but please give this a chance. Hank's dying, Julie."

Her distressed expression showed she hadn't expected that news. "I don't know how to respond to that."

I nodded. "He's at the nursing home in hospice care."

Then Momma called, "Sadie, who's at the door?"

Julie tensed and inhaled sharply.

"She loves you, Julie. I'm not defending what happened, but she did what she believed was best for you at the time, and she's regretted it every day since."

Julie's gaze was fierce, but she nodded. "I can't promise how it will go, but I'll see her."

"Let me go in and prepare her a little. You can get to know my Daisy Mae." I pointed to the tail-wagging pup beside us, currently sniffing the situation.

I SUCKED IN a breath, all the emotions whirling in my heart, and shut the door, leaving Julie on the porch. I turned and called, "Momma, can you come here for a minute?"

Momma wiped her hands on her apron as she entered the room. Chase, on alert, stood and moved from the dining room table. He asked, "Is everything okay?"

I barely spared him a glance as I grabbed Momma by the arm and said, "You might want to sit down for a second."

"Is it Hank? Is he dead?" I couldn't tell if she would've been upset or not if that really were the news I had to break.

"It's not Hank, Momma. It's...Julie. She's home." I smiled then, believing I'd given her the best news possible.

Hope and joy filled her expression, and then almost instantly, it changed to sadness. "She's finally come home, has she? After all this time? I guess she saw you were here."

Oh dear. This hadn't gone nearly as I'd believed. "Yes. She's back."

"She's outside?" Momma asked.

"Yes, she's on the porch." Now my voice sounded falsely excited.

"Well, you might as well let your sister in. It's hot out there."

Thoroughly confused, I opened the front door. Julie indeed did look hot. Her cheeks were red and there was perspiration at the sides of her temples and across the bridge of her nose. "Sorry to keep you out here in the heat." I smiled.

"No worries. Am I going in?" she asked, her tone was

wry, but her expression appeared anxious.

"Of course." We entered the air-conditioned house where Momma was waiting.

"I thought I'd never see you again." Their embrace seemed intense but awkward. There was so much between them. Julie was now an adult instead of a young child.

"Hi, Momma," Julie said, her voice shaking with emotion.

Chase had stood to the side and kept quiet during this entire exchange. Bless him for realizing that now was a good time for a distraction from the awkward drama.

"It's nice to see you again, Julie. I'm happy that you're well," Chase said.

Julie turned as if she'd just noticed his presence, which likely was the case. "Hi. Chase, right? I remember you from when we were kids. And I saw you on TV during the press conference. Thanks for helping Sadie."

"Of course. Her return has caused quite a stir," he said.

"I can imagine it has."

"And yours will too, so be prepared," I said. "Everyone will be dying to know every detail since you left. I hope you can stay awhile so we can catch up."

"Yes, I hope you can stay at least for the night," Chase said. Momma was quiet, which wasn't surprising given the situation. "I'm going to head out now. I know Becky will be thrilled to know you're back safe and sound, Julie. Don't worry, we'll keep it quiet so y'all can take some time and get reacquainted."

"Please give your mother my best," Julie said.

I followed Chase to the door and stepped outside onto

the porch, letting the screen slap shut behind me, leaving Julie sitting on the couch in the family room with Momma.

"Are you all right?" he asked. "I know how happy you must be that Julie's come back."

"It's been the craziest day, but having her here is going to help us; I know it will. At least it will eventually. She and Momma have some really complicated stuff to work out. I have a feeling this isn't going to happen overnight."

Chase's expression lost its humor then. "There's not always a happy ending just because we think there should be one. Be patient and remember that your relationships with family members aren't going to be the same as theirs with each other. You need to do you and let them work on them."

"Sounds like you've had personal experiences with not-so-happy endings."

"Let's just say things don't always go how we want or how we expect. And with those mysterious words, I'll leave you with this mess."

"Gee, thanks," I joked.

He gave a little mock salute and a quick pat to Daisy Mae.

"See you tomorrow. Hope nothing else blows up before then." It had been quite a day of surprises, some not so good.

"Yeah. No kidding."

I waved as he climbed into his sheriff's vehicle. His easy smile calmed my turbulence. With Chase around, I somehow knew I was safe. He wouldn't allow anyone to hurt me. Maybe that was ridiculous and naïve thinking, but since it had proved true thus far, I would go with it for now.

Not to say bad things weren't happening all around me,

things he couldn't control. But when they did, he continued to be nearby and supportive, which gave me peace of mind.

Daisy Mae sat beside me and reminded me how badly she needed some loving support of her own. The dog couldn't bathe herself, and she wasn't coming inside after communing with the dead—at least not until the dead had been thoroughly exorcised from her entire body.

The smell was enough to knock a buzzard off a wagon full of fresh fertilizer. The thought made me smile. I'd have never come out with that one back in Nebraska. It seemed Sadie was creeping in and taking root.

Before I grabbed a hose and bucket, I wanted to check in on Momma and Julie. Leaving them alone was a roll of the dice, but it had been good manners to see Chase out after his kindness today.

Plus, I was still buzzing inside at the idea that Julie was back. Memories had begun flooding my mind at seeing her again. I'd remembered her the first time I saw Momma, but because we didn't know where she was, it had been painful to think about her too much, so I'd tried hard not to.

I pushed open the screen, only to find Julie sitting on the couch alone, texting someone on her phone.

"Hey there. Everything okay?" I asked.

"Um, yeah. I was texting my husband to let him know that I'm here," she said.

"You're married?" I asked, trying not to sound surprised. Of course she would be. Look at her—she was stunning.

She smiled, despite the strain around her eyes. "Yes. His name is Gray. I have a daughter too. Suzy. She's five and reminds me so much of you." She proudly told me about her family.

I sat beside her and grabbed her hand. "I'm so happy for you and I can't wait to meet them." I meant it too. "When they told me you were taken away, I felt so guilty that I left you behind."

Julie dashed away a tear with her fingertips. "I thought my life had ended. I curled up in a ball after I'd screamed and begged them to take me back home. Then, I didn't speak for weeks."

The silence was crushing between us. Because my sister's pain had been the consequence of my running away. "I'm sorry."

"No. You had to go. I remember how violent Daddy was with you, and I remember how awful that night was," Julie said sadly.

"I don't remember much about what led up to it, but I remember Hank attacking me. I know he tried to kill me. I stabbed him with the screwdriver that he'd attacked me with and thought I'd killed him for sure because of all the blood. So, I ran. It's bits and pieces from there. I hit my head."

Julie put her arms around me. "You did what you had to. I was a mess, but I was safe. I was always safe. I never had to worry about the same things as you."

Momma stifled a sob. We hadn't realized she'd been standing there. "I know you don't understand why I let you go, but after the night in the barn, Hank really lost it. He made threats against you to hurt me when I threatened to leave or take out a restraining order." She directed her words to Julie.

I felt Julie stiffen. "He wouldn't have hurt me."

"He changed after Sadie stabbed him that night in the barn. He lost a lot of blood but refused to let me take him to the hospital. He was weak but so angry. And when they took you a couple of weeks later, he swore on his mother's grave that he'd have his revenge."

"How could you not have protected Sadie from that kind of abuse?" Julie demanded, her tone scathing.

Even though I had a sudden urge to defend Momma, I stayed silent, waiting to hear her answer. I'd wondered the same thing over and over. I now remembered flashes from my childhood of standing in front of Momma as *her* protector. Honestly, it did chafe still that she'd not been the adult and done what was necessary at the time when I was threatened.

"I can't defend myself. I wasn't a good mother to either of you—I admit that. But no matter how I tried to be strong, I never seemed to manage standing up to his rage. I wish I had a better answer." Her posture was defeated. Gone was the woman who'd finally found a sliver of confidence in the last few weeks and had begun to stand a little straighter. I couldn't let her slip backward.

Julie closed her eyes and took a breath, as if she were trying to regain her composure. "I'm sorry. I shouldn't have said that. But I've wondered all these years. I have a daughter, and if anyone threatened her in any way, I'd do whatever was necessary to make it stop and make certain they paid a high price. I know you were a victim of violence, and I was there to see it firsthand, but the child I was is still struggling to understand."

"You have a daughter?" Momma's eyes widened as she

latched on to the idea of a granddaughter instead of what Julie had just said to her.

"Yes. Suzy. She's five."

"Could you show us a picture?"

Julie's expression showed that she was annoyed at Momma for not addressing the point. But she pulled her phone out of her pocket and scrolled until she found the photo she was looking for. Turning the screen toward us, she said, "This was at her birthday party." The photo showed a little dark-haired beauty with big blue eyes dressed in pink with pink balloons and a pink cake with the number five atop it.

"Why, she looks so much like Sadie as a child. Such a beauty." Momma's eyes glazed with tears.

"Yes, I think so too. Her daddy has dark hair and blue eyes." Since Julie and I didn't share a father, that made sense. Hank's hair was always a dirty blond and he had brown eyes.

"Oh, I can't wait to meet her," Momma said.

"You will, eventually. But we've got some things to work out before that happens." Julie had always been a quiet, sweet child, but I now remembered how stubborn she could be.

I could see both sides of this. Because I felt the same way. "Momma, I know getting Hank out of the house when I got back was a huge step. After the progress you've made the past several weeks, the last thing I want is to push you back down. We were all victims of Hank's abuse in one way or another. I know we can agree on that."

"I've been in and out of therapy for years. It's the only thing that got me through those terrible times after—after I left home. Maybe you could see a therapist," Julie suggested.

"I don't know about all that," Momma said, her tone doubtful. "What could they tell me that I don't already know about my own life?"

"Nothing can change our past. But maybe some counseling would help with making peace for you." Julie was still hurt and angry, and it was likely going to take a lot more therapy for her to resolve years of wondering why her mother gave her up.

"Maybe I'll try therapy if you girls think it will help us." Momma turned to Julie. "Signing that paper to give you up was the hardest thing I ever did. But I did it because I thought you would be better off away from this house and the things that went on here. And I couldn't imagine you being here without Sadie. Y'all were so close."

"I don't think you have any idea what that was like for me. This was my home, and you were my family. You gave me away. *This*—" Julie waved her hand around the room at the unseen drama that hung in the air "—was all I knew."

Momma frowned. "I thought it would only be for a few years, and then you would come back once you were old enough. And we could start over. There wasn't any way of finding you until then, and I didn't think you would stay away forever." Momma's voice broke on a sob.

I intervened before Julie had a chance to answer. "Well, she's back now. And we're going to go slow," I said, hoping it wasn't too late for our family. But what did I expect? For things to fall into place once we were thrown back together after thirteen years? Once I'd gotten my memory back?

Chapter Nineteen

C HASE DIALED HIS mother's number as soon as he got on the highway from leaving Mary Frances's house. He was treating her to a meal at Jeb's Diner because it was nearly dinnertime and Becky had been out in her garden all afternoon.

Jeb's was a town institution, as were the two near-ancient waiters, Myrtis and Maevis, who were identical twins. At eighty-two, they were still hard to tell apart, except Myrtis had several more teeth, and never hesitated to point out that fact in front of her sister, who was also her roommate. Neither had ever married that anyone knew about.

Jeb's was known far and wide for their world-famous fried banana and peanut butter sandwich, and though it was printed on the menu, Chase couldn't say he'd actually seen anyone but tourists order one.

Maevis squeaked up in her well-worn orthopedic shoes. "What'll it be, Sheriff? The usual?"

"I'll take a sweet tea for now. I'm waiting on Momma. She oughta be here soon."

"Sure thing, baby." Maevis flashed him a two-tooth smile and scooted off toward the pickup/drop-off window where their much younger brother Max worked the kitchen. At seventy-three, Max still had most of his teeth but none of his hair, and very little of his hearing left.

The place was bustling with the senior crowd. They normally arrived by five to take advantage of the early-bird special before portions ran out. Chase nodded to several of the old-timers as he'd come in. Most were supportive to his post as sheriff, and he'd done his best to earn their trust.

His job often involved the occasional wild goose chase. Truly, it mostly had him dealing with folks' animals. Cats, livestock, and dogs. Either somebody's varmint got hold of another's or was on somebody's property tearing up or digging something up. Cows got out of their fences and trampled vegetable gardens and blocked traffic. It was endless.

"Hey there, Sheriff. Got pot roast on the menu today. Your favorite." Chase noticed the worn nametag identified Myrtis. The two women became mortally offended if he ever mixed them up.

"Thanks, Myrtis. Sounds fantastic. Give me a couple minutes. Momma's coming."

"*I'm* waiting on the sheriff in case you missed it. Can't you see he already has his tea?" Maevis's approach was pure stealth. "You know this is my table, *heifer*." She hissed the last word.

"Well, hello, girls. Are y'all fussing over my boy, here?" His momma's timing couldn't have been more perfect.

Chase breathed a sigh of relief at his mother's arrival. The idea of breaking up a catfight between the ancient siblings made him cringe. "Hey there, Momma. Glad you made it. Myrtis here was telling me about the pot roast, and

Maevis brought me some sweet tea."

Both women beamed.

"Well, ladies, let me slide in here across from my son and see what's what. I'm starving too. That iced tea looks downright refreshing. Maevis, might I have a glass?"

"Of course. I was telling my sister, here, that it's my table. I would be happy to take your order when you're ready." Maevis shot her sibling a hard stink eye.

"Oh look, Myrtis, looks like you might be needed by Mr. James. He's waving at you. Quite a hottie, that Jesse James."

Sure enough, the elderly widower, Jesse James—one of the few single and eligible men of age in the community—was working hard to get noticed across the diner. "I'll bet he prefers his women with teeth." Myrtis shot her zinger and moved away faster than any woman her age that Chase had ever seen.

"That woman is a menace. I wish she would find a man. Then, she might leave me in peace, so I can watch whatever I want on Netflix," Maevis muttered.

"I'll have the post roast special, please," Chase said.

"Me too. Can't beat that with a stick," Mom chimed in.

"Two pot roast specials and a sweet tea for Becky; got it." Maevis shuffled off, still grumbling about her unrepentant sister.

"Wow, never a dull moment around here, is there?" Mom asked.

"Nice distraction to Mr. James over there. How did you know Myrtis was sweet on him?"

"I think the whole town knows, except you." She laughed then. "It's okay, honey. You're busy dealing with everybody's obvious problems, so it's okay if you miss the subtleties of elderly crushes."

He actually could feel the blush rising in his cheeks. "I'm a bit clueless when it comes to that sort of thing."

"Yes, you are. Intentionally sometimes, I believe. It's about time you moved on, don't you think?" She nailed him with a wise-but-sympathetic stare, no longer referring to the elderly. She wanted him to get a love life of his own again.

His single status caused some frustration for his mother. She'd been there to pick up the pieces after his marriage collapsed. But she'd also been there during the collapse. Trying to point out ways to prevent said collapse. Now that his love life was a cold, dead, pile of rubble, and Chase was still single, she encouraged him to try again.

"I'm content now, Mom. If I meet someone, it will happen naturally. I don't want to try and force something."

She rolled her eyes. This wasn't a new conversation. "She's not gonna come gift-wrapped with a bow. This is a small town, son. Not much is going to change unless you make it change."

Desperate to *change* the subject, he remembered why he'd invited her here. "I have some news you'll be interested to hear, but for now, they don't want it getting out."

"Don't make me beg."

He leaned in so no one else would hear. "Julie Brubaker showed up at the Brubaker farm today completely unexpected." His mother was a vault. Information went in and never saw the light of day unless she was given permission to share.

"You're shitting me, son." She whooped a laugh and

slapped her leg in glee.

"Shhh, Mom. I told them we would keep it quiet so they had time to get reacquainted."

"Wow. That's some news. You should have led with that, and we wouldn't have had to discuss your love life," she said quietly and looked around. "How's Julie? She okay?"

"Seems to be. Pretty sure she and Mary Frances are going to have some issues to work out." That was all he felt comfortable sharing.

"Sorry to hear it. What a terrible thing for them both," she said and took a sip of her tea. "Lots of water under that bridge, I'll bet. I can't imagine losing my child."

He nodded. He didn't want to gossip about the particulars, even with his mother. The family would share what they chose when they wanted to do so. He just happened to be there to witness a private moment.

Chase told her about Sadie's account being frozen by the IRS.

"Does she need money?"

"Not at the moment," he said. "Says she's got a stash."

"You'll let me know if she gets in a bind?"

He nodded. Becky had a stash too.

"Two blue-plate specials." Maevis returned with their meals. Chase wondered again at her stealth, especially with those squeaky shoes.

"Thanks, Maevis. Looks amazing as always," Becky said.

"Y'all let us know if you need anything else." The woman grinned and sashayed away.

Just then, Jasper Weston, Jason's dad, entered the diner. The atmosphere in the room changed immediately. The locals considered the Weston family their own brand of royalty. Mr. Weston's eyes went to Momma's, and they shared a meaningful look, which made Chase's blood run cold.

"Mom, you and Mr. Weston aren't—"

"Leave it, son. It doesn't concern you. Jasper and I have history, but that's all I'm saying about it." She nearly whispered the last words as they were in the middle of the diner. And while most of the crowd this time of the day was hearing-impaired, having forgotten their hearing aids at home, there were always those who found a way to learn new information, or to confirm what they suspected and use it as fodder.

Jasper nodded to them both as he passed them on his way to his booth.

Add to the fact that Jason Weston was married to Chase's ex-wife, their parents had *history*. Maybe Jason knew more about it than Chase, and he didn't like it either.

"Don't say I didn't warn you about him."

She placed a hand over his. "Honey, Annie seems to be happy with Jason, as strange as it seems. You need to let that go."

Chase had let it go, mostly. "I want her to be happy, Mom. I pushed Annie away. That was on me. It's just hard to believe she fell for Jason of all people." He tried to avoid the cringe that threatened every time he heard about or encountered Jason.

"If you ask me, Annie didn't stick by you like she should have." She held up her hands as if to ward off an attack. "I know, I know. Nobody's supposed to criticize Saint Annie.

But, son, you went through a lot, and she was your wife. She gave up on you. Now here you are, doing fine with no wife to show for it. Don't you think you might have done better and gotten through it quicker if she'd been there for you?"

He stared at his mother. She'd never said this before, or anything like it. Her words were honest, and he didn't take offense, but they did impact him to his core.

"I hadn't thought about it like that." Well, maybe he had a few times, but Annie convinced him that his inability to kick his sadness and depression down the road quickly enough had chased her away.

"Maybe if you'd stop mooning over what you did wrong and realize you've got more than half your life to live and start looking ahead, things will seem brighter."

He raised his hand to flag down Maevis for the check as she passed their booth.

"I hope it's not weird to say that my mom's my best friend." He laughed.

"Oh, it's weird all right, but we'll keep it between the two of us. We make a great team, don't we?"

"That we do."

As Chase drove to his house, the one he'd bought a year after Annie suggested he move out, he realized how accurate his mom had been in her statements regarding his former wife. She'd been impatient with him to rebound from his father's illness and death. And he'd struggled. Had she believed he'd never recover? People eventually recovered from the passing of parents, so why had she thought he wouldn't? Why had she given up on him? It hadn't been *that* much time, all told. He'd finally even gotten on an antidepressant. But by then, she was already one foot out the door.

As many years as they'd spent together, he simply couldn't believe she'd decided to end their marriage so easily. They'd wanted children, but when his dad got sick, they'd put a family on the back burner. Then, Chase had become depressed. He'd never consider that maybe it wasn't him. Maybe it was both of them, or maybe it *was* her. She and Jason hadn't had children yet and Chase wondered if they would.

A pair of clear blue eyes appeared in his mind, wiping away the face of his ex. Sadie was popping into his head more and more lately. He couldn't deny that the more time he spent with her, the more he liked her. She was refreshing and honest and had no guile about her. Of course, she'd lived a life that lacked much social interaction for many years, which likely accounted for some of it. But he had to admit, as much as she'd been through, she'd come out surprisingly normal, for lack of a better word. At least from the outside.

Sure, she dimmed a little when she remembered Hank's physical and emotional abuse, but she was able to discuss it and how it made her feel, and she'd *faced* him with such bravery. So many who'd survived similar experiences hadn't done nearly so well. He was proud of her. And something else. He had to admit that when she smiled at him, it wasn't brotherly or fatherly. He was attracted to Sadie Brubaker. What in the world was he supposed to do with that?

Nothing. As long as she needs my protection as sheriff, there isn't a damn thing I can do about it. Or was there?

Either way, something had lifted from his soul. A weight

of burden he'd been hefting around these past years. What a revelation to have over pot roast with one's mother at the diner on a Tuesday evening.

"How would you feel about my going to the nursing home to see Hank?" Julie appeared a little nervous asking the question. We were sitting on the porch swing. It was shaded now that the sun wasn't so high in the sky. She appeared nervous.

I wasn't quite sure how to answer her, but I figured that she got to decide how she dealt with Hank. "Julie, don't not see Hank because of me. I know you hated how he treated me. But he's your father and he's dying. You have to make your peace."

Julie frowned. "I don't know how to feel about Hank, honestly. I remember him as someone who was moody and unpredictable on a good day. Kind and mean, to me, anyway. But I guess I should see him."

"This situation is so messed up; we've got to do what drives out the demons." I shrugged.

Momma stepped outside then and muttered, "And Lord knows we've got enough demons to scare the devil himself. I can take you over to the nursing home now if you want."

Julie nodded. "Okay. I guess I'd like to get it over with."

"I'll stay here and start dinner while the two of you do that," I said. "I'm waiting to hear back from my attorney about my frozen bank accounts and meeting with the FBI. Fun stuff happening around here."

"Sounds like things are complicated for you right now." Julie frowned.

"Ha, complicated doesn't begin to cover it," Momma said. "Right now, we hope she doesn't get arrested for identity theft and fraud."

Julie hadn't any idea what she'd walked into. "Oh my. I guess my coming back kind of added to the stress around here. My timing stinks pretty badly, doesn't it?" she asked.

"Are you kidding? Your coming home has been a happy distraction from my own messy life." It was true. Having Julie here with us had helped push thoughts of my situation to the back of my brain.

"Do you need to freshen up before we head to Moonshine Manor?" Mom asked Julie.

Julie shook her head. "I'll grab my purse and keys from inside. I'll drive if you want."

"Don't want to ride in Hank's old beater, eh? I don't blame you." Momma's embarrassment showed by her words and the edge in her voice.

"Uh, no, it's not that—"

"Don't worry about it. It's a piece of shit, all right. As soon as I can, I'm gonna trade it in and buy myself one of those little crossovers."

Julie didn't say anything to that. What was there to say? We'd ridden shotgun in that old red truck so many times as kids…and we'd both been embarrassed by it. Some of the kids in town made no secret of their contempt of the Brubaker family's meager circumstances. We'd been poor.

There were others who weren't much better off, but our family was notorious in that Hank was our father. And Hank took top billing over anybody else's dire straits.

Perhaps our social pariah status in town had played a part in Julie's less-than-eager attitude about returning once she was old enough. It was a lot to overcome.

Chapter Twenty

ONCE THEY'D GONE, I examined the options in the refrigerator and made the decision to head into town to the grocery to grab something to fix for dinner. Plus, I was antsy and wanted to get out of the house, so I pulled some cash from inside the secret lining pocket of my suitcase before I left home, considering my newly frozen credit cards and bank accounts.

Frustration and anger surged through me at someone—anyone—having control of my life like that again. I'd spent my entire twenty-nine years under someone else's control, whether I'd known it or not, and whether I'd fought against it or not.

First, Hank's violence, which even as a young child, I'd railed and struggled against. Then, my loss of memory that put me under Mom's—Thelma's—loving protection but also her control, with no say whether I should come back here and rescue my family from the hell they were living. Without a memory, I'd been as weak and powerless as a newborn. Certainly, over time, Thelma had fostered some independence in me, but she'd definitely called the shots in the name of protecting me.

Since I'd come here, I'd regained some power, and definitely independence. I had most of my memories, I'd faced my greatest fear in Hank, and I knew who I was. I had my business and my own money. I was capable for the first time of making decisions, although limited, until I figured out the identity stuff. But now, the government had me pinned like a butterfly in a case until they decided what to do with me.

This could turn out quite terrible if things went awry. So, here I was, stuffing cash into my purse so I could buy groceries and pay for the purchases at the hardware store I still owed Betsy, the owner, for—since the awful day the press descended on Moonshine.

As I drove toward town, I made a call to Jenny, who answered on the first ring. "Hi there, stranger. How's it going?" she asked.

"I've certainly had better days." I quickly told her about the feds and their demands for proof of my amnesia from early on. I asked about her notes from when we'd met, and she'd tried to do some hypnotherapy with me.

"I'm not sure how helpful they would be, but I still have them in my old stuff."

"I appreciate anything you could tell them to corroborate my story since you were familiar with my situation back then."

"I'll give the notes a once-over tonight to make sure there's nothing that would be unhelpful."

"How could it not help?" I asked but wasn't certain I wanted to know.

"It *should* help to show that you lost your memory way back and that I tried to help you, but the notes were my observations about your condition, and were meant to only be seen by me. They weren't records. The writing is casual and personal."

"Was I part of your case study or something?" I asked, since so much time had passed, and I didn't remember the exact circumstances of our therapy sessions. Jenny had been fascinated by my history as we'd gotten to know one another during college and hoped she could help me while she was finishing up her clinical work.

"Yes and no. I wrote my notes and put you in my clinical rotation for a few sessions to see if we could jar loose some of your suppressed memories. But since you showed no change or progress, I chose not to use your case in my final group of clinical patient reports. So, you never showed up as a true case study at the end of my clinicals even though you were one of the patients of record I treated during that period."

"Oh, kind of like some of the projects I attempted while working on my final design portfolio but then scrapped because they didn't turn out like I'd hoped," I said.

"Well, I guess." Jenny laughed just a little. "But I didn't scrap you, for the record. I included the patients that showed a response to treatment mostly, either positive or negative, as we were directed. You simply had no change during that time."

"Well, I always appreciated that you tried," I said. "And since we have some record of the fact that you treated me for amnesia, hopefully it will be helpful."

"Yes, I hope so. I'll have a look at the notes and get back to you ASAP."

"Thanks, Jenny."

As I hung up, the phone buzzed in my hand. "Hello?"

"Hi, Sadie. Everything okay?" Chase asked.

A tiny thrill shot through me at the sound of his deep voice. I was so lame. "Um, yes. I just got off the phone with Jenny about her therapy notes."

"Oh, okay. Are you driving?" he asked.

"I'm just getting into town. I wanted to pay Betsy for the stuff I got the other day when the press showed up."

"I took care of it," he said. "You're all square with Betsy."

I was quiet a minute, and not sure how to respond. "What do you mean you took care of it?"

"I stopped by the hardware store a couple days later and paid the bill. I meant to let you know, but things have been crazy since then, and I forgot to say something about it."

I pulled into the grocery store parking lot outside of town and put my Jeep in park. "Did I ask you to pay my bill?" I spoke a little sharply, which was rare for me as either Sadie or Randi.

"No. I just thought it might help since I was already there. You've had a lot going on."

"I don't need you to rescue me, Sheriff. I appreciate everything you've done, but it's time for me to handle my own problems now. So, don't do me those kinds of favors unless you check with me first."

He was silent for a second, then he said, "Listen, Sadie, I'm sorry if I overstepped. I apologize. The last thing I wanted to do was upset you."

My God, I was acting like a bitchy woman. I'd not yelled at anyone since I'd been a teen, and *he'd* beaten me.

"Chase—" My voice cracked. *Oh, my God, was I going to cry?* I drew a shuddering breath before I tried that again. "I-

I'm so sorry. That was kind of you. I know you weren't trying to do anything but be a friend to me."

"Is that you sitting in the store parking lot?" he asked.

I looked up and saw him sitting across the row in his sheriff's vehicle. "Yep, it's me." I waved a small acknowledgment but wanted to shrink down into a puddle on the seat.

"You want some company?" he asked in a way that made me want to burst into the tears I worked hard to stifle.

"Um, I'm headed inside to grab something to cook for dinner while Momma and Julie visit Hank." The sun was setting, and the sky was on fire in the late summer sky.

I ended our call then cut my engine and climbed down.

Chase met me at the front of the Jeep.

"Friends?" He put his hand out.

I took it and nodded. He held my hand in an awkward, non-handshake kind of way.

"I'm sorry for behaving like that," I said, my lower lip wobbling like a child fighting tears.

Before I realized what was happening, he pulled me into his warm, strong arms. A hug. He was hugging me. My legs threatened to give way.

"You've had quite a day, haven't you?"

I nodded, feeling a single tear leak out of my eye.

I was *not* going to cry.

Another tear. And then another.

And then I hiccupped. An unmistakable sob.

He led me to his vehicle. Where I cried shamelessly in his arms for at least fifteen minutes.

It was horrible. It was heaven. I was feeling new things with my body so close to his. He was warm, and he smelled like man soap. And I'd never gotten this close to any of that. Or experienced any of *this*. Was it desire?

"I-I'm s-so s-sorry." But I wasn't.

"Are you kidding? After everything you've been through since you came back to Moonshine, the only time I've seen you shed a tear was when you saw your momma for the first time."

"For years, I was kind of...emotionally stunted. I didn't cry much while I was with Thelma. Until she died, and then my emotions sort of kicked into overdrive. But once I arrived here, I've had to work to keep myself in check. I didn't know what the day would bring or who I would meet."

"Sounds like you've gone a long time without people around that you can trust."

I guessed that was true in some ways. "I like it here. Most people are pretty nice. You've been especially nice." I think I was flirting. Badly, I was sure.

"So, how about I grab some stuff and cook you ladies dinner?" he offered.

"You don't have to do that," I protested.

"I insist. Plus, I'm not quite ready to go home to my empty house yet. It will be nice to spend some time with you." *Ooohh. He* was flirting with *me.*

I stupidly wanted to giggle. Wanted by the FBI for treachery and fraud, but I was straight-up giddy because a man was flirting with me. I was a hot mess in every direction. "Okay. Let me wipe my eyes so I don't look like I've come from a funeral."

He reached in the back seat and grabbed a box of tissues.

"Thanks."

We entered the grocery store together a few minutes later, with no one the wiser to our hugs out in the car. Well, someone was always the wiser in a town this size, but mostly no one.

My face was hot, and I wondered if Chase experienced any similar...discomfort.

I couldn't wait to experience it again. Hopefully, without crying next time. As usual, Chase said hello and responded to the many nods and single-worded "Sheriff" or "Evenin', Sheriff." Several included me in their greeting. I guess it wasn't unusual for folks to see us together in public because from the moment I got here, Chase had stuck pretty close, of course, and so had Becky. I hated to think how I might have been treated otherwise.

Remembering some of my childhood treatment at the hands of Moonshine residents wasn't pleasant, although many had offered heartfelt apologies for their behavior at our expense. I chose to forgive them. It might have been easy to hold a grudge, but I was looking for a new start. Grudges seemed to hold people back.

"What do you think about tacos?" Chase asked.

"I've never met a taco I didn't like."

"Taco Tuesday it is," he said, and proceeded to the lettuce, tomatoes, shells, sauce, and ground beef like an old pro.

"Not your first fiesta, eh?" I asked.

"Not hardly. In fact, I'm going to make homemade guac that will knock your socks off."

"Who doesn't like some good guac?" I asked, playing along.

We were laughing, and gently squeezing avocados when

it happened.

"Well, well, Annie, looks like you've finally been replaced in the sheriff's heart." The words were uttered with sarcasm, and I nearly dropped my avocado. The mayor and a blonde woman had approached while we'd been goofing off.

"Hi, Chase," she said softly, a look of embarrassment and possibly curiosity in her gaze.

"Hello, Annie," he said, as one does when encountering an ex-wife with her husband while shopping with another woman in the grocery store. Awkward. "This is Sadie."

"You're the famous Sadie Brubaker everyone's been talking about. Welcome home." She grinned at me and offered her hand. "Chase spent years wondering where you'd gone and trying to find you."

I shook it. "Hi. Nice to meet you, Annie."

"Hope all is well over at the farm," Jason said, but somehow his tone didn't carry off his good tidings. "Be sure and tell your momma I said hello."

I nodded. "Thanks, I will."

"Y'all have a good night now." Jason gave Chase a kind of quasi-military salute.

"Nice to meet you, Sadie." Annie waved as Jason all but dragged her away alongside their grocery cart.

"You too," I whispered, but I'm pretty sure she didn't hear me.

Chase was quiet for a minute as we picked out another couple of avocados.

"She seems nice," I said.

"She was—is."

"I'm sorry. We can do this another time if you want," I

said. The fun of the evening had suddenly evaporated.

"Are you kidding? Taco Tuesday is a go." He shook off the dark cloud the Westons had managed to leave behind them.

We picked up the last few items for dinner and the milk Momma'd asked me to get, and then checked out. Fortunately, we did so without running into Jason and Annie again.

Chase loaded the bags in the back of his car and I returned the cart. "I'll see you there," he said with a smile.

That smile brought me back to our earlier encounter.

"See you in a bit." I waved and turned toward my Jeep while I dialed Momma's number to check in with her and Julie.

As I started the engine, Momma answered the call. "Hey there, Sadie. Sorry we're not back yet. Hank's not doing so well this evening."

"Oh. Sorry. Did he recognize Julie?" I asked, wondering how their reunion went, because I was morbidly curious how he would react to seeing her.

"He knows her. They did some talking, just the two of them. But his breathing isn't good tonight, and they've called in the hospice nurse to see what can be done to make him more comfortable."

"Okay. Let me know if you want me to come over or if you need anything. I'll leave you something out for dinner. I ran into Chase at the grocery store, and he's offered to cook for us."

"That's sweet of him. Tell him we said thanks. It's likely we'll eat when we get home later. Enjoy your dinner."

"Okay. Keep me posted." I'd driven the short way home during our conversation.

I climbed out of the Jeep. Now it would only be Chase and me for dinner. The idea thrilled and terrified me equally, even as I worried for Momma and Julie. "I just spoke with Momma. They're going to be later than expected," I told Chase when he arrived.

He nodded. "How'd it go between Hank and Julie?"

We pulled the bags from his car and carried them inside where Daisy Mae met us with great enthusiasm. "Hi, girl." While I gave her her due, I told him about Hank's condition and what Momma had said about Julie visiting in private with him.

"So, it's just us for dinner. I hope you don't mind."

"Not a bit. It will be nice." Then he said, "Sorry to hear about Hank for Mary Frances's and Julie's sakes, but I know how hard it's been for you to come back here and face him."

"It's been a lot easier knowing he's out of the house and I don't have to deal with him. And Momma's like a different person without him here yelling at her. She's not afraid anymore. I mean, she goes to visit him most days for an hour or so but doesn't spend all day there or give in to his tantrums to buy liquor for him. If he gets nasty, she leaves. She's in control for the first time since she married him I think."

"I know there's a lot going on, and now with Julie coming back, it's got to be even more complicated," he said.

"I hate that Julie's first day back ended like this. I knew she wanted to see Hank and make some kind of peace with him, or with herself about him. I guess it was a good thing at least that she was able to make it here before he died."

"You know what I think?" he asked.

"What?"

"I think it's time for tacos and guacamole."

I laughed out loud. "I think you're right. I can worry more later when I have to."

Chapter Twenty-One

C HASE DIDN'T BOTHER to tell Sadie that he'd eaten an early dinner already with his mother at the diner. Not that it mattered. The blue-plate special was hours ago, and he wouldn't have missed this evening with her for anything.

"Holy cow, I'm stuffed," Sadie groaned. The dining table was crowded with various dishes of sour cream, shredded cheese, tomatoes, ground beef, guacamole, and taco shells. There were refried beans and Spanish rice in addition to the taco fixings.

"Me too. Looks like I overshot the portions again," he said.

"I hope Momma and Julie are hungry when they get here."

Chase tried to take Sadie's mind off her troubles and not discuss anything that might worry or stress her further this evening. He'd also worked hard to keep things light between them. He'd been aware of his growing attraction to Sadie, and obviously Chase wasn't a stranger to sexual desire. But tonight was the first time their bodies had connected for more than just a moment—long enough for him to actually become aroused. The tension between them had been unmistakable. She'd melted into his embrace as if they were a couple of matched puzzle pieces. A perfect fit.

With the chaos surrounding them, Chase understood how foolish it would be to pursue any kind of relationship, sexual or otherwise, with Sadie right now. He had no idea if she planned to stay in Moonshine beyond sorting out the whole mess she had going on. She had a house and a life back in Hickman. Maybe she intended to return to it.

What he did know was that she'd gotten under his skin, and that he liked her. If he let it go beyond that, he might get hurt or hurt her. And after the years of regret and healing it had taken to get over Annie, Chase figured there was no sense jumping back in with both feet unless he was sure the odds were in their favor.

He'd made dinner because Sadie'd had a tough day and he'd wanted to cheer her up. And to apologize for overstepping by paying her bill without asking.

"I think taco Tuesday should be a weekly thing. Maybe with margaritas next time." Sadie appeared happy and relaxed.

"I agree. And you're on for the margaritas," he said.

Neither of them heard Julie and Mary Frances enter the room. "Wow, this looks fantastic. I'm starved," Julie said.

"There's way more food than any of us can finish. Dig in," Chase said.

"Momma, how's Hank?" Sadie asked.

"He's breathing a little better. Julie went in to speak with him and he had a coughing spell, but they managed to get him calmed down just as we left."

Sadie's gaze switched to Julie. "How did it go?"

Julie gave her a tight smile. "Just because he's dying

doesn't make him repentant. He didn't show a bit of remorse for any of it. Somehow he believes himself the victim after everything that's happened." Julie paused. "I wasn't allowed back to my home as a child because of how he'd treated our family. And Sadie, you disappeared because of his abuse."

"He's a narcissist without a conscience, according to what I've read on the subject," Momma interjected.

They all stared at her in surprise.

"I've been doing a little research on the computer when things are slow at work. Narcissists aren't capable of accepting blame for their actions no matter how terrible or obvious that things were their fault." She said this as if reciting from a book.

"Well, that does explain a lot," Chase said. "Sounds like a few other people I've known in my life."

"It's caused by a young child not getting enough emotional or physical attention when they are at a critical point in their development. Or too much attention and being excessively spoiled," Mary Frances supplied, continuing her encyclopedic explanation.

"That goes with what my therapist said," Julie agreed. "We've discussed what might have been Hank's major malfunction over the years."

"The hospice nurse believes he will pass in the next few days," Mary Frances said. She sounded accepting, but not devastated.

"I'm sorry," he said.

"Thank you," she answered.

Julie and Sadie were silent. Likely their thoughts on the matter were best kept to themselves at the moment.

"Thanks for taco Tuesday, Chase," Julie said, scooping guacamole with a chip. "This is delicious."

"Thanks. It's Momma's recipe. Here, let me help y'all clean some of this up since I made such a big mess," he offered.

"Nonsense. We're glad you were here to be with Sadie. She's had a tough few days. We'll have this cleaned up in no time," Mary Frances said.

"It was my pleasure."

Sadie chimed in, "Yes, you've got another busy day tomorrow solving the population of Moonshine's crimes and misdemeanors." She grinned at him and a pang of the same desire he'd experienced earlier hit him straight in the groin.

"Good night, ladies. I'll head home now. Have a nice evening." He waved and turned toward the door, intending to give them some privacy. Hard to believe it was only today that Julie had returned.

"I'll walk you out," Sadie said.

They stepped out onto the porch, along with Daisy Mae, who'd happily chewed through a huge rawhide bone while they'd made dinner and eaten.

The evening was hot and humid compared to the air-conditioned interior, and the stars were bright in the clear mountain sky. It was a beautiful night.

"Thanks for everything today."

Her voice was soft and husky and his attraction to her was strong.

She approached until they were toe-to-toe. "Uh, Sadie—"

She appeared uncertain then, her eyes faltered. "Do you know that I've never kissed a man?"

It hit him then. Her sheltered life with Thelma. This was all new to her. She wasn't flirting, not really. She was attracted to him but didn't know what to do with it.

"Never?" he asked.

He lifted her chin with his finger. The least he could do was talk her through it.

"Sadie, do you want me to kiss you?" he asked her. Doing this right was important.

Her breathing was a slight pant, and her tongue flicked her bottom lip. "I think I want that more than anything right now."

Controlling the urge to crush her in his arms, he very gently lowered his lips to hers and softly kissed her. She leaned in and moaned. *Dear God.* He deepened the kiss enough that they were both breathing hard, and then pulled away.

"Sadie, kissing leads to touching, and touching leads to much more. And we are standing outside your momma's front door."

"Mmm. I like the kissing, and I'm pretty sure I want the touching and more. Something about you makes me want those things. I like you, Chase. Nobody else I've met has made my body feel like this." She did a little wiggle to show what she meant.

Which made his body stand at complete attention. And made him want to teach her about all the things she'd been missing.

"You're making it very hard for me to be a gentleman about this. You're inexperienced, and I don't want to take advantage of your innocence, Sadie."

"So if I ask you to teach me about the things I've never done, would you? Because I trust you and I believe you wouldn't take advantage of me."

He groaned. "How about we take this slow? I don't want to rush into a physical relationship neither of us is emotionally ready for." He honestly didn't want either of them to get hurt.

"I think I'm ready. If I'm not, I'm ready to find out that I'm not ready," she said.

He laughed softly at her eagerness. "Let's start out by going to dinner at a restaurant together. A date is a good first step. Okay?" he suggested. That was the best he could do in his current state.

"Okay. I'm sorry if I've made you uncomfortable. I've never felt this way. I want to see where this goes."

"You are a beautiful, desirable, and sexy woman, Sadie Brubaker. And I want you in my arms more than I can say. I'm not rejecting you. When this happens for us, I want it to be more than physical. Okay?"

She nodded, her face flushing. She opened the screen door, allowing Daisy Mae to precede her, then grinned at him before going inside.

"Dear God, help me." He stood, staring after the amazing woman who'd never had a man's touch. She trusted him and asked him to show her what she'd been missing. He had an idea she was about to show him what *he'd* been missing.

Chapter Twenty-Two

I HAD MY appointment with Bree, the therapist, later today in town. I'd tossed and turned last night, maybe because Bree might be tapping back into the years I'd spent away from home. I didn't look forward to it. I still carried the fear inside that I might find out something even worse than I had so far.

As I stepped out on the porch in my robe and bare feet, a steaming cup of coffee in my hands, I smiled. How I'd missed sitting outside in the early mornings with Thelma in the garden. But I had to say, this time with Momma here in my childhood home had done a lot to calm my hurt for missing Thelma.

Leaving the heavy interior wood door propped open, I allowed the screen to shut as I took a seat on the porch swing.

Momma joined me a few minutes later. We'd gotten in the habit of coming out here in the mornings before the heat and humidity became overwhelming. It was still coolish and the wildlife hadn't yet gone deeper into the woods for shade. Crickets and tree frogs chirped leftover songs from the night, while birds welcomed the day with enthusiasm. It was a golden hour easily missed.

"What's your day looking like?" I asked. Momma sat in the cheerful yellow metal chair we'd freshened up with a good sanding and a can of spray paint. It was a sturdy chair that had been around since my childhood. No amount of rust seemed to be able to take it down.

"I should spend some time at the nursing home with Hank today since they say he's failing," Momma said.

I couldn't tell if she was apologetic or resigned. But she was no longer defensive about her need to put time in while Hank still lived.

"Of course," I said. I wasn't a monster, after all. Whatever her reasons for seeing him through these last days were hers. I'd felt some tinges of regret and a need to let go of my terrible anger toward a sad, old man, despite the fact that he was still raging against us all. Forgiveness might be the thing that would make life more bearable for our family.

"What about you? I saw the light under your door late last night," she said.

"Yes. I'm finishing a couple of projects for clients and starting a new one." Obviously there were some days that required me to work more than others. Clients were still able to pay me in the normal ways, but I couldn't access the money currently. "Today, I've got a meeting with the therapist."

She nodded and looked around the freshly painted porch where we'd hung four Boston ferns across the front. "It's looking good out here. Your daddy would've been so proud of you. He loved this house." I noticed her dreamy expression then. It was one I hadn't seen before.

"Did you buy the house right after you married him?" I

asked. I hadn't given my birth father much thought since I'd been home. I mean, in the scheme of things, he'd never been discussed, since Hank had always been lurking. But her words made me curious.

"Yes, we moved here not long after we married. He wanted the house to go to you someday. Of course, to me if anything ever happened to him, but then to you, so your name is also on the title."

Her words were so unexpected and spoken in such a matter-of-fact tone, I nearly missed what she'd said. I stared for a second before responding. "I had no idea." I wanted to weep for a father who loved me and who intended that I have a home no matter what.

"I never told you because of Hank. He adopted you, but that didn't matter. When you turned eighteen, the house still became half yours. That's why he wouldn't leave later when you went away. He didn't have a claim on anything if we divorced. As long as he stayed, he had a home."

This new information made actual sense as to why Hank was so adamant to stay when he was clearly miserable, and why he might have actually wanted me dead.

But I now wondered about my own dad.

"Do you have a photo of my father?" I asked. Suddenly I wanted desperately to know him, to see him.

She nodded. "I've had to keep them well hidden from Hank all these years, but I do have a few. Give me a few minutes to dig them up."

"I'll get dressed while you're looking."

Momma knocked on my door a half hour later, just as I was slipping on my shoes. "Come in."

"I found a few of them. The pictures of your dad. I know there were more, but I don't know where they went. Could be Hank found them and burned them."

Excitement fluttered in my chest. I smiled and took them from her outstretched hand.

"His name was Randall, but we called him Randy."

I raised my eyebrows in surprise. "How strange that I've been called Randi all these years too."

"I thought so, but I didn't say anything because of everything else that was going on. It certainly is such a coincidence."

I looked down at the photos in my grasp. The one on top was a faded color photo of a man with black hair, holding a baby and smiling, happiness shining in his obviously light eyes. My eyes.

"I have his eyes." I looked up to see tears welled in Momma's eyes.

"You do."

The next one was rather faded. It was of Momma and Daddy on a beach in swimsuits. They were arm in arm, unmistakably in love, and laughing. She was so young.

The third and final photo was at their wedding. They were cutting the cake, her hand atop his, both smiling into the lens.

Something about him was so familiar, but I couldn't decide what it was, other than our possible resemblance. Maybe it was the kinship, as I was drawn toward his infectious grin.

"Thanks, Momma," I whispered. "These are treasures."

"We'll get up in the attic one day soon and see if we can find some more." She smiled at me. "There's more to us than the bad things that have happened, you know."

"I know. Let's try and get the rest of the bad things taken care of so we can work on the good ones, okay?" I said and picked up my purse.

I HAD TO admit to being a little nervous at seeing Chase again. Since the night I'd made a fool of myself on Momma's porch, I'd stayed pretty much out of sight, making a point to stick close to home and focus on working on the house and online with my clients.

My tactics had been, well, embarrassing and ineffective, to say the least. I'd been told on a number of occasions that the Sadie Brubaker they'd known had been unafraid of danger and consequences. I remember that to some degree. But I also remember how it felt to push forward toward something I wanted or to defend myself or my family under humiliating circumstances. Much of it had been bravado, and my inability to back down from a fight.

I'd been foolish to stand up to an adult who was bigger and stronger than I was. Maybe I could have saved myself a lot of pain, and ultimately not ended up needing to leave home had I been more agreeable. More like Momma and Julie.

But the past was over. And so much had happened since then. Now I had new battles to fight. These battles wouldn't end in my death, but they were terribly important to my future, and to Momma's security and happiness.

The appointment with Bree was at ten. Her office was

just off the town square, which happened to be near Chase's office. His vehicle was already there, sitting in front of the bright gold star painted on the plate-glass window.

I couldn't think of anyone who was better suited for being sheriff. He was honest and of the best character. He could have taken advantage of my innocence, but he didn't, and I was thankful for it. Well, somewhat thankful. My physical response to him had been overwhelming. Of course I knew what sex was, but I'd never had any close calls with it as I'd grown into adulthood.

Chase had mentioned our going on a date, but so far, he hadn't called with specifics. Maybe he was giving me a chance to get over my mortification. Or maybe he was letting me down easy. It had been a week. I'd not gone a whole week without seeing him since my arrival in Moonshine.

I checked the time. I had twenty minutes before my meeting with Bree. Just enough time to pop in and say hello. Who was I kidding? I wanted to lay eyes on the man. All the television I'd watched with Thelma through the years hadn't prepared me for my palpitating-heart reaction for a man. But I seemed powerless to stop what seemed like foolishness.

The jingling of the door's bells didn't shock my system like they had the first time I'd heard them. My eyes adjusted from the bright sunshine to the fluorescent lighting.

"Hey there, Sadie. Are you looking for the sheriff?" Hannah asked.

"Oh, hi. Yes. I just had something I wanted to tell him."

Hannah grinned at her. "Well, he's gone over to the courthouse this morning. They're trying Grover Dixon today."

I guess she noticed my non-comprehension.

"You may have heard the stories. Grover had a meth lab up in the woods in an old RV. Says he got the idea from watching that show on Netflix. Only Grover didn't take the necessary safety precautions and nearly blinded himself when the whole darn thing blew up in his face, quite literally and started a forest fire."

"Oh dear. Sounds like he learned his lesson," I said.

"Not Grover. He isn't very smart, apparently. After he got out of the hospital, he was caught trying to sell a bunch of pain meds he stole from the old people in his trailer park."

"Ouch."

Hannah rolled her eyes at Grover's apparent stupidity. "Anyway, the sheriff's gone to testify at court again today. Don't know how long it's going to take but I'll tell him you stopped by. The trial's been going on all week."

Ah. No wonder he'd been tied up. "Oh, okay. No worries. I'll catch up with him later."

"I know he will want to see you," Hannah said.

"He will?" I asked, unable to help it.

"I'll tell you a secret. Since you've been in Moonshine, it's the first time since he and Annie split that left that he's been whistling."

"Whistling?"

"When he comes in in the morning. He whistles, in a cheerful way."

I tried to suppress my grin. "How does that have anything to do with me?" I asked, but secretly I was whistling inside.

"Oh my God, you're nuts about him too. This is perfect."

"Hannah—don't say anything—"

She made a little *my lips are sealed* gesture by pressing her fingers together and pulling them across her own lips.

"Seriously—" I began.

"Honey, I want Chase to be happy. And if you're the one who makes him whistle, then I'm all the way on board. I just don't want him to get hurt again."

"This is all new to me. I mean, we haven't even gone on a date yet," I said.

"I saw him online looking at restaurants when court was in recess, so you should expect him to call. He's a good man and deserves happiness, and from what I understand, so do you."

I smiled at Hannah as a little thrill shot through me. "Thank you."

"Where are you headed this morning?" she asked.

"I have an appointment with Bree down the way. She's going to do an evaluation for the FBI's investigation to help prove I didn't recover any of my memories until shortly after I arrived in Moonshine."

"Sorry, I wasn't trying to get in your business." Hannah looked a little embarrassed.

I waved a hand as if it wasn't a big deal. "It's not like you don't know what's been going on. Like anybody around here doesn't."

I felt like I had back when Merilee told everybody Julie was wearing her hand-me-downs. Like they were pointing and laughing at us again.

"Don't let anyone's gossip get you down. Right now, it's about getting your momma back on her feet. This will get worked out, you hear? Most folks are on your side, and those that aren't are going to hell anyway, so don't worry about them."

I snorted at her words. I wouldn't want anyone to go to hell on our account. "Thanks, Hannah, you've been a good friend through all of this mess. And I do think we can get this straightened out."

"Go get your head shrunk now, missy. I'll tell Chase you stopped by."

I exited the office with a grin. This town and its odd people seemed to cheer me at every turn, no matter what blows came my way.

Chapter Twenty-Three

I WASN'T SURE what to expect with a new therapist. Bree Hawthorne wasn't it. Big blonde hair and very Southern—Dolly Partonesque.

As soon as I met her, I recognized her, at least I thought so.

"Hi, Sadie. I'm so glad to have the opportunity to work with you." Her manner was warm and professional.

"Thanks for seeing me. Hey, I think I recognize you from the morning after I arrived in town." She'd been the blonde who'd waved at me through the window from outside the bed-and-breakfast—I was sure of it.

"Um, yes. Though I must say I'm a little embarrassed that I was loitering on the street that morning to get a glimpse of you like the rest of the town. I've been fascinated by your story since day one."

"I have a friend who's a psychologist. I've fascinated her for years." I laughed.

"Well, it's not every day one gets to hear a firsthand clinical account of someone who's experienced your condition, Sadie. Your kind of long-term memory loss is incredibly rare. There are a significant number of people who experience a dissociative fugue state after a traumatic experience, but almost none of them fail to recover their memories, at least mostly, within a few months to a year."

"What can I say? I'm that weird girl," I joked.

Bree laughed.

She read over my paperwork and said, "The request is for a full evaluation of your psychological status, as in emotional stability, missing memories, a timeline from when you went missing from Moonshine. I know you gave a statement to your attorney, but the investigators want a professional clinical therapist's evaluation. Obviously we can't tackle it all in one day. So, I want to begin by making sure you feel comfortable. Normally, with new patients, we would have several sessions geared toward establishing trust."

I just wanted to get the show on the road, honestly. "You don't seem intimidating, and you come highly recommended from people whose opinions I trust, so I'm okay with jumping right in. I wouldn't say that I'm especially fragile at this point. This has been going on for a while now."

Bree nodded but frowned just a little. "Unfortunately, some of what I will ask might dig into issues that are highly personal and sensitive. I want you to understand that while nothing in this town seems private, our sessions will be. My conversations with you are confidential. I will produce a report at the end that supplies my professional opinion regarding the requested information. I might be called upon to answer questions pertaining to the report. But I won't reveal our private conversations specifically."

"That sounds fine, but a lot more like therapy than I'd expected," I admitted.

"You said you had a psychologist friend. Has she been

your therapist?"

"Only briefly. But mostly, she's my friend." I described Jenny's early sessions and attempts at hypnotherapy.

"I also had a therapist not long after I lost my memory and came to live with Thelma. Her name was Bev, but she's been dead for several years. She wasn't able to do much toward helping with my memory either."

"Sorry to hear of her passing. Sounds like you know the drill though, and you don't need me to tell you that trust is essential. And I'm hoping to help you fill in the gaps with anything you still haven't remembered."

I experienced a tiny frisson of excitement. "I want to get my full memory back, but I'm a little nervous to find out the stuff I don't know firsthand. I'm frustrated that I still have so many gaps. More and more, I feel like some of the missing memories are the most important ones to help me understand what happened to me and finish the puzzle. Deep down, I think there is something huge that I'm skipping over."

"Now that your past is resurfacing, you're more likely to find what's missing. When you remembered nothing, everything was buried deep and tight. It's all coming loose now."

"So how do we start?" I asked.

"Let's figure out where your obvious gaps in memory are. I've read your statement from the attorney, so I've marked areas we might discuss. Why don't you settle in on the sofa. Slip off your shoes if you'd like and assume whatever position you feel most comfortable. You can close your eyes or keep them open—it's up to you."

I decided to put my feet up and lie back. The leather was soft and warm.

"It says you rode your bicycle to a bus station the night your stepdad, Hank, attacked you, but no details of how you acquired the bicycle. What about money? Do you know how you came to have bus ticket money that night? Or how you chose your destination?" she asked in a gentle tone. "Think back and try to picture the situation unfolding. Try to see it all as if you were watching from the outside and not part of the drama. Maybe with the sound turned off. From a less-emotional state. As if you needed to describe every detail."

I closed my eyes, picturing the scene in the barn, watching Hank come at me. I hovered above. I'd decided that I couldn't stay any longer.

I could feel the memory as it surrounded me.

My hands shook, and I whimpered. I'd probably killed Hank, or maybe he would die later, because he was still yelling. He might even follow me until he lost enough blood to weaken. But nobody could bleed like that and not die, could they?

My backpack. I had to get my backpack. It had everything I needed. The money and clothes. I'd made a list and planned. This day had been coming. And I was ready. The lady had told me what to do. She'd warned me Hank would get worse.

My bike was parked in the shed at an old, abandoned deer camp down the trail deeper in the woods.

My eyes popped open. "I had it all planned. I had an escaped mapped out."

Bree's eyes widened. "Until now, you believed you were running away randomly because of Hank's attack?"

I nodded. "Yes. That's why none of it made sense. But I

was prepared." I told Bree about the backpack and my bike.

"That definitely makes more sense. What about your destination? You were picked up outside Oklahoma City?"

"I don't know. I can't remember where I planned to go or who helped me, but I got the sense that someone had given me advice on what to do if I needed to escape Hank. I can't hear a voice or see a face, but I'm pretty sure it was a woman." The who was a blank.

Bree looked down at the notes in her lap. "Okay. You say you fell off your bike and hit your head as you rode on the trail toward the road."

"Yes. I remembered that when I got here and saw Hank the first time. And then I woke up on the bus and didn't remember anything that had happened before."

"It's likely you had a concussion."

"I remember being in pain from the beating Hank had given me. Before he'd gotten his hands on the screwdriver, he'd knocked me around pretty good. Blows to the face and body. I tried to evade him, but he grabbed hold of my hair and wouldn't let go."

"So it was likely you were pretty bruised up, bloody, even? Enough that anyone who took a good look at you would have noticed?" she asked.

"I'm not sure. I knew how to dress to hide the bruises. I wore a baseball cap, and I'm pretty sure I pulled on a long-sleeved shirt, so my arms and legs would have been covered. I don't remember if I was bleeding. Maybe from my head, where I hit it, or my lip where he hit me. But I don't specifically remember my own blood, only Hank's that night. I changed clothes in the shed where I'd stashed my bike because he'd bled on me. I shoved the clothes into my bag and took off."

"These are very important and helpful clues, Sadie. Your disappearance has been a mystery for some of the best detectives for years. Knowing that you had a well-laid plan in place for a night like the one you and Hank fought will help them realize you worked to evade the obvious roadblocks and cover your tracks without leaving a trace that normally would have made finding you a no-brainer."

"I don't think what I'd planned had anything to do with evading the police. I think I just wanted to disappear so that Hank wouldn't be able to find me and bring me back to finish me off." At least that was the intrinsic feel I got from the memories. But I did remember someone giving me guidance in the matter. But I couldn't remember who.

"What can you tell me about your mental condition when Thelma found you, and shortly after? And did she try to seek help for you?"

"I was terrified, confused, and I hardly spoke. Thelma brought me to the hospital, and everyone just assumed she was my mom. When I told her that I didn't remember my name or her, she supplied me with a fairly simple story: that I'd been in a car accident and that she was my adopted mother. I assumed she meant from when I was a baby. Everyone at the hospital assumed the same."

Bree nodded. "I'm guessing it was all pretty fuzzy at that point."

I nodded. "We were home after the 'accident' for a while before she brought me to a therapist to address my memory loss. It made me uncomfortable since I didn't remember who

I was after the accident. Now that I think about it, I'm not sure why I was in such a state. I'd always been so—brave—I guess that's the word. I mean, I'd never backed down from a physical altercation with Hank from what I remember and have been told by my mother. So, why would I have become so squeamish suddenly?" I asked.

Bree's expression held a wealth of compassion. "You were a child, Sadie. You'd been forced to physically fight off a strong, grown man by any means necessary, drunk or not. That kind of repeated trauma causes a kind of inability for a young person to trust and relax."

I nodded, understanding her line of reasoning. "I remember never knowing when Hank's next tantrum was coming. The signs weren't always the same. The drinking, the agitation about something that had happened during the day, or someone he'd had an altercation with in town maybe. But sometimes it came out of the blue."

"So, you had to always be on guard for what might come. Either toward you or your mom. That creates a restlessness and overstimulation that is utterly exhausting to anyone. I have a theory that once you believed he was dead or dying, paired with your head injury, your little body and brain went into self-protection mode. Part of you knew he wasn't coming after you, and you'd been so exhausted for so long that you closed it off."

"I hadn't thought of it like that. I wasn't especially nervous or worried once I was a couple thousand miles away with Thelma. She worried constantly, but I never did. I didn't ask a lot of questions either. Like I didn't want to find out anything that might push me back to that state of constant edginess again, I guess."

"Yes, the self-protection," Bree confirmed.

"Makes sense."

"I think we've made great progress for one session."

"So, how many sessions do you think this will take to get what they require?"

"Honestly, you seem stable. And if you weren't it wouldn't be something you could fake with me, especially after that memory flashback you just had. And there's no doubt, in my professional opinion that you lost your memory, based on your statement to the FBI and our discussions today. That's what they really want to know."

"So you have enough information for a report?"

"*I'm* confident I could make an honest professional evaluation, but they will require at least one more session before accepting a legitimate opinion. And remember, you're not on trial, so we don't have the burden of proving you innocent, only that you're not intentionally defrauding the government. There's no prosecutor trying to throw you in a cell."

This did put a new perspective on it in my mind. I had felt on trial.

"It's all about what you knew and when you knew it. Between your therapist friend back in Hickman, your statement to the FBI, and my evaluation, and any other pertinent information they gather, this should be over soon."

I exhaled. "It can't be soon enough. I'm ready to figure out what to do with my life, such as it is."

"You've got a career that you enjoy, right? Family?" Bree asked.

"I do. But I have a house in Hickman that I shared with Thelma. I lived there since I was sixteen, and I love the place. But now I have memories and family here. It's confusing."

"Sounds like you're fusing two lives and two sets of memories, the before and after, into a new one."

"I was a completely different person before I lost my memory, not just because I was a child. I changed after that as I grew up. While I lived as Randi, I was calm and less emotional. I didn't react or respond to things passionately. Now that my memories are coming back, so are my thoughts and emotions from my Sadie life. Sadie—I—am far more extreme in temperament than Randi."

"Fascinating. I hadn't heard about any of this. You must let me work with you to integrate your two lives. Clinically, I am giddy." She made a note on the page where she'd been writing.

"Is that a clinical term?" I asked, smiling.

"It is now. I won't charge you. I'll call it research." There was a gleam of excitement I recognized, the same as when I got a client with a challenging creative project I couldn't wait to dive into.

"Well, I have to come back again anyway, so I guess it couldn't hurt to speak with someone about this bizarre mess." I sat up and slipped on my shoes.

"You are an amazingly strong person, Randi-Sadie." Bree closed her notebook where she'd been handwriting notes as I spoke.

"Thanks, though sometimes I wonder if I can handle one more thing showing up."

I stood and smoothed a hand down the back of my long

hair to make sure it hadn't gotten knotted up from lying on the couch.

"Do you want to come back in a couple of days?" Bree asked.

"Let me check on some things and I'll give you a call or text as soon as I know what works," I said, thinking about the things that might prevent me from confirming an appointment.

"You have my number?" she asked.

"Right here." I patted the outside of my small cross-body bag I carried with me everywhere. I had one of her cards, given to me by Chase.

"Well, good luck until I see you next time. If anything comes up between now and then, feel free to call."

"Thanks, Bree."

GROVER DIXON'S IDIOCY was one for Moonshine's, and maybe the state of Georgia's record books. Keeping a straight face during his trial had been…a trial…for lack of a better word. Grover's bright idea to run a meth lab out of an old broken-down RV he'd towed out to the middle of nowhere in the woods hadn't panned out quite like he'd intended. Of course, *he'd* had no knowledgeable mentor like on the Netflix show to teach him how deadly meth making could be.

Sadly, Grover's scarred face proved the point that perhaps he should have paid more attention in chemistry class during the lab portion.

"This never happened to Jesse and Walt, you know. I blame Netflix for not explaining how it all works better," Grover whined to the judge as he mentioned the names of the characters in the TV show where he'd gotten his bright ideas.

Unfortunately, Grover had made a few somewhat successful batches and found distribution for those deadly drugs before he'd blown himself and his ratchet RV to the sky. He'd also set a forest fire that had had to be contained after burning twenty or so acres of surrounding pines and brush on the side of the mountain, leaving a scarred, bald area on the earth that would take five or six years to fill in after replanting.

Grover had immediately squealed on his dealers without waiting for an offer of a deal from the prosecution, so here he sat, on trial for all means of crimes. The main one, in Chase's eyes, was the crime of idiocy, though regrettably, they couldn't add that one to the list.

Since the events mostly took place outside of town, besides some of the actual drug dealing, they were within Chase's jurisdiction. His office covered the entire county, though most of it was forest and lake, with help from the Georgia Wildlife and Fisheries Department.

Court was in recess, so he'd gone downstairs to check in with Hannah and get a cup of coffee when he spotted Sadie just outside his office.

Curious, Chase followed to see where she was headed.

"Oh, hi," she said, obviously surprised by his sudden appearance.

"I just got out of court and followed you."

"That's not creepy at all." She laughed.

"I guess that didn't come out quite right. What brings you into town?"

"I had an appointment with Bree this morning."

"Oh, yeah. How did it go?" he asked.

"Intense. I remembered a few more details about the night I left Moonshine. I know you'll want that for your report. I'll fill you in when we have more time to talk," she said.

"Absolutely. I'll need to get you on record with that information. But I wanted to talk to you about something else," he said.

"Oh?" she asked, her innocent eyes widening.

"I've been meaning to call. About our date. Are you free this evening?"

Sadie's cheeks flamed and she slipped her hands inside her jean pockets. "Um, sure. I think so." He was making her uncomfortable.

"Can I take you to dinner?" he asked. Several times this week he'd picked up his phone to call her and chickened out.

"O-okay."

"Great! I'll pick you up at seven." Perspiration began to bead between his shoulder blades.

"Sure. What should I wear?"

He hadn't considered that. "I'm thinking about a place with a killer view on the side of the mountain. It's less casual than most, so it's up to you." He'd made the reservation a few days ago but hadn't called Sadie yet to confirm with her.

"Real specific, thanks." But she laughed. "It's okay, I'll figure it out."

"I'll see you later," he said, nearly doing a fist pump.

He waved instead but couldn't help grinning like a weir-do.

Chapter Twenty-Four

I NEARLY BUMPED into Merilee Bell as soon as I stepped onto the street from the sidewalk where I'd been speaking with Chase. I was distracted and possibly panicked by the upcoming need to choose something killer from my meager wardrobe.

"Well, hey there, Sadie. You're moving like a long-tailed cat in a room fulla rocking chairs, girl."

I stared at her for a full three seconds trying to figure out what she'd just said, then grinned at the mental image. "Oh-oh. I get it. Sorry about that. I've got something on my mind."

"Well, I hope you'll let me do your hair sometime. You know that even the best hair needs maintenance."

I stopped then. "Wait. Do you have time to do it today?" I asked. I had a date tonight, and Merilee possessed the skills I needed.

"Huh? Oh, you really want me to do your hair?" She seemed surprised. "Well, I was just running over to the post office, but yeah, I've got a break now. Are you free?"

I nodded. "Yes."

She led me to her shop, which was only a block away. More bells on the door jingled when she opened it. The place was adorable. The walls were painted a light turquoise and the shabby-chic décor featured several Southernisms hand-lettered on the wall, a couple of crystal chandeliers, and dried flowers were set about in mason jars and other containers.

Merilee had two shampoo bowls, two hairdryers, and two styling stations. There was a nail station and a large chair for pedicures. "Wow, this is amazing, Merilee. It's so…charming and cozy," I said, wanting to describe how it made me feel. As a graphic designer, I could truly appreciate the style and creative vision that went into her establishment.

"Thank you, Sadie. It's my pride and joy. I didn't finish college, but I've worked hard to make this place a success."

"Well, you've certainly done an amazing job of creating a great space for it."

"So, are you going to tell me what to do, or are you going to let me have my way with that gorgeous hair of yours?" she asked.

I hadn't thought about it until now. "I—uh—I've never been to a salon. My friend always cut my hair in the past." Jenny had been hesitant at first, but she'd turned out to be pretty good at it.

Merilee blinked at me like she had no idea what planet I'd just landed from. "Never been to a salon? Like, in your life?"

I shook my head in the negative. "Certainly not when I lived here, and never since."

She rubbed her hands together. "Am I gonna have fun with you. But first let me say that you aren't going to pay me a red cent, you hear? The first time's on me."

"But—" I was done with charity, even though I had to be careful with my cash until my assets were released.

"Shh. Let a girl with a guilty conscience do a favor for a friend, okay? I was unkind to you when we were kids and I want a chance to make it up to you. I know it's a tough thing in our past, but I *need* to do this. Please." Merilee had teared up. This was clearly no joke to her.

"I've forgiven you, Merilee. But I accept your generosity since it's important to you. But no more talk of the unpleasantness between us in the past after today, okay? It's over. We're square."

"Agreed. Now, please let me have my way with you."

I sat in her chair staring at my reflection. I wasn't wearing any makeup today, as usual. Maybe I should try a little harder. My hair was straight and black. My eyes a light blue. Everything else was just—normal. I was ready for something a little less normal maybe.

"Any thoughts?" I asked.

"Are you kidding? You're gorgeous just like you are. But I'm a magician, so off to the shampoo bowl with you, first-timer."

I called Momma to check on her and to let her know I would be a while longer.

"Is everything okay?" she asked.

"Yes. I'm just getting my hair cut," I said.

"You are? You never wanted your hair cut as a girl." Momma sounded surprised.

A ponytail hurt less than a handful of hair when getting pulled around by it. *I don't have anyone to pull me around by it anymore.* "I've never been to a salon before, so I thought it was time."

"Well. I haven't regular-like either, but it's a real treat, so have fun, love. I'll see you back at home. Did you manage to get the uh, stuff done?" she asked.

"Yes. We can discuss it when I see you this evening." I tried not to let on what "stuff" to which we referred. As good of friends as Merilee and I might become, I wasn't testing it by sharing my identity issue and mental health eval on the first day.

That seemed to satisfy Momma without further discussion. "Okay, see you later."

I hadn't asked about Hank, and she hadn't offered, so either he was the same or she'd been sitting next to him while we spoke.

"Lean back and relax," Merilee said as she snapped the plastic cape under my chin and tucked a dry towel into the front of the cape. When she pulled my hair back and began rinsing it with warm water and massaging my scalp with her fingers, the tension drained away. Why had I never done this before?

CHASE KNOCKED ON Sadie's front door a minute before seven, a bouquet of flowers from the Moonshine Florist in his slightly sweaty grasp. He'd swapped out his usual jeans for dark chinos and a sport coat with a button-down white shirt. He still wore boots, but for tonight, he was wearing what Momma had always called his "church boots."

Mary Frances greeted him with a smile. It occurred to

him how different she seemed now that Sadie had returned. "Hello, Chase. Sadie said you were coming over. She'll be out in a minute."

"Thanks, Mary Frances. How's Hank faring today?" he asked, slightly afraid to dim her smile.

She shrugged. "The same. He's lost more weight, but they say that's to be expected. Mean as ever. They keep saying he's near the end, but the Lord must have other plans."

"Sorry to hear it." Wait, maybe that wasn't the right thing to say.

They turned at the sound of a door opening. "Oh, look, here she is."

Chase followed her gaze and was nearly struck dumb. He'd expected Sadie as he'd left her at the courthouse this afternoon. *Not* the woman who emerged in a black dress that gently hugged every curve, and she wore high heels. And her hair—it was shorter and shiny and she looked like she'd stepped out of some fashion magazine. "Wow."

She did a slow spin, but it amused him that she wobbled slightly in her heels. "Oops. That was supposed to be graceful."

"Doesn't she look amazing?" Mary Frances gushed.

"Uh-mazing, yes. I'll say. Who did this to you?" he asked.

"Merilee," she said. "She asked that I allow her to do her thing without my interference."

"Good call."

"Are those for me?" she asked.

"Huh? Oh…yes." Chase handed her the bouquet. He'd

completely forgotten about the flowers once he'd gotten a look at her.

"They're beautiful. Thank you."

"I'll just go put these in some water for you." Mary Frances took the nosegay and hurried into the kitchen with them.

"Do you like my hair?" she asked, and bit her lip.

While it was shorter and had been cut in layers, it was extremely flattering. It fell just above her shoulders and framed her gorgeous features. Her nose was pert and perfect, and she had the lushest lips. And those eyes… "Merilee deserves an award. I didn't think anything could make you more attractive."

Color splashed across Sadie's cheeks. "You're doing it again. Making me feel all squishy inside."

"Good. But we have dinner reservations on the mountain before we address that." He leaned forward and kissed the tip of her nose just as Mary Frances returned from the kitchen.

"Oh. I'm sorry."

Chase smiled at the woman. "It's okay. We're headed out to dinner. I'll have her home by midnight," he said.

"How lovely." Mary Frances sighed and waved them out the door.

Chase helped Sadie into the passenger's side of his four-wheel-drive vehicle, which was more of a challenge considering her dress and high heels.

"Thanks. I hope I don't embarrass you. This is my first date you know."

"Are you kidding? Embarrass me?" This hadn't occurred to him but based on what she'd told him about her life with

Thelma, it made sense. "I assume you didn't do any dating before you left Moonshine?" he asked once he was inside behind the wheel.

"Are you kidding? With Hank as my dad? No boy would've had the nerve to ask, much less the courage to see it through. Plus, I wasn't exactly a popular girl if you remember."

They were driving down the dirt driveway, so he stopped the car. And he took her hand. "I want to set the record straight, Sadie—you were beautiful. I was too old to date you then, but even so, you were so far beyond any of the other girls your age. You think they were mean to you because you were poor? Ha. They were insanely jealous of your looks. Of course you had a huge chip on your shoulder by then from childhood and had no way of knowing the source of their nastiness."

"I don't see myself as beautiful at all. I guess I've worked pretty hard to hide from the world."

"You've lived your adult life under a rock and ball cap."

She laughed. "You're right. I have. I've kept my head down and not made eye contact."

He laughed at his own early words to her. He pulled back onto the road and headed onto the highway toward the restaurant.

"When Merilee let me look in the mirror after she'd waxed my eyebrows, my lip, and done my makeup and hair, I felt like a movie star."

"I didn't notice that you needed a lip wax." He laughed at her honesty. That was something he liked most about her. She didn't hold her words in or pretend.

"According to Merilee it was essential," she assured him.

"And yes, you do look like a movie star. But then, you always have."

Instead of smiling, her eyes suddenly filled as if she were going to cry. "Whoa, no. Not that again. I said that because it's true."

She dashed her fingertips at her eyes. "No, I'm sorry. It's just so nice to hear. It makes me feel…normal. It's the one thing I've never been, you know. Normal. I've been weird Sadie or weird Randi with no memory my entire life."

"You've had a strange life, yes. But you're one of the most grounded and *normal* people I know. *Weirdly* so."

She laughed at that. "I have Thelma to thank for that, I think. She was so grounding during those years. Even though I missed out on so many things. This." She motioned to the interior of the vehicle. "Dating. Relationships with boys, men."

"I'm somewhat thankful for meeting you without a lot of baggage and expectations, truth be told." He did hate that she'd missed out on normal things, and that it had worked on her confidence, but no other guy had ever smashed her heart either. That was a specific pain in addition to any other kind. With everything else she'd experienced, she didn't deserve heartache.

"I see your point. And I never missed it before I came back here. When I didn't have a memory, my affect was lower and I didn't crave that kind of human connection or passion, which I guess was a blessing in some ways."

"In a cocoon maybe. Now you're a butterfly who's emerged and ready to experience everything in living color."

She nodded. "Exactly. The good and the bad. So far, I've had plenty of both."

As they pulled into the parking lot, Chase noticed it was already nearly full.

"Well, in my experience this restaurant is amazing. If food is your thing, prepare for more of the good stuff this evening."

"Food is definitely my thing. It was one pleasure I could always appreciate to the fullest because it didn't involve a lot of emotion. It was pure enjoyment. And Thelma was an incredible cook. She made lots of Creole and Cajun dishes."

"Do you cook?" he asked.

"Yes. Remember, I was a homebody, so cooking, gardening, and home projects were how we spent our time when I wasn't studying or working. I'm pretty sure it's how I developed my artist's skills."

"No wonder you've been so capable in getting your momma's house whipped into shape so quickly."

"I've done for Momma a lot of what Thelma and I did at our own house over the years."

They'd parked and had just entered the restaurant when Chase heard *the voice*. "Oh, Sheriff, yoo-hoo, Chase." He took a breath, exhaled, then turned to face Cindy Hayes. She'd approached quickly and likely, with great intent.

"Hello, Cindy. How are you?" he asked.

"I'm well, thank you for asking. *Well*, I declare. Is this— *Sadie Brubaker*?" She drew out Sadie's name as if she'd discovered expired salad dressing being served at a dinner party and was caught between the disgust of it and the exciting revelation of exposing her host.

Sadie stepped up then, not Randi. "Hi there, aren't you Cindy Hayes? Yes, I remember you from when I was young." She left it at that, causing a mottled red to creep up Cindy's neck.

"Oh. That was a long time ago. I'm a good Christian woman now. Ask Chase. I run the ladies' auxiliary at church. Why, we've even gone out and tried to help your momma. Well, as much as we could." Cindy couldn't quite keep the sneer from her voice.

"I've heard about your Christian charity," Sadie said with a radiant smile at Cindy, who was at least two inches shorter in her heels, and whose skin was sadly mottled all the way to her forehead by now.

Chase had a working knowledge of women's cerebral warfare, but this exchange was filled with unsaid poison darts thrown with accuracy and venom.

"It's nice to see you're back home to help your own momma now instead of leaving her care to the kindness of strangers. I heard your sister, Julie, stopped in too. Two grown daughters and y'all left her alone with that animal all these years."

Wow. That was going too far.

Chase put a hand on Sadie's arm, afraid she might punch Cindy. Certainly she deserved it, but he'd hate to have to arrest his date for assault. Sadie shook off his hand.

"I remember a time, Cindy, when you were a senior in high school—" Sadie began.

Cindy held up a hand. "Fine. That was a low blow. I apologize," Cindy gritted out through her teeth. "We should let bygones be gone."

Sadie gave what Chase knew to be a phony smile, leaned down into Cindy's personal space, and uttered through her own gritted teeth, "Before you speak another foul word about my family, which you know nothing about, remember what happened under the bleachers your senior year, okay? Because I do."

"Fine." Cindy backed down as if she'd been slapped. She spun on her heel, grabbing the hand of her dinner companion, an older man Chase didn't recognize, and nearly dragged him from the restaurant. He'd been standing several feet away during the short exchange and likely didn't hear much of what had passed between the women.

"Wow. That was...intense," he said to Sadie, whose fierce expression hadn't quite smoothed out yet.

"That...woman...is a nasty cow." She nearly spat every word.

He worked hard to prevent the laughter from bursting forth at her utterance. His distaste for Cindy now had a rival.

"You can't imagine how great it is to know that someone finally understands what a pain in my ass she is."

The host interrupted then. "Are y'all ready to be seated?" she asked.

They followed her to the table by the window.

Once seated, Sadie asked, "I assume from what you said that you don't care for Cindy either?"

He did laugh then. "She's horrible. Comes by my office to complain incessantly about potholes and people in town that annoy her. As if my law-keeping ability extends to her happiness."

"Does she have a crush on you?" Sadie asked, eyes narrowed, but there was a little sparkle in them. "She's attractive."

He thought about that for a minute. "I guess it's possible, but I've only ever thought of her as a pain in the ass."

They shared a laugh.

"Not the best way to flirt, I guess," Sadie said.

"Guess not."

Chapter Twenty-Five

S ADIE GAZED OUT the window then and gasped. The sun was setting over the lake, which mirrored the flipside of the lush green mountain layered with streaks of blues, yellows, and oranges; it was perfect. He'd planned their reservation and reserved this table in hopes she would appreciate this sunset. "Wow. It's...amazing."

"It's my favorite view."

She continued to stare at nature's excellence, nodding slowly. "I remember sitting on the lake's edge as a teenager wishing for the courage to join in with all the other kids on the boats. I wanted to learn to ski so badly. It looked like so much fun."

"You never went out on a boat?"

A shadow passed over her expression. Anger? Pain? "I couldn't wear a swimsuit in public. I always had bruises I was trying to cover up. Either new ones or fading ones. And if I'd been able to avoid Hank long enough to not have marks, I didn't have the confidence to take off my clothes in front of my peers."

He grimaced at the thought of Hank laying a hand on her small body in anger. And how nobody had been the wiser. "I'm so sorry."

"He was careful. There's no way you could have known," she said. Her smile was sad but not broken.

"You were always an attractive girl."

She shrugged. "I'd been burned too many times by snide comments about my clothes, my hair, and so many other things that I wasn't taking any chances by showing up in a swimsuit."

"How do you feel about yourself now?" he asked.

A slow smile spread across her lips that activated dimples on both sides of her mouth and lit up her eyes to sparkle. "Better now."

"That's good, because none of those people who gave you shit in your past life here hold a candle to you, in looks or otherwise. I mean, you persevered in ways they never could. They hid behind their nicer clothes and easier lives and used unkind words to slay you."

"Not all of them." She continued to smile at him in ways that made him wish they'd already eaten.

"You overcame enormous odds to get back here. You've got a college degree and own a successful business. And you've forgiven them for their hateful behavior."

"I have moments that I'm not proud of—when I still let things get to me. When memories hit out of the blue of something awful one of them said or did to me or Julie, and I want to claw their eyes out. Or if they make nasty comments about Momma."

"Who could blame you? I think you handled Cindy perfectly, without a scene. She's unrepentant and bitter about how her life turned out. She hates your beauty and success."

"And she's jealous that we're out on a date," Sadie added.

Chase hadn't asked what past event Sadie'd used to rein Cindy's hatefulness in, and he'd rather let that lie.

He shifted in his chair uncomfortably. "Yeah. Probably that too."

"So, what happened to Cindy that made her so bitter?" Sadie asked.

"Her husband ran off with the preacher's son." He normally didn't like gossiping about folks in town, but it was common knowledge, true, and she'd asked.

"Oh. Well, maybe I shouldn't have been so hard on her back there. That's quite a blow to a woman—any woman."

He shrugged. "She ignored the warning signs and bulldozed him into marriage." That was also commonly known and had been well observed. The results had only surprised Cindy.

"I guess love makes people blind to things they might otherwise see. Or so I've seen on television."

Chase laughed. She'd shared with him her screen fascination, and how it had allowed her to learn a somewhat dramatic view of how the world turned. While she was holed up most of that time in Hickman with Thelma.

"I'd have to support that statement for the most part," he agreed. "Love can make the smartest of us drooling idiots."

They'd ordered a nice bottle of white, which had been poured by the server while they were chatting. He picked up his glass and held it aloft. "Here's to moving forward, a day at a time, and finding our own way the best we can."

She lifted her glass, newly manicured nails glinting in the candlelight from the table. "That was a lovely toast."

"I was inspired."

"Your words are a testament to my life every single day. It's nice to have someone understand that."

"You've taken your blows with grace and courage, Sadie. You don't whine and ask, 'Why me?' I respect your confidence things will work out."

"That's one of the nicest things anyone's ever said to me. Thanks, Chase." Her eyes were a little misty from his observation. It wasn't a compliment, only the truth. And he wanted her to understand how much he admired her as a human being, whether or not they ever became anything more than friends.

"You're welcome. Now, I think we should have a look at the menu before someone gets hangry."

She frowned. "Are you implying I get testy when I'm hungry?"

"Oh, I was talking about me. I skipped lunch today."

IF I NEVER went on another date, I could die happy. Tonight had been perfect. Well, besides the Cindy Hayes episode, but I'd decided she was to be forgiven once I discovered about her husband running off on her and all.

The restaurant, the sunset, and the food and wine. All perfect. The man, well, he'd gone all out to make sure I'd had a wonderful first date. I'd had tingles since he'd kissed my nose in front of Momma at the house before we'd left for the restaurant.

I hoped he would kiss me tonight—really kiss me. I'd been watching his lips all night and imagining that kiss. And more. I felt a little buzzy from the wine, so that might have loosened me up a little for the drive home. Maybe he would stop someplace and we could make out.

Dear God, I'd reverted to my sixteen-year-old fantasies. Because I wasn't such an odd girl that I hadn't liked boys or had crushes. It'd just taken until now to remember them. I hadn't wanted to admit to myself or anyone else the now-gross crush I'd recently remembered having on Jason Weston.

I experienced no attraction toward Jason now. Plus, I'd been a much younger girl admiring a cool, older guy. Chase had been rather intimidating and serious, though striking in his dark good looks back then. Jason had been blond, tanned, and carefree. He'd seemed to always be laughing, an arm slung casually around a gorgeous girl or two. Of course, he hadn't had a lot of worries. His parents had paved the way for his happiness and success.

I hadn't known Chase well, but he was always polite when our paths crossed. I wish I could have said that I'd been above a crush on someone like Jason, but I envied his happy demeanor. He made me wish I could be more like him, whereas Chase reminded me too much of myself. Too deep-thinking and serious. He suited me perfectly now.

I felt Chase's hand on mine. "Deep thoughts?" he asked.

"Not so much. Just sifting through some teenage memories. It's strange that for all the time I lived away from here, my mind was erased. Now that I'm back, I live in a constant state of recovering new bits and pieces of my past. I sometimes have to figure out the timeline and catalog the items for things to make sense. It truly is like a jigsaw puzzle, but a long, linear one."

The moment we pulled onto the drive leading to Momma's house, my palms slickened with sweat. Had I reverted back to my sixteen-year-old self? Grown women with my body and haircut should probably act a bit more sophisticated. *Right?* But this was truly new territory for me. This was grown-up Sadie stuff. Boring Randi who didn't feel passion hit the road a while ago.

Randi had less experience than even teenage Sadie. Merging the two of me was like trying to combine a staid, steady, but unsophisticated matron with a fearless, headstrong, hormonal teen. Sometimes that worked and sometimes it was a process in conflict.

Chase slowed the SUV and pulled over to the side of the road just around the curve from Momma's house, which excited and thrilled me. Maybe he would kiss me now.

My mouth couldn't help itself as I began to babble. "It's been quiet this evening. You haven't gotten a single call," I said. Normally, he was putting out fires and giving directions to one or the other of his deputies regarding calls that came in on the radio.

"I've got someone covering for me."

"Oh. That's nice."

He turned the headlights off, which caused me to jump just a little. "Wow, would you look at those stars tonight?" I continued to jabber.

"Would you like to get out and have a closer look?"

I nodded but realized he couldn't see me. "O-okay. That sounds nice."

"Be there in a sec." He opened his door, climbed out,

then shut it. About two seconds later he appeared outside my window and opened my door.

"Oh. Hi," I said, stupidly, as he helped me down from my seat onto the gravel. I didn't care much about my shoes at the moment. Maybe I would later.

We made our way in the pitch-dark to the back of the vehicle, where Chase let down the tailgate on the SUV. His big hands went around my waist, and he lifted me up to sit on the bench-like seat.

I might have squealed just a little at the unexpected manhandling.

"Are you comfortable?" he asked.

"Yes," I whooshed out.

"I would like to kiss you, if that's okay, Sadie."

"Yes," I whooshed again.

He continued to stand very close, then lowered his lips to mine, gently. They were warm and soft, and I felt his breath catch. His hands were on my shoulders but slipped around my back then and pulled me closer. I did not resist—any of it. Truth be told, I wanted to drag him up on the tailgate and find out what Eve had done to Adam after they'd eaten the apple that had gotten them thrown out of the Garden of Eden.

I leaned closer and sighed, kissing him deeper. I'd watched a lot of kissing on TV and hoped I was doing it right. It certainly felt right. Funny how kissing wasn't only about the lips. I was tingling and wanting everywhere. Hoping Chase would move those big hands and touch me someplace besides my shoulders.

"I don't want to go too fast," he said, sounding a little

breathless.

"I'm turning thirty. You can speed this up a little." I groaned just a little as I said it, my frustration likely apparent.

He laughed at that. "I don't want you to feel cheated out of anything."

"But I'm so *ready*."

He seemed to consider this a moment. "It's a little too soon for more than kissing. I'm a little old-fashioned like that."

"I guess I should be grateful, but I'm not."

THEY'D MANAGED TO kiss good night in front of her momma's front door as if nothing odd had happened and made plans to meet for lunch the next day. Only Sadie's flushed cheeks and possibly a slight case of whisker burn on her smooth, otherwise unblemished skin gave an indication that anything more had occurred than a nice dinner out together.

Getting to know Sadie again was going to be fun, and he'd decided that they'd moved past the point where they could be only friends. He understood himself well enough to know he had real feelings for her. But he refused to rush this, even if it nearly killed him.

As he drove home, he whistled along to the song on the radio, believing finally things were heading in the right direction.

His brain didn't register the large, dark object in time—

not until he'd slammed into it, reacted by turning his steering wheel, and jamming his foot so hard on the brake that the SUV swerved hard. The deer hit the windshield and shattered it as his airbags deployed and he careened through the guardrail around the curve and down the side of the steep dead-man's-curve a mile from his house.

Holy Shit.

All he could think about before the world went black was how glad he was that he'd kissed Sadie tonight. And how sorry he was that he hadn't called his mom today.

I'D GONE TO bed shortly after telling Momma about my date with Chase. I'd skipped the part about running into Cindy or making out with Chase. *That* had been unexpected and—well—mind-blowing, to say the least. No, I'd stayed with the G-rated stuff. The view, the sunset, the wine, and the dinner.

She'd sighed and told me how happy for me she was and what a wonderful man Chase was. I had to agree.

The promise of more made me giddy with our moving forward dating.

I couldn't stop smiling. I was in the middle of an FBI fraud investigation, I had no legal identity or access to my money, and I might be indicted. But I was lying in my bed grinning like a loon because now I understood so much more about the world of women and men. I wonder how Thelma would have reacted to that. And I wonder why she hadn't told me about it.

Thelma. How I missed her. And I still couldn't figure

out our past together. My memory failed me when it came to her. Something was still missing. Something important.

I fell asleep caught between delicious thoughts of Chase and confusing ones of Thelma.

Chapter Twenty-Six

I HEARD MOMMA speaking to someone on the phone, which I guess is what woke me initially. But the tone of her voice, kind of frantic and upset, pulled me out of any remaining sleep. Something was wrong. I wondered if maybe Hank had passed or was about to.

I quickly pulled on a pair of sweatpants under my over-sized T-shirt and headed out to see if I could help with the situation.

Momma sat on the sofa speaking quietly into the phone now, obviously trying not to wake me. "What is it?" I asked, softly, so as not to interrupt her conversation but also letting her know I was in the room.

She startled, and quickly said into the phone, "Sadie's just come in. Yes, we'll be there soon. Hang in there, honey."

There were tears in Momma's eyes as she took a big breath and faced me.

"What's happened? Is it Julie?" I asked, my heart begin-ning to pound.

"No, darling, it's Chase. He was in an accident last night after he left our house."

Chase. "What? No—he—" I couldn't process her words.

Momma said softly, "He's in the hospital. He hit a big

deer and went off the road."

"But he's okay, right? I mean, he'll be all right." Of course he would.

Momma's lip quivered. And she burst into tears. "I'm so sorry, Sadie. They just can't say. The truck flipped over the guardrail on the big curve between here and town."

I swallowed, not believing. "I need to see him. What about Becky?" I could only imagine what she must be going through.

Momma wiped her eyes and worked to be the strong one. "I just hung up with her. I told her we were on our way."

"I'll get dressed," I said, and then willed my feet to move back toward my bedroom. But they were stuck in concrete, the dread was so thick.

"I'll bring you some coffee."

"Momma, what if he's—"

She frowned then, and said, "He's not. And we're not gonna think like that. I didn't mean to scare you with my hysterics. Chase is a strong man, the strongest. If anybody can survive a tumble down the side of a mountain, he can. Now, get dressed and let's go support Becky. She needs us right now, and so does Chase."

My fingers shook as I zipped my jeans. I shoved my hair back into a ponytail, even though tendrils tried to escape since it was shorter now. I grabbed a button-up long-sleeved shirt to wear over my T-shirt in case it was cold at the hospital. I had no intention of leaving Chase or Becky. They'd become my family, almost as much as Momma since I'd come back to Moonshine.

I pulled a little cash from the hidden pocket in my suitcase, thankful that Thelma had hammered the idea of keeping cash on hand "just in case." If I hadn't kept her words in mind, I'd have been in a real pickle while my fate was decided, and my accounts remained frozen. My little nest egg was dwindling, but at least I hadn't run through it all yet.

I also packed a change of clothes and my toothbrush as soon as I finished with it in a small backpack, along with my laptop and charger.

"Are you ready?" Momma tapped on my door just as I was slinging the backpack on my shoulder.

"Yes. Don't you have a shift at the dollar store this afternoon?" I worried that she'd taken so much time off with Hank's illness.

"I do, and I'm planning to go in once I check on Becky and Chase. If you're there with them, I'll feel okay about going to work."

"Okay. I will too." Momma's job didn't pay much, but it seemed to be a source of pride for her. Losing her job at this point wouldn't be good for her.

I fed Daisy Mae and set her up with a couple of chew toys that still had their squeakers, and a mega-bone that would keep her in ecstasy most of the day.

Momma and I decided to take separate vehicles since Momma would need to go in to work later and let Daisy Mae out in a few hours. I planned to install a doggie door where she could enter and exit freely at will whenever we were gone during the day but hadn't done so yet. There was a fence around the backyard, which had some grass, though not the kind of lawn grass I'd been used to in Hickman. It was more a kind of dirt/grass/weed mixture that wasn't uncommon on acreage out in the country.

There used to be chickens who roamed in the fenced area, and a goat when I was little, but neither were there now.

As I drove toward town, my blood ran cold at the detour around the bright orange cones and Georgia State Patrol with their blue flashing lights where Chase's vehicle had broken through the guardrail at the steepest curve in the area. There was a flatbed tow truck with its yellow lights and a couple of large trucks with wenches that appeared to be working to pull up a truck from below. But it was beyond my view from the road. I wanted to throw up.

Chase had been down there in the dark. Alone. Hurt. I wondered how long it was before someone found him. Had he been able to call for help? How badly hurt was he? *Is he going to die?*

If not for me, he wouldn't have been on the road when that deer crossed. Oh, God. *It's my fault!* My breathing became more like panting by the time I arrived at the hospital on the other side of town. Moonshine General was a small, regional hospital from what I remembered. If Chase was badly hurt, wouldn't he need more care?

I couldn't get out of my Jeep quickly enough to get more information. Momma parked next to me and we walked together toward the entrance.

As we approached the sliding front doors, the memory hit me like a nightmare.

It's okay, Sadie. Remember, just tell them you tripped and fell when they ask what happened. If you tell them Hank did it, they'll put him in jail, and he'll lose his job again.

I glared at Momma as if she'd lost her mind. How could she protect him like this? I had a bump on the back of my head the size of a duck's egg, and my hair was matted with blood. My whole body shook with pain and terror at what Hank had done this time. I had thrown up twice already and my sight was blurry.

"Momma, he threw me against the side of the house. Shouldn't he go to jail?" I'd sobbed.

"Yes, baby, he should. But if he goes, they'll just let him out in a few days, and he'll be even madder when he gets home. We don't want that, do we?"

I threw up on her shoes then.

"Sadie?" Momma's voice brought me out of the fog of the past.

I'd stopped dead. "This place. You brought me here after Hank hurt me—gave me what must have been a concussion. I was probably twelve."

"Yes." Her voice was hollow, and she stared at the ground.

"You told me to say I fell."

"Yes. But since it was your only visit, and I was the one who brought you in, they believed us."

"And that was a *good* thing?" If she'd made eye contact with me then she would have seen my horrified expression.

"It kept us off the radar from child protection services," Momma said, as if slipping back into the secret society of protecting-the-child-abuser mode. "I'm not saying it was good, but in the scheme of things back then, I thought it would've been worse if they hadn't believed us. I think about these things a lot now. I remember and it hurts that I was so stupid and scared."

"I don't even know how to respond to that."

Momma said nothing, only continued looking at her shoes.

So many of my memories hurt me. And I wanted to lash out and protect that child who'd been wronged by all the adults in my life. No one had protected me. The law hadn't protected me. Momma certainly hadn't.

But here I was. None of it had been fair or right. I could tear into Momma again about what a horrible mother she'd been. That wouldn't solve anything. She would cry. I would feel like crap, and Chase would still be lying in a hospital bed someplace in this establishment.

"Let's find Chase," I said, keeping it simple.

Momma nodded, not making eye contact with anyone in the immediate area. They all knew her and Hank here. Hell, most of them knew me from the past. But I had one goal in mind—finding Chase.

There was blood in the emergency room waiting area, which normally wouldn't have bothered me. But the sickly smell brought back a memory—a particularly unpleasant one I squelched down.

The cold tiles echoed a crying child. An orderly was mopping up a red puddle. There was no filter here. It was raw and real.

Swallowing down my bile, I noticed Becky slumped in an uncomfortable-looking black chair over to the side in the small waiting area. "Look, there's Becky," I said.

As we approached, Becky stood and tried to smile, but

the lines on her face were deeper than usual with worry and her lip quivered just a little.

"How is he?" Momma asked.

"I'm not sure yet. They've taken him back to surgery. Had to call in a surgeon from Atlanta because they didn't want to move him. And he's got a broken arm and foot—maybe some internal injuries."

I wrapped my arms around my middle and closed my eyes and absorbed the impact of her words like body blows. Would he be okay? I couldn't ask Becky. Maybe the answer wasn't even clear to the doctors yet. I couldn't process moving forward without Chase's steady presence in my life. It's like I'd known him forever. I had, actually, but our recent relationship had become something vital in my life. He was precious.

"He's strong, that boy of yours." Momma put her arms around Becky.

"He must have hit the deer not long after he left our house last night." My guilt was creeping up again and threatened to strangle me. "We went on a date." I tried to smile.

She took my hands in hers and smiled through tears. "Honey, my boy is smitten with you. You've finally broken through to healing something I worried would never mend. So, thank you. And I'm tickled y'all were out together last night. We all know the risks of these roads and the large animals that can come out at us without any warning. Could've been anybody."

Her words soothed me, but it didn't change the fact that Chase might be fighting for his life because of me. "Thanks for saying that."

"How long until they found him?" Momma asked, and I wanted to pinch her.

Becky shuddered. "At least four hours. It's so dark on that road and nobody saw it happen. Some guys were coming home from spotlighting for frogs in the middle of the night and noticed heavy skid marks and that the guard-rail was out. They pulled out their lights and saw Chase's vehicle down in the trees, wheels up."

The mental picture of passing the dead man's curve just minutes ago still lodged inside my brain and weakened my knees, causing me to find the nearest chair. I breathed in and out quickly, sweat popping out on my face.

"Easy, Sadie. I had the same reaction. But they're taking good care of him, and we have to believe in his stubborn nature." Becky's expression told me she was equally trying to convince herself.

I couldn't believe *she* was reassuring *me*. "I'm sorry. I...just didn't expect this." I turned away and paced for a few seconds. "We had such a nice time at dinner. It's hard to believe."

The front doors to the ER swished, causing us to all briefly glance toward them. Annie Weston entered. She was distraught, judging by her movements, and rushed toward the registration desk. The volunteer pointed toward Becky.

"Oh Lord," Becky whispered. "This is all I need."

Annie's gaze followed the woman's finger and she hur-ried toward our small, tight group, sitting in chairs together in the waiting area.

Annie glanced at the three women, and briefly nodded,

homing in on Becky. "How is he? Is he going to be all right?"

"Hi, Annie," Becky answered her. "He's in surgery now, and we'll know more soon." Becky was polite—I'd give her that.

"Surgery? What kind of surgery?" she demanded.

"Annie, we're all upset and have to be patient until the surgeon gives us an update," Momma chimed in, obviously trying to take the heat off Becky.

"Why don't you join us?" I gestured to a chair beside me. It was clear she wasn't planning to leave until she got a report on Chase's condition. I didn't blame her, after all, she'd been married to him. Divorce didn't always mean you quit caring about the other person, did it? Certainly, it didn't in Annie's case.

So we waited.

Chapter Twenty-Seven

"MRS. BLACKBURN?" THE woman at the desk called to Becky.

"Yes?" Both Becky and Annie answered simultaneously.

"Y'all can go on up to the third-floor surgical waiting area."

Our small group moved en masse to the elevators after thanking the woman bearing directions.

We rode up to the third floor and stepped out before the elevator doors had opened completely. I was just as freaked out about his being in surgery as Becky, but he was her son and I was—well, I wasn't quite sure what I was besides the girl who was crazy about her son.

I spotted a sign with arrows pointing to the Surgical ICU Waiting Area. It was a quiet, carpeted area, where people spoke in hushed tones and the décor was tastefully appointed in pale blues and cream. Such a contrast from the loud, injured mess of the emergency department.

I figured the ER was the first point of contact, before the blood was squelched, before emotions were calmed, and before folks knew if it was going to be okay. Maybe the farther we moved into the depths of the hospital, the more information about a loved one's condition was processed.

Even if the news was bad, at least by then, it gave us a chance to calm down and for the bleeding to slow or stop.

There wasn't any insulation in the ER. The floors were tiled, lacking any softness, and the big room with all the hurt people butted right up to the outside where the bad things had happened. The cries echoed with nothing to absorb them. The entire place was like an exposed nerve.

Here, the décor was more tasteful, and there was more protection against the pain. Rugs, draperies, and soft music. Art. It was all intentional.

Becky spoke with the male attendant at the desk, who pointed to a carpeted waiting area with cushioned chairs and lamp lighting.

"He's checking with the surgical team for an update on Chase's condition," Becky said. We found a comfortable spot in the corner of the small area. A man, who appeared to be about my age, sat beside a little boy who might have been five or six. The man glanced up briefly and offered up a half-smile to the newcomers. Worry lines were etched into his forehead and around his mouth. The child bounced in his seat as he played a game on an electronic tablet, seemingly oblivious to the tension around him.

I wondered if his wife was in surgery. His mom?

"Ms. Blackburn?" A tall, elegant black woman in scrubs with a mask pulled down around her neck addressed the room almost immediately. She would have fit in on a runway in a fashion show in New York just as seamlessly. But she was using her powers for good, apparently.

Becky popped right back up from the chair she'd sat down in. "Yes. I'm Becky Blackburn, Chase's mother."

"Hi, I'm Dr. Casey. Can we speak privately?" she asked.

Becky turned and motioned for me to accompany her. I wondered how that made Annie feel but I didn't look to see her reaction.

Dr. Casey led us into a tiny consultation room and shut the door.

"I've scrubbed out for a few minutes to update you on your son's status. We're currently repairing a compound tibia fracture. Are you familiar with that terminology?" she asked.

We both nodded. I cringed inwardly, picturing it. Big bone sticking out. Blood. Ghastly. I'd watched a lot of medical dramas with Thelma.

"Chase is young and strong, and putting his leg back together should go smoothly, but he's lost a lot of blood from the injury, so we're working to transfuse him as quickly as we can, but only so much new blood can be introduced into the body at a time."

"What does that mean?" Becky asked.

"It means we can't work as quickly as we'd like."

"What are his other injuries?" Becky asked, her voice thready.

"He has multiple deep contusions, a fractured elbow, and several lacerations."

"No internal injuries?" I asked, clarifying.

"We're hoping not," she said. "We're going to do a high-resolution doppler ultrasound of his chest and abdomen before he comes out of anesthesia."

Becky's lip quivered, and her posture slumped just a little at hearing the extent of Chase's injuries. "When can we see him?" she asked.

"Once he's out of recovery and in the ICU, you'll have limited visitation. He's going to be only semi-conscious for several days, as we're going to try and control his pain that way, so it's unlikely he'll remember your being here. But as soon as he's awake, you'll have more access. Plan for him to be in intensive care for the better part of the week because of the leg break."

"Should I donate blood? Anything? What can I do?" I asked, hating the helplessness that surrounded us.

"A blood drive here in his hometown would be very helpful. He's going to require a lot of blood products, such as plasma and clotting factors throughout his recovery. It will also assist with the supply and expenses."

"Okay. We can get that started immediately. You know he's the sheriff of Moonshine?" Becky informed the doctor.

She nodded and smiled unexpectedly. "I love this town. We have a cabin on the lake here, and we go in the summers and on holidays when I can get time off, and I've met Chase before on a trip into town. I promise you, Ms. Blackburn, we're doing everything we can to help him recover as quickly as possible." The surgeon then turned to me. "You look very familiar, have we met?"

"I'm Sadie Brubaker." That's all I had. I couldn't even say I was Chase's girlfriend.

"Chase is very fond of Sadie," Becky supplied in the awkward moment. She added, "Sadie has been on the news lately. She was missing from Moonshine for a long time and has just come home. You might have seen it on TV or read about it someplace."

The doctor's eyes widened. "Oh, yes. I did hear about

your situation. Well, welcome home, Sadie. I'm so happy to hear that you're back safely. Such a fascinating story you've lived. Of course, I'm sure not all of it was fascinating to you. But it's very nice to meet you."

"Thank you. And thanks for taking good care of Chase. He's important to a lot of people."

She smiled again. "I'll get back to surgery now. We'll send someone to the waiting area periodically to update you on his progress. Make sure to give the charge nurse at the desk your contact information in case you leave the area."

We thanked her again.

"What a lovely woman," Becky commented after she'd gone.

"He certainly seems to be in good hands," I agreed.

"I guess we won't hear anything for a while. Do you want to go find the cafeteria and the coffee machine?" Becky asked. "I don't think I can sit still right now."

"Yes. Maybe we should give them both our numbers, just in case," I suggested as we moved toward the large C-shaped desk with several employees of all ages, both male and female, sporting combinations of pink or turquoise scrubs, white lab coats, and stethoscopes looped around their necks.

"Good idea. I wouldn't want to miss a text or call because my shitty provider doesn't get service in one corner or another of the hospital."

That was Becky, always real. "Hopefully one or the other of our shitty providers will have us covered wherever we go around here," I said.

"My phone has been buzzing nonstop with folks asking how Chase is doing. I didn't have anything to tell them until now. I guess I'd better get on top of answering them now," she said.

"Maybe you should put it in the newspaper if Jason will allow it," I suggested.

"That's an efficient idea. We'll tell Hannah to post information on the sheriff's office webpage and send her updates if there are any changes," Becky agreed.

Remaining optimistic made sense, of course, because the alternative was beyond unthinkable. But the gravity of the situation remained. Chase was in a very serious condition.

We reported to Momma and Annie exactly what the surgeon had communicated to us. Annie cried just a little and asked if there was anything she could do for Becky.

Momma decided to head home and let Daisy Mae out before she went to work and made us promise to text or call with any updates.

BECKY AND I dragged ourselves slowly toward the hospital cafeteria as directed by the signs along the way. The last thing I'd eaten was the mouthwatering crème brûlée from the dessert menu with Chase last night. It had a raspberry topping I'd wanted to lick the remnants of from the plate.

Fortunately, they'd just opened for the lunch crowd, so the food was fresh and hot, and smelled amazing, even for hospital fare. Becky said she wasn't very hungry and opted for a small sandwich and piece of fruit in the prepared section. I was ravenous, on the other hand, and took full advantage of the evening's special. I filled a Styrofoam

container with black-eyed peas, green beans, mashed potatoes, a large baked chicken breast, and a huge square of corn
bread.

We found a small table in the corner of the dining area
to eat and begin our planning. "Who should we call about
the blood drive?" I asked Becky.

"Call Hannah. She has Chase's contacts for everybody in
town. She's a whiz at getting things rolling when something
like this happens. Mention posting a basic version of Chase's
condition on the website too. We might just say he's having
surgery to fix his broken leg, and that he's got several other
serious injuries. Say he's stable but in serious condition. I'll
say the same for the newspaper story."

Posting such personal things seemed strange and inva-
sive, probably because I'd lived so many years in extreme
privacy with Thelma. But I guess since Chase was such a
public figure and the people in town cared so much about
his well-being, letting them know his condition made sense.
Otherwise, Becky might be inundated with half the town
inquiring about his status.

I ate quickly, surprised by my appetite, but still couldn't
begin to finish the huge plate of food, so I closed the container for later.

We made our phone calls, and each took about fifteen
minutes. But as I hung up with Hannah, another call came
through. "Hello?"

"Sadie?" It was Julie.

"Hi, Julie. How are you?" She was the last person I expected to hear from at that moment.

"Hi there. Everything okay?" she asked. I guess she could

hear something in my voice. We'd always known if something was off with the other.

I stood and walked a short distance from the table. Becky had made another call. "Um. No, honey. Chase was in a serious car accident last night. I'm at the hospital here in Moonshine with Becky. Mom was here earlier."

"Oh, no. Is he okay?" Julie's sweet, compassionate voice melted my brave front and I nearly choked on a sob. So unlike how functional and together I was only a few minutes ago.

"I-I don't know. I hope so."

"I'll be there as soon as I can. Where are you in the hospital?" Her tone announced that her coming wasn't up for discussion.

"The surgical ICU waiting area."

"Sit tight, Sadie. Do you need anything? Clothes? Money?" she asked.

"No. I've got some cash with me."

"Tell Mrs. Blackburn my thoughts and prayers are with her," Julie instructed.

"Okay. Julie, thanks for coming. I've missed you so much since you left."

"You too. I was planning to come back and visit tomorrow. That's why I was calling." Today was Saturday, so a Sunday dinner with Julie would have been nice. Momma would have been so happy to have her two girls together, despite our still-lingering and long-standing issues.

We hung up and relief washed over me. The idea that Julie would be beside me for the next several hours gave me comfort.

"Everything okay?" Becky asked.

I nodded. "My sister's driving up from Alpharetta."

"It will be nice to see Julie," Becky said.

"Yes. I've been missing her already." Funny how small talk became the norm while we avoided the obvious bigger, more terrible things looming over us. We clung on to the subject at hand instead of facing our fears.

This waiting was like a physical hunger that gnawed at my insides and could only be satiated with good news. Chase's smile flashed repeatedly in my mind's eye from last night. Our evening together had been almost perfect. *Almost* because I didn't know what perfect looked like. Maybe it had been perfect, or as much as something can be.

Looking back on events, I guess it was possible our memories, in general, sifted through and extracted the little details that made things imperfect or mundane. When I reflected on my time with Thelma, the years appeared now as series of smoothness and ease, though I know they weren't always. Of times spent together cooking, crafting, and watching television. While I hadn't been one to display overt emotions, there was an easy humor that ran between us, a certain overriding happy essence in our days.

Yes, she'd warned me to be careful. But *I* hadn't been afraid. Thelma's perspective likely would've looked completely different.

Even my questionable childhood in Moonshine hadn't been all bad. Now that the lion's share of memories had returned, I'd retained a fondness for my home, a place where I'd been beaten throughout several years of my childhood. I'd held on to love for my mother and sister and compartmentalized the terror and anger Hank had caused me.

Maybe the years of forgetting had given me a break from it, enough to not let those awful events ruin what was left of my life. A blessing?

These thoughts and ideas came to me as I waited to hear dire news about the man who had come into my life and introduced me to love. A kind of love and new set of emotions I'd never expected to experience. Such a gift after my bizarre life thus far. Chase had known me before. And he'd understood my journey to this point. It was a near-miracle that he'd still been willing to take a chance on my brokenness.

"Are you okay?" Becky asked.

"Yes. I was just thinking about Chase. And how he's been so amazing since I got here. He never treated me like a weirdo, or doubted my story," I said.

"Honey, he searched for you for years. It was as if the two of you already had a strong connection. He didn't want them to declare you dead. He fought against it. Even after his dad passed and he married, the search for you was a constant in his life. During the worst time."

"I had no idea." Chase had mentioned helping with the search, but not that he'd invested a part of himself in finding me over several years.

"When he went through the depression after his daddy died, it was about the same time they closed your case file. I can't help but think that the world giving up on finding you had something to do with his hopelessness. Not that he knew you well. It was just part of the whole, you know? Your showing up here was healing to him."

"Is that why he's dating me? Because I was his lost cause? Some weird savior-obsession thing?" The thought became words and spit out of my mouth.

Becky's eyes widened. "What? No! Of course not." She put an arm around my shoulders. "He was dumbfounded the day you arrived out of the clear blue. I could see it in his bearing—like a ghost had come back to haunt him. But the more time he spent with you, the real you, he became enchanted with how special you are."

"Oh."

"Sadie, you are a unique girl. We all recognize it. Chase is smitten with the person you are, not the *missing* person you've been all these years. Please don't confuse this. I'm sorry if I mucked up explaining that to you. I wanted you to understand that he never gave up on you."

That was the impression I'd gotten from him but Becky's describing what sounded like an obsession on Chase's part had thrown me for a loop.

If Chase had worked that hard for so long to find me and the town was aware of it, who else believed his interest in me might stem from a weird savior complex?

It still left me uncomfortable, though my gut told me otherwise and that I was overblowing the situation. I'd *felt* the electricity and emotion between us. But feelings, possibly mostly sexual, might not be trustworthy on my end.

"HOW IS HE?" Julie approached where we were sitting quietly. She appeared to be carrying luggage. She carried a giant bag slung over one shoulder and rolled another.

Before I could answer, she busied herself with unzipping the luggage, and pulled out a plate of sandwiches and brownies tucked inside a bag that would have done Mary Poppins proud. She immediately zeroed in on the little boy sitting with his dad in the waiting room, whose name she immediately learned was Jeffrey. Jeffrey was tucked under the waiting room's coffee table with a tiny ham sandwich, brownie, and water bottle, all neatly sitting on a paper towel before we had the chance to properly greet her.

I understood Julie's superpower then. It was being a mom. To everyone's children. I could only imagine what a great kid her Suzy must be. Or maybe a terrible one with all that *super-momming* going on all the time. Hopefully she'd harnessed her powers for good in her own home.

It made me that much more eager to meet my niece.

Julie had seemed so out of place and uncomfortable at Momma's house, but here she was a different person. Confident, as if this was part of her normal day. "How can I help?" she asked Becky and me.

"Thanks for coming so quickly. Unfortunately, there's nothing we can do now but wait."

"How long's he been in surgery?" she asked.

I looked at Becky for confirmation. "Three hours?"

Becky nodded. "Thereabouts."

They'd brought out a mountain of paperwork a little while ago for Becky to fill out and sign since she was Chase's next of kin. That had kept her distracted.

I'd made small talk with Jeffrey's dad, David, whose wife was back in surgery after complications from a colon cancer surgery. Her prognosis was somewhat grim, which he'd managed to keep from Jeffrey thus far.

A crappy day all around, to be sure.

"Sandwich? Brownie?" Julie offered to us. I declined, still so full after my large lunch from the cafeteria, the leftovers still sitting beside my things under the chair.

"Thank you, Julie." Becky took a large divine-smelling square from the smart, yellow plastic container that must have come from one of those suburban-Mom parties where everyone drank wine and ordered cool stuff from catalogs.

"Cute container," I remarked.

"Yes. It's part of a set."

Bingo.

Maybe I would be a mom one day and go to parties with other women. This occurred to me even as my situation mocked me. I'd not thought much over the years about becoming a mother. I mean, why would I? The possibility seemed ridiculous when I'd lived in such a limbo with no memory. I'd not dated besides a few surface flirtations in high school and college.

I'd understood that I wasn't normal and that I didn't have normal emotions, but did I want them? I'd been so shut down that I hadn't allowed myself to dream like that—about a family of my own. Children. A partner.

Now that I'd recovered a little of what I'd lost emotionally and most of my memories, I wondered now. It surprised me what I was feeling toward Chase right now. It wasn't just sexual. It felt real and strong, and the idea that he could be taken from my life in an instant terrified me.

"Sadie, are you okay?" Julie moved beside me and took

my hand.

I shrugged. "I was watching you and wondering if I would ever have a normal life after everything that's happened—after the way I've lived my adult life so far."

Julie gave me a sad smile. "I never thought things would get better after they took me away, and I'd lost you and Momma. I spent so much time grieving for y'all and for my home. My adoptive family was so patient with me and spent endless time and energy showing me that I could live again. It took years, Sadie. You have over half your life to live still. You can find love, have children if you want. I see you, my big-hearted sister, and you have more empathy and kindness inside than anybody I've ever met."

Her words gave me hope. I knew that what she said was true. I was kind and empathetic, and despite my odd past, I realized that I had the tools and needed to learn how to use them. "Thanks, Julie. I look back sometimes and feel like I spent all those years living in a vacuum. I realize that Thelma was trying to protect me from the memories and from Hank. But she kept me from facing my life."

We sat in silence for a while as I pondered how much my life had changed in a few months. And then again overnight. Thelma had passed away in mid-April, which seemed so long ago now. It was already midsummer here and I had memories of the heat as a child.

By the end of the school year when Julie and I were kids and then again when it started back in the fall, the elementary school we attended didn't have air-conditioning, and we came home wringing wet with sweat every day. Hank refused to let Momma run the air-conditioning during the day because of the electric bill. I guess running it while he was there for his comfort made more sense to him. So many of my memories now revolved around myself and Julie as sad little girls who'd deserved better.

So, my thoughts meandered until my phone buzzed and startled me out of them.

I excused myself from our stoic seating circle.

Chapter Twenty-Eight

"HELLO?" I DIDN'T recognize the number, but to be honest, I didn't know that many people.

"Sadie, this is Paul. I'm conferenced in with someone from Social Security. They are recording the call. Are you okay with that?"

"Yes, that's fine."

"They need to collect DNA samples from you and compare them to the evidence that was collected from the scene when you disappeared."

That made sense. I was ready to get my identity sorted once and for all. "Do you think there's anything left in evidence?"

"Seems there's baby teeth and a hairbrush, so hopefully that's all they'll need." I heard Paul pause. "Randi, they want to test Thelma Collins's DNA. If you have something that belonged to her, it would be helpful."

"Why do you need to test Thelma's DNA?" I asked, completely confused.

Nate Bascombe from the SSA answered, "We are working to figure out what happened to Randi Collins, Thelma's daughter. Since a death certificate was never filed, she is now considered a missing person. Matching Thelma's DNA to our missing person database might help put the pieces together."

"Thelma's personal items are still inside our home in Hickman. I haven't gone through everything yet and cleaned them out. I could have someone get what you need, I guess."

"We would prefer to accompany your representative inside to collect the samples ourselves," Bascombe replied. "We can't take the chance of contamination."

"Sadie has an attorney who oversees the property. Let me contact him and I'll give you a call back once I set it up. Does that work for you, Sadie?" Paul asked, but it was more of an order than a request.

"I would like to be in on that call too, Paul, if you don't mind." I asserted myself finally after they'd pushed and pulled me around long enough.

Paul must have recognized his bullyish tone and backed off a notch. "Of course, Sadie. I'll be in touch shortly."

"And I want to know if my calls are being monitored. Can we find this out?" I asked.

"Uh. Sure. I'm not aware of any monitoring, but I can check with our associates at the FBI. We've opened a joint file on your identity case. Let me reassure you that we're not investigating you for any wrongdoing in the disappearance of Randi Collins. That's a separate matter. We simply don't know what happened to her before you took over her identity, and since her mother is now deceased, we must investigate fully," the agent said.

"Thank you. I wish I'd known about Thelma's daughter before I became her, but I had no idea," I said.

"We believe that. But we do our due diligence to account

for citizens," he said.

"Nate, we're pushing hard to allow Sadie access to her funds and assets. It's become a hardship for her."

"I understand, and I apologize. As soon as her DNA comes back clean as Sadie Brubaker, and the reports from both psychologists are examined, and it's determined the amnesia was legitimate, and the fraudulent identity was unintentional, we should be able to lift the freeze. I just can't say how quickly that can all be accomplished."

This all sounded ridiculous and complicated, but at least things were moving forward.

"Okay, thanks, Nate. We'll be in touch once we work it all out. Will you send someone out to collect samples?" Paul asked.

"Yes. As soon as you determine where and when, we'll send someone from our lab in Atlanta."

"Got it. Sadie, is there anything else you want to ask?" Paul asked.

"No. But since we're being recorded, I want to say that if this is how you treat innocent people, I'd hate to see how you treat those who intentionally steal identities or break laws."

"Noted," Agent Bascombe replied, but there was a tiny bit of humor in his tone. "I'll let you confer with your attorney, Sadie. Nice speaking with you. Hopefully we can clear this up soon."

"Thanks," I said.

There was a click that I assumed meant that call was disconnected.

"Sadie?" It was Paul.

"I'm here."

"Sorry about that. Now that we're all on the same page, I'll contact Whitaker in Hickman. If he's working with us officially, they can't record his phone calls with me due to client confidentiality."

"Thanks."

"Okay. Hey, I tried to call the sheriff earlier and got his voicemail. Have you heard from him?" Paul asked.

As I REJOINED the others, I noticed that Julie had moved close to Becky, and they were speaking in hushed tones. Becky's shoulders had relaxed, and she appeared to have lost some of her tension. Julie's other superpower seemed to be putting others at ease like she'd done a few minutes ago with me. Her calming effect on the room when she'd entered bearing food earlier had been palpable.

I wondered at her peaceful nature after the hell she'd endured as a child coming from an obviously unpeaceful environment. She'd confessed her anger and resentment at having been torn from her home and family, and the struggle she'd had adjusting for years. But watching her now, it was hard to reconcile her calm with that troubled child.

I guess the same could be said about me if somebody assessed my behavior from the outside. Admittedly, I'd not had enough time to reacquaint with my sister. She was still Julie, but so much more polished than the little girl in the raggedy clothes who hung on my every word and giggled under the covers at night. I'd missed her since we'd parted a couple weeks ago, but I'd wanted to give her space to adjust to my return and all the emotions toward Momma, and Hank, and coming back to Moonshine.

Even when I hadn't remembered her, while I'd been almost a thousand miles from home, I believe I'd missed her. There had been an emptiness, a void where somebody should have been. I believe it was Julie I'd longed for. Thelma had become my family, but still…

"Everything okay?" Julie asked as I sat down in the chair beside her.

"My attorney and the Social Security agent asking for DNA, from me and from Thelma."

"Wow. That's a big ask," Becky said. She'd been in the loop on everything that had gone down with my situation since I'd rolled into town, so I felt comfortable sharing information with her. I guess our new friend, David, was likely to overhear some of it too, but it wasn't to be helped in such a tight space.

"What do they hope to find out from Thelma's DNA?" Julie asked. "And how will they get it?"

I shared most of our conversation with them, as quietly as possible.

"Hopefully you'll get your life back and be able to figure out your options," Julie said.

I nodded. What were my options? Would I stay here? Move in with Momma? For how long? Take care of Chase when he got out of the hospital, or help Becky? Continue to run my business and put off making any new decisions about the house in Hickman? Move back to Hickman if—if… I couldn't think about anything beyond Chase being okay.

"Will you live in Moonshine?" Julie asked, her expression hopeful.

"I…just don't know what's going to happen. I'm in a weird place right now." I lowered my head, unable to meet their eyes. I saw expectation in them. Becky hoped things would work out between Chase and me, and Julie couldn't bear the thought that I might leave again.

I agreed with them both. But the idea that I wouldn't ever return to the house Thelma and I shared for so many years in Hickman crushed me. And it was too far to maintain from across the country long term. My roots were growing deeper and stronger here every day with every memory, both good and bad, so to say I was torn would be a massive understatement.

To lose what remained of my life with Thelma would break my heart. It wasn't so much the things, but our environment together. Our life space. It would be like erasing important and precious time. When I'd left Hickman, it had only been a few weeks since her death, and things had happened so quickly once I'd gotten to Moonshine. Once my memory began to return, I was so distracted that it had allowed me to push my grief into an isolated corner.

No, Thelma shouldn't have kept me from my life in Moonshine and the people who loved me. But she'd been so good to me, always encouraging, and never demanding that I try to retrieve painful memories. I wonder now that those memories were back what she might've known about my past. It was still a mystery, but somewhere deep down, I still trusted that she had no ill intentions. There must've been a reason she'd done it.

I'd compartmentalized our life together since Thelma had passed and I'd found out so many confusing things about our time together. When I wasn't thinking about her specifically, it was like I'd left Thelma safe and sound in the house in Hickman with all her things. In her garden, with her clothes, her kitchen where she'd cooked our meals. In front of our television where we still had shows and movies recorded that we'd never watched together. That's where I still pictured her waiting for me. It's how I coped most of the time. Of course I understood she was gone, but I pretended with myself when it got hard.

And I had people here. I had a mother and a sister, and Chase had been by my side from the moment my foot hit the pavement in the Moonshine town square. These people were alive. But Thelma wasn't back at the house in Hickman, and my fear was that when I returned, I would realize it. For real.

Sitting around, even with such great company, was crazy making, so I checked the time and took a chance that Jenny might be finished for the day or between patients. We'd spoken less lately, but I knew she was eager to know what was happening here with me. And since there was a lot right now to catch up on, it might be beneficial to get her opinion on the DNA situation, in addition to the rest.

"I'm going to give Jenny a quick call while we're waiting," I said to Becky and Julie. They were still chatting quietly, so they looked up and smiled. "I'll be just over there." I pointed.

I found a quiet, unoccupied spot down the hall with a

couple chairs. Hopefully, no one would join me. These little nooks proved useful for snatches of privacy in a busy hospital. My stomach fluttered as I dialed.

"Well hello, stranger. Any news on the handsome sheriff?"

I bit my lip, literally and tried not to cry. But of course, I did, a lot. I'd done the same thing right after Thelma died while I waited for the ambulance. I told her what happened to Chase and was thankful for the box of tissues on the small table beside my chair.

Jenny had been my friend and confidante for such a long time, and my trust in her was complete. She'd always kept my best interests in her heart.

"You have to believe Chase is going to recover, Randi. I know it's hard, but he needs your faith in him right now." Her words were strong and backed with love.

It was weird to hear her call me Randi. Here, no one really had since my arrival. "Thanks. I needed to hear that. It's just a powerless feeling, this waiting."

"I know. I hate to ask, but how's your identity quest going?" she asked.

"I just a got a call this morning asking for DNA."

I described the situation as it had been laid out for me by the government agents.

"So you have to prove you're you, and prove Thelma was Thelma, and Thelma has to posthumously prove that her Randi was Randi so they can figure out what happened to her?" Jenny asked.

"Something like that. They want to tie up all the loose ends with a report, including the psychologist's reports that say I really did lose my memory the night I left Moonshine and all the years until I came back."

"That shouldn't be hard to convince them of. I also have the notes ready to send from when we did the hypnotherapy several years ago that might help. I outlined your clinical situation before our sessions. It's solid irrefutable documentation. You had nothing to gain by pretending for thirteen years," Jenny said.

"I still have a strange feeling that I'm missing a big piece of this puzzle though. There are still several gaps in my memory and some things that don't make sense. I'm supposed to meet with Bree, the psychologist, here again in a few days. She did some hypnosis and brought back a few things that helped some of it fall into place. I can feel how everything has loosened up and is waiting to return. It's so close I can almost touch it."

"Sometimes we miss what's right in front of us. It's our humanness," Jenny said.

"Is there something I don't want to see?" I asked. Maybe my brain continued to protect me from another truth, though I couldn't imagine anything worse than what Hank had put our family through over time.

"You'll get to it soon, I feel certain. Moonshine has softened you up. Missing information has a way of revealing itself. I know that sounds funny in your case because it's taken so long, but your being back home among the people who love you has changed you."

"It has, Jenny. The two of me are merging. It's like two different worlds and lives coming together. Randi, the adult me, knew nothing of Sadie, the child. Randi protected that child and her experiences until I could handle them again—I'm sure of it."

"That's a lovely way to comprehend what's happened. And it makes sense," Jenny agreed.

"Thanks for letting me unload on you," I said.

"Hey, it's my pleasure. I miss you." I could hear a sadness in Jenny's tone.

"I miss you too. You should come to visit as soon as things calm down. I think you would like it here." And I did. I could see Jenny at home with this town and its people.

"You never know when I might show up. And let me know if you need any help on this end with anything. Take care and keep me posted on Chase's condition. I'm thinking good thoughts over here."

As I spoke with Jenny, my life in Hickman flashed within my mind, as clear as flipping through a photo album. The house, the garden, and times with Thelma and Jenny. It was hard to believe I'd lived so many years away from here without a clue. From my real home.

As I made my way back to the waiting area, I wondered what was going through Chase's mind, if he was experiencing pain, worry, or if he was just blessedly asleep. Surely they would let us see him soon.

❧

CHASE WAS IN jail. No, he was underground. But there were sounds. Beeps and buzzers. Sometimes it was dark, but then there were flashes of bright light. And pain. *Holy Hell!* He'd been kidnapped, yes, that was it. They were torturing him.

He was cold, freezing, and his teeth chattered. Then, the searing, knives in his leg, belly, and arm. Who was he kidding—he hurt all over. He wanted to tell what he knew, but this wasn't an interrogation, it was only torture.

For a little while the sounds and the pain calmed and muted. Maybe he'd passed out. But then, it began again. He tried to get up, to escape, but he was tied down, arms and legs. No sound came when he screamed. His mouth had cotton inside, or something. How could he endure this much longer? Should he call someone? Did he have his cell phone with him, or did they take it when they captured him? If he could only figure out a way to let them know where he was. Becky would call in the cavalry and then, once he was home, Sadie would marry him.

Sadie. She was home, wasn't she? And she loved him. Didn't she? He had to find a way back to her.

"Chase? We need you to calm down now. We've had to put restraints on you since you've just had surgery. Can you open your eyes for me?"

Chase heard his name and the voice that penetrated wasn't Sadie's. He moved his dried-out lips, trying to speak.

"What's he saying?" he heard a male voice ask.

"Chase, you're waking up from anesthesia now. Open your eyes. You're safe. You had a car accident and broke your leg."

He heard them but didn't quite understand. Maybe they would take him to Sadie. She would help him. He took a breath and exhaled her name: "Zhaaa—dee."

Wait, that didn't sound right.

"What's that, Chase? Are you asking for something,

someone?"

He tried again: "Shaa—dee." Better, to his ears.

"I think he might have said Sadie. You know, the Brubaker gal who got kidnapped?"

Chase grinned. "Shaa—dee."

"Bingo. Does anyone know if she's here?" the voice asked. "Chase, I'm Dr. Casey. We just fixed up your leg and took out your spleen, so you might be a little uncomfortable as you wake up more fully. Don't worry, we've got some good pain meds coming your way as soon as we check you out."

"She's here with his mother in the waiting area. Do think we should bring them back yet? I mean, he's not quite coherent and he's still restrained."

"I think it would go a long way to assist in his recovery at this point," the sage Dr. Casey asserted.

Chase tried to nod at her wisdom, but it caused such pain in his head. He whispered, "Shaa—dee," again.

Chase tried to relax, despite the pain still stabbing his left shin, belly, and right arm. *What the devil?* Car crash, surgery they'd said. At least he wasn't chained in a dungeon someplace awaiting more brutal torture at the hands of some cartoonish evil madman.

"Chase, someone has gone to get Sadie and your mother. They've been waiting to see you. Can you open your eyes?"

Weren't they open? He saw colors, but no people, only heard them. Did they have his lids taped shut? Geez, they weighed a ton. Finally, after several tries, he managed to open his left eye just a little. The right one must have something heavy sitting on top of it.

A group he didn't recognize was gathered in a semicircle above him.

"That's great, Chase," a woman's voice encouraged him, and as a reward, she shined a light directly into his opened eye, which caused him to groan loudly. "Sorry about that. Just checking your pupil dilation. Can you manage the other eye yet?"

And have her do that again? No thank you.

"Aw, c'mon. You can do it," the woman encouraged. She was persistent—he would give her that.

Just as the right lid began to cooperate, he heard a familiar voice, causing both his eyes to pop open.

"Chase? It's Momma, honey. I'm here. Oh, my love, you gave us a scare." She took his hand gently.

A calm settled in his chest. If his momma was here, no captors stood a chance. He tried to smile, but his mouth worked about as well as his eyes right now. Momma's eyes were red, like she'd been crying. Momma never cried.

Then he saw her, his Sadie. And he managed, "Sha-dee."

"Hi there," she whispered, then leaned close and kissed him on his cheek. He smelled shampoo and soap, and whatever that irresistible scent was that signaled to his soul whenever she was near.

"He's still coming out of the anesthesia and his jaw is swollen and bruised but not broken, so his speech will improve in the coming hours and days," the doctor said to explain his poor language skills.

He tried an eye-roll that caused laughter all around but cost him a shooting pain in his right temple. Why were they laughing?

"I'll leave you to visit for a few minutes while he contin-ues to wake up fully but then we'll give him a hit of morphine to help with the pain and let him rest," the doctor said.

Chase was uncertain at this point whether he wanted the company of his most beloved or morphine. He leaned strongly toward morphine.

Chapter Twenty-Nine

TWO WEEKS PASSED in a blur of sleepless worry. I spent every possible moment at the hospital with Chase but tried not to overstep when it came to Becky's need to mother him back to health.

I'd given my samples of DNA to the lab technicians who'd come around to collect them as scheduled. Momma had weirdly kept some items of mine from my childhood, which indeed had included a hairbrush and a pillowcase, of all things. Anyway, the lab folks determined they'd collected plenty of *before* samples to compare with the current ones in addition to comparing Momma's DNA to mine.

Mr. Whitaker was officially on the case with Paul Bristol's office in Atlanta. And he took his job quite seriously. It seemed that protecting Thelma's reputation and memory became his top priority. "I'm personally meeting the lab technicians at the house tomorrow to supervise the gathering of possible DNA from Thelma's things."

But the stickiness of gathering DNA, especially from someone who wasn't alive, and who couldn't speak for herself, and answer questions somehow seemed wrong. Thelma had been an incredibly private person, and I envisioned the interlopers invading Thelma's and my house, digging through her most personal items. My stomach hurt and I wanted to punch someone as I thought about it.

"Thank you, Mr. Whitaker, for being there. I hate the idea that strangers will be inside our home, going through Thelma's things. I'm glad to know you'll be there with them to keep a close eye on things."

"You bet I will, darling girl. I got to know Thelma well enough to know how important her privacy was and how much she'd have resented this kind of invasion."

"I couldn't have said it better. This would have been her worst nightmare," I agreed.

"I plan to photograph and video everything they do as the family's representative."

"That's great, thanks."

We hung up and I felt a little better knowing someone Thelma trusted would be there to make sure the awful process would be completed with a minimum of upset to our home.

The agents promised to fast-track the DNA results, whatever that meant.

I'd just left Daisy Mae at home with Momma and was on my way back to the hospital when Jenny's number popped up on my phone screen.

"Hi there." We'd spoken more recently since our tearful conversation the day after Chase's accident.

"Are you up for a visitor?" she asked.

"I'm headed to the hospital to check in on Chase right now. Who's visiting?" I asked, uncertain as to whom she referred.

"I know this isn't likely the best of times, but my schedule was light and none of my patients seemed to be in immediate crisis—"

"You mean—you're coming here?" I nearly shrieked, but in a good way.

"The truth is, I *am* here. I flew into Atlanta a couple hours ago and drove on up. I'm in the middle of this pretty little town. You didn't tell me it was so adorable."

"Oh, my gosh. I'm headed into town now. Where are you?" I asked her, barely able to control my delight.

"I'm parked outside the sheriff's office."

That made me smile, thinking about the day I arrived here and parked near the exact same spot. "I'll be there in five minutes." I couldn't believe Jenny had come all this way.

"I can't wait." Jenny sounded excited, almost as much as me.

I worked to keep my speed down, which I'd become far more aware of since Chase's accident. The drive to town seemed to take forever, instead of the normal few minutes.

As I pulled around the square, I noticed a Mustang GT sitting just outside Chase's office. I lucked out finding a spot in front of the B&B across the square. Summer tourist season was in full swing, and Moonshine blossomed with music, food, and arts of every kind. The air was heavy and humid, and extremely hot this time of day. I could only imagine Jenny's first impression of the town.

The shops were overflowing with handmade gifts, candles, and textiles, and the restaurants and cafés lined the square, their tables and umbrellas bright and welcoming guests to sit under the shade and order a cool drink.

By the time I'd parked and moved toward her car, Jenny

had met me halfway. "You look wonderful. Oh, look at your hair!"

She grabbed me up in a big hug. We held on for a minute. "I'm so happy you came. I've missed you," I said.

Jenny wore a wide-brimmed straw hat. "Look at this place. Who knew? But it's so hot!"

I nodded. Georgia heat wasn't the kind one became accustomed to. There wasn't a way to do that. "Yes, it's hot. I remember this heat from my childhood. Let's grab a sweet tea."

Jenny laughed. "Oh, you've gone and gotten all Southern on me, haven't you?"

I hadn't thought about it. Sweet tea was a thing from my childhood that came back like a reflex. "I have to admit there are some things a body never forgets."

Jenny held her hands up. "I'll pass, but a lemonade sounds nice."

"Perfect." We stepped inside the ice cream shop, and I greeted the owner, Patty.

"Hey there, Sadie, you want the usual?" she asked.

I nodded. "Thanks, Patty."

A few other locals nodded toward us and said hello to me. We sat down at a tiny table in the corner.

"You've taken to this place like a duck to water."

That wasn't a question. "I guess so. I'm home here."

Jenny smiled. "I had to come and see this for myself. This town that has brought you such peace."

"I don't know about peace. There's a lot here that still isn't so peaceful," I reminded her.

As if right on cue, Jason and Annie Weston entered.

I sank down in my chair, wishing myself instantly invisible.

"What is it?" Jenny asked and followed my gaze. "Who are they?"

"Chase's ex, and the mayor who married her. Long story," I muttered.

Just then, Annie spotted me and came over. I didn't believe in fakeness at all, but I didn't have much choice in this situation. Making nice here was pretty much the only way to behave.

"Hey there, Sadie. How's Chase? I heard he's going home soon."

I nodded. "Yes, he's doing much better."

Jason made his way over with two mint chocolate chip cones and handed one to Annie.

"Hey, tell Chase I'm glad he's improving."

I didn't know how to take that. I'd never seen Jason behave in what seemed like a conciliatory way.

"I'll let him know you send your best wishes," I said.

"Hi, I'm Jenny." Jenny stuck out her hand. "Just got in from Hickman, Nebraska."

Annie responded in kind. "Annie Weston. And this is my husband, Jason."

"Sorry, I was getting around to it." I turned a little pink. Jenny wanted in here and wasn't waiting on me to do the honors, apparently.

"So, Jenny, you've known our Sadie while she didn't know who she was. That's so interesting," Jason said.

"Yes, for many years. I came here to see her in her natural habitat," Jenny said, seriously eyeballing the mayor.

"Cute town you've got here."

"We think so," he replied.

"Listen, Sadie, I think it's time we buried the hatchet, and not in Chase's head, if you know what I'm saying," Jason directed his words to me.

My surprise must have shown.

"His near-death experience has made me realize I prefer our fair town with him in it than without. So, let's have a cease-fire and behave like adults moving forward, okay?"

I stared hard at him, then at Annie, who appeared just as stunned as me. "I'll pass it on to Chase, but it sounds like the two of you might need to speak in person about something this long-standing and important. Just my thought."

Jason nodded. "When he's up to it, we'll plan a dinner. How's that?" he suggested.

"Yes," Annie agreed, recovering her wits. "You should both come and have dinner at our house. This is long overdue." Her surprise had turned to relief if I was reading her body language and expression correctly.

"This sounds better than warfare," I said. "I'll let Chase know."

When they retreated, found a table, and sat down, I stared after them, open-mouthed. "We can take these to go if you want to," Jenny said.

I nodded.

"So, I take it that was unexpected?"

I nodded, still not trusting myself to comment on what just happened. In fact, I decided to think on it before discussing it further.

We stood and exited the shop and were instantly enveloped by the oppressive heat. I found my voice then. "I want you to meet Chase," I said. "I was headed to see him when you called."

"I don't want to intrude. I can check in to the bed-and-breakfast while you visit."

"No way. They're going to let him come home in a day or two. He's doing better now. We had a tough week after his accident, but he's beginning to heal."

Now, the memories of this hospital were replaced with visiting Chase as he improved, minus the ones from the first few days of hell right after his accident. I guess most memories of hospitals weren't so great for people.

"I'm thrilled to hear he's doing well. How are the two of you as a couple?" she asked.

I thought about that. "Honestly, he's had such traumatic injuries that I've been switching shifts with his mother, Becky, and most of the time when I've been here he's slept." I'd taken my laptop with me and worked at the tiny desk in Chase's room a lot of the time to catch up with my clients. It figured that my services were in higher demand now that I was distracted with so many other things.

"Do you love him?" she asked.

"I think so. I can't see living here without him in my life. So, I guess so." We'd had so little time together before the accident and almost none since. "I'm crazy about him, and I guess I just hope when he's home and feeling better, he feels the same."

"Look at you, Randi—I mean Sadie. How could he not?"

I didn't have an answer for that. Jenny got in the passenger's side of the Jeep. I'd taken off the top, so the breeze whipped through as we drove. Jenny held her hat on.

"I freaking love this place." Jenny grinned all the way to the hospital as we passed the local attractions. I remember how picturesque it was the first time I drove through town. Like a set from a Hallmark or Lifetime movie.

"I know. It's got a great vibe, doesn't it?"

"Totally. So, I'd love to meet with the psychologist you've been seeing since our reports are an important sticking point for them to let you off the hook if that's okay with you," Jenny said.

"I think it's a great idea. In fact, I'm scheduled to see Bree tomorrow for our last session before she completes her report. You should come along. There's nothing I'm sharing with her that you haven't already heard, unless something new pops up with my memory, which can always happen."

This would be our third session, and the sense that the missing things were on the verge of flooding back continued, though nothing new had come to me last time.

Jenny nodded. "Great. I've brought my notes along to share as well. I didn't feel comfortable sending them to anyone I hadn't met. And by law, they must be sent through a secure server or email, so regular personal email won't work."

"What about Bev's notes?" I'd asked Jenny to inquire if the records from my initial therapist, Bev, were still stored someplace and might be retrieved.

She shook her head. "They were destroyed several years ago, unfortunately, according to the family."

I'd done some research and learned that Nebraska law

required they be kept for eight years after a patient stopped seeing the therapist. Now that Bev had been deceased for such a long time, I'd figured it was unlikely we would be able to get them, but it had been worth a try because Bev's records would have been the most legitimate way to prove my memory loss to the government.

We pulled into the hospital lot just as Becky was exiting the front door. "Hi, Becky, everything okay?" I asked.

"Oh, hi, Sadie. He's getting ornery, and he needs a shave." She laughed.

"Becky, this is my dearest friend, Jenny. She just arrived from Hickman."

Becky grinned at Jenny and pulled her into a bear hug. "I've heard so much about you, darlin'! Welcome to Moonshine. I wish we were in a better position to give you a proper introduction to our community, but I guess you've heard about our recent troubles around here."

"Yes. Sorry about showing up with no notice but I hope my coming here will be helpful to Ra—Sadie."

"From what she's told me about the two of you, I imagine your coming here will be good for her," Becky said. "Oh, Sadie, they may let him out today. I'm headed over to his place to make sure things are ready. He refuses to let me take care of him at my house."

I nodded. "Wow. I thought it would be early next week. Is there anything I can do?" I asked.

"Nope. You just pop in and let him see your pretty face. That always cheers him up. I know getting out of the hospital will do him the most good."

"Okay. Thanks, Becky."

"See you girls later," she said.

"Bye. Nice to meet you, Becky," Jenny said.

Becky waved as she headed toward her truck.

"She's his mom?" Jenny asked. "Wow."

"Yes, she's impressive."

We continued inside the hospital and headed for the elevators. I waved, spoke to, and nodded at several staff members on the way upstairs as I encountered folks I knew.

I stopped by the nurses' station briefly to inquire about Chase's release.

"Oh, hey there, Sadie. Did you see Becky? She just left here." George, the charge nurse sat in front of his computer, typing. "They're getting his release paperwork together. Good thing too because he's a grumpy goat." George made a face.

"Uh-oh. I hope he hasn't given anyone too hard a time this morning," I said.

"Just the usual grumbles about everybody seeing his ass." George snorted a laugh. "Hey there, sweetie, I'm George." He waved to Jenny, who was standing beside me, taking it all in.

"I'm Jenny, nice to meet you." She waved from the other side of the counter. "Just in from Nebraska."

"Girl, that's a long way from Georgia. Either you're family or a *very* good friend."

"She's my very best friend," I told George.

"Welcome to hell, honey. It's so hot around here it would make the devil himself beg for mercy." George's tone was droll, but his eyes twinkled.

"Yes. I've already noticed I'm not in the Midwest anymore," Jenny agreed. "But so far, I've hardly noticed the heat because this town is so adorable."

George grinned at her then. "Yes, we are adorable. Thanks for noticing."

"Is Chase decent for visitors?" I asked.

"Sheriff has a cute ass. Sure you don't want to take your chances and pop in?" George winked. "Just kidding, girl. I'll check."

Jenny choked on her laughter. I rolled my eyes. "People are more likely to say what they mean here. Just so you know."

"I noticed. I like it."

"He's just had a shave and shower. Lunch is being served now if y'all want a tray, just let somebody know."

"Thanks, George."

"Sure, honey."

We moved down the hallway past a couple of gowned patients doing the same IV-pole shuffle poor Chase had been for the past two weeks. Ever since they'd gotten him up and walking after surgery. Well, not exactly walking. More like knee-scooter and wheelchair-rolling. That compound fracture of the lower big bone in his leg was no joke and still had a ways to go. But it had been important that he move around as much as possible, which had been painful and challenging, considering he also had a broken arm.

I knocked softly on his door before pushing it open. "Hello?" I singsonged softly in case he'd gotten back in bed and fallen asleep.

"Sadie?"

"Hey there. I brought a friend with me." He was in bed,

but had his bad leg stretched out in front of him and elevated. His right arm hung in a sling and was casted. The bruises on his face were still pretty dark but had just begun to yellow around the edges. Honestly, he still looked pretty rough. But to me, so handsome.

"Oh, hi." He tried to sit up taller.

"No, don't get up on my account," Jenny put her hands out as if to keep him down.

"Chase, this is Jenny. She flew in from Hickman to surprise me, and to bring me the notes from those hypnotherapy sessions I told you about."

Chase grinned, despite his bruising and swelling. "It's great to finally meet you, Jenny. Sorry I'm not in a better state."

"Are you kidding? I'm thrilled to be here and meet you. Sadie has been giving me a play-by-play over the phone since I watched her drive away three months ago. She's been worried sick about you."

I blushed then.

"Well, I know Sadie's missed you, Jenny," Chase said.

"Hey, I hear you might actually get sprung from here today," I said.

Chase grinned at me. My heart went pitty-pat. "I'm trying not to get too excited. The wheels move slowly sometimes."

"Ah, c'mon, you're the law around here. Surely, you can get some results," I teased.

"They like to remind me my badge has no authority here." He made a face.

"Are you sure you're ready to be home alone?" I asked.

"Ha. Do you think my mother will allow me to be alone for much of the time? According to the doctors, they're sending a home care nurse three times a week for wound care and bathing. But my plan is to go back to work as soon as possible."

"I hope you won't try to push yourself too hard too soon. I know you're still in a lot of pain sometimes," I said, trying not to sound naggy. But I did worry about Chase. He wanted to take care of his town and not leave his job to Hannah and the deputies.

Chase sighed. "I'll be fine. Better as soon as I can get back to some kind of normal and sleep in my bed and recliner. I know y'all are all worried, but I'm gonna be okay."

"I'm just glad you're awake and talking finally. It seemed like you slept until just a few days ago. Or maybe you just always seemed to sleep while I was here." My eyes teared up unexpectedly.

"Now, stop that. No crying. They kept me so drugged up after surgery I could hardly stay awake. And yes, I get tired easily and still hurt—a lot. But things are improving. Going home will be hard, but I can't get back to normal until I feel normal."

"I know. I'm happy you're going home. I'm just a worried mother hen," I said.

"There's nothing motherly about you." He winked then.

I blushed again. He'd not said or done anything remotely flirty since his accident and I hadn't either, so it surprised me a little. And with Jenny here, especially.

"Should I give you some privacy?" Jenny laughed.

"Sadly, I'm a man who's been reduced to sponge baths

by women named Marguerite and Hazel, who were friends of my grandmother."

We all giggled at that.

***

AS CHASE EYED Sadie, he noticed a worried expression on her face. During his time in the hospital, she'd kept busy working on her computer while he mostly slept. She appeared anxious and edgy now. He wondered what was up. Her friend Jenny seemed nice, and he didn't get the impression her arrival had anything to do with Sadie's upset.

Was it his impending discharge that had her stirred up? Had anything else happened that he was unaware of? He knew she was waiting for DNA results, as she'd told him about that, and agents collecting Thelma's samples.

He wished they were alone so he could ask what her deal was.

Certainly, he was antsy to get back to the office and take back the job of running the county. And he did have a few concerns that he might not yet be physically up to the challenge.

Between medication-induced naps, Chase had been taking calls from the office since a week after surgery and giving orders to his staff. Hannah had prudently determined if he'd been on pain meds at the time, and whether or not that advice had been solid. Fortunately, nothing of grave importance had gone down in his absence. Cows had gotten out on the south highway and traffic had to be controlled for a couple hours. And there'd been a two-car crash up the mountain when it had rained last week requiring some assistance from the sheriff's department. Nothing the deputies couldn't handle.

Hannah fielded the calls from citizens with varied complaints that usually necessitated little more than her using her magical skills of diplomacy and kindness to smooth ruffled feathers between two parties. She promised to loop him in on anything that truly required his decision-making authority.

Sadie and Jenny were quietly discussing something as Sadie pointed out the window of his hospital room. Chase hoped she wasn't having second thoughts about the two of them beginning a relationship, because he was more convinced than ever that he wanted to be with her. Was that why she seemed bothered? Was she reconsidering it now that he would be available? Did she feel like she owed him something while he'd been laid up in the hospital convalescing?

"Here's your lunch, Sheriff." A smiling staff member entered carrying a covered plate and placed it on his rolling tray. His stomach rumbled at the smell. The food here was pretty good, aside from a few oddball items he'd requested they not bring him.

The women turned and greeted the food-bearing staff member, who smiled and said, "Hi, ladies, y'all want some lunch with this handsome guy?"

"Oh, no thanks, Brenda. My friend Jenny and I will leave him to eat in peace and head into town to the diner. But thanks."

"Nice to meet you, Jenny. See y'all later," Brenda said

and moved on with her lunch bearing.

Chase enjoyed how Sadie had gotten to know almost everyone in town, whether she'd known them before, remembered them, or not. Everyone seemed to love her.

"Well, this handsome sheriff is hungry, so I hope you don't mind if I eat in front of you," he said, pulling the top off his plate.

"Can I get you anything else before we head over to the diner?" Sadie asked.

"No, I've got all I need. They take good care of me at mealtime."

"It was great to meet you, Chase. I'm sure I'll see you again before I leave town." Jenny shook his good hand.

"Definitely, Jenny." Then he turned to Sadie. "Hey, don't feel like you have to babysit me while Jenny's in town. I'm fine, and you know Momma's got it all handled and then some."

She gave him a funny look and said, "I'll be back later, or I'll see you at home when you get there. You're not getting rid of me that easy, big guy." She was on the other side of the food tray and leaned forward and kissed him on his forehead, lingering a second. "Mmm. You smell good," she said.

He pulled her a little closer with his good arm and whispered, "You feel good."

She giggled then. And he had hope.

"All right, you two, I'd say get a room, but nah," Jenny said.

"See you later," Sadie said and waved, her sexy hair bouncing as she turned her head.

He guessed parts of him worked just fine.

Chapter Thirty

MAEVIS GOT TO us first at the diner. "Here you go. Sweet tea for my sweet pea. Extra lemon, just how you like it." Maevis grinned at me, showing her remaining teeth.

"Thanks, Maevis."

"What would your friend like to drink?" she asked.

"This is Jenny."

"Hi, Maevis. I'll have a lemonade. Thanks."

As soon as Maevis squeaked away, Myrtis approached, which caused Jenny to do a quick double take.

"Hi there, Sugar. Did that demon-sister of mine take care of y'all?" She winked at Jenny.

"Yes, ma'am, she did. Thanks," I said.

"Good gracious, they're identical," Jenny said, her expression showing wonder.

"Well, almost. There's the shoes, and one has a few more teeth. But pretty much," I agreed, not mentioning the heavier purple tone in Myrtis's hair.

"This *place*. I swear it's right out of a Southern comedy." Jenny wheezed laughter.

"It's entertaining on a good day, for sure," I agreed. "The sisters don't always get along so well."

"You really are Sadie Brubaker, aren't you?" she asked, but it wasn't a question. "I mean, she's you, and the Randi I knew has morphed into her and into this place. No offense, but you're a lot more fun these days."

"None taken. It's nice to let Sadie take over. I understand her and my sensible Randi parts still come in handy." I looked around the diner, filled with the lunchtime faces, many of whom I knew. Sure, some were tourists, but they were part of this place too. "I belong here, Jenny. It's my home now."

"Yes, it is. And as sad as that makes me, I'm so happy for you. And that *sheriff*. Could you have found anybody hotter?" she whispered loudly.

"I don't think I could have, honestly. He lights me up, I have to admit. And that was a real surprise. It wasn't something I expected to find anywhere. In fact, at my age, I doubted I ever would."

"Are you kidding, Sadie? You are a knockout. I've always known it, but you were so introverted, and Thelma kept you so sheltered that you didn't have much chance to meet anyone."

"I never cared to until now."

"Yeah. I hated that you felt you couldn't branch out socially. Thelma must've lived with the worry that somehow Hank would find you or that she would get busted for kidnapping a minor."

"I still don't quite understand it all. But I'm glad to be here now. It's right."

"Well, you're making up for lost time, girlfriend. And I wanted to tell you something about me too."

"What?" I asked. We'd focused so much on my life that Jenny hadn't recently discussed what was happening in her own sphere.

"I have a boyfriend," she announced, her face suffusing with color.

"Wait, when? How? You never said anything."

"Things have been pretty intense on your end, so I kept it on the down-low. We've been seeing each other since right after you left. I met him online."

"I'm so happy for you, Jenny. Wow, that's amazing. I feel like the worst friend ever. I haven't even asked how things were going for you." I couldn't have been more surprised, honestly. And thrilled for Jenny. I'd begun to feel guilty leaving her in Hickman on her own. She had a few friends, I knew, but not so many.

"Stop. You're forgiven. Jared and I are exclusive. Here's a picture." She tapped her smart phone screen and slid it over to show me a photo of her hugging a balding guy with large-rimmed glasses. "Oh, he's—"

"He's no Sheriff Hottie, but he's wonderful and adores me. We like the same movies and foods, and he gets my sense of humor. And the sex is *hot*."

I choked on my tea. "Well, that's good."

"I'll bet the sheriff is something else, huh?" she asked.

"Uh, we haven't done that yet."

Jenny grinned. "Oh, you will."

We thankfully moved on from the subject because we were interrupted by Maevis waiting to take our order. The daily special of collard greens with ham and black-eyed peas and a side of corn bread was strongly suggested, and we complied.

"I'm dying to meet your momma and Julie, and I miss Daisy Mae, even though she makes me sneeze. I don't care to meet Hank though. I'm pretty sure I couldn't be nice."

I shook my head. "I don't blame you. They say he's hanging on by a thread, but we're not sure why or how. He should have passed away a month or so ago. I haven't seen him since Momma moved him out of the house. I made what little peace I could with him if you could call it that. But something is tugging at me with Hank. Like I want to let the past go and the anger at what he did to us. I'm struggling with it."

"The fact that you could even consider forgiving him is pretty miraculous. What about Julie? Does she see him?" Jenny asked.

"She did once. Whatever they talked about upset Hank, and Julie's never wanted to go back. And since then, Hank hasn't made any noise about talking to the press about my trying to murder him."

"Do you think it was something Julie said to him?" she asked.

"I don't know if that was it, or if the last person in the world who he thought might believe him told him to shove it. I figured if Julie wanted to discuss it, she would have."

"She might one day," Jenny said.

"Maybe."

"This food is amazing. Jared would love it," Jenny said as she took a picture with her phone of her plate and texted it.

"You should bring him to visit soon," I said.

"Maybe I will."

I ANSWERED A call from Paul, my attorney, on our way back to Momma's house. We'd gotten Jenny checked in to the B&B. I offered to have her stay with us, but she insisted that she wanted the full Moonshine experience. She was lucky to have gotten a room on such short notice, but it was getting late in the season, so things were loosening up a little.

"Hi, Paul, what's up?" I asked.

"The DNA results have come back. I've agreed to set up a meeting with all parties there in Moonshine as soon as the reports from the psychologists are in. Do you know when your therapist in Nebraska will send in her records?"

His words were a punch in my gut though I couldn't say why.

"You're on my speakerphone with my friend Jenny and me. She's the therapist, and she's flown in to hand-deliver the notes. And I'm seeing Bree for our last session tomorrow.

"Hi, Jenny. How long are you going to be there in Moonshine?" Paul asked.

"Up to a week unless Sadie needs me to leave sooner. My ticket is for next Sunday."

"Awesome," I mouthed.

"Okay. If y'all can get those reports to me by tomorrow at five p.m., that should wrap things up. If the agents can't come here, they should be able to do a Zoom with us so we're all on the same page."

"Do you know anything about the results?" I asked.

"Not yet. I just know they're back. If I hear anything, I'll let you know. How's the sheriff?"

"He's supposed to get out of the hospital sometime to-day. Thanks for asking."

"Give him my best. Bye, Jenny."

I disconnected the call and pulled into Momma's drive at the same time.

"Before we get to Momma's, I wanted to give you a heads-up about the condition of our house. I mean, it's seen better days."

"Are you embarrassed about where you live?" Jenny asked.

"Not really. Well, kind of. I mean, I was when I was growing up because Hank didn't take care of the place and people made fun of us for being poor." I babbled and sounded ridiculous to my own ears.

"Sadie, I don't care where you live. Do you think for a minute it would change my opinion of you in any way?" Jenny sounded incredulous.

That did sound stupid. "No. It's a throwback to my childhood insecurities, and I need to try and control it or get past it, I know."

As we finally drove up to the house, I tried to see it as Jenny might, and found myself pleasantly surprised. The farmhouse still had a bit of a sagging porch, but we'd fixed the rotted boards and painted the trim and exterior, including the porch swing. We'd even brought in some soil, mulch and planted some flowering perennials and planted some beds with annuals in addition to the hanging ferns and pots of red geraniums.

"Sadie, the house is charming. Why on earth would you apologize that you live here?" Jenny chided me.

"I guess I still see it the way it was when I got here. We've been working to fix things up since Hank went into the nursing home."

"Well, get past it and live in the present. It's lovely."

It *was* in the process of becoming lovely. And it made me proud for Momma.

Hank's old red pickup was parked in front of the house. Momma'd had it cleaned up both inside and out and it looked much better than before. Some might even call it vintage. I couldn't wait to help her buy a car of her own choosing once I was able.

Momma stepped out on the porch as we got out of the Jeep, and Daisy Mae ran to greet us. She had better manners than to jump on us but there was much tail-wagging and excitement, both for me and Jenny.

"Hi there, pretty girl. Yes, I've missed you. Yes, I have." Jenny patted Daisy Mae and immediately sneezed twice. "And you still make me sneeze."

"C'mon, girl, we'll have to let Aunty Jenny adore you from afar."

"Well, hey there, is this Jenny?" Momma grabbed Jenny in a big bear hug. "Aren't you pretty?"

Jenny laughed, caught off guard by the hug. "Yes, hi, Mrs. Brubaker. I surprised Sadie. I hope you don't mind my barging in without any notice."

"Honey, any friend of my girl's is family around here. And from what she's told me, you've been more like family to her these many years, so I can't thank you enough." Momma had tears in her eyes.

"Well, if the truth be known, she's been my family too."

"Where's your suitcase?" Momma asked.

"Oh, I'm staying at the bed-and-breakfast in town," Jenny said.

"*Whaaat?*" Momma nearly screeched. "Sadie Ann, I can't believe what I'm hearing. How could you not invite Jenny to stay here with us at the house?"

"Momma, Jenny insists on staying in town. It's her vacation, and she wants to enjoy Moonshine."

"Yes, ma'am, I love the town so much already and can't wait to go exploring and listen to some bands and wander around the shops."

"Well, as long as you know you're welcome here any time."

"Thank you. I appreciate it. I haven't had a real vacation in years, so I researched the area before I left and decided this would be a perfect getaway."

"I agree. If you don't burst into flames. Make sure you drink plenty. If you're not used to the heat, it can really put you down," Momma warned her. "Y'all come on in and have a glass of tea."

Jenny laughed at that.

"Jenny hasn't quite caught on to our sweet tea habit yet," I said.

"Give me some time. Water will work just fine, thanks."

Once we were inside Momma asked, "How's Chase today?"

"Hopefully he's going home today," I said.

"So soon? Gosh, seems like he should take it easy after how bad he was hurt. Hope he doesn't do too much."

"Me too. But Becky will be hovering, so I can't imagine

she'll allow it," I said.

"No, likely not," Momma agreed.

"How's Hank today?" I asked because I should.

Momma shook her head. "Not good. They're saying it's gonna be days now and that we should call in the family. Thing is, the only family he has is Julie and me. I guess I should make some kind of arrangements for…after."

I placed an arm gently around her. "I know this is hard for you. It's okay to be sad."

Momma smiled slightly. "I'm sad, but mainly because I wish things could've been different for me and Hank and our family. I knew him before he changed into what he became."

"We can't go back and change anything as much as we wish it. And believe me, I wish it a lot," I said.

"Me too," Momma sighed. "But Hank will be better off after he leaves the earth. I don't know much about heaven or hell, but I hope God understands that he was broken. Surely there's a place for broken souls who just don't know any other way to be but bad. Not that he deserves that kind of grace or mercy, I'd just like to think he couldn't do any better."

I thought about her words. Were broken people to blame for their terrible deeds? Even if they knew what they did was wrong? The suffering Hank put us all through for most of our lives surely didn't deserve mercy or pity. But maybe if we could all just release our anger and blame, we could live better.

"Maybe he couldn't do better, Momma. But it's unlikely he'll have a big turnout if you have a service." I wanted to prepare her for this truth.

"Then I'll plan small. But we have to do something," she said.

I nodded. "Yes, you should. And Julie and I will be there."

Jenny's sob broke the silence.

"Jenny? Are you okay, honey?" Momma went to her and put an arm around her shoulders.

"I-I j-just haven't ever heard any-anything so b-beautiful in m-my life."

"Aw, we say stuff like that around here all the time. We're mushy and weird like that."

Jenny just stared at me through her puffy eyes. "You're so different, Sadie. I mean, so different."

I guessed she was right. "I didn't understand myself or how to love and protect my people now that I have people. I loved Thelma, but until she died, I didn't know how much. And you, Jenny, I love you. So much."

Jenny wailed. "This is so pro-profound. My h-heart. I can't take it. What's happened to you—it's the stuff of epic novels and movies. So rich and p-poetic."

"Is she pregnant?" Momma asked, and we both stared at Jenny.

Jenny's eyes popped wide. "Oh my God, I'm pregnant."

"You are?" Nothing could have shocked me more in that moment. Or thrilled me. "A baby, Jenny. Wait, you didn't know?"

She hadn't moved and her expression hadn't changed for a full ten seconds. "Jenny? Are you all right?"

"Pregnant," she whispered, and then stared down at her flat belly. "I hadn't even thought of that. I mean, I haven't taken a test, but my period—I haven't had one lately. We weren't doing anything to prevent having a baby. It just didn't occur to me that I would become a mom at this point in my life."

I hoped this was a good thing. I mean, I couldn't think of anything better. "Jenny, are you okay with this?" I asked, becoming slightly concerned by her reaction.

Her gaze flew to mine. "I'm pregnant, Randi—Sadie." Then she began to laugh like a loon. A great big belly laugh like she'd just heard the most hilarious joke ever. Momma and I shared a look of concern for her state of mind, and possibly for her baby.

I sat down beside her on the sofa. "Jenny, you're starting to scare me. Should I call Jared?" I asked in a gentle tone.

Jenny stopped laughing but continued to smile as a tear formed in the corner of her eye and slid down her cheek. "I never even bothered to hope—I mean, wow. The fact that I found Jared felt like a miracle. But this—this is beyond a dream, Sadie. And yes, I need to call Jared. I'm almost afraid to hope it's true, but it all makes sense now. I know the symptoms. He's going to be over the moon at this news. I was getting older, and just never thought—"

I laughed then. "You're going to be a fantastic mom, Jenny. I'm so happy for you!" Jenny was thirty-six, and certainly not weirdly old to get pregnant, which immediately brought thoughts of such to my own mind. I quickly banished them. I couldn't go there right now.

Jenny grabbed her phone and excused herself to the front porch to make the phone call.

"Well, that was exciting. I can't wait until you get that

news one day," Momma said.

"Whoa, wait now. I'm not sure how this became about me." I turned bright red though, as if she knew my top-secret longing for a baby to love. "You haven't met your granddaughter yet." There, that would throw her off my scent.

She grinned. I knew how much she anticipated the day that Julie would show up with Suzy in tow. "I'm dying to meet Suzy, but I know you will make a wonderful mother someday too."

"I'd almost given up on having a family," I said. But what I'd just witnessed with Jenny had secretly renewed my hope.

She waved her hand at me as if to ward off such an obviously stupid notion. "Oh, bologna. You'd better use protection with Chase, or you'll be pregnant in no time flat. We're fertile women in our family, and I'll just bet he's not one to sit around and watch Netflix after dinner if you know what I mean." Momma wiggled her eyebrows suggestively.

"*Momma.* What a thing to say to your daughter." I sounded like the outraged maiden I was.

"Oh, come on, Sadie. Do we need to have *the talk*? I know you've missed out on a lot of things, but I thought by now you would know about the birds and the bees."

"I know all I need to know, thank you," I said more stiffly than I intended. "I'm going to get Daisy Mae her chew toy.

Momma's laughter followed me into the kitchen, and my face continued to flame.

Chapter Thirty-One

C HASE WAS FINALLY home. The getting here wasn't an experience he cared to repeat, but now that he was sitting in his recliner in front of the seventy-five-inch TV, things were looking better than they had been an hour before.

The house was clean and smelled like, what? Cinnamon? Mom must have lit a candle or two because he knew she hadn't had time to bake. Then he remembered. The ladies from the Methodist Church had taken the first week of his home convalescence to organize a meal train.

Just as he'd gotten to ESPN's SportsCenter, Cindy Hayes arrived with casserole dishes. She informed him that there would be a nourishing, home-cooked meal delivered, complete with salad and dessert, daily for an entire week. Tonight's feast was a chicken casserole (her grandmother's recipe), a green salad, and pecan brownies, she'd explained.

It was as if the incident at the restaurant with Sadie hadn't happened. Or Cindy's memory had been wiped blessedly cleaned. Chase hadn't remembered going over the guardrail or even leaving Sadie's house exactly. But he did recall the uncomfortable exchange between the two women that night.

Cindy, apparently, chose to let the bygones go, which normally would have been a relief, but this was Cindy, and he'd never known her to let a good grudge go to waste. Then again, this was his food and his health at stake, so maybe best to let it lie for now.

"Did you hear me?" she asked, blinking at him.

"Uh, sorry. I'm a little worn out. Thanks again for arranging things." He plead the tired patient excuse. And he had just taken a painkiller. It was likely affecting his responses.

"Oh, you poor thing. I'll fix you right up." She picked up a pillow and moved closer. His heartbeat became more rapid, but not from excitement. Was she going to smother him with that pillow?

"I'll take it from here, Cindy. Thanks for your help," Sadie said, appearing out of nowhere.

Chase was instantly giddy with relief. He would not die here today at the hands of an angry church relief worker.

Cindy's mouth tightened, but she smiled tightly and handed over the pillow. Now he'd never know her intentions.

"I'm a phone call away if you need anything," she said and marched out of the room, then they heard the front door slam.

"I might have drawn my last breath had it not been for your arrival," he joked, but not really.

"I guess we'll always wonder," Sadie said with a laugh, then helped him sit up a little higher with the possible murder pillow.

"Thanks. That's better." He gently grasped her hand before she moved away. "I've missed you."

She sat down on the arm of his recliner. "I've seen you every day."

"No. I've *missed* you. As in, being awake and spending time with you. Talking. I know we were just starting to date, but I still want to do that, if you do," he said.

He hoped this stupid accident hadn't derailed things with Sadie. Because even though he'd been incapacitated, it hadn't lessened his interest in her as a person, nor had it cooled his desire for her.

He stared at her intently, hoping she'd reveal something.

"I-I didn't know if I'd imagined what happened between us the night of the accident. How it felt. I kept thinking about it, about you. But I was so scared to lose you," she said, and her lip trembled.

He reached up and touched her face with his good hand. "It wasn't your imagination, Sadie. I'm crazy about you. And I'm leaving it up to you to pace our relationship according to your comfort. I know it's all new for you, so I'm yours to do with as you please."

She grinned at him then. "Sounds…appealing."

Then she leaned down and gave him the softest of kisses, which caused both an immediate physical and emotional response.

He exhaled when she pulled back and stood. "The accident didn't kill me, but waiting for this leg to heal might," he groaned.

"Don't worry, I'll be around to help you in the meantime," she promised. "Now, can I get you anything while I'm here?" she asked.

He guessed that would do for now. The long game was his strategy with Sadie. He'd been waiting for her to come back all this time and hadn't understood why it was so important. She was his destiny. And yes, that sounded like a goofy lovestruck epic thing in his mind, but in this case, considering everything she'd gone through and his unwavering hope that one day she'd come home, it was getting closer and closer to sounding like a solid fact.

"I'm assuming you've got some good Methodist cooking waiting for you in the kitchen. Are you hungry?" she asked, a twinkle in her eye.

"A special family recipe for chicken casserole, if I'm not mistaken."

"Should I test it first? The town can't afford to lose its sheriff."

"The sheriff can't afford to lose Sadie Brubaker again," he said. But it was true.

"If we go, we can go together. I'll have a taste too," she said as she found her way to the kitchen. "Mmm. Smells good," she called out.

He couldn't imagine going back to a solitary life without the anticipation of Sadie's showing up at some point during the day. Because that's what she'd done every day since he'd woken up from the accident. She'd come in and brightened his days—even the toughest ones.

"Oh, I didn't get a chance to tell you that Mayor Jason wants to be your friend and let bygones be gone," she said.

Chase laughed out loud at that. "He said *what?*"

"I think he was serious. Jenny and I ran into him and Annie at the ice cream place, and he went out of his way to tell me that your accident gave him a new perspective on things and that when you're back on your feet, they want to have us over for dinner in a real effort at burying the past. Said he'd rather live here in Moonshine with you in it."

"Well, isn't that an unexpected turn of events?" Chase would believe it when he saw it, but the idea of forgiveness and letting go of anger made for a nice idea.

The front door slammed, and he heard another female voice he assumed was his mother's.

The two of them got along very well to Chase's relief. Momma had made a strong effort where Annie was concerned, but it hadn't ever been as effortless as with Sadie.

"Wow. Those women have this meal delivery down to a science. It's impressive," Sadie said. She carried a lap tray Chase assumed came as part of the meal service.

His mother came in right behind Sadie. "Hey there, Chase. I brought you some peach pie from Myrtis and Maevis down at the diner. They send their best wishes. I knew you were supposed to have a meal delivered today but I didn't realize Cindy would be doing the honors herself since she's normally the one who delegates."

"I guess she's got a soft spot for me, or she's trying to kill me. I haven't decided what her motive is yet."

"Cindy has a crush on Chase, but he sees it as overt aggression," Sadie said.

"Ah. Like when little boys pull on girls' ponytails to get their attention but end up making them cry. It's opposite with Cindy, I think. It's toxic femininity instead of toxic masculinity."

"Momma, where on earth did you hear that terminology?"

"I watch talk shows and listen to podcasts and keep up with the world. Just because I live out here in the middle of nowhere, doesn't mean I'm not current. We've got the internet after all," Becky huffed.

Chase just stared at his mother. "Podcasts?"

"On that note, I'll head out. I just stopped by to make sure you were settling in. Jenny will be here all week. We're meeting in the square for some music and food," Sadie said. She still stood next to his chair but hadn't touched him while his mother was in the room. I'm sorry I can't just stay here and hang out."

He was a little disappointed Sadie wasn't spending the evening, but he understood how thrilled she was that Jenny had come to visit from Nebraska. "You ladies have fun and watch your drinks." Concerts, even those in Moonshine, still presented opportunities for predators.

"Yes, Sheriff. And I know you'll be in the best hands, so listen to your momma and don't try to do too much the first night home."

"I've got him. Been bossing him around since he was a baby, so he shouldn't be too hard to handle," Becky said. "You girls go have fun."

Sadie bent down then and kissed him on the cheek. "See you tomorrow. I've got to meet with Bree so she can finalize the report. They're ready to give us the DNA results as soon as they get both therapists' final reports. And hopefully unfreeze my accounts."

"I wish there was something I could do for y'all," he said.

"Just get better, please. We're at the home stretch with all this and I'm looking forward to learning what people call normal."

"Amen to that," Becky agreed.

CHASE LIVED ONLY a couple of miles up the mountain. As I sang to a country song on the radio, I reflected on our brief interaction before Becky had arrived. It seemed we were on the same page when it came to moving forward romantically.

I sighed. And grinned. I might as well have been a love-sick character on a romantic movie. I totally got it now. Totally.

It was dusk, and parking was at a premium, so I found a space in the alley behind the sheriff's department and then walked around to the center of the square where a band was warming up and tuning their instruments. The worst of the day's heat had subsided, though it couldn't be called cool out here by any stretch of the imagination.

I wore the same flip-flops, shorts and T-shirt I'd visited Chase in, so I was pretty comfortable and casual. I'd pulled out a lightweight blanket for us to sit on the grass under the stars. The crowd was thickening as I searched for Jenny. This was a mostly tourist and younger generation audience, so I was less likely to run into many people I knew. But it was Moonshine, so familiar faces were always a possibility.

My phone buzzed. Text from Jenny. I followed her directions as to her location based on descriptions of building landmarks and a woman with a bright red wig, which Jenny swore I couldn't miss. And I recognized that dazzler the moment it ran across my line of vision. "Oh, there you are," Jenny grabbed my arm as I continued to stare, mesmerized by the shiny, unnatural tresses as we passed. "Look away. It'll lure you in."

We laughed and found a square of space to spread the blanket. Jenny handed me a beer and she took a sip of her lemonade. "You're not pregnant, are you?" she asked. Of course she knew better from our conversation at the diner.

I laughed and shook my head. I wouldn't be driving for several hours so I figured one wouldn't hurt. Any more than that and I would stay in town with Jenny.

We'd spent some time talking about her shocking yet wonderful news after she'd gotten off the phone with Jared. Come to find out, they were both over the moon about the baby. Jenny was scheduled to see a local doctor at Moonshine General before she left town just to be sure everything was okay with her pregnancy before she flew back to Atlanta.

"I'm still pinching myself every half hour or so to be sure this is real," Jenny said.

I couldn't grin big enough. "It couldn't have happened to a nicer or more deserving person. You'll be the best mom ever."

"Speaking of moms, I like yours," she said. "I know it's been a weird reunion and there's a lot to get through there, but Mary Frances seems crazy about you."

"Yeah. She is. And I feel the same. I mean, she's my mom and I have all those memories back now from my childhood both good and bad. But lately when she slips and tries to make excuses or defend Hank, she usually catches herself doing it. And I catch myself controlling the urge to yell at her for being weak and unable to hit him over the head with a baseball bat in his sleep." This was a light version but still all true.

Jenny snorted. "After the hell you lived at that man's hands, I can't blame you one bit. And I hate playing devil's advocate because I have to do it way too much, but she's lived the battered woman's life. It's affected her mental state. It's like brain damage to some degree. She can no more completely change how she is with Hank than you could make your memories reappear at will."

"This is why I keep you around. You center me and make me see what I should already know. I've learned and grown so much since coming back here. I've...filled in. When Thelma died, I was only a part of a person. The rest has come back and more. I understand how to communicate with people, and how much I've missed for so long. I've been starved for all kinds of human connection and didn't even realize it."

Jenny threw an arm around my shoulder. "You were always more than you knew. I've valued our friendship all these years. You were Randi without Sadie. And Randi just needed Sadie to come in to help her loosen up and laugh again."

"And cry. Lord, have I learned to cry."

The band launched into its intro and cut off the words. But no more were needed then. The music was loud and fun, and it was a wonderful reprieve to just sit back and enjoy it with my best friend in the middle of Moonshine, staring at the stars.

AS SOON AS I introduced Jenny to Bree, I may as well have left the room. Since each knew my story so well, they could hardly contain themselves from discussing it from all aspects. That was okay, I guess, since helping me figure out this mess was the goal.

"I always believed the missing piece lay in what happened between the bike ride and her getting on the bus," Jenny said to Bree.

Bree nodded and finally looked at me. "Do you want to try some hypnotherapy today?" she asked.

"Sure. I guess it couldn't hurt at this point." I took my position on the sofa and kicked off my sandals. Having Jenny there was reassuring because I knew a hundred percent that she had my best interests at heart.

We went through the deep breathing and focusing steps until I was ready.

"Okay, Sadie, let's focus on the bike ride again. On your determination to get away. How far and fast you rode, and what happened when you fell down, when you got back up. I know you were hurt, and your head was bleeding. Deep breaths."

I had to hurry. I'd left Hank bleeding, but knowing him, he could be right behind me in that red truck of his. If he found me out here in the woods, I'd never be seen again and there'd be no witnesses.

My head hurt so much. The blood on my fingers confused me. Was it from Hank or from me? I wasn't sure. It didn't matter. All I cared about was getting away. I had the bus schedule, just like she told me. Every week, I'd gone into town and gotten a new one in case the time came that Hank went too far. The station was on the outside of Moonshine, so I hoped no one would know me.

My lungs were burning, and the ride seemed endless. But thankfully, it wasn't up the mountain, just on the other side of the valley, way on the edge. By car, it would be no problem. Not the best part of town though.

"Sadie, tell us what you see."

"I'm so tired. It was such a long way, and my head hurts. My backpack's heavy and I'm looking for a phone now."

"Who are you planning to call?"

"She said to call when I got there. Near the bus station and then she would tell me what to do."

"Who are you supposed to call?"

"I found the phone. It's long distance and it takes a lot of quarters. It's hard to put them in—my hands are shaking."

My eyes popped open then. Jenny and Bree stared at me with such anticipation that I wanted to apologize. "I-I'm okay," I said, wide awake and totally in the now. I remembered the bike ride and trying to find the phone in the dark. "I had to use a pay phone." I remembered how hard it was to slide those quarters in the skinny slot because I was seeing double."

"How do you feel? Do you need to go back and transition from then to now? It's odd that you woke up so abruptly," Bree said.

I shook my head. "I remember everything up to the point of dialing the number. But I've hit that blank wall again."

"Do you know who you were supposed to call?" Jenny asked.

"No." Just a blank.

Bree asked, "Did you get a sense of emotion for the person you were calling? Like, it was someone you loved or knew well?"

"No. Not really. In fact, just the opposite. It was like I was calling someone I hardly knew and grasping a lifeline."

"Initially you believed your escape was random. Now, we know you had an exit plan, and now someone helping you with that plan, and possibly on the other end to pick you up. This is leading us someplace significant," Bree said.

"It scares me though. I mean, the idea that I still don't remember something that important," I said.

"You will, Sadie. This missing key is coming," Jenny said.

"I agree. But solving this isn't dependent on getting your identity restored. I've completed the report for the feds. They required the two visits, and this was your official third." Bree sounded so positive now.

"And I've got my notes from years ago when we did some hypnotherapy. The therapist, Beverly, she saw early on died and they've been unable to get her records. But Beverly wasn't especially helpful, except to show that Sadie's memory was missing then." Jenny addressed Bree with this information.

"They've supplied us with a secure portal to upload the documents," Bree said.

"I just received the email. I was worried about sending them," Jenny said.

"The next step will be a meeting with the attorney and agents about DNA results. Those are in and all this should be over soon. I know the FBI wants a full accounting of the facts as my memory returns so they can close the case. I've answered all their questions, but I'm supposed to supply any new information," I said.

"Aren't they going to investigate the missing person's case for Randi Collins?" Jenny asked.

I nodded. "Yes. But that shouldn't include me unless I remember something important about it."

"It sounds like they'll have to do some digging into Thelma's past in Louisiana. How do you feel about learning more about her life, Sadie?" Jenny asked.

I wasn't sure about that can of worms at all. "Ask me once I'm in the clear and it's all I have to worry about. Right now, I've got all I can handle figuring out my own past."

They both nodded at my understatement.

"Let me know if you want me to attend the meeting for support," Bree said. "I assume it will take place within the next week or so."

"Paul suggested it would be soon after they received your reports, so yes, I believe it will happen pretty quickly. Most likely when they can get everyone together." Part of me was champing at the bit to get past this final hurdle, but a tiny voice whispered that there was more to this whole DNA thing than just closing my file and giving me back my money and official name and birth certificate. They were the government after all. Surely it couldn't be that simple.

Chapter Thirty-Two

THE MEETING FINALLY took place one day shy of two weeks after my meeting with Bree and Jenny. I was told I could bring my attorney and anyone I felt strongly should be with me during the reading of the DNA results and the findings of the small committee that had been assembled to decide my fate. I was also informed this situation was not a usual one, and therefore required some out-of-the-box *development* by the departments involved.

A neatly dressed female agent named Priscilla Gans was part of the small group assembled, along with the usual group of men. Ms. Gans's brown hair was scraped back into a ballet bun, and she wore wire-rimmed spectacles over her piercing gray eyes. But she threw me off when she smiled warmly during introductions.

"I'm fascinated by your case, Ms. Brubaker. It's very nice to meet you."

"Uh…thank you," I said, still unsure of how to respond to this odd woman.

Chase had accompanied me, though he was using his knee scooter and had to elevate his leg on a chair after he sat. He'd insisted as soon as he learned it was allowed. My relief at having him there was immense.

There was a knock on the door, just as we were about to get started and the door opened. Surprisingly, Mr. Whitaker entered, his pristine white hair a little rumpled, along with his suit. "Excuse me, everyone. I'm counsel representing the deceased, Thelma Collins LaFleur, as well as co-counsel for Sadie Brubaker. My flight was delayed, and well, Atlanta traffic was…troublesome."

"Troublesome, indeed, Mr. Whitaker. We're glad you could join us. I wish I'd known you were coming. I would have sent a car." Paul stood and shook the older man's hand.

"Hi, Mr. Whitaker, I'm so glad you came. Thanks for traveling all this way," I said. And I also wondered why he didn't let anyone know about his plans.

"Closure is important, Sadie. I'm assuming you're going strictly by Sadie now?" he asked.

I nodded. "Yes."

"Shall we proceed?" Ms. Gans took the lead.

Everyone nodded their assent.

This meeting is to determine that Sadie Brubaker is recognized by this committee and by the United States Department of Social Services as legally alive and to reinstate all her rights and privileges as such. This has been proven by DNA samples taken from Ms. Brubaker and compared to hair cuticle and teeth saved by her mother, Mary Frances Brubaker, from her childhood and from evidence gathered at the time of her disappearance. Our sample from Mary Frances Brubaker is a maternal match as well."

I tried not to get excited that this all sounded like what I needed to hear. It was proven that I was me. Not that there was any doubt about that.

"There's a packet of information set out in the folder in front of you. Please open it to page one, section one." Ms. Gans passed a folder down to Mr. Whitaker.

We did as she directed. There was a lot of jargon about matching strands and such.

"Congratulations, Ms. Brubaker, you're officially declared alive and a citizen of this United States with all your rights and privileges reinstated."

There was a mild round of applause, which was unusual, in my opinion. But Ms. Gans smiled.

"Now, to the matter of Thelma LaFleur. We have made a discovery in the DNA. It seems that Mrs. LaFleur's DNA matches with a hundred percent accuracy a familial connection to Ms. Brubaker's DNA. We've done some research, and it seems that Ms. Lafleur was your biological aunt on your father's side, Ms. Brubaker. We understand you've had an unreliable memory and thus far you've not made anyone on this committee aware of this connection. Were you aware of this connection?"

I stared at the woman. *Thelma was my aunt.* "N-no." But was I? Did I know? "I-I didn't know. I wondered why, for all those years, she would have picked me up out of the clear blue and kept me. But I didn't remember her from—before." I felt Chase's hand on my shoulder.

"Did you know Ms. Lafleur had a biological daughter?" Ms. Gans asked.

"N-no, not until I was told by Mr. Whitaker after she died. I thought Thelma was my adoptive mother until she died. And I didn't remember anything until I came here. But I never remembered her as my aunt."

"This is obviously a huge shock to my client. You've proven that Sadie is Sadie and you've restored her rights. One of those rights is to consult with me, as her attorney. If you wish to question her further, it will have to be at a later date."

"Very well. Our other purpose today was to clear Sadie of any intentional fraudulent identity activities by showing she had complete memory loss and no knowledge that she was impersonating Randi Collins until just before she was made aware of her true identity. This was documented through two separate clinical therapists' reports and has been accepted by the committee. It has also been well documented by statements taken by citizens," Ms. Gans stated.

Agent Nate Bascombe piped up then. "The Social Security Administration would like to reserve the right to question Ms. Brubaker at a later date regarding her knowledge of Thelma Lafleur's activities while in her care, should she remember any new information."

"Noted, Agent Bascombe. Is that acceptable with you and your client, Mr. Bristol?" she asked Paul.

I nodded. "That's fine with us."

"The Georgia Bureau of Investigation, acting on behalf of the Federal Bureau of Investigation reserves the right to document the full sequence of events as Ms. Brubaker's memory evolves as well. We have a very sketchy retelling of her disappearance thus far, as we feel it's imperative to learn more information," the GBI agent said, but I didn't get his name.

I was still reeling from the idea that Thelma my dad's sister. Why didn't Momma say anything about it when

I talked about her? Surely she must have known her. Why didn't I remember?

Chase squeezed my shoulder then. "You okay?" he asked.

I just stared at him. I wasn't nearly okay, and he knew it.

The meeting concluded and those people congratulated me. Of course, they wanted more information about Thelma and our relationship, but it didn't keep me from turning back into me. Everybody there knew I was a kid who ran away from abuse and called my aunt to come get me in Oklahoma City at a bus stop. Nothing so sinister on my end of things in their view. But for me, this whole thing had taken a shocking turn.

Mr. Whitaker stopped me before I flew out of the conference room. "Sadie, I brought you something from the house in Hickman. Actually, I came because of this, mostly."

I took a deep breath and resisted the urge to sprint away from any more bombshells, as Mr. Whitaker had a habit of landing on me.

"At the risk of sounding rude, *what now*?" I asked.

Mr. Whitaker had the grace to laugh. "I deserve that, don't I? I've hit you with more than a person should learn in a lifetime, and I'm sorry for it. But in the spirit of adventure, and I'm certain you have one by now, I have a letter and a gift for you."

My stomach curdled. No adventure, please.

He reached into an oversized briefcase and pulled out a letter and Thelma's old Bible. It brought tears to my eyes. "Thanks for bringing me her Bible."

He grinned then. "Dear girl, it's not a Bible. It's only made to look like one. It's the story of Thelma's life. I haven't read it, as it wasn't my place, but I thought you might want to."

As he handed it over, I opened the cover and noticed there was a veneer of The HOLY BIBLE glued on top of what was a thick journal. It was hundreds of pages written in Thelma's own handwriting. I flipped to the back and saw that her last entry was the night before she'd passed away.

Tears streamed down my cheeks. Chase approached then. He'd been speaking with my attorney, Paul, across the room, giving me time with Mr. Whitaker. "Are you ready to go?" he asked.

I held up the book. "It's Thelma's diary. It's everything."

He smiled. "Now you'll know."

"Let's not forget the letter. I wasn't to mention it until three months after her death. I'm telling you, if she didn't know she was scheduled to pass, she wanted to make sure she went the right way. I don't know its contents, but I assume it will assist in answering more questions," Mr. Whitaker said.

"Thank you for everything," I said, then: "What will I do about the house?"

"The house is being cared for as if someone was living in it, as is the garden. Take your time, come visit. You can decide how best to proceed at your own pace."

My eyes were still full of emotion and tears. "Thelma picked the right man for this job."

"How kind of you to say."

CHASE WAS WITH me when I arrived back at Momma's

house since I'd driven him. I'd spent more and more time with him as he'd recovered these past couple of weeks, so our being together had begun to feel natural, and nearly perfect.

Julie's car sat in Momma's driveway, which was a wonderful surprise after such a crazy day. But I hadn't expected her.

Daisy Mae came out to greet us, as did Julie and Momma. But I could tell as soon as I saw them that something was off—way off. My phone had been shut down, as had Chase's, during the meeting.

"Something's wrong," I muttered as I helped Chase out of the car.

"I can manage. Go see what's up," he said and waved me toward my family.

I met them both on the porch. "What's happened?" I asked.

Momma took my hands, and I noticed her eyes were red. "Honey, we wanted to wait to tell you until you got home because your meeting was so important. Hank passed this afternoon. About two hours ago."

I didn't know how to feel. Mostly, I wanted to know how she felt.

"Momma, are you okay?" I hugged her and her shoulders sagged as she cried softly.

"I've been told he would die for so long I almost stopped believing it."

"It's okay, Momma, we're here for you," Julie said, but Julie looked like she could use some cheering up too.

"Julie, I'm sorry. He was your father. You don't have to be strong," I said and hugged my sister.

She wiped a tear but smiled. "I'm okay. I just wished he'd turned out better in the end. You know?" she asked.

"Boy, don't I?" I said. And I meant it. If Hank had been able to make peace with Momma and Julie it would have gone a long way in healing us. It might have closed the breach and allowed for more complete forgiveness and understanding instead of leaving a still-yawning gap of hurt. But over the last month or so he'd lost his grasp on reality—and his memory. Stroke-induced dementia, they'd called it. So, any possibility for remorse or admission of guilt he might've made was now out of the realm of possibility.

We'd come a long way, but traces of his evil and violence still permeated our relationships. It was early yet, and time would surely help because we wanted to rid ourselves of the past, but it was some past and would take effort. I could feel the need to forgive creeping up on me, but I wasn't there yet. I'm not sure to what degree I would be in the future, but now that I had my mother and sister back, Hank's abuse didn't seem to matter as much. It would always be with me. It had been the catalyst for everything I was dealing with now, but wallowing in it didn't seem productive. Giving him power wasn't productive.

Chase had obviously overheard what had happened. "I'm so sorry for your loss. Is it okay if I call Becky? She'll want to know," Chase said.

"Of course. She's family," Momma said.

He hopped up onto the porch and sat down awkwardly and made the call.

"Let's go inside and see what's what," Julie said. "Momma called me right after you left for your meeting this morning to tell me Hank had taken a bad turn."

The cool interior was a relief from the heat outdoors. I could hear Chase's deep voice as he spoke to Becky on the porch.

Momma said the hospice care folks had put her in touch with the nursing home just after Hank had drawn his last breath, and they were sending out a representative this evening to finalize things. She'd already made plans for cremation, and only needed to sign the paperwork for it and the death certificates.

"There's not much else to do now. Y'all know Hank wasn't a religious man, and folks around here would've laughed us out of town if we'd have tried to do a church service."

Not that I thought he deserved one, but if it made Momma feel like she'd properly put him to rest, then she should do what she thought was right. "It's entirely up to you, Momma."

"I-I don't know what would be proper."

"Don't worry about what people will think. Do what will bring you peace," Julie said.

We sat together, one on each side of Momma on the sofa. "I'm just so thankful you're both here with me. And I'm a little bit thankful Hank's finally gone. That makes me a terrible person, I guess. I say we cremate and decide on a time after we get his ashes back. Once things settle down."

"You're not a terrible person. Maybe you'll both find some peace now," Julie said.

"Sounds sensible. There's no rush since you're having him cremated," I agreed.

"Sadie, tell Chase to come on inside from the heat before he burns up out there. I know he's probably trying to give us some privacy, and that's sweet, but he'll die of heatstroke."

I went out to where I'd left Chase, and sure enough, his face was beet red as he waited. My heart nearly melted in my chest at his generous nature. I smiled. "Momma says you're going to die of heatstroke and to come inside now," I said, and went to help him up.

"It's hot as blazing hell out here, for sure. Is she okay?" he asked.

"She's going to be fine."

THAT EVENING, I hated to leave Chase's house, but I was needed at home. So, after our usual, lengthy and very hot kiss, I reluctantly pulled away. "I'll see you tomorrow."

"Mmm. G'nite, beautiful Sadie. Give your family my best. I'm sorry about Hank, you know."

"Yeah? I'm not sure how I feel about his passing. I'm sorry for Momma and Julie, and I'm sorry that Hank hurt so many people during his lifetime."

"I'm sorry he hurt you." There was a lot in those words.

"Thank you." I believed him with my whole heart.

"So, you know our relationship isn't built on my desire to save you, right?" he asked. We'd had our lengthy conversation about his obsessive search for me. Becky had told him I'd gotten a little creeped out by it.

But he'd helped me understand it by showing me the files on my missing person's cold case. He'd let me go through the notes he'd made after I'd disappeared. They'd shown his frustration at the lack of leads or witnesses. There were blood traces—my blood. Other blood. I could imagine how exhausting it must have been to a lawman of his intellect. Plus, he had known me as a young girl. He'd even defended me from Hank, I discovered. He'd been invested. He'd worried. He'd obsessed. And he'd never understood how a young girl could have just disappeared and never returned. Until one day I had.

So, as much as my disappearance had haunted him, my return had healed him. But our blooming relationship was ours. Not because of the missing child I was, but because of the woman I was now.

"No. I'm good now," I said.

"I wish you could understand how important finding you was to me. I had such a strong belief that you were still alive and couldn't find your way home."

"Thank you for believing in me when I didn't know where I belonged."

✤

WE MET IN the evening with Eula from the Moonshine Mortuary and Crematorium. "Are you sure you don't want to go ahead with a date for the service? People will be asking what the plans are."

"Listen, Eula Jean, if anybody says anything, tell them we'll put it in the paper and give them plenty enough time to clear their schedule so they can attend. Okay?" Momma said, frowning hard at the woman.

"Well, Mary Frances, I meant no disrespect. It's just that people ask, you know?"

"People didn't care a whit about Hank or likely me for that matter. It's not about paying respects, it's about being nosy."

"Eula, if you'll please post the obituary in the newspaper and online and state he's to be cremated and that details of his service will be announced at a later date, that will be fine," Julie said, smiling at the older woman.

Julie had a way about her. Her voice was lovely and kind, but she took no guff from anyone.

"Well, I guess that would be fine. Just keep in mind we don't want to wait too long to plan the service," Eula said. Likely Eula was thinking about all of the little upgrades and extras she would get a commission on if she sold them before she walked out the door. I didn't resent someone making a living, but the grief business felt kind of icky just now.

"We'll certainly keep that in mind," I said. "Thanks so much for coming out. We'll be by next week to pick out an urn and pick up Hank's remains."

Momma signed more papers that gave the crematorium permission to handle the remains, and then there was the issue of the bill. Momma's panicked look let me know she didn't have the money on hand to pay the thousand-plus dollars to settle up with Eula.

"I should have my accounts unfrozen by Monday," I said quietly to Momma and Julie.

"Not another word. He was my father, no matter how we felt about him." She went over to the kitchen table where her purse sat and pulled out her wallet. "How do you prefer to take payment?" she asked.

"We take Visa, Mastercard, checks, or cash," Eula said, but it was clear by the lifting of her brows when Julie had whipped out her wallet that she'd not expected such prompt payment from the Brubaker household.

Chapter Thirty-Three

I WOKE SLOWLY to the smell of bacon. For a second, I was back in Hickman and Thelma was singing softly in Cajun French as she made pancakes. A profound sadness permeated my heart at the memory, but only briefly as I realized I was actually tucked in my childhood bedroom with my sister next door and my own momma cooking bacon in the kitchen.

And I had a boyfriend. Thelma would be tickled about that despite the fact that she'd sheltered me. I knew now that she'd wanted me to regain my memory and my life. Especially now that I was safe. I just knew she would adore Chase. Maybe that's why she'd set him up as my contact from the beginning. I had no idea if she knew folks here in Moonshine from before.

I rolled out of bed and stretched. I hadn't had the courage to open Thelma's diary yet. It was like I had a secret story to anticipate meant for my eyes only. I wanted to read the letter first. Yesterday was filled with the tragedy and emotion of Hank's passing. And yes, it was a tragedy for our family. Daisy Mae still lay at the foot of my bed, where she opened one eye and yawned.

Today, I would gather my mother and sister and share

the letter with them. I felt certain it would help me fill in some of my gaps. If I had any surges of memory, I needed family around me. The memories were often unpredictable, and sometimes unpleasant. I'd learned to be patient until now. But today was the day I hoped to learn the truth.

But first, bacon.

Julie's door was open, and her room was empty, but her clothes were still there, so she hadn't gone back home yet. I lingered for a moment, before leaving her room. She was always a neat child, and that hadn't changed. I noticed her shoes were tucked under the edge of the bed, and that she'd folded yesterday's clothes instead of throwing them in a heap. Her bed was made already, the pillows arranged perfectly. I hadn't gotten quite that far yet this morning.

This sense of perfect order made me a little sad. Julie hadn't opened up about how her life had been, other than her anguish over being taken away after I left home. I hoped she'd never felt like she had to be this good for people to love her. We loved her no matter if she made her bed and folded her clothes. I hoped she knew that.

I turned and followed my nose to where they were in the kitchen. The initial angst between Momma and Julie had settled, it seemed. I didn't doubt there were unresolved emotions simmering below the surface, as there were with me and Momma from time to time, mostly on my end, I guess. But we'd all come together since I'd been home, and I hoped that over time we could work out some of the upset and move along as best we could.

"There you are, sleepyhead." Julie turned from the refrigerator, the container of orange juice in her hand. Her blonde hair was neat, but she was still in her matching pajamas. I, on the other hand, was wearing a pair of sweatpants and a ratty T-shirt. And my hair was likely sticking straight out in all directions. Now that it was cut shorter, it tended to do that.

"Good morning, y'all." Y'all had become my go-to word since my memories had returned. I don't think I'd ever uttered it in Hickman. Maybe when I'd first arrived there? I don't recall.

I let Daisy Mae out the kitchen door, which led to the backyard where she could run around and go potty.

"Mornin', Sadie. You hungry?" Momma asked from in front of the stove, still in her robe and slippers. This was a throwback from our childhood, but without Hank's ominous presence to cast a shadow of worry about what might happen at any moment.

"Bacon? You bet. Can I do anything to help?" I asked.

"You can grab those pot holders and pull the biscuits out of the oven." She pointed to the ancient tightly crocheted squares that hung from a magnetic hook that hung on the exterior of the oven. I remembered those same pot holders from childhood, hanging in the same spot.

"Wow, how old are these things?" I asked as I flapped them around and prepared to pull the fragrant biscuits from the oven.

"Almost as old as you are, I guess," Momma said. "Might be time to update a few things around here."

"Might be." Julie laughed.

I inhaled deeply as I set the hot pan of biscuits on the trivet by the sink. Momma's biscuits were a real thing of beauty and melted in your mouth.

"So, after we clean up and get dressed, I hoped I might ask you both a favor," I said.

They turned to stare at me in question. "Of course, Sadie," Julie said.

"What is it, honey?" Momma asked.

"At the meeting yesterday, the attorney from Hickman showed up with a letter from Thelma, a new one that he was supposed to give me three months after her death. Of course, she never thought she was going to die before I learned about my past, but she'd planned for it all the same. Anyway, I hoped you would be with me when I read it."

"Absolutely. Are you afraid of what she might say?" Momma asked.

"Not afraid really. More nervous about what my reaction might be. The missing memories could come back, and that worries me a little."

It occurred to me then that they didn't know about the DNA results. Momma and I had some real hashing out to do. I would tell them after breakfast.

"Okay. We'll eat and then you can read the letter," Julie said.

I TOOK A quick shower, which helped me gather my thoughts. I didn't want to go at Momma with accusations about Thelma being my aunt. She might not even know about any of it. I'd pushed yesterday's meeting to the very back of my mind once I'd arrived home and found out about

Hank. But now it was time for some answers.

I called Chase, and Becky answered. "Hey there honey. He just got in the shower. Well, the home health nurses are here and he's cussing in there with them. So, I guess he's *trying* to take a shower. Everything okay?" she asked.

With the broken leg still in a cast, albeit a waterproof one, Chase struggled to shower himself safely. He was a big guy, and maneuvering the slippery surface without bearing weight on two legs required lots of help.

I didn't want to bother him with my worries, so I said, "Yes, I was calling to say hi. Tell him I'll see him later. I'm spending this morning with my momma and sister."

"Please send my best and let them know how sorry I am about Hank. I plan to drop off a casserole this afternoon."

"That would be lovely. Thanks, Becky." I'd learned never to turn down an offer of bereavement or "helping" food. Apparently, it was a rude thing to do should someone offer.

I picked up the letter and the diary and found Momma and Julie waiting for me at the dining room table. Both were fully dressed.

They each sat on one side toward the end, leaving me to take the head-of-table chair. "Thanks for this," I said, my hands trembling slightly.

"Honey, don't be nervous. Anything you find out, we can help you with," Momma said.

I noticed then that there was a good-sized box of photos sitting on the table next to Julie. "What's that?" I asked.

"These must belong to you and Momma. I brought them with me from home. The social worker sent them when they—when I left home. She thought they were mine.

But I'm sure some of them are pictures of you and your father, Sadie. Maybe they will help your memory, even though you look too young to remember in most of them. At the very least, they belong to you and Momma."

I nodded. "Thanks."

I looked over at Momma. "I found out something very important yesterday in the meeting with the agents. They told me that Thelma was my paternal aunt—my father's sister."

Something flickered in Momma's eyes. "Your what? No, it can't be. He didn't have a sister—" Then she put her hands to her cheeks. "Wait. Lordy be, Sadie. Her name wasn't Thelma, and she was your daddy's half-sister. She was Creole, and she was older by nearly fifteen years. I'd nearly forgotten about her. I assume your Thelma was a black woman?"

A deep recognition hit me then. "Yes, she was Creole. Or Cajun, I guess. I don't honestly know the distinction, but I know there is one. She was from the southernmost part of Louisiana." I hadn't shared anything about Thelma, other than her name with my family, or anyone, for that matter. Thelma had been too personal, and mine only. I hadn't wanted to talk about her because everyone assumed she'd done wrong by keeping me.

"Wait. Hang on. There's a picture in here," Julie said, and began to flip through photos. "Yes, here it is." She handed me an old, somewhat faded color photo of my father, a much-younger Thelma, and who I assumed was me at around two years old, because of my blue eyes, and a tiny, frail-looking baby, who was about a year old. I turned it over, and in faded blue ballpoint it read: *Tilly, Miranda, Sadie, and Randy.*

I handed it to Momma, who squinted her eyes. "Tilly. Yes, that was her name. Tilly LaFleur, and she had a baby named Miranda—whom she called Randi. A sickly little thing. They came to visit once or twice ages ago. I'd forgotten. Just forgotten about them. She was very protective of your daddy, now that I think about it. She'd helped raised him on the bayou, he'd once said."

"He was from Louisiana?" I asked, puzzle pieces clicking into place.

"Yes, but I never went there. He left when he was young and didn't return. Didn't like to talk about it."

"Did I ever meet Tilly later? When I was older?" I asked. "Maybe after my father passed away?"

"Not that I know of. Of course you know how Hank felt about anybody with a drop of colored blood. That's probably why he held such a grudge against you. Because you've got some Creole blood."

"I *do*?" I hadn't yet gone through the full DNA report, but I couldn't wait to now.

"Well, Sadie, I don't think discussing it out in the open would've gone over so well around here, do you? With Hank. Your father was a quarter Creole, whatever that meant. He was very tan, but you'd never have known it by looking at him. But Hank knew about it. I'm not sure how. Maybe he'd seen a picture of your grandparents."

"I had no idea. He said I had devil eyes." Hank hated when I stared at him. Sometimes I did it just to freak him out as a kid.

"He was convinced you had some kind of voodoo power or other because of your heritage. Of course, he pretty much thought everybody who had any color to them at all was of the devil."

I remembered Thelma's letter. I nearly tore into it and began to read silently, my heart pounding:

Dear Sadie,

Have you come to know yourself as Sadie by now? This letter is to ensure you understand who you are and where you came from. And, if you haven't remembered by now who I am—was—and how we came to be to-gether in Hickman, here are your answers. When I picked you up in Oklahoma City, you didn't recognize me. You were so vulnerable and scared. You seemed to accept my explanations, and I didn't want to try to force any memories on you, hoping they would come naturally in time.

I am your aunt Tilly, dear. But Thelma worked better for legal purposes. I promised my brother, Randy, when you were a baby that I would protect you should you ever need me to. When you were fifteen years old, I came to Moonshine and found you home alone. You were sick and hadn't gone to school. But what I found was that you had been abused. I wanted to take you that minute, but it would have been kidnapping and caused a big stir. So, I gave you my phone number and we hatched a plan. No one ever knew about my coming to town.

You called me from near the bus station on the night Hank beat you in the barn. I told you where to go.

When you arrived, you were in desperate shape. The rest, shall we say, is history. Except, you don't know about my Miranda, my Randi. I lost her during a terrible hurricane the week after 9/11. I've written about it in my diary, and you'll learn more there about our family history.

What I most want you to know and remember some day is that I needed to keep my promise to my brother, Randy. To protect you. To love you when he couldn't. I did that. I only wish my life circumstances had allowed me to come to your aid sooner.

We did pretty well together, did we not, ma cher? I hope you do not question my love for you, nor my best intentions. If only I could have seen it through. I wish for you to find happiness and love for the rest of your life.

Aunt Tilly (Thelma)

Tears fell silently down my face. Because as I'd read the letter, the memories of that night swarmed back. I knew. I remembered. There were no more secrets or lies. I'd just been made whole by Thelma's words.

I stood and handed the letter to Momma and went outside where Daisy Mae waited for me. She understood. She'd known the good in Thelma. Dogs knew.

It was over. But now I had a need to understand Thelma's pain. Her life. And she'd left me the opportunity to uncover Randi's fate. Was there something I could do for her? Why hadn't there been a death certificate filed? Had she been lost during a hurricane? Did I still have more family in

Louisiana?

Maybe it wasn't as over as I'd believed. Maybe this diary signaled a beginning of sorts.

I knew who I was now, really knew. I had support. A family who loved me. Peace in my soul, and a man I adored and could count on. I possessed all the tools to help someone else, even though she was departed from this world. The one who'd stood by me when she was alive and believed I could find my home.

I had Thelma's diary, and perhaps a mystery to uncover.

Epilogue

I GRINNED UP at Chase as we clasped hands in front of half the town of Moonshine, Georgia. I marveled at my great fortune as we exchanged vows surrounded by the North Georgia Mountains. This man. He was pure gold, and I knew I'd been waiting only for him.

Momma was beautiful in a pale blue mother-of-the-bride gown, and Julie stood beside me as my maid of honor. My six-year-old niece, Suzy, stood in front of Julie as junior bridesmaid. Julie's husband, Gray, was handsome in a black suit. Julie was loved and cherished by her family, which is what I'd hoped for.

I was fully and completely Sadie Brubaker-Blackburn. A mouthful, but I'd decided to keep the Brubaker name, despite the fact that it had belonged to Hank. It was our family name. I'd forgiven Hank Brubaker sometime after I'd learned everything about Thelma—Aunt Tilly. Hers was a fascinating story and I intended to learn more when the time was right.

Jenny sat on the pew with her newborn son, Jeremy, along with her recent husband, Jared. Lot of Js. They'd decided to relocate to Moonshine after spending a week here in town together a few months ago. The feeling of community was a powerful draw for them, and I was over the moon when she'd told me.

Everything we'd all endured had led us here together. No more missing pieces.

This was the happy ending I never thought possible.

A Georgia Christmas, book #2 in the *Moonshine* series, is coming soon!

Merilee Bell has worked hard to establish her salon in her hometown of Moonshine, Georgia. It's Christmastime—her busiest time of the year. She's made her peace with living and working in the small town where she's known every eligible male since Kindergarten, so finding love isn't high on her list. Until the new sheriff's deputy, Randy Slade, parks his three-quarter-ton pickup in her salon's allotted parking space. He's not there for a haircut…and she's not good with trusting anybody she doesn't know.

Georgia Bureau of Investigation (GBI) agent Randy Slade is invited by the local Sheriff in Moonshine to help with an undercover investigation into a group of scammers who've been taking over empty properties and leasing them to unsuspecting renters during the holiday season. He's posing as a local sheriff's deputy, so nobody in town knows he's not there to stay. When Merilee Bell offers her garage apartment for him to "rent", he uses it to bait the scammers. Randy tells her half-truths to protect the investigation, so she thinks he's a deputy who's come to live in Moonshine.

Merilee and Randy are drawn to each other, but will his omissions and her past prevent the two lonely souls from a Christmas love match?

A Georgia Christmas, is book #2 in the *Moonshine* series, will be available in the absolutely gorgeous
A Southern Christmas Anthology!

If you enjoyed *Her Missing Pieces*,
you'll love the other books in the…

Moonshine series

Book 1: *Her Missing Pieces*

Book 2: *A Georgia Christmas in the
A Southern Christmas Anthology*

Available now at your favorite online retailer!

More Books by Susan Sands

Louisiana series

Book 1: *Home to Cypress Bayou*
Book 2: *Secrets in Cypress Bayou*
Book 3: *A Bayou Christmas*
Book 4: *Bayou Redemption*

The Alabama series

Book 1: *Again, Alabama*
Book 2: *Love, Alabama*
Book 3: *Forever, Alabama*
Book 4: *Christmas, Alabama*
Book 5: *Noel, Alabama*

Available now at your favorite online retailer!

About the Author

Susan Sands grew up in a real life Southern Footloose town, complete with her senior class hosting the first ever prom in the history of their tiny public school. Is it any wonder she writes Southern small town stories full of porch swings, fun and romance?

Susan lives in suburban Atlanta surrounded by her husband, three young adult kiddos and lots of material for her next book.

Thank you for reading

Her Missing Pieces

If you enjoyed this book, you can find more from all our great authors at TulePublishing.com, or from your favorite online retailer.

TULE
PUBLISHING